John Galsworthy was born on 14 Aug[...] Surrey, the son of John and Blanche Gal[...] children. John Galsworthy senior, whose family came from Devon, was a successful solicitor in London and a man of 'new money', determined to provide privilege and security for his family. They idolised him. By contrast, their mother Blanche was a more difficult woman, strict and distant. Galsworthy commented that 'My father really predominated in me from the start . . . I was so truly and deeply fond of him that I seemed not to have a fair share of love left to give my mother.'

Young Johnny enjoyed the happy, secure childhood of a Victorian, upper-middle-class family. Educated at Harrow, he was popular at school and a good sportsman. Holidays were spent with family and friends, moving between their country houses. After finishing school, John went up to New College, Oxford to read law. There he enjoyed the carefree life of a privileged student, not working particularly hard, gambling and becoming known as 'the best dressed man in College'. But he could also be quiet and serious, a contemporary describing how 'He moved among us somewhat withdrawn . . . a sensitive, amused, somewhat cynical spectator of the human scene'.

The period after university was one of indecision for Galsworthy. Although his father wanted him to become a barrister, the law held little appeal. So he decided to get away from it all and travel. It was on a voyage in the South Seas in 1893 that he met Joseph Conrad, and the two became close friends. It was a crucial friendship in Galsworthy's life. Conrad encouraged his love of writing, but Galsworthy attributes his final inspiration to the woman he was falling in love with: Ada.

Ada Nemesis Pearson Cooper married Major Arthur Galsworthy, John's cousin, in 1891. But the marriage was a tragic mistake. Embraced by the entire family, Ada became close friends with John's beloved sisters, Lilian and Mabel, and through them John heard of her increasing misery, fixing in his imagination the pain of an unhappy marriage. Thrown together more and more, John and Ada eventually became lovers in September 1895. They were unafraid of declaring their relationship and facing the consequences, but the only person they couldn't bear to hurt was John's adored father, with his traditional values. And so they endured ten years of secrecy until Galsworthy's father died in December 1904. By September 1905 Ada's divorce had come through and they were finally able to marry.

It was around this time, in 1906, that Galsworthy's writing career flourished. During the previous decade he had been a man 'in chains', emotionally and professionally, having finally abandoned law in 1894. He struggled to establish himself as an author. But after many false starts and battling a lifelong insecurity about his writing, Galsworthy turned an affectionately satirical eye on the world he knew best and created the indomitable Forsytes, a mirror image of his own relations – old Jolyon: his father; Irene: his beloved Ada, to name but a few. On reading the manuscript, his sister Lilian was alarmed that he could so expose their private lives, but John dismissed her fears saying only herself, Mabel and their mother, 'who perhaps had better not read the book', knew enough to draw comparisons. *The Man of Property*, the first book in *The Forsyte Saga*, was published to instant acclaim; Galsworthy's fame as an author was now sealed.

By the time the first Forsyte trilogy had been completed, with *In Chancery* (1920) and *To Let* (1921), sales of *The Forsyte Saga* had reached one million on both sides of the Atlantic. With the public clamouring for more, Galsworthy followed these with six more Forsyte novels, the last of which, *Over The River*, was completed just before his death in 1933. And their appeal endures, immortalised on screen in much-loved adaptations such as the film *That Forsyte Woman* (1949), starring Errol Flynn. The celebrated BBC drama in 1967 with Kenneth More and Eric Porter was a phenomenal success, emptying the pubs and churches of Britain on a Sunday evening, and reaching an estimated worldwide audience of 160 million. The recent popular 2002 production starred Damien Lewis, Rupert Graves and Ioan Gruffudd and won a Bafta TV award.

Undoubtedly *The Forsyte Saga* is Galsworthy's most distinguished work, but he was well known, if not more successful in his time, as a dramatist. His inherent compassion meant Galsworthy was always involved in one cause or another, from women's suffrage to a ban on ponies in mines, and his plays very much focus on the social injustices of his day. *The Silver Box* (1906) was his first major success, but *Justice* (1910), a stark depiction of prison life, had an even bigger impact. Winston Churchill was so impressed by it that he immediately arranged for prison reform, reducing the hours of solitary confinement. *The Skin Game* (1920) was another big hit and later adapted into a film, under the same title, by Alfred Hitchcock.

Despite Galsworthy's literary success, his personal life was still troubled. Although he and Ada were deeply in love, the years of uncertainty had taken their toll. They never had children and their marriage reached a crisis in 1910 when Galsworthy formed a close friendship with a young dancer called Margaret Morris while working on one of his plays with her. But John, confused and tortured by the thought of betraying Ada, broke off all contact with Margaret in 1912 and went abroad with his wife. The rest of their lives were spent constantly on the move; travelling in America, Europe, or at home in London, Dartmoor and later Sussex. Numerous trips were made in connection with PEN, the international writers' club, after Galsworthy was elected its first president in 1921. Many people have seen the constant travelling as unsettling for Galsworthy and destructive to his writing, but being with Ada was all that mattered to him: 'This is what comes of giving yourself to a woman body and soul. A. paralyses and has always paralysed me. I have never been able to face the idea of being cut off from her.'

By the end of his life, Galsworthy, the man who had railed against poverty and injustice, had become an established, reputable figure in privileged society. Having earlier refused a knighthood, he was presented with an Order of Merit in 1929. And in 1932 he was awarded the Nobel Prize for literature. Although it was fashionable for younger writers to mock the traditional Edwardian authors, Virginia Woolf dismissing Galsworthy as a 'stuffed shirt', J.M. Barrie perceived his contradictory nature: 'A queer fish, like the rest of us. So sincerely weighed down by the out-of-jointness of things socially . . . but outwardly a man-about-town, so neat, so correct – he would go to the stake for his opinions but he would go courteously raising his hat.'

John Galsworthy died on 31 January 1933, at the age of sixty-five, at Grove Lodge in Hampstead, with Ada by his side. At his request, his ashes were scattered over Bury Hill in Sussex. *The Times* hailed him as the 'mouthpiece' of his age, 'the interpreter in drama, and in fiction of a definite phase in English social history'.

Other Forsyte novels by John Galsworthy and available from Headline Review

The Man Of Property
In Chancery
To Let
The White Monkey
The Silver Spoon
Swan Song
Flowering Wilderness
Over The River

The Forsyte Saga
Maid in Waiting

John Galsworthy

headline
review

First published in Great Britain in 1931

This paperback edition published in 2007 by HEADLINE REVIEW
An imprint of HEADLINE PUBLISHING GROUP

1

ISBN 978 0 7553 4091 0

Typeset in Sabon by Palimpsest Book Production Limited,
Grangemouth, Stirlingshire

Printed and bound in Great Britain by
Clays Ltd, St Ives plc

Headline's policy is to use papers that are natural, renewable
and recyclable products and made from wood grown in
sustainable forests. The logging and manufacturing processes
are expected to conform to the environmental regulations
of the country of origin.

HEADLINE PUBLISHING GROUP
An Hachette Livre UK Company
338 Euston Road
London NW1 3BH

www.reviewbooks.co.uk
www.headline.co.uk

To
Frank Galsworthy

Chapter One

The Bishop of Porthminster was sinking fast; they had sent for his four nephews, his two nieces and their one husband. It was not thought that he would last the night.

He who had been 'Cuffs' Cherrell (for so the name Charwell is pronounced) to his cronies at Harrow and Cambridge in the 'sixties, the Reverend Cuthbert Cherrell in his two London parishes, Canon Cherrell in the days of his efflorescence as a preacher, and Cuthbert Porthminster for the last eighteen years, had never married. For eighty-two years he had lived and for fifty-five, having been ordained rather late, had represented God upon certain portions of the earth. This and the control of his normal instincts since the age of twenty-six had given to his face a repressed dignity which the approach of death did not disturb. He awaited it almost quizzically, judging from the twist of his eyebrow and the tone in which he said so faintly to his nurse:

'You will get a good sleep tomorrow, nurse. I shall be punctual, no robes to put on.'

The best wearer of robes in the whole episcopacy, the most distinguished in face and figure, maintaining to the end the dandyism which had procured him the nickname 'Cuffs', lay quite still, his grey hair brushed and his face like ivory. He had been a bishop so long that no one knew now what he thought about death, or indeed about anything, except the prayer book, any change in which he had deprecated with determination.

In one never remarkable for expressing his feelings the ceremony of life had overlaid the natural reticence, as embroidery and jewels will disguise the foundation stuff of vestment.

He lay in a room with mullion windows, an ascetic room in a sixteenth-century house, close to the Cathedral, whose scent of age was tempered but imperfectly by the September air coming in. Some zinnias in an old vase on the window-sill made the only splash of colour, and it was noticed by the nurse that his eyes scarcely left it, except to close from time to time. About six o'clock they informed him that all the family of his long-dead elder brother had arrived.

'Ah! See that they are comfortable. I should like to see Adrian.'

When an hour later he opened his eyes again, they fell on his nephew Adrian seated at the foot of the bed. For some minutes he contemplated the lean and wrinkled brownness of a thin bearded face, topped with grizzling hair, with a sort of faint astonishment, as though finding his nephew older than he had expected. Then, with lifted eyebrows and the same just quizzical tone in his faint voice, he said:

'My dear Adrian! Good of you! Would you mind coming closer? Ah! I haven't much strength, but what I have I wanted you to have the benefit of; or perhaps, as you may think, the reverse. I must speak to the point or not at all. You are not a Churchman, so what I have to say I will put in the words of a man of the world, which once I was myself, perhaps have always been. I have heard that you have an affection, or may I say infatuation, for a lady who is not in a position to marry you – is that so?'

The face of his nephew, kindly and wrinkled, was gentle with an expression of concern.

'It is, Uncle Cuthbert. I am sorry if it troubles you.'

'A mutual affection?'

His nephew shrugged.

'My dear Adrian, the world has changed in its judgments since my young days, but there is still a halo around marriage. That, however, is a matter for your conscience and is not my point. Give me a little water.'

When he had drunk from the glass held out, he went on more feebly:

'Since your father died I have been somewhat *in loco parentis* to you all, and the chief repository, I suppose, of such traditions as attach to our name. I wanted to say to you that our name goes back very far and very honourably. A certain inherited sense of duty is all that is left to old families now; what is sometimes excused to a young man is not excused to those of mature age and a certain position like your own. I should be sorry to be leaving this life knowing that our name was likely to be taken in vain by the Press, or bandied about. Forgive me for intruding on your privacy, and let me now say good-bye to you all. It will be less painful if you will give the others my blessing for what it is worth – very little, I'm afraid. Good-bye, my dear Adrian, good-bye!'

The voice dropped to a whisper. The speaker closed his eyes, and Adrian, after standing a minute looking down at the carved waxen face, stole, tall and a little stooping, to the door, opened it gently and was gone.

The nurse came back. The Bishop's lips moved and his eyebrows twitched now and then, but he spoke only once:

'I shall be glad if you will kindly see that my neck is straight, and my teeth in place. Forgive these details, but I do not wish to offend the sight . . .'

Adrian went down to the long panelled room where the family was waiting.

'Sinking. He sent his blessing to you all.'

Sir Conway cleared his throat. Hilary pressed Adrian's arm. Lionel went to the window. Emily Mont took out a tiny handkerchief and passed her other hand into Sir Lawrence's. Wilmet alone spoke:

'How does he look, Adrian?'

'Like the ghost of a warrior on his shield.'

Again Sir Conway cleared his throat.

'Fine old boy!' said Sir Lawrence, softly.

'Ah!' said Adrian.

They remained, silently sitting and standing in the compulsory discomfort of a house where death is visiting. Tea was brought in, but, as if by tacit agreement, no one touched it. And, suddenly, the bell tolled. The seven in that room looked up. At one blank spot in the air their glances met and crossed, as though fixed on something there and yet not there.

A voice from the doorway said:

'Now please, if you wish to see him.'

Sir Conway, the eldest, followed the bishop's chaplain; the others followed Sir Conway.

In his narrow bed jutting from the centre of the wall opposite the mullion windows the bishop lay, white and straight and narrow, with just the added dignity of death. He graced his last state even more than he had graced existence. None of those present, not even his chaplain, who made the eighth spectator, knew whether Cuthbert Porthminster had really had faith, except in that temporal dignity of the Church which he had so faithfully served. They looked at him now with all the different feelings death produces in varying temperaments, and with only one feeling in common, aesthetic pleasure at the sight of such memorable dignity.

Conway – General Sir Conway Cherrell – had seen much death. He stood with his hands crossed before him, as if once more at Sandhurst in the old-time attitude of 'stand at ease'. His face was thin-templed and ascetic, for a soldier's; the darkened furrowed cheeks ran from wide cheek-bones to the point of a firm chin, the dark eyes were steady, the nose and lips thin; he wore a little close grizzly dark moustache – his face was perhaps the stillest of the eight faces, the face of the taller Adrian beside him, the least still. Sir Lawrence Mont had his arm through that of Emily his wife, the expression on his thin twisting countenance was as of one saying: 'A very beautiful performance – don't cry, my dear.'

The faces of Hilary and Lionel, one on each side of Wilmet, a seamed face and a smooth face, both long and thin and decisive, wore a sort of sorry scepticism, as if expecting those eyes to open. Wilmet had flushed deep pink; her lips were pursed. She was a tall thin woman. The chaplain stood with bent head, moving his lips as though telling over internal beads. They stayed thus perhaps three minutes, then as it were with a single indrawn breath filed to the door. They went each to the room assigned.

They met again at dinner, thinking and speaking once more in terms of life. Uncle Cuthbert, except as a family figure-head, had never been very near to any one of them. The question whether he was to be buried with his fathers at Condaford or here in the Cathedral was debated. Probably his will would decide. All but the General and Lionel, who were the executors, returned to London the same evening.

The two brothers, having read through the will, which was short, for there was nothing much to leave, sat on in the library, silent, till the General said:

'I want to consult you, Lionel. It's about my boy, Hubert. Did you read that attack made on him in the House before it rose?'

Lionel, sparing of words, and now on the eve of a Judgeship, nodded.

'I saw there was a question asked, but I don't know Hubert's version of the affair.'

'I can give it you. The whole thing is damnable. The boy's got a temper, of course, but he's straight as a die. What he says you can rely on. And all I can say is that if I'd been in his place, I should probably have done the same.'

Lionel nodded. 'Go ahead.'

'Well, as you know, he went straight from Harrow into the War, and had one year in the R.A.F. under age, got wounded, went back and stayed on in the army after the war. He was out in Mespot, then went on to Egypt and India. He got malaria badly, and last October had a year's sick leave given him, which will be up on October first. He was recommended for a long voyage. He got leave for it and went out through the Panama Canal to Lima. There he met that American professor, Hallorsen, who came over here some time ago and gave some lectures, it appears, about some queer remains in Bolivia; he was going to take an expedition there. This expedition was just starting when Hubert got to Lima, and Hallorsen wanted a transport officer. Hubert was fit enough after his voyage and jumped at the chance. He can't bear idleness. Hallorsen took him on; that was in December last. After a bit Hallorsen left him in charge of his base camp with a lot of half-caste Indian mule men. Hubert was the only white man, and he got fever badly. Some of those half-caste Indian fellows are devils, according to his account; no sense of discipline and perfect brutes with animals. Hubert got wrong with them – he's a hot-tempered chap, as I told you, and, as it happens, particularly fond of animals. The half-castes got more and more out of hand, till finally one of them, whom he'd had to have flogged for ill-treating mules and who was stirring up mutiny, attacked him with a knife. Luckily Hubert had his revolver handy and shot him dead. And on that the whole blessed lot of them, except three, cleared out, taking the mules with them. Mind you, he'd been left there alone for nearly three months without support or news of any kind from Hallorsen. Well, he hung on somehow, half dead, with his remaining men. At last Hallorsen came back, and instead of trying to understand his difficulties, pitched into him. Hubert wouldn't stand for it; gave him as good as he got, and left. He came straight home, and is down with us at Condaford. He's lost the fever, luckily, but he's pretty well worn out, even now. And now that fellow Hallorsen has attacked him in his book; practically thrown the blame of failure on him, implies he was tyrannical and no good at handling men, calls him a hot-tempered aristocrat – all that bunkum that goes down these days. Well, some Service member got hold of this and asked that question about it in Parliament. One expects Socialists to make themselves unpleasant, but when it comes to a Service member alluding to conduct unbecoming to a British officer, it's another matter altogether. Hallorsen's in the States. There's nobody to bring an action against: besides, Hubert could get no witnesses. It looks to me as if the thing has cut right across his career.'

Lionel Cherrell's long face lengthened.

'Has he tried Headquarters?'

'Yes, he went up on Wednesday. They were chilly. Any popular gup about high-handedness scares them nowadays. I daresay they'd come round if no more were said, but how's that possible? He's been publicly criticised in that book, and practically accused in Parliament of violent conduct unbecoming to an officer and gentleman. He can't sit down under that; and yet – what can he do?'

Lionel drew deeply at his pipe.

'D'you know,' he said, 'I think he'd better take no notice.'

The General clenched his fist. 'Damn it, Lionel, I don't see that!'

'But he admits the shooting and the flogging. The public has no imagination, Con – they'll never see his side of the thing. All they'll swallow is that on a civilian expedition he shot one man and flogged others. You can't expect them to understand the conditions or the pressure there was.'

'Then you seriously advise him to take it lying down?'

'As a man, no; as a man of the world, yes.'

'Good Lord! What's England coming to? I wonder what old Uncle Cuffs would have said? He thought a lot of our name.'

'So do I. But how is Hubert to get even with them?'

The General was silent for a little while and then said:

'This charge is a slur on the Service, and yet his hands seem tied. If he handed in his Commission he could stand up to it, but his whole heart's in the Army. It's a bad business. By the way, Lawrence has been talking to me about Adrian. Diana Ferse was Diana Montjoy, wasn't she?'

'Yes, second cousin to Lawrence – very pretty woman, Con. Ever see her?'

'As a girl, yes. What's her position now, then?'

'Married widow – two children, and a husband in a Mental Home.'

'That's lively. Incurable?'

Lionel nodded. 'They say so. But of course, you never know.'

'Good Lord!'

'That's just about it. She's poor and Adrian's poorer; it's a very old affection on Adrian's part, dates from before her marriage. If he does anything foolish, he'll lose his curatorship.'

'Go off with her, you mean? Why, he must be fifty!'

'No fool like an— She's an attractive creature. Those Montjoys are celebrated for their charm. Would he listen to you, Con?'

The General shook his head.

'More likely to Hilary.'

'Poor old Adrian – one of the best men on earth. I'll talk to Hilary, but his hands are always full.'

The General rose. 'I'm going to bed. We don't smell of age at the Grange like this place – though the Grange is older.'

'Too much original wood here. Good-night, old man.'

The brothers shook hands, and, grasping each a candle, sought their rooms.

Chapter Two

Condaford Grange had passed from the de Campforts (whence its name) into possession of the Cherrells in 1217, when their name was spelt Kerwell and still at times Keroual, as the spirit moved the scribe. The story of its passing was romantic, for the Kerwell who got it by marrying a de Campfort had got the de Campfort by rescuing her from a wild boar. He had been a landless wight whose father, a Frenchman from Guienne, had come to England after Richard's crusade; and she had been the heiress of the landed de Campforts. The boar was incorporated on the family 'shield', and some doubted whether the boar on the shield did not give rise to the story, rather than the story to the boar. In any case parts of the house were certified by expert masons to go back to the twelfth century. It had undoubtedly been moated; but under Queen Anne a restorative Cherrell, convinced of the millennium perhaps, and possibly inconvenienced by insects, had drained off the water, and there was now little sign that a moat had ever been.

The late Sir Conway, elder brother of the bishop, knighted in 1901 on his appointment to Spain, had been in the diplomatic service. He had therefore let the place down badly. He had died in 1904, at his post, and the letting-down process had been continued by his eldest son, the present Sir Conway, who, continually on Service, had enjoyed only spasmodic chances of living at Condaford till after the Great War. Now that he did live there, the knowledge that folk of his blood had been encamped there practically since the Conquest had spurred him to do his best to put it in order, so that it was by now unpretentiously trim without and comfortable within, and he was almost too poor to live in it. The estate contained too much covert to be profitable, and, though unencumbered, brought in but a few hundreds a year of net revenue. The pension of a General and the slender income of his wife (by birth the Honourable Elizabeth Frensham) enabled the General to incur a very small amount of supertax, to keep two hunters, and live quietly on the extreme edge of his means. His wife was one of those Englishwomen who seem to count for little, but for that very reason count for a good deal. She was unobtrusive, gentle, and always busy. In a word, she was background; and her pale face, reposeful, sensitive, a little timid, was a continual reminder that culture depends but slightly on wealth or intellect. Her husband and her three children had implicit confidence in her coherent sympathy. They were all of more vivid nature, more strongly coloured, and she was a relief.

She had not accompanied the General to Porthminster and was therefore awaiting his return. The furniture was about to come out of chintz, and she was standing in the tea room wondering whether that chintz would last another season, when a Scotch terrier came in, followed by her eldest daughter Elizabeth – better known as 'Dinny'. Dinny was slight and rather tall; she had hair the colour of chestnuts, an imperfect nose, a Botticellian mouth, eyes cornflower blue and widely set, and a look rather of a flower on a long stalk that might easily be broken off, but never was. Her expression suggested that she went through life trying not to see it as a joke. She was, in fact, like one of those natural wells, or springs, whence one cannot procure water without bubbles: 'Dinny's bubble and squeak', her uncle Sir Lawrence Mont called it. She was by now twenty-four.

'Mother, do we have to go into black edging for Uncle Cuffs?'

'I don't think so, Dinny; or very slight.'

'Is he to be planted here?'

'I expect in the Cathedral, but Father will know.'

'Tea, darling? Scaramouch, up you come, and don't bob your nose into the Gentleman's Relish.'

'Dinny, I'm so worried about Hubert.'

'So am I, dear; he isn't Hubert at all, he's like a sketch of himself by Thom the painter, all on one side. He ought never to have gone on that ghastly expedition, Mother. There's a limit to hitting it off with Americans, and Hubert reaches it sooner than almost anybody I know. He never could get on with them. Besides, I don't believe civilians ever ought to have soldiers with them.'

'Why, Dinny?'

'Well, soldiers have the static mind. They know God from Mammon. Haven't you noticed it, dear?'

Lady Cherrell had. She smiled timidly, and asked:

'Where is Hubert? Father will be home directly.'

'He went out with Don, to get a leash of partridges for dinner. Ten to one he'll forget to shoot them, and anyway they'll be too fresh. He's in that state of mind into which it has pleased God to call him; except that for God read the devil. He broods over that business, Mother. Only one thing would do him good, and that's to fall in love. Can't we find the perfect girl for him? Shall I ring for tea?'

'Yes, dear. And this room wants fresh flowers.'

'I'll get them. Come along, Scaramouch!'

Passing out into September sunshine, Dinny noted a green woodpecker on the lower lawn, and thought: 'If seven birds with seven beaks should peck for half a term, do you suppose, the lady thought, that they could find a worm?' It *was* dry! All the same the zinnias were gorgeous this year; and she proceeded to pick some. They ran the gamut in her hand from deepest red through pink to lemon-yellow – handsome blossoms, but not endearing. 'Pity,' she thought, 'we can't go to some bed of modern maids and pick one for Hubert.' She seldom showed her feelings, but she had two deep feelings not for show – one for her brother, the other for Condaford, and they were radically entwined. All the coherence of her life belonged to Condaford; she had a passion for the place which no one would have suspected from her way of talking of it, and she had a deep and jealous desire to bind her only brother to the same devotion. After all, she had been born there while it was shabby and run-down, and had survived into the period of renovation. To Hubert it had only been a holiday and leave-time perch. Dinny, though the last person in the world to talk of her roots, or to take them seriously in public, had a private faith in the Cherrells, their belongings and their works, which nothing could shake. Every Condaford beast, bird and tree, even the flowers she was plucking, were a part of her, just as were the simple folk around in their thatched cottages, and the Early-English church, where she attended without belief to speak of, and the grey Condaford dawns which she seldom saw, the moonlit, owl-haunted nights, the long sunlight over the stubble, and the scents and the sounds and the feel of the air. When she was away from home she never said she was homesick, but she was; when she was at home she never said she revelled in it, but she did. If Condaford should pass from the Cherrells, she would not moan, but would feel like a plant pulled up by its roots. Her father had for it the indifferent affection of a man whose active life had been passed elsewhere; her mother the acquiescence of one who had always done her duty by what had kept her nose to the grindstone and was not exactly hers; her sister treated it with the matter-of-fact tolerance of one who would rather be somewhere more exciting; and Hubert – what had Hubert? She really did not know. With her hands full of zinnias and her neck warm from the lingering sunshine, she returned to the drawing room.

Her mother was standing by the tea table.

'The train's late,' she said. 'I do wish Clare wouldn't drive so fast.'

'I don't see the connection, darling.' But she did. Mother was always fidgety when Father was behind time.

'Mother, I'm all for Hubert sending his version to the papers.'

'We shall see what your Father says – he'll have talked to your Uncle Lionel.'

'I hear the car now,' said Dinny.

The General was followed into the room by his younger daughter. Clare was the most vivid member of the family. She had dark fine shingled hair and a pale expressive face, of which the lips were slightly brightened. The eyes were brown, with a straight and eager glance, the brow low and very white. Her expression was old for a girl of twenty, being calm and yet adventurous. She had an excellent figure and walked with an air.

'This poor dear has had no lunch, Mother,' she said.

'Horrible cross-country journey, Liz. Whisky-and-soda and a biscuit's all I've had since breakfast.'

'You shall have an egg-nogg, darling,' said Dinny, and left the room. Clare followed her.

The General kissed his wife. 'The old boy looked very fine, my dear, though, except for Adrian, we only saw him after. I shall have to go back for the funeral. It'll be a swell affair, I expect. Great figure – Uncle Cuffs. I spoke to Lionel about Hubert; he doesn't see what can be done. But I've been thinking.'

'Yes, Con?'

'The whole point is whether or not the Authorities are going to take any notice of that attack in the House. They might ask him to send in his commission. That'd be fatal. Sooner than that he'd better hand it in himself. He's due for his medical on October the first. Can we pull any strings without his knowing? – the boy's proud. I can go and see Topsham and you could get at Follanby, couldn't you?'

Lady Cherrell made wry her face.

'I know,' said the General, 'it's rotten; but the real chance would be Saxenden, only I don't know how to get at him.'

'Dinny might suggest something.'

'Dinny? Well, I suppose she *has* more brains than any of us, except you, my dear.'

'I,' said Lady Cherrell, 'have no brains at all.'

'Bosh! Oh! Here she is.'

Dinny advanced, bearing a frothy liquor in a glass.

'Dinny, I was saying to your mother that we want to get into touch with Lord Saxenden about Hubert's position. Can you suggest any way?'

'Through a country neighbour, Dad. Has he any?'

'His place marches with Wilfred Bentworth's.'

'There it is, then. Uncle Hilary or Uncle Lawrence.'

'How?'

'Wilfred Bentworth is Chairman of Uncle Hilary's Slum Conversion Committee. A little judicious nepotism, dear.'

'Um! Hilary and Lawrence were both at Porthminster – wish I'd thought of that.'

'Shall I talk to them for you, Father?'

'By George, if you would, Dinny! I hate pushing our affairs.'

'Yes, dear. It's a woman's job, isn't it?'

The General looked at his daughter dubiously – he never quite knew when she was serious.

'Here's Hubert,' said Dinny, quickly.

Chapter Three

Hubert Cherrell, followed by a spaniel dog and carrying a gun, was crossing the old grey flagstones of the terrace. Rather over middle height, lean and erect, with a head not very large and a face weathered and seamed for so young a man, he wore a little darkish moustache cut just to the edge of his lips, which were thin and sensitive, and hair with already a touch of grey at the sides. His browned cheeks were thin too, but with rather high cheek-bones, and his eyes hazel, quick and glancing, set rather wide apart over a straight thin nose under gabled eyebrows. He was, in fact, a younger edition of his father. A man of action, forced into a state of thought, is unhappy until he can get out of it; and, ever since his late leader had launched that attack on his conduct, he had chafed, conscious of having acted rightly, or rather, in accordance with necessity. And he chafed the more because his training and his disposition forbade him giving tongue. A soldier by choice, not accident, he saw his soldiering imperilled, his name as an officer, and even as a gentleman, aspersed, and no way of hitting back at those who had aspersed it. His head seemed to him to be in Chancery for anyone to punch, most galling of experiences to anyone of high spirit. He came in through the French window, leaving dog and gun outside, aware that he was being talked about. He was now constantly interrupting discussions on his position, for in this family the troubles of one were the troubles of all. Having taken a cup of tea from his mother, he remarked that birds were getting wild already, covert was so sparse, and there was silence.

'Well, I'm going to look at my letters,' said the General, and went out followed by his wife.

Left alone with her brother, Dinny hardened her heart, and said:

'Something must be done, Hubert.'

'Don't worry, old girl; it's rotten, but there's nothing one can do.'

'Why don't you write your own account of what happened, from your diary? I could type it, and Michael will find you a publisher, he knows all those sort of people. We simply can't sit down under this.'

'I loathe the idea of trotting my private feelings into the open; and it means that or nothing.'

Dinny wrinkled her brows.

'I loathe letting that Yank put his failure on to you. You owe it to the British Army, Hubert.'

'Bad as that? I went as a civilian.'

'Why not publish your diary as it is?'

'That'd be worse. You haven't seen it.'

'We could expurgate, and embroider, and all that. You see, the Dad feels this.'

'Perhaps you'd better read the thing. It's full of "miserable Starkey". When one's alone like that, one lets oneself go.'

'You can cut out what you like.'

'It's no end good of you, Dinny.'

Dinny stroked his sleeve.

'What sort of man is this Hallorsen?'

'To be just, he has lots of qualities: hard as nails, plenty of pluck, and no nerves; but it's Hallorsen first with him all the time. It's not in him to fail, and when he does, someone else has to stand the racket. According to him, he failed for want of transport: and I was his transport officer. But if he'd left the Angel Gabriel as he left me, he'd have done no better. He just miscalculated, and won't admit it. You'll find it all in my diary.'

'Have you seen this?' She held up a newspaper cutting, and read:

'"We understand that action will be taken by Captain Charwell, D.S.O., to vindicate his honour in face of the statements made in Professor Hallorsen's book on his Bolivian Expedition, the failure of which he attributed to Captain Charwell's failure to support him at the critical moment.' Someone's trying to get a dog-fight out of it, you see.'

'Where was that?'

'In the *Evening Sun.*'

'Steps!' said Hubert bitterly; 'what steps? I've nothing but my word, he took care of that when he left me alone with all those dagoes.'

'It's the diary then, or nothing.'

'I'll get you the damned thing . . .'

That night Dinny sat at her window reading 'the damned thing'. A full moon rode between the elm trees and there was silence as of the grave. Just one sheep-bell tinkled from a fold on the rise; just one magnolia flower bloomed close to her window. All seemed unearthly, and now and then she stopped reading to gaze at the unreality. So had some ten thousand full moons ridden since her forebears received this patch of ground; the changeless security of so old a home heightened the lonely discomfort, the tribulation in the pages she was reading. Stark notes about stark things – one white man among a crew of half-caste savages, one animal-lover among half-starved animals and such men as knew not compassion. And with that cold and settled loveliness out there to look upon, she read and grew hot and miserable.

'That lousy brute Castro has been digging his infernal knife into the mules again. The poor brutes are thin as rails, and haven't half their strength. Warned him for the last time. If he does it again, he'll get the lash . . . Had fever.'

'Castro got it good and strong this morning – a dozen; we'll see if that will stop him. Can't get on with these brutes; they don't seem human. Oh! for a day on a horse at Condaford and forget these swamps and poor ghastly skeletons of mules . . .'

'Had to flog another of these brutes – their treatment of the mules is simply devilish, blast them! . . . Fever again . . .'

'Hell and Tommy to pay – had mutiny this morning. They laid for me. Luckily Manuel had warned me – he's a good boy. As it was, Castro nearly had his knife through my gizzard. Got my left arm badly. Shot him with my own hand. Now perhaps they'll toe the mark. Nothing from Hallorsen. How much longer does he expect me to hold on in this dump of hell? My arm is giving me proper gee-up . . .'

'The lid is on at last, those devils stampeded the mules in the dark while I was asleep, and cleared out. Manuel and two other boys are all that's left. We trailed them a long way – came on the carcasses of two mules, that's all; the beggars have dispersed and you might as well look for a star in the Milky Way. Got back to camp dead beat . . . Whether we shall ever get out of this alive, goodness knows. My arm is very painful, hope it doesn't mean blood-poisoning . . .'

'Meant to trek today as best we could. Set up a pile of stones and left despatch for Hallorsen, telling him the whole story in case he ever does send back for me; then changed my mind. I shall stick it out here till he comes or till we're dead, which is on the whole more likely . . .'

And so on through a tale of struggle to the end. Dinny laid down the dim and yellowed record and leaned her elbow on the sill. The silence and the coldness of the light out there had chilled her spirit. She no longer felt in fighting mood. Hubert was right. Why show one's naked soul, one's sore finger, to the public? No! Better anything than that. Private strings – yes, they should be pulled; and she would pull them for all she was worth.

Chapter Four

Adrian Cherrell was one of those confirmed countrymen who live in towns. His job confined him to London, where he presided over a collection of anthropological remains. He was poring over a maxilla from New Guinea, which had been accorded a very fine reception in the Press, and had just said to himself: 'The thing's a phlizz. Just a low type of Homo Sapiens,' when his janitor announced:

'Young lady to see you, sir – Miss Cherrell, I think.'

'Ask her in, James'; and he thought: 'If that's Dinny, where did I put my wits?'

'Oh! Dinny! Canrobert says that this maxilla is pre-Trinil. Mokley says Paulo-post-Piltdown; and Eldon P. Burbank says propter Rhodesian. I say Sapiens; observe that molar.'

'I do, Uncle Adrian.'

'Too human altogether. That man had toothache. Toothache was probably the result of artistic development. Altamiran art and Cromagnon cavities are found together. Homo Sapiens, this chap.'

'No toothache without wisdom – how cheery! I've come up to see Uncle Hilary and Uncle Lawrence, but I thought if I had lunch with you first, I should feel stronger.'

'We shall,' said Adrian, 'therefore go to the Bulgarian café.'

'Why?'

'Because for the moment we shall get good food there. It's the latest propaganda restaurant, my dear, so we are probably safe at a moderate price. Do you want to powder your nose?'

'Yes.'

'In here, then.'

While she was gone Adrian stood and stroked his goatee and wondered exactly what he could order for eighteen and sixpence; for, being a public servant without private means, he rarely had more than a pound in his pocket.

'What,' said Dinny, when they were seated before an omelette Bulgarienne, 'do you know about Professor Hallorsen, Uncle Adrian?'

'The man who set out to discover the sources of civilisation in Bolivia?'

'Yes; and took Hubert with him.'

'Ah! But left him behind, I gather?'

'Did you ever meet him?'

'I did. I met him in 1920, climbing the "Little Sinner" in the Dolomites.'

'Did you like him?'

'No.'

'Why?'

'Well, he was so aggressively young, he beat me to the top, and – he reminded me of baseball. Did you ever see baseball played?'

'No.'

'I saw it once in Washington. You insult your opponent so as to shake his nerve. You call him doughboy and attaboy, and President Wilson and Old Man Ribber, and things like that, just when he's going to hit the ball. It's ritual. The point is to win at any cost.'

'Don't you believe in winning at any cost?'

'Nobody says they do, Dinny.'

'And we all try to when it comes to the point?'

'I have known it occur, even with politicians, Dinny.'

'Would you try to win at any cost, Uncle?'

'Probably.'

'You wouldn't. I should.'

'You are very kind, my dear; but why this local disparagement?'

'Because I feel as bloodthirsty as a mosquito about Hubert's case. I spent last night reading his diary.'

'Woman,' said Adrian, slowly, 'has not yet lost her divine irresponsibility.'

'Do you think we're in danger of losing it?'

'No, because whatever your sex may say, you never will annihilate man's innate sense of leading you about.'

'What is the best way to annihilate a man like Hallorsen, Uncle Adrian?'

'Apart from a club, ridicule.'

'His notion about Bolivian civilisation was absurd, I suppose?'

'Wholly. There are, we know, some curious and unexplained stone monsters up there, but his theory, if I understand it, won't wash at all. Only, my dear, Hubert would appear to be involved in it.'

'Not scientifically; he just went as transport officer.' And Dinny levelled a smile at her Uncle's eyes. 'It wouldn't do any harm, would it, to hold up a stunt like that to ridicule? You could do it so beautifully, Uncle.'

'Serpent!'

'But isn't it the duty of serious scientists to ridicule stunts?'

'If Hallorsen were an Englishman – perhaps; but his being an American brings in other considerations.'

'Why? I thought Science paid no regard to frontiers.'

'In theory. In practice we close the other eye. Americans are very touchy. You remember a certain recent attitude towards Evolution; if we had let out our shout of laughter over that, there might almost have been a war.'

'But most Americans laughed at it too.'

'Yes; but they won't stand for outsiders laughing at their kith and kin. Have some of this soufflé Sofia?'

They ate in silence, each studying sympathetically the other's face. Dinny was thinking: 'I love his wrinkles, and it's a nice little beard for a beard.' Adrian was thinking: 'I'm glad her nose turns up a little. I have very engaging nieces and nephews.' At last she said:

'Well, Uncle Adrian, will you try and think of any way of strafing that man for the scurvy way he's treated Hubert?'

'Where is he?'

'Hubert says in the States.'

'Have you considered, my dear, that nepotism is undesirable?'

'So is injustice, Uncle; and blood is thicker than water.'

'And this wine,' said Adrian, with a grimace, 'is thicker than either. What are you going to see Hilary about?'

'I want to scrounge an introduction to Lord Saxenden.'

'Why?'

'Father says he's important.'

'So you are out to "pull strings", as they say?'

Dinny nodded.

'No sensitive and honest person can pull strings successfully, Dinny.'

Her eyebrows twitched and her teeth, very white and even, appeared in a broad smile.

'But I'm neither, dear.'

'We shall see. In the meantime these cigarettes are really tiptop propaganda. Have one?'

Dinny took a cigarette, and, with a long puff, said:

'You saw great-Uncle "Cuffs", didn't you, Uncle Adrian?'

'Yes. A dignified departure. He died in amber, as you might say. Wasted on the Church; he was the perfect diplomat, was Uncle "Cuffs".'

'I only saw him twice. But do you mean to say that *he* couldn't get what he wanted, without loss of dignity, by pulling strings?'

'It wasn't exactly pulling strings with him, my dear; it was suavity and power of personality.'

'Manners?'

'Manner – the Grand; it about died with him.'

'Well, Uncle, I must be going; wish me dishonesty and a thick skin.'

'And I,' said Adrian, 'will return to the jawbone of the New Guinean with which I hope to smite my learned brethren. If I can help Hubert in any decent way, I will. At all events I'll think about it. Give him my love, and good-bye, my dear!'

They parted, and Adrian went back to his museum. Regaining his position above the maxilla, he thought of a very different jawbone. Having reached an age when the blood of spare men with moderate habits has an even-tempered flow, his 'infatuation' with Diana Ferse, dating back to years before her fatal marriage, had a certain quality of altruism. He desired her happiness before his own. In his almost continual thoughts about her the consideration 'What's best for her?' was ever foremost. He had done without her for so long that importunity (never in his character) was out of the question where she was concerned. But her face, oval and dark-eyed, delicious in lip and nose, and a little sad in repose, constantly blurred the outlines of maxillae, thighbones, and the other interesting phenomena of his job. She and her two children lived in a small Chelsea house on the income of a husband who for four years had been a patient in a private Mental Home, and was never expected to recover his equilibrium. She was nearly forty, and had been through dreadful times before Ferse had definitely toppled over the edge. Of the old school in thought and manner, and trained to a coherent view of human history, Adrian accepted life with half-humorous fatalism. He was not of the reforming type, and the position of his lady love did not inspire him with a desire for the scalp of marriage. He wanted her to be happy, but did not see how in the existing circumstances he could make her so. She had at least peace and the sufficient income of him who had been smitten by Fate. Moreover, Adrian had something of the superstitious regard felt by primitive men for those afflicted with this particular form

of misfortune. Ferse had been a decent fellow till the taint began
to wear through the coatings of health and education, and his
conduct for the two years before his eclipse was only too liber-
ally explained by that eclipse. He was one of God's afflicted; and
his helplessness demanded of one the utmost scrupulosity. Adrian
turned from the maxilla and took down a built-up cast of
Pithecanthropus, that curious being from Trinil, Java, who for
so long has divided opinion as to whether he shall be called man-
ape or ape-man. What a distance from him to that modern English
skull over the mantelpiece! Ransack the authorities as one might,
one never received an answer to the question: Where was the
cradle of Homo Sapiens, the nest where he had developed from
Trinil, Piltdown, Neanderthal man, or from some other undis-
covered collateral of those creatures? If Adrian had a passion,
indeed, except for Diana Ferse, it was a burning desire to fix
that breeding spot. They were toying now with the idea of descent
from Neanderthal man, but he felt it wouldn't do. When special-
isation had reached a stage so definite as that disclosed by those
brutish specimens, it did not swerve to type so different. As well
expect development of red-deer from elk! He turned to that huge
globe whereon were marked all discoveries of moment concerning
the origin of modern Man, annotated in his own neat hand-
writing with notes on geological changes, time and climate. Where
– where to look? It was a detective problem, soluble only in the
French fashion by instinctive appreciation of the inherently prob-
able locality, ratified by research at the selected spot – the greatest
detective problem in the world. The foothills of the Himalayas,
the Fayoum, or somewhere now submerged beneath the sea? If,
indeed, it were under the sea, then it would never be established
to certainty. Academic – the whole thing? Not quite, for with it
was conjoined the question of man's essence, the real primitive
nature of the human being, on which social philosophy might
and should be founded – a question nicely revived of late: Whether,
indeed, man was fundamentally decent and peaceful, as examin-
ation into the lives of animals and some so-called savage peoples

seemed to suggest, or fundamentally aggressive and restless, as that lugubrious record, History, seemed to assert? Find the breeding nest of Homo Sapiens, and there would emerge perhaps some evidence to decide whether he was devil-angel or angel-devil. To one with Adrian's instincts there was great attraction in this revived thesis of the inherent gentleness of man, but his habit of mind refused to subscribe easily or wholesale to any kind of thesis. Even gentle beasts and birds lived by the law of self-preservation; so did primitive man; the devilries of sophisticated man began naturally with the extension of his activities and the increase of his competitions – in other words, with the ramifications of self-preservation induced by so-called civilised life. The uncomplicated existence of uncivilised man might well afford less chance to the instinct of self-preservation to be sinister in its manifestations, but you could hardly argue anything from that. Better to accept modern man as he was and try to curb his opportunities for mischief. Nor would it do to bank too much on the natural gentleness of primitive peoples. Only last night he had read of an elephant hunt in Central Africa, wherein the primitive negroes, men and women, who were beating for the white hunters, had fallen upon the carcasses of the slain elephants, torn them limb from limb, flesh from flesh, eaten it all dripping and raw, then vanished into the woods, couple by couple, to complete their orgy. After all, there was something in civilisation! But at this moment his janitor announced:

'A Professor 'Allorsen to see you, sir. He wants to look at the Peruvian skulls.'

'Hallorsen!' said Adrian, startled. 'Are you sure? I thought he was in America, James.'

''Allorsen was the name, sir; tall gentleman, speaks like an American. Here's his card.'

'H'm! I'll see him, James.' And he thought: 'Shade of Dinny! What am I going to say?'

The very tall and very good-looking man who entered seemed

about thirty-eight years old. His clean-shaven face was full of health, his eyes full of light, his dark hair had a fleck or two of premature grey in it. A breeze seemed to come in with him. He spoke at once:

'Mr Curator?'

Adrian bowed.

'Why! Surely we've met; up a mountain, wasn't it?'

'Yes,' said Adrian.

'Well, well! My name's Hallorsen – Bolivian expedition. I'm told your Peruvian skulls are bully. I brought my little Bolivian lot along; thought I'd like to compare them with your Peruvians right here. There's such a lot of bunk written about skulls by people who haven't seen the originals.'

'Very true, Professor. I shall be delighted to see your Bolivians. By the way, you never knew my name, I think. This is it.'

Adrian handed him a card. Hallorsen took it.

'Gee! Are you related to the Captain Charwell who's got his knife into me?'

'His uncle. But I was under the impression that it was your knife that was into him.'

'Well, he let me down.'

'I understand he thinks you let him down.'

'See here, Mr Charwell—'

'We pronounce the name Cherrell, if you don't mind.'

'Cherrell – yes, I remember now. But if you hire a man to do a job, Mr Curator, and that job's too much for him, and because it's too much for him you get left, what do you do – pass him a gold medal?'

'You find out, I think, whether the job you hired him to do was humanly possible, before you take out your knife, anyway.'

'That's up to the man who takes the job. And what was it? Just to keep a tight rein on a few dagoes.'

'I don't know very much about it, but I understand he had charge of the transport animals as well.'

'He surely did; and let the whole thing slip out of his hand.

Well, I don't expect you to side against your nephew. But can I see your Peruvians?'

'Certainly.'

'That's nice of you.'

During the mutual inspection which followed Adrian frequently glanced at the magnificent specimen of Homo Sapiens who stood beside him. A man so overflowing with health and life he had seldom seen. Natural enough that any check should gall him. Sheer vitality would prevent him from seeing the other side of things. Like his nation, matters must move his way, because there was no other way that seemed possible to his superabundance.

'After all,' he thought, 'he can't help being God's own specimen – Homo transatlanticus superbus'; and he said slyly: 'So the sun is going to travel West to East in future, Professor?'

Hallorsen smiled, and his smile had an exuberant sweetness.

'Well, Mr Curator, we're agreed, I guess, that civilisation started with agriculture. If we can show that we raised Indian corn on the American continent way back, maybe thousands of years before the old Nile civilisation of barley and wheat, why shouldn't the stream be the other way?'

'And can you?'

'Why, we have twenty to twenty-five types of Indian corn. Hrwdlicka claims that some twenty thousand years was necessary to differentiate them. That puts us way ahead as the parents of agriculture, anyway.'

'But alas! no type of Indian corn existed in the old world till after the discovery of America.'

'No, sir; nor did any old-world type cereal exist in America till after that. Now, if the old-world culture seeped its way across the Pacific, why didn't it bring along its cereals?'

'But that doesn't make America the light-bringer to the rest of the world, does it?'

'Maybe not; but if not, she just developed her own old civilisations out of her own discovery of cereals; and they were the first.'

'Are you an Atlantean, Professor?'

'I sometimes toy with the idea, Mr Curator.'

'Well, well! May I ask if you are quite happy about your attack on my nephew?'

'Why, I certainly had a sore head when I wrote it. Your nephew and I didn't click.'

'That, I should think, might make you all the more doubtful as to whether you were just.'

'If I withdrew my criticism, I wouldn't be saying what I really thought.'

'You are convinced that you had no hand in your failure to reach your objective?'

The frown on the giant's brow had a puzzled quality, and Adrian thought: 'An honest man, anyway.'

'I don't see what you're getting at,' said Hallorsen, slowly.

'You chose my nephew, I believe?'

'Yes, out of twenty others.'

'Precisely. You chose the wrong man, then?'

'I surely did.'

'Bad judgment?'

Hallorsen laughed.

'That's very acute, Mr Curator. But I'm not the man to advertise my own failings.'

'What you wanted,' said Adrian, dryly, 'was a man without the bowels of compassion; well, I admit, you didn't get him.'

Hallorsen flushed.

'We shan't agree about this, sir. I'll just take my little lot of skulls away. And I thank you for your courtesy.'

A few minutes later he was gone.

Adrian was left to tangled meditation. The fellow was better than he had remembered. Physically a splendid specimen, mentally not to be despised, spiritually – well, typical of a new world where each immediate objective was the most important thing on earth till it was attained, and attainment more important than the methods of attainment employed. 'Pity,' he thought, 'if there's going to be a dog-fight. Still, the fellow's in the wrong; one ought to be more charitable than to attack like that in public print. Too much ego in friend Hallorsen.' So thinking, he put the maxilla into a drawer.

Chapter Five

Dinny pursued her way towards St Augustine's-in-the-Meads. On that fine day the poverty of the district she was entering seemed to her country-nurtured eyes intensely cheerless. She was the more surprised by the hilarity of the children playing in the streets. Asking one of them the way to the Vicarage, she was escorted by five. They did not leave her when she rang the bell, and she was forced to conclude that they were actuated by motives not entirely connected with altruism. They attempted, indeed, to go in with her, and only left when she gave them each a penny. She was ushered into a pleasant room which looked as though it would be glad if someone had the time to enter it some day, and was contemplating a reproduction of the Castelfranco Francesca, when a voice said:

'Dinny!' and she saw her Aunt May. Mrs Hilary Cherrell had her usual air of surmounting the need for being in three places at once; she looked leisurely, detached, and pleased – not unnaturally, for she liked her niece.

'Up for shopping, dear?'

'No, Aunt May, I've come to win an introduction off Uncle Hilary.'

'Your Uncle's in the Police Court.'

A bubble rose to Dinny's surface.

'Why, what's he done, Aunt May?'

Mrs Hilary smiled.

'Nothing at present, but I won't answer for him if the magistrate isn't sensible. One of our young women has been charged with accosting.'

'Not Uncle Hilary?'

'No, dear, hardly that. Your uncle is a witness to her character.'

'And is there really a character to witness to, Aunt May?'

'Well, that's the point. Hilary says so; but I'm not so sure.'

'Men are very trustful. I've never been in a Police Court. I should love to go and catch Uncle there.'

'Well, I'm going in that direction. We might go together as far as the Court.'

Five minutes later they issued, and proceeded by way of streets ever more arresting to the eyes of Dinny, accustomed only to the picturesque poverty of the countryside.

'I never quite realised before,' she said, suddenly, 'that London was such a bad dream.'

'From which there is no awakening. That's the chilling part of it. Why on earth, with all this unemployment, don't they organise a national Slum Clearance Scheme? It would pay for itself within twenty years. Politicians are marvels of energy and principle when they're out of office, but when they get in, they simply run behind the machine.'

'They're not women, you see, Auntie.'

'Are you chaffing, Dinny?'

'Oh! no. Women haven't the sense of difficulty that men have; women's difficulties are physical and real, men's difficulties are mental and formal, they always say: "It'll never do!" Women never say that. They act, and find out whether it will do or not.'

Mrs Hilary was silent a moment.

'I suppose women *are* more actual; they have a fresher eye, and less sense of responsibility.'

'I wouldn't be a man for anything.'

'That's refreshing; but on the whole they get a better time, my dear, even now.'

'They think so, but I doubt it. Men are awfully like ostriches, it seems to me. They can refuse to see what they don't want to, better than we can; but I don't think that's an advantage.'

'If you lived in the Meads, Dinny, you might.'

'If I lived in the Meads, dear, I should die.'

Mrs Hilary contemplated her niece by marriage. Certainly she looked a little transparent and as if she could be snapped off, but she also had a look of 'breeding', as if her flesh were dominated by her spirit. She might be unexpectedly durable, and impermeable by outside things.

'I'm not so sure, Dinny; yours is a toughened breed. But for that your uncle would have been dead long ago. Well! Here's the Police Court. I'm sorry I can't spare time to come in. But everybody will be nice to you. It's a very human place, if somewhat indelicate. Be a little careful about your next-door neighbours.'

Dinny raised an eyebrow: 'Lousy, Aunt May?'

'Well, I wouldn't go so far as to say not. Come back to tea, if you can.'

She was gone.

The exchange and mart of human indelicacy was crowded, for with the infallible flair of the Public for anything dramatic, the case in which Hilary was a witness to character had caught on, since it involved the integrity of the Police. Its second remand was in progress when Dinny took the last remaining fifteen square inches of standing room. Her neighbours on the right reminded her of the nursery rhyme: 'The butcher, the baker, the candlestick-maker.' Her neighbour on the left was a tall policeman. Many women were among the throng at the back of the Court. The air was close and smelled of clothes. Dinny looked at the magistrate, ascetic and as if pickled, and wondered why he did not have incense fuming on his desk. Her eyes passed on to the figure in the dock, a girl of about her own age and height, neatly dressed, with good features except that her mouth was perhaps more sensuous than was fortunate for one in her position. Dinny estimated that her hair was probably fair. She stood very still, with a slight fixed flush on her pale cheeks, and a frightened restlessness in her eyes. Her name appeared to be Millicent Pole. Dinny gathered that she was alleged by a police constable to have accosted two men in the Euston Road, neither of whom had appeared to give evidence. In the witness-box a young man who resembled a tobacconist was testifying that he had seen the girl pass twice or three times – had noticed her specially as a 'nice bit'; she had seemed worried, as if looking for something.

For somebody, did he mean?

That or the other, how should he know? No, she wasn't looking on the pavement; no, she didn't stop, she passed *him*, anyway, without a look. Had he spoken to her? No fear! Doing? Oh, he was just outside his shop for a breath of air after closing. Did he see her speak to anyone? No, he didn't, but he wasn't there long.

'The Reverend Hilary Charwell.'

Dinny saw her uncle rise from a bench and step up under the canopy of the witness box. He looked active and unclerical, and her eyes rested with pleasure on his long firm face, so wrinkled and humorous.

'Your name is Hilary Charwell?'

'Cherrell, if you don't mind.'

'Quite. And you are the incumbent of St Augustine's-in-the-Meads?'

Hilary bowed.

'For how long?'

'Thirteen years.'

'You are acquainted with the defendant?'

'Since she was a child.'

'Tell us, please, Mr Cherrell, what you know of her?'

Dinny saw her uncle turn more definitely to the magistrate.

'Her father and mother, sir, were people for whom I had every respect; they brought up their children well. He was a shoemaker – poor, of course; we're all poor in my parish. I might almost say they died of poverty five and six years ago, and their two daughters have been more or less under my eye since. They work at Petter and Poplin's. I've never heard anything against Millicent here. So far as I know, she's a good honest girl.'

'I take it, Mr Cherrell, your opportunities of judging of her are not very great?'

'Well, I visit the house in which she lodges with her sister. If you saw it, sir, you would agree that it requires some self-respect to deal as well as they do with the conditions there.'

'Is she a member of your congregation?'

A smile came on her uncle's lips, and was reflected on the magistrate's.

'Hardly, sir. Their Sundays are too precious to young people nowadays. But Millicent is one of the girls who goes for her holidays to our Rest House near Dorking. They are always very good girls down there. My niece by marriage, Mrs Michael Mont, who runs the house, has reported well of her. Shall I read what she says?

DEAR UNCLE HILARY,

You ask about Millicent Pole. She has been down three times, and the matron reports that she is a nice girl and not at all flighty. My own impression of her is the same.

'Then it comes to this, Mr Cherrell: in your view a mistake has been made in this case?'

'Yes, sir; I am convinced of it.'

The girl in the dock put her handkerchief to her eyes. And Dinny felt, suddenly, indignant at the extreme wretchedness of her position. To stand there before all those people, even if she had done as they said! And why shouldn't a girl ask a man for his companionship? He wasn't obliged to give it.

The tall policeman stirred, looked down at her, as if scenting unorthodoxy, and cleared his throat.

'Thank you, Mr Cherrell.'

Hilary stepped out of the witness box and in doing so caught sight of his niece and waved a finger. Dinny became aware that the case was over, the magistrate making up his mind. He sat perfectly silent, pressing his finger-tips together and staring at the girl, who had finished mopping her eyes and was staring back at him. Dinny held her breath. On the next minute – a life, perhaps, hung in the balance! The tall policeman changed his feet. Was his sympathy with his fellow in the force, or with that girl? All the little noises in the Court had ceased, the only sound was the scratching of a pen. The magistrate held his finger-tips apart and spoke:

'I am not satisfied that this case has been made out. The defendant will be dismissed. You may go.'

The girl made a little choking sound. To her right the candle-stick-maker uttered a hoarse: ''Ear! 'ear!'

''Ush!' said the tall policeman. Dinny saw her uncle walking out beside the girl; he smiled as he passed.

'Wait for me, Dinny – shan't be two minutes!'

Slipping out behind the tall policeman, Dinny waited in the lobby. The nature of things around gave her the shuddery feeling one had turning up the light in a kitchen at night; the scent of Condy's Fluid assailed her nostrils; she moved nearer to the outer door. A police sergeant said:

'Anything I can do for you, Miss?'

'Thank you, I'm waiting for my uncle; he's just coming.'

'The reverend gentleman?'

Dinny nodded.

'Ah! He's a good man, is the Vicar. That girl got off?'

'Yes.'

'Well! Mistakes will 'appen. Here he is, Miss.'

Hilary came up and put his arm through Dinny's.

'Ah! Sergeant,' he said, 'how's the Missis?'

'Prime, Sir. So you pulled her out of it?'

'Yes,' said Hilary; 'and I want a pipe. Come along, Dinny.' And, nodding to the sergeant, he led her into the air.

'What brought *you* into this galley, Dinny?'

'I came after you, Uncle. Aunt May brought me. Did that girl really not do it?'

'Ask me another. But to convict her was the surest way to send her to hell. She's behind with her rent, and her sister's ill. Hold on a minute while I light up.' He emitted a cloud of smoke and resumed her arm. 'What do you want of me, my dear?'

'An introduction to Lord Saxenden.'

'Snubby Bantham? Why?'

'Because of Hubert.'

'Oh! Going to vamp him?'

'If you'll bring us together.'

'I was at Harrow with Snubby, he was only a baronet then – I haven't seen him since.'

'But you've got Wilfred Bentworth in your pocket, Uncle, and their estates march.'

'Well, I daresay Bentworth will give me a note to him for you.'

'That's not what I want. I want to meet him socially.'

'Um! Yes, you can hardly vamp him without. What's the point, exactly?'

'Hubert's future. We want to get at the fountain-head before worse befalls.'

'I see. But look here, Dinny, Lawrence is your man. He has Bentworth going to them at Lippinghall on Tuesday next week, for partridge driving. You could go too.'

'I thought of Uncle Lawrence, but I couldn't miss the chance of seeing you, Uncle.'

'My dear,' said Hilary, 'attractive nymphs mustn't say things like that. They go to the head. Well, here we are! Come in and have tea.'

In the drawing room of the Vicarage Dinny was startled to see again her Uncle Adrian. He was sitting in a corner with his long legs drawn in, surrounded by two young women who looked like teachers. He waved his spoon, and presently came over to her.

'After we parted, Dinny, who should appear but the man of wrath himself, to see my Peruvians.'

'Not Hallorsen?'

Adrian held out a card: 'Professor Edward Hallorsen', and in pencil, 'Piedmont Hotel'.

'He's a much more personable bloke than I thought when I met him husky and bearded in the Dolomites; and I should say he's no bad chap if taken the right way. And what I was going to say to you was: Why not take him the right way?'

'You haven't read Hubert's diary, Uncle.'

'I should like to.'

'You probably will. It may be published.'

Adrian whistled faintly.

'Perpend, my dear. Dog-fighting is excellent for all except the dogs.'

'Hallorsen's had his innings. It's Hubert's turn to bat.'

'Well, Dinny – no harm in having a look at the bowling before he goes in. Let me arrange a little dinner. Diana Ferse will have us at her house, and you can stay the night with her for it. So what about Monday?'

Dinny wrinkled her rather tip-tilted nose. If, as she intended, she went to Lippinghall next week, Monday *would* be handy. It might, after all, be as well to see this American before declaring war on him.

'All right, Uncle, and thank you very much. If you're going West may I come with you? I want to see Aunt Emily and Uncle Lawrence. Mount Street's on your way home.'

'Right! When you've had your fill, we'll start.'

'I'm quite full,' said Dinny, and got up.

Chapter Six

Her luck held, and she flushed her third Uncle contemplating his own house in Mount Street, as if he were about to make an offer for it.

'Ah! Dinny, come along; your Aunt's moulting, and she'll be glad to see you. I miss old Forsyte,' he added in the hall. 'I was just considering what I ought to ask for this house if we let it next season. You didn't know old Forsyte – Fleur's father: he was a character.'

'What is the matter with Aunt Em, Uncle Lawrence?'

'Nothing, my dear. I think the sight of poor old Uncle "Cuffs" has made her dwell on the future. Ever dwell on the future, Dinny? It's a dismal period, after a certain age.'

He opened a door.

'My dear, here's Dinny.'

Emily, Lady Mont, was standing in her panelled drawing room flicking a feather brush over a bit of Famille Verte, with her parakeet perched on her shoulder. She lowered the brush, advanced with a far-away look in her eyes, said 'Mind, Polly,' and kissed her niece. The parakeet transferred itself to Dinny's shoulder and bent its head round enquiringly to look in her face.

'He's such a dear,' said Lady Mont; 'you won't mind if he tweaks your ear? I'm so glad you came, Dinny; I've been so thinking of funerals. Do tell me your idea about the hereafter.'

'Is there one, Auntie?'

'Dinny! That's so depressing.'

'Perhaps those who want one have it.'

'You're like Michael. He's so mental. Where did you pick Dinny up, Lawrence?'

'In the street.'

'That sounds improper. How is your father, Dinny? I hope he isn't any the worse for that dreadful house at Porthminster. It did so smell of preserved mice.'

'We're all very worried about Hubert, Aunt Em.'

'Ah! Hubert, yes. You know, I think he made a mistake to flog those men. Shootin' them one can quite understand, but floggin' is so physical and like the old Duke.'

'Don't you feel inclined to flog carters when they lash over-loaded horses uphill, Auntie?'

'Yes, I do. Was that what they were doin'?'

'Practically, only worse. They used to twist the mules' tails and stick their knives into them, and generally play hell with the poor brutes.'

'Did they? I'm so glad he flogged them; though I've never liked mules ever since we went up the Gemmi. Do you remember, Lawrence?'

Sir Lawrence nodded. On his face was the look, affectionate but quizzical, which Dinny always connected with Aunt Em.

'Why, Auntie?'

'They rolled on me; not they exactly, but the one I was ridin'. They tell me it's the only time a mule has ever rolled on anybody – surefooted.'

'Dreadful taste, Auntie!'

'Yes; and most unpleasant – so internal. Do you think Hubert would like to come and shoot partridges at Lippinghall next week?'

'I don't think you could get Hubert to go anywhere just now. He's got a terrible hump. But if you have a cubby-hole left for me, could *I* come?'

'Of course. There'll be plenty of room. Let's see: just Charlie

Muskham and his new wife, Mr Bentworth and Hen, Michael and Fleur, and Diana Ferse, and perhaps Adrian because he doesn't shoot, and your Aunt Wilmet. Oh! ah! And Lord Saxenden.'

'What!' cried Dinny.

'Why? Isn't he respectable?'

'But, Auntie – that's perfect! He's my objective.'

'What a dreadful word; I never heard it called that before. Besides, there's a Lady Saxenden, on her back somewhere.'

'No, no, Aunt Em. I want to get at him about Hubert. Father says he's the nod.'

'Dinny, you and Michael use the oddest expressions. What nod?'

Sir Lawrence broke the petrified silence he usually observed in the presence of his wife.

'Dinny means, my dear, that Saxenden is a big noise behind the scenes in military matters.'

'What is he like, Uncle Lawrence?'

'Snubby? I've known him many years – quite a lad.'

'This is very agitatin',' said Lady Mont, resuming the parakeet.

'Dear Auntie, I'm quite safe.'

'But is Lord – er – Snubby? I've always tried to keep Lippin'hall respectable. I'm very doubtful about Adrian as it is, but' – she placed the parakeet on the mantelpiece – 'he's my favourite brother. For a favourite brother one does things.'

'One does,' said Dinny.

'That'll be all right, Em,' put in Sir Lawrence. 'I'll watch over Dinny and Diana, and you can watch over Adrian and Snubby.'

'Your uncle gets more frivolous every year, Dinny; he tells me the most dreadful stories.' She stood still alongside Sir Lawrence and he put his hand through her arm.

Dinny thought: 'The Red King and the White Queen.'

'Well, good-bye, Dinny,' said her Aunt, suddenly; 'I have to go to bed. My Swedish masseuse is takin' me off three times a week. I really am reducin'.' Her eyes roved over Dinny: 'I wonder if she could put you on a bit!'

'I'm fatter than I look, Auntie.'

'So am I – it's distressin'. If your uncle wasn't a hop-pole I shouldn't mind so much.' She inclined her cheek, and Dinny gave it a smacking kiss.

'What a nice kiss!' said Lady Mont. 'I haven't had a kiss like that for years. People do peck so! Come, Polly!' and, with the parakeet upon her shoulder, she swayed away.

'Aunt Em looks awfully well.'

'She is, my dear. It's her mania – getting stout; she fights it tooth and nail. We live on the most variegated cookery. It's better at Lippinghall, because Augustine leads us by the nose, and she's as French as she was thirty-five years ago when we brought her back from our honeymoon. Cooks like a bird, still. Fortunately nothing makes me fat.'

'Aunt Em isn't fat.'

'M-no.'

'And she carries herself beautifully. We don't carry ourselves like that.'

'Carriage went out with Edward,' said Sir Lawrence; 'it was succeeded by the lope. All you young women lope as if you were about to spring on to something and make a get-away. I've been trying to foresee what will come next. Logically it should be the bound, but it may quite well revert and be the languish.'

'What sort of man is Lord Saxenden, really, Uncle Lawrence?'

'One of those who won the war by never having his opinion taken. You know the sort of thing: "Went down for week-end to Cooquers. The Capers were there, and Gwen Blandish; she was in force and had much to say about the Polish front. I had more. Talked with Capers; he thinks the Boches have had enough. I disagreed with him; he is very down on Lord T. Arthur Prose came over on Sunday; he estimates that the Russians now have two million rifles but no bullets. The war, he says, will be over by January. He is appalled by our losses. If he only knew what

I know! Lady Thripp was there with her son, who has lost his left foot. She is most engaging; promised to go and see her hospital and tell her how to run it. Very pleasant dinner on Sunday – everybody in great form; we played at comfits. Alick came in after; he says we lost forty thousand men in the last attack, but the French lost more. I expressed the opinion that it was very serious. No one took it."'

Dinny laughed. 'Were there such people?'

'Were there not, my dear! Most valuable fellows; what we should have done without them – the way they kept their ends up and their courage and their conversation – the thing had to be seen to be believed. And almost all of them won the war. Saxenden was especially responsible. He had an active job all the time.'

'What job?'

'Being in the know. He was probably more in the know than anybody else on earth, judging by what he says. Remarkable constitution, too, and lets you see it: great yachtsman.'

'I shall look forward to him.'

'Snubby,' sighed her uncle, 'is one of those persons at whom it is better to look back. Would you like to stay the night, Dinny, or are you going home?'

'Oh, I must go back tonight. My train's at eight from Paddington.'

'In that case I'll lope you across the Park, give you a snack at Paddington, and put you into the train.'

'Oh! don't bother about me, Uncle Lawrence.'

'Let you cross the Park without me, and miss the chance of being arrested for walking with a young female! Never! We might even sit, and try our luck. You're just the type that gets the aged into trouble. There's something Botticellian about you, Dinny. Come along.'

It was seven o'clock of the September evening when they debouched into Hyde Park, and, passing under the plane trees, walked on its withered grass.

'Too early,' said Sir Lawrence, 'owing to Daylight Saving.

Indecorum isn't billed till eight. I doubt if it will be any use to sit, Dinny. Can you tell a disguised copper when you see him? It's very necessary. The bowler hat – for fear of being hit on the head too suddenly; they always fall off in books; tendency to look as if he weren't a copper; touch of efficiency about the mouth – they complete their teeth in the force; eyes a trifle on the ground when they're not on you; the main man dwelling a little on both feet, and looking as if he had been measured for something. Boots of course – proverbial.'

Dinny gurgled.

'I tell you what we might do, Uncle Lawrence. Stage an accost. There'll be a policeman at the Paddington Gate. I'll loiter a little, and accost you as you come up. What ought I to say?'

Sir Lawrence wrinkled up an eyebrow.

'So far as I can recollect, something like: "How do, ducky? Your night out?"'

'I'll go on, then, and let that off on you under the policeman's nose.'

'He'd see through it, Dinny.'

'You're trying to back out.'

'Well, no one has taken a proposition of mine seriously for so long. Besides, "Life is real, life is earnest, and the end is not the gaol"!'

'I'm disappointed in you, Uncle.'

'I'm used to that, my dear. Wait till you're grave and reverend, and see how continually you will disappoint youth.'

'But think: we could have whole columns of the newspapers devoted to us for days. "Paddington Gate accosting incident: Alleged Uncle." Don't you hanker to be an alleged uncle and supersede the affairs of Europe? Don't you even want to get the Police into trouble? Uncle, it's pusillanimous.'

'*Soit!*' said Sir Lawrence: 'One uncle in the Police Court per day is enough. You're more dangerous than I thought, Dinny.'

'But, really, why should those girls be arrested? That all belongs to the past, when women *were* under-dogs.'

'I am entirely of your way of thinking, Dinny, but the Nonconformist conscience is still with us, and the Police must have something to do. Without adding to unemployment it's impossible to reduce their numbers. And an idle police force is dangerous to cooks.'

'Do be serious, Uncle!'

'Not that, my dear! Whatever else life holds for us – not that! But I do foresee the age when we shall all be free to accost each other, limited only by common civility. Instead of the present Vulgate, there will be revised versions for men and women. "Madam, will you walk?" "Sir, do you desire my company?" It will be an age not perhaps of gold, but at least of glitter. This is Paddington Gate. Could you have had the heart to spoof that noble-looking copper? Come along, let's cross.'

'Your Aunt,' he resumed, as they entered Paddington Station, 'won't rise again, so I'll dine with you in the buffet. We'll have a spot of the "boy", and for the rest, if I know our railway stations, oxtail soup, white fish, roast beef, greens, browned potatoes, and plum tart – all good, if somewhat English.'

'Uncle Lawrence,' said Dinny, when they had reached the roast beef, 'what do *you* think of Americans?'

'No patriotic man, Dinny, speaks the truth, the whole truth, and nothing but the truth, on that subject. Americans, however, like Englishmen, may be divided into two classes – Americans and Americans. In other words, some are nice and some are nasty.'

'Why don't we get on better with them?'

'That's an easy one. The nasty English don't get on better with them because they have more money than we have. The nice English don't get on as well as they ought with them, because Americans are so responsive and the tone of the American voice is not pleasing to the English ear. Or take it the other way round. The nasty Americans don't get on well with the English because the tone of the English voice is unpleasing to them. The nice Americans don't get on as well with us as they should, because we're so unresponsive and sniffy.'

'Don't you think they want to have things their own way too much?'

'So do we. It isn't that. It's manner, my dear, that divides us, manner and language.'

'How?'

'Having what used to be the same language is undoubtedly a snare. We must hope for such a development of the American lingo as will necessitate our both learning each other's.'

'But we always talk about the link of a common tongue.'

'Why this curiosity about Americans?'

'I'm to meet Professor Hallorsen on Monday.'

'The Bolivian bloke. A word of advice then, Dinny: Let him be in the right, and he'll feed out of your hand. Put him in the wrong, and you'll not feed out of his.'

'Oh! I mean to keep my temper.'

'Keep your left up, and don't rush in. Now, if you've finished, my dear, we ought to go; it's five minutes to eight.'

He put her into her carriage and supplied her with an evening paper. As the train moved out, he added:

'Give him the Botticellian eye, Dinny. Give him the Botticellian eye!'

Chapter Seven

Adrian brooded over Chelsea as he approached it on Monday evening. It was not what it used to be. Even in late Victorian days he remembered its inhabitants as somewhat troglodytic – persons inclined to duck their heads, with here and there a high light or historian. Charwomen, artists hoping to pay their rent, writers living on four-and-sevenpence a day, ladies prepared to shed their clothes at a shilling an hour, couples maturing for the Divorce Court, people who liked a draught, together with the worshippers of Turner, Carlyle, Rossetti, and Whistler; some publicans, not a few sinners, and the usual sprinkling of those who eat mutton four times a week. Behind a river façade hardening into the palatial, respectability had gradually thickened, till it was now lapping the incurable King's Road and emerging even there in bastions of Art and Fashion.

Diana's house was in Oakley Street. He could remember it as having no individuality whatever, and inhabited by a family of strict mutton-eaters; but in the six years of Diana's residence it had become one of the charming nests of London. He had known all the pretty Montjoy sisters scattered over Society, but of them all Diana was the youngest, the prettiest, most tasteful, and wittiest – one of those women who, without money to speak of or impeachment of virtue, contrive that all about them shall be elegant to the point of exciting jealousy. From her two children and her Collie dog (almost the only one left in London), from her harpsichord, four-poster, Bristol glass, and the stuff on her chairs and floors, taste always seemed to him to radiate and give comfort to the beholder. She, too, gave comfort, with her still perfect figure, dark eyes clear and quick, oval face, ivory complexion, and little crisp trick of speech. All the Montjoy sisters had that trick, it came from their mother, of Highland stock, and had undoubtedly in the course of thirty years made a considerable effect on the accent of Society, converting it from the g-dropping yaw-yaw of the 'nineties into a rather charming r- and l-pinching dialect. When he considered why Diana, with her scant income and her husband in a Mental Home, was received everywhere in Society, Adrian was accustomed to take the image of a Bactrian camel. That animal's two humps were like the two sections of Society (with the big S) joined by a bridge, seldom used after the first crossing. The Montjoys, a very old landed family in Dumfriesshire innumerably allied in the past with the nobility, had something of an hereditary perch on the foremost hump – a somewhat dull position from which there was very little view, because of the camel's head – and Diana was often invited to great houses where the chief works were hunting, shooting, hospitals, Court functions, and giving debutantes a chance. As Adrian well knew, she seldom went. She was far more constantly seated on the second hump, with its wide and stimulating view over the camel's tail. Ah! They were a queer collection on that back hump! Many, like Diana herself, crossed from the first hump by the bridge, others came up the camel's tail, a few were dropped from Heaven, or – as people sometimes called it – America. To qualify for that back hump Adrian, who had never qualified, knew that you needed a certain liveliness on several fronts; either a first-rate memory so that anything you read or listened to could be retailed with ready accuracy; or a natural spring of wit. If you had neither of these you might appear on the hump once, but never again. Personality of course, you must have, though without real eccentricity; but it must not be personality which hid its light under a bushel. Eminence in some branch of activity was desirable, but not a *sine qua non*. Breeding again was welcome, but not if it made you dull. Beauty was a passport, but it had to be allied with animation. Money was desirable, but money alone wouldn't get you a seat. Adrian had noted that knowledge of Art, if vocal, was of greater value than the power to produce it; and directive ability acceptable if it were not too silent or too dry. Then, again, some people seemed to get there out of an aptitude for the 'coulisses', and for having a finger in every pie. But first and last the great thing was to be able to talk. Innumerable strings were pulled from this back hump, but whether they guided the camel's progress at all he was never sure, however much those who pulled them thought so. Diana, he knew, had so safe a seat among this heterogeneous group, given to constant meals, that she might have fed without expense from Christmas to Christmas, nor need ever have passed a week-end in Oakley Street. And he was the more grateful in that she so constantly sacrificed all that to be with her children and himself. The war had broken out just after her marriage with Ronald Ferse, and Sheila and Ronald had not been born till after his return from it. They were now seven and six, and, as Adrian was always careful to tell her, 'regular little Montjoys'. They certainly had her looks and animation. But he alone knew that the shadow on her face in repose was due more to the fear that she ought not to have had them than to anything else in her situation. He, too, alone knew that the strain of living with one unbalanced as Ferse had become had so killed the sex impulse in her that she had lived these four years of practical widowhood without any urge towards love. He believed she had for himself a real affection, but he knew that so far it stopped short of passion.

He arrived half an hour before dinner time, and went up to the schoolroom at the top of the house, to see the children. They were receiving bed-time rusks and milk from their French governess, welcomed him with acclamation and clamoured for him to go on with the story he was telling them. The French governess, who knew what to expect, withdrew. Adrian sat down opposite the two small sparkling faces, and began where he had left off: 'So the man who had charge of the canoes was a tremendous fellow, brown all over, who had been selected for his strength, because of the white unicorns which infested that coast.'

'Boo! Uncle Adrian – unicorns are imaginative.'

'Not in those days, Sheila.'

'Then what's become of them?'

'There is only about one left, and he lives where white men cannot go, because of the "Bu-bu" fly.'

'What is the "Bu-bu" fly?'

'The "Bu-bu" fly, Ronald, is remarkable for settling in the calf of the leg and founding a family there.'

'Oh!'

'Unicorns – as I said before I was interrupted – which infested that coast. His name was Mattagor, and this was his way with unicorns. After luring them down to the beach with crinibobs—'

'What are crinibobs?'

'They look like strawberries and taste like carrots – crinibobs – he would steal up behind them—'

'If he was in front of them with the crinibobs, how could he steal up behind them?'

'He used to thread the crinibobs through a string made out of fibre, and hang them in a row between two charm trees. As soon as the unicorns were nibbling, he would emerge from the bush where he would be hiding, and, making no noise with his bare feet, tie their tails together two by two.'

'But they would feel their tails being tied!'

'No, Sheila; white unicorns don't feel with their tails. Then he would retire to the bush, and click his tongue against his teeth, and the unicorns would dash forward in wild confusion.'

'Did their tails ever come out?'

'Never. That was the great thing, because he was very fond of animals.'

'I expect the unicorns never came again?'

'Wrong, Ronny. Their love of crinibobs was too great.'

'Did he ever ride on them?'

'Yes; sometimes he would leap lightly on to two of their backs and ride off into the jungle with one foot on each back, laughing drily to himself. So under his charge, as you may imagine, the canoes were safe. It was not the wet season, so that the land-sharks would not be so numerous, and the expedition was about to start when—'

'When what, Uncle Adrian? It's only Mummy.'

'Go on, Adrian.'

But Adrian remained silent, with his eyes fixed on the advancing vision. Then, averting from it his eyes and fixing them on Sheila, he proceeded:

'I must now pause to tell you why the moon was so important. They could not start the expedition till the half-moon was seen advancing towards them through the charm trees.'

'Why not?'

'That is what I am going to tell you. In those days people, and especially this tribe of Phwatabhoys, paid a great deal of attention to what was beautiful – things like Mummy, or Christmas carols, or little new potatoes, had a great effect on them. And before they did anything they had to have an omen.'

'What is an omen?'

'You know what an amen is – it comes at the end: well, an omen comes at the beginning, to bring luck. And the omen had to be beautiful. Now the half-moon was considered to be the most beautiful thing in the dry season, so they had to wait till it came advancing to them through the charm trees, as you saw Mummy just now walking towards us through the door.'

'But the moon hasn't got feet.'

'No; she floats. And one fine evening she came floating, like nothing else on earth, so lovely and so slim, and with such an expression in her eyes that they all knew their expedition was bound to be successful; and they abased themselves before her, saying: "Omen! if thou wilt be with us, then shall we pass over

the wilderness of the waters and the sands with thee in our eyes,
and be happy in the happiness that comes with thee for ever and
ever. Amen!" And when they had put it like that, they got into
the canoes, Phwatabhoy by Phwatabhoy and Phwatanymph by
Phwatanymph, till they were all in. And the half-moon stayed
there at the edge of the charm trees and blessed them with her
eyes. But one man stopped behind. He was an old Phwatabhoy
who wished for the half-moon so much that he forgot everything, and started crawling towards her, hoping to touch her
feet.'

'But she hadn't feet!'

'He thought she had, for to him she was like a woman made
of silver and ivory. And he crawled in and out of the charm trees,
but never could he quite reach her, because she was the half-
moon.'

Adrian paused, and there was for a moment no sound; then
he said: 'To be continued in our next,' and went out. Diana
joined him in the hall.

'Adrian, you are corrupting the children. Don't you know that
fables and fairy-tales are no longer to be allowed to interfere
with their interest in machines? After you'd gone Ronald said:
"Does Uncle Adrian really believe you are the half-moon,
Mummy?"'

'And you answered?'

'Diplomatically. But they're as sharp as squirrels.'

'Well! Sing me "Waterboy" before Dinny and her swain come.'

And while she sat and sang, Adrian gazed and worshipped.
Her voice was good and she sang well that strange and haunting
song. The last 'Waterboy' had barely died away when the maid
announced:

'Miss Cherrell. Professor Hallorsen.'

Dinny came in with her head held high, and Adrian augured but
poorly from the expression of her eyes. He had seen schoolboys
look like that when they were going to 'roast' a new-comer. After
her came Hallorsen, immensely tall in that small drawing room, his

eyes swimming with health. He bowed low when presented to Dinny.
'Your daughter, I presume, Mr Curator?'

'No, my niece; a sister of Captain Hubert Cherrell.'

'Is that so? I am honoured to make your acquaintance, Ma'am.'

Adrian, noting that their eyes, having crossed, seemed to find
it difficult to disengage, said:

'How are you liking the Piedmont, Professor?'

'The cooking's fine, but there are too many of us Americans.'

'Perching just now like the swallows?'

'Ah! In a fortnight we'll all have flitted.'

Dinny had come brimful of Anglo-femininity, and the contrast
between Hallorsen's overpowering health and Hubert's haggard
looks had at once sharpened the edge of her temper. She sat
down beside that embodiment of the conquering male with the
full intention of planting every dart she could in his epidermis.
He was, however, at once engaged in conversation by Diana, and
she had not finished her soup (clear, with a prune in it) before,
stealing a look round at him, she revised her plan. After all, he
was a stranger and a guest, and she was supposed to be a lady;
there were other ways of killing a cat beside hanging it. She
would not plant darts, she would 'charm him with smiles and
soap'; that would be more considerate towards Diana and her
uncle, and more effective warfare in the long run. With a cunning
worthy of her cause, she waited till he was in deep water over
British politics, which he seemed to regard as serious manifestations of human activity; then, turning on him the Botticellian
eye, she said:

'We should treat American politics just as seriously, Professor.
But surely they're not serious, are they?'

'I believe you are right, Miss Cherrell. There's just one rule
for politicians all over the world: Don't say in Power what you
say in Opposition; if you do, you only have to carry out what
the other fellows have found impossible. The only real difference, I judge, between Parties is that one Party sits in the National
Bus, and the other Party strap-hangs.'

'In Russia, what's left of the other Party lies under the seat, doesn't it?'

'So it does in Italy,' said Diana.

'And what about Spain?' added Adrian.

Hallorsen uttered his infectious laugh. 'Dictatorships aren't politics. They're jokes.'

'*No* jokes, Professor.'

'Bad jokes, Professor.'

'How do you *mean* – jokes, Professor?'

'Bluff. Just one long assumption that human nature's on the mark the Dictator makes for it. The moment his bluff's called – Why! Wump!'

'But,' said Diana, 'suppose a majority of the people approve of their dictator, isn't that democracy, or government by consent of the governed?'

'I would say no, Mrs Ferse, unless he was confirmed by majority every year.'

'Dictators get things done,' said Adrian.

'At a price, Mr Curator. But look at Diaz in Mexico. For twenty years he made it the Garden of Eden, but see what it's been ever since he went. You can't get out of a people for keeps what isn't yet in them.'

'The fault,' replied Adrian, 'in our political system and in yours, Professor, is that a whole lot of reforms latent in the common-sense of the people don't get a chance of being carried out because our short-term politicians won't give a lead, for fear of losing the power they haven't got.'

'Aunt May,' Dinny murmured, 'was saying: Why not cure Unemployment by a National Slum Clearance effort, and kill the two birds with one stone?'

'My! But that's a mighty fine idea!' said Hallorsen, turning on her the full of his brimming face.

'Vested interests,' said Diana, 'slum landlordism and the building trades are too strong for that.'

Adrian added: 'And there's the cash required.'

'Why! that's all easy. Your Parliament could take what powers they need for a big national thing like that; and what's wrong with a Loan, anyway? – the money would come back; it's not like a Loan for war, all shot away in powder. What do you pay in doles?'

No one could answer him.

'I judge the saving would pay the interest on a pretty big Loan.'

'It just, in fact,' said Dinny, sweetly, 'needs simple faith. That's where you Americans beat us, Professor Hallorsen.'

A look slid over the American's face as though he were saying: 'Cats!'

'Well, we certainly had a pieful of simple faith when we came over to fight in France. But we ate the lot. It'll be the home fires we keep burning next time.'

'Was your faith so simple even last time?'

'I fear it was, Miss Cherrell. Not one in twenty of us ever believed the Germans could get a cinch on us away over there.'

'I sit rebuked, Professor.'

'Why! Not at all! You judge America by Europe.'

'There was Belgium, Professor,' said Diana; 'even we had some simple faith at the start.'

'Pardon me, but did the case of Belgium really move you, Ma'am?'

Adrian was drawing circles with a fork; he looked up.

'Speaking for oneself, yes. I don't suppose it made any difference to the Army people, Navy people, big business people, or even to a large section of Society, political and otherwise. They all knew that if war came we were practically committed to France. But to simple folk like myself and some two-thirds of the population not in the know, to the working classes, in fact, generally, it made all the difference. It was like seeing What's-his-name – the Man Mountain – advancing on the smallest Flyweight in the ring, who was standing firm and squaring up like a man.'

'Mighty well put, Mr Curator.'

Dinny flushed. Was there generosity in this man? Then, as if conscious of treachery to Hubert, she said acidly:

'I've read that the sight even ruffled Roosevelt.'

'It ruffled quite a few of us, Miss Cherrell; but we're a long way off over there, and things have to be near before they stir the imagination.'

'Yes, and after all, as you said just now, you did come in at the end.'

Hallorsen looked fixedly at her ingenuous face, bowed and was silent.

But when, at the end of that peculiar evening, he was saying good-night, he added:

'I fear you've gotten a grouch against me, Miss Cherrell.'

Dinny smiled, without reply.

'All the same, I hope I may meet you again.'

'Oh! But why?'

'Well, I kind of have the feeling that I might change the view you have of me.'

'I am very fond of my brother, Professor Hallorsen.'

'I still think I've more against your brother than he has against me.'

'I hope you may be right before long.'

'That sounds like trouble.'

Dinny tilted her head.

She went up to bed, biting her lip with vexation. She had neither charmed nor assailed the enemy; and instead of clean-cut animosity, she had confused feelings about him.

His inches gave him a disconcerting domination. 'He's like those creatures in hairy trousers on the films,' she thought, 'carrying off the semi-distressed cow-girls – looks at one as if he thought one was on his pillion.' Primitive Force in swallow-tails and a white waistcoat! A strong but not a silent man.

Her room looked over the street, and from her window she could see the plane trees on the Embankment, the river, and the wide expanse of starry night.

'Perhaps,' she said to herself, aloud, 'you won't leave England so soon as you thought.'

'Can I come in?'

She turned to see Diana in the doorway.

'Well, Dinny, what think you of our friend the enemy?'

'Tom Mix, mixed with the Giant that Jack killed.'

'Adrian likes him.'

'Uncle Adrian lives too much with bones. The sight of red blood goes to his head.'

'Yes; this is the sort of "he-man" women are supposed to fall for. But you behaved well, Dinny, though your eyes looked very green at first.'

'They feel greener now I've let him go without a scratch.'

'Never mind! You'll have other chances. Adrian's got him asked to Lippinghall tomorrow.'

'What!'

'You've only to embroil him with Saxenden there, and Hubert's trick is done. Adrian didn't tell you, for fear your joy might show itself. The Professor wants to sample British "hunting". The poor man doesn't in the least realise that he's walking into a lioness's den. Your Aunt Em will be delicious with him.'

'Hallorsen!' murmured Dinny: 'He must have Scandinavian blood.'

'He says his mother was old New England, but married out of the direct succession. Wyoming's his State. Delightful word, Wyoming.'

'"The great open spaces." What is there about the expression "he-man" which infuriates me, Diana?'

'Well, it's like being in a room with a burst of sunflowers. But "he-men" aren't confined to the great open spaces; you'll find Saxenden one.'

'Really!'

'Yes. Good-night, my dear. And may no "he-men" come to you in dreams!'

When Dinny had disrobed, she again took out the diary and

re-read a passage she had turned down. It ran thus: 'Feel very low tonight – as if all my sap had run out. Can only keep my pecker up by thinking of Condaford. Wonder what old Foxham would say if he could see me doctoring the mules! The stuff I've invented for their colic would raise hair on a billiard ball, but it stops the thing all right. God was in luck when He planned the inside of a mule. Dreamed last night I was standing at the end of the home spinney with pheasants coming over in a stream, and for the life of me I couldn't pull my trigger; ghastly sort of paralysis. Keep thinking of old Haddon and his: "Go it, Master Bertie. Stick your 'eels in and take 'old of 'is 'ead!" Good old Haddon! He was a character. The rain's stopped. Dry – first time for ten days. And the stars are out.

A ship, an isle, a sickle moon,
With few but with how splendid stars.

If only I could sleep! . . .'

Chapter Eight

hat essential private irregularity, room by room, which differentiates the old English from every other variety of country house, was patent at Lippinghall Manor. People went into rooms as if they meant to stay there, and while there inhaled an atmosphere and fitted into garniture different from those in any of the other rooms; nor did they feel that they must leave the room as they found it, if indeed they knew how that was. Fine old furniture stood in careless partnership with fill-up stuff acquired for the purposes of use or ease. Portraits of ancestors, dark or yellow, confronted Dutch or French landscapes still more yellow or dark, with here and there delightful old prints, and miniatures not without charm. In two rooms at least were beautiful old fireplaces, defiled by the comfort of a fender which could be sat on. Staircases appeared unexpectedly in the dark. The position of a bedroom was learned with difficulty and soon forgotten. In it would be, perhaps, a priceless old chestnut wood wardrobe and a four-poster bed of an excellent period; a window-seat with cushions, and some French prints. To it would be conjoined a small room with narrow bed; and bathroom that might or might not need a stroll, but would have salts in it. One of the Monts had been an Admiral; queer old charts, therefore, with dragons lashing the seas, lurked in odd corners of the corridors; one of the Monts, Sir Lawrence's grandfather, seventh baronet, had been a racing man, and the anatomy of the thoroughbred horse, and jockey of his period (1860–1883) could be studied on the walls. The sixth baronet, who, being in politics, had lived longer than the rest, had left imprints of the earlier Victorian period, his wife and daughters in crinolines, himself in whiskers. The outside of the house was Carolean, tempered here and there by Georgian, and even Victorian fragments where the sixth baronet had given way to his feeling for improvement. The only thing definitely modern was the plumbing.

When Dinny came down to breakfast on the Wednesday morning – the shoot being timed to start at ten – three of the ladies and all the men except Hallorsen were already sitting or wandering to the side-tables. She slipped into a chair next to Lord Saxenden, who rose slightly with the word:

'Morning!'

'Dinny,' called Michael from a sideboard, 'coffee, cocoatina or ginger beer?'

'Coffee and a kipper, Michael.'

'There are no kippers.'

Lord Saxenden looked up: 'No kippers?' he muttered, and resumed his sausage.

'Haddock?' said Michael.

'No, thank you.'

'Anything for you, Aunt Wilmet?'

'Kedgeree.'

'There is no kedgeree. Kidneys, bacon, scrambled eggs, haddock, ham, cold partridge pie.'

Lord Saxenden rose. 'Ah! Ham!' and went over to the side-table.

'Well, Dinny?'

'Just some jam, please, Michael.'

'Goose-gog, strawberry, black currant, marmalade.'

'Gooseberry.'

Lord Saxenden resumed his seat with a plate of ham, and began reading a letter as he ate. She did not quite know what to make of his face, because she could not see his eyes, and his mouth was so full. But she seemed to gather why he had been nicknamed 'Snubby'. He was red, had a light moustache and hair, both going grey, and a square seat at table. Suddenly he turned to her and said:

'Excuse my reading this. It's from my wife. She's on her back, you know.'

'I'm so sorry.'

'Horrible business! Poor thing!'

He put the letter in his pocket, filled his mouth with ham, and looked at Dinny. She saw that his eyes were blue, and that his eyebrows, darker than his hair, looked like clumps of fish-hooks. His eyes goggled a little, as though he were saying: 'I'm a lad – I'm a lad.' But at this moment she noticed Hallorsen coming in. He stood uncertain, then, seeing her, came to the empty seat on her other side.

'Miss Cherrell,' he said, with a bow, 'can I sit right here?'

'Of course: the food is all over there, if you're thinking of any.'

'Who's that fellow?' said Lord Saxenden, as Hallorsen went foraging: 'He's an American.'

'Professor Hallorsen.'

'Oh! Ah! Wrote a book on Bolivia? What!'

'Yes.'

'Good-looking chap.'

'A he-man.'

He looked round at her with surprise.

'Try this ham. I used to know an uncle of yours at Harrow, I think.'

'Uncle Hilary!' said Dinny. 'He told me.'

'I once laid him three strawberry mashes to two on myself in a race down the Hill steps to the Gym.'

'Did you win, Lord Saxenden?'

'No; and I never paid your uncle.'

'Why not?'

'He sprained his ankle and I put my knee out. He hopped to the Gym door; but I couldn't move. We were both laid up till the end of term, and then I left.' Lord Saxenden chuckled. 'So I still owe him three strawberry mashes.'

'I thought we had "some" breakfast in America, but it's nil to this,' said Hallorsen, sitting down.

'Do you know Lord Saxenden?'

'Lord Saxenden,' repeated Hallorsen with a bow.

'How de do? You haven't got our partridge in America, have you?'

'Why, no, I believe not. I am looking forward to hunting that bird. This is mighty fine coffee, Miss Cherrell.'

'Yes,' said Dinny. 'Aunt Em prides herself on her coffee.'

Lord Saxenden squared his seat. 'Try this ham. I haven't read your book.'

'Let me send it you; I'll be proud to have you read it.'

Lord Saxenden ate on.

'Yes, you ought to read it, Lord Saxenden,' said Dinny; 'and I'll send you another book that bears on the same subject.'

Lord Saxenden glared.

'Charming of you both,' he said. 'Is that strawberry jam?' and he reached for it.

'Miss Cherrell,' said Hallorsen, in a low voice, 'I'd like to have you go through my book and mark the passages you think are prejudicial to your brother. I wrote that book when I had a pretty sore head.'

'I'm afraid that I don't see what good that would do now.'

'So I could get them cut out, if you wish, for the second edition.'

'That's very good of you,' said Dinny, icily, 'but the harm is done, Professor.'

Hallorsen said, still lower: 'I'm just terribly sorry to have hurt you.'

A sensation, perhaps only to be summed up in the words: 'You are – are you!' flushed Dinny from top to toe with anger, triumph, calculation, humour.

'It's my brother you've hurt.'

'Maybe that could be mended if we could get together about it.'

'I wonder.' And Dinny rose.

Hallorsen stood up too, and bowed as she passed.

'Terribly polite,' she thought.

She spent her morning with the diary in a part of the garden so sunk within yew hedges that it formed a perfect refuge. The sun was warm there, and the humming of the bees over zinnias, pentstemons, hollyhocks, asters, Michaelmas daisies, was very soothing. In that so sheltered garden the dislike of casting Hubert's intimate feelings to the world's opinion came on her again. Not that the diary whined; but it revealed the hurts of mind and body with the sharpness of a record meant for no eye but the recorder's. The sound of shots kept floating to her; and presently, leaning her elbows on the top of the yew hedge, she looked out over the fields towards where they were shooting.

A voice said:

'There you are!'

Her aunt, in a straw hat so broad that it covered her to the very edges of her shoulders, was standing below with two gardeners behind her.

'I'm coming round to you, Dinny; Boswell, you and Johnson can go now. We'll look at the Portulaca this afternoon.' And she gazed up from under the tilted and enormous halo of her hat. 'It's Majorcan,' she said, 'so shelterin'.'

'Boswell and Johnson, Auntie!'

'We had Boswell, and your uncle would look till we found Johnson. He makes them go about together. Do you believe in Doctor Johnson, Dinny?'

'I think he used the word "Sir" too much.'

'Fleur's got my gardenin' scissors. What's that, Dinny?'

'Hubert's diary.'

'Depressin'?'

'Yes.'

'I've been lookin' at Professor Hallorsen – he wants takin' in.'

'Begin with his cheek, Aunt Em.'

'I hope they'll shoot some hares,' said Lady Mont; 'hare soup is such a stand-by. Wilmet and Henrietta Bentworth have agreed to differ already.'

'What about?'

'Well, I couldn't be bothered, but I think it was about the P.M., or was it Portulaca? – they differ about everything. Hen's always been about Court, you know.'

'Is that fatal?'

'She's a nice woman. I'm fond of Hen, but she does cluck. What are you doin' with that diary?'

'I'm going to show it to Michael and ask his advice.'

'Don't take it,' said Lady Mont; 'he's a dear boy, but don't take it; he knows a lot of funny people – publishers and that.'

'That's why I'm asking him.'

'Ask Fleur, she has a head. Have you got this zinnia at Condaford? D'you know, Dinny, I think Adrian's goin' potty.'

'Aunt Em!'

'He moons so; and I don't believe there's anywhere you could stick a pin into him. Of course I mustn't say it to you, but I think he ought to have her.'

'So do I, Auntie.'

'Well, he won't.'

'Or she won't.'

'They neither of them will; so how it's to be managed I don't know. She's forty.'

'How old is Uncle Adrian?'

'He's the baby, all but Lionel. I'm fifty-nine,' said Lady Mont decisively. 'I know I'm fifty-nine, and your father is sixty; your grandmother must have been in a great tear at that time, she kept on havin' us. What do *you* think about this question of havin' children?'

Dinny swallowed a bubble and said:

'Well, for married people, perhaps, in moderation.'

'Fleur's going to have another in March; it's a bad month – careless! When are you goin' to get married, Dinny?'

'When my young affections are engaged, not before.'

'That's very prudent. But not an American.'

Dinny flushed, smiled dangerously and said:

'Why on earth should I marry an American?'

'You never know,' said Lady Mont, twisting off a faded aster; 'it depends on what there is about. When I married Lawrence, he was so about!'

'And still is, Aunt Em; wonderful, isn't it?'

'Don't be sharp!'

And Lady Mont seemed to go into a dream, so that her hat looked more enormous than ever.

'Talking of marriage, Aunt Em, I wish I knew of a girl for Hubert. He does so want distracting.'

'Your uncle,' said Lady Mont, 'would say distract him with a dancer.'

'Perhaps Uncle Hilary knows one that he could highly recommend.'

'You're naughty, Dinny. I always thought you were naughty. But let me think: there *was* a girl; no, she married.'

'Perhaps she's divorced by now.'

'No. I think she's divorcin' him, but it takes time. Charmin' little creature.'

'I'm sure. Do think again, Auntie.'

'These bees,' replied her aunt, 'belong to Boswell. They're Italian. Lawrence says they're Fascists.'

'Black shirts and no after-thoughts. They certainly seem very active bees.'

'Yes; they fly a lot and sting you at once if you annoy them. Bees are nice to me.'

'You've got one on your hat, dear. Shall I take it off?'

'Stop!' said Lady Mont, tilting her hat back, with her mouth slightly open: 'I've thought of one.'

'One what?'

'Jean Tasburgh, the daughter of our Rector here – very good family. No money, of course.'

'None at all?'

Lady Mont shook her head, and the hat wobbled. 'No Jean never has money. She's pretty. Rather like a leopardess.'

'Could I look her over, Auntie? I know fairly well what Hubert wouldn't like.'

'I'll ask her to dinner. They feed badly. We married a Tasburgh once. I think it was under James, so she'll be a cousin, but terribly removed. There's a son, too; in the Navy, all there, you know, and no moustache. I believe he's stayin' at the Rectory on furlong.'

'Furlough, Aunt Em.'

'I knew that word was wrong. Take that bee off my hat, there's a dear.'

Dinny took the small bee off the large hat with her handkerchief, and put it to her ear.

'I still like to hear them buzz,' she said.

'I'll ask him too,' answered her aunt; 'his name's Alan, a nice fellow.' And she looked at Dinny's hair. 'Medlar-coloured, I call it. I think he's got prospects, but I don't know what they are. Blown up in the war.'

'He came down again whole, I hope, Auntie?'

'Yes; they gave him something or other for it. He says it's very stuffy in the Navy now. All angles, you know, and wheels, and smells. You must ask him.'

'About the girl, Aunt Em, how do you mean, a leopardess?'

'Well, she looks at you, and you expect to see a cub comin' round the corner. Her mother's dead. She runs the parish.'

'Would she run Hubert?'

'No; she'd run anybody who tried to run him.'

'That might do. Can I take a note for you to the Rectory?'

'I'll send Boswell and Johnson,' Lady Mont looked at her wrist. 'No, they'll have gone to dinner. I always set my watch by them. We'll go ourselves, Dinny; it's only quarter of a mile. Does my hat matter?'

'On the contrary, dear.'

'Very well, then; we can get out this way,' and moving to the far end of the yew-treed garden, they descended some steps into a long grassy avenue, and, passing through a wicket gate, had soon arrived at the Rectory. Dinny stood in its creepered porch, behind her aunt's hat. The door stood open, and a dim panelled hallway with a scent of pot-pourri and old wood, conveyed a kind of invitation. A female voice from within called:

'A—lan!'

A male voice answered: 'Hal—lo!'

'D'you mind cold lunch?'

'There's no bell,' said Lady Mont; 'we'd better clap.' They clapped in unison.

'What the deuce?' A young man in grey flannels had appeared in a doorway. He had a broad brown face, dark hair, and grey eyes, deep and direct.

'Oh!' he said. 'Lady Mont . . . Hi! Jean!' Then, meeting Dinny's eyes round the edge of the hat, he smiled as they do in the Navy.

'Alan, can you and Jean dine tonight? Dinny, this is Alan Tasburgh. D'you like my hat?'

'It's a topper, Lady Mont.'

A girl, made all of a piece and moving as if on steel springs, was coming towards them. She wore a fawn-coloured sleeveless jumper and skirt, and her arms and cheeks were fully as brown. Dinny saw what her aunt meant. The face, broad across the cheek-bones, tapered to the chin, the eyes were greenish grey and sunk right in under long black lashes; they looked straight out with a light in them; the nose was fine, the brow low and broad, the shingled hair dark brown. 'I wonder!' thought Dinny. Then, as the girl smiled, a little thrill went through her.

'This is Jean,' said her aunt: 'my niece, Dinny Cherrell.'

A slim brown hand clasped Dinny's firmly.

'Where's your father?' continued Lady Mont.

'Dad's away at some parsonical Conference. I wanted him to take me, but he wouldn't.'

'Then I expect he's in London really, doin' theatres.'

Dinny saw the girl flash a look at her aunt, decide that it was Lady Mont, and smiled. The young man laughed.

'So you'll both come to dinner? Eight-fifteen. Dinny, we must go back to lunch. Swallows!' added Lady Mont round the brim of her hat, and passed out through the porch.

'There's a house-party,' said Dinny to the young man's elevated eyebrows. 'She means tails and white tie.'

'Oh! Ah! Best bib and tucker, Jean.'

The two stood in the porchway arm in arm. 'Very attractive!' Dinny thought.

'Well?' said her aunt, in the grass avenue again.

'Yes, I quite saw the cub. She's beautiful, I think. But I should keep her on a lead.'

'There's Boswell and Johnson!' exclaimed Lady Mont, as if they were in the singular. 'Gracious! It must be past two, then!'

Chapter Nine

Some time after lunch, for which Dinny and her aunt were late, Adrian and the four younger ladies, armed with such shooting sticks as had been left by the 'guns', proceeded down a farm lane towards where the main 'drive' of the afternoon would debouch. Adrian walked with Diana and Cicely Muskham, and ahead of them Dinny walked with Fleur. These cousins by marriage had not met for nearly a year, and had in any case but slender knowledge of each other. Dinny studied the head which her aunt had recommended to her. It was round and firm and well carried under a small hat. The pretty face wore a rather hard but, she decided, very capable expression. The trim figure was as beautifully tailored as if it had belonged to an American.

Dinny felt that she would at least get common-sense from a source so neat.

'I heard your testimonial read in the Police Court, Fleur.'

'Oh! that. It was what Hilary wanted, of course. I really don't know anything about those girls. They simply don't let one. Some people, of course, can worm themselves into anybody's confidence. I can't; and I certainly don't want to. Do you find the country girls about you any easier?'

'Round us they've all had to do with our family so long that one knows pretty well all there is to know before they do themselves.'

Fleur scrutinised her.

'Yes, I daresay you've got the knack, Dinny. You'll make a wonderful ancestress; but I don't quite know who ought to paint you. It's time someone came along with the Early Italian touch. The pre-Raphaelites hadn't got it a bit; their pictures lacked music and humour. *You'll* have to be done with both.'

'Do tell me,' said Dinny, disconcerted, 'was Michael in the House when those questions were asked about Hubert?'

'Yes; he came home very angry.'

'Good!'

'He thought of bringing the thing up again, but it was the day but one before they rose. Besides, what does the House matter? It's about the last thing people pay attention to nowadays.'

'My father, I'm afraid, paid terrific attention to those questions.'

'Yes, the last generation. But the only thing Parliament does that really gets the Public now, is the Budget. And no wonder; it all comes back to money.'

'Do you say that to Michael?'

'I don't have to. Parliament now is just a taxing machine.'

'Surely it still makes laws?'

'Yes, my dear; but always after the event; it consolidates what has become public practice, or at least public feeling. It never initiates. How can it? That's not a democratic function. If you want proof, look at the state of the country! It's the last thing Parliament bothers about.'

'Who does initiate, then?'

'Whence doth the wind blow? Well, the draughts begin in the coulisses. Great places, the coulisses! Whom do you want to stand with when we get to the guns?'

'Lord Saxenden.'

Fleur gazed at her: 'Not for his *beaux jeux*, and not for his *beau titre*. Why, then?'

'Because I've got to get at him about Hubert, and I haven't much time.'

'I see. Well, I'll give you a warning, my dear. Don't take Saxenden at his face value. He's an astute old fox, and not so old either. And if there is one thing he enjoys more than another, it's his quid pro quo. Have you got a quid for him? He'll want cash down.'

Dinny grimaced.

'I shall do what I can. Uncle Lawrence has already given me some pointers.'

'"Have a care; she's fooling thee,"' hummed Fleur. 'Well, I shall go to Michael; it makes him shoot better, and he wants it, poor dear. The Squire and Bart will be glad to do without us. Cicely, of course, will go to Charles; she's still honeymoonish. That leaves Diana for the American.'

'And I hope,' said Dinny, 'she'll put him off his shots.'

'I should say nothing would. I forgot Adrian; he'll have to sit on his stick and think about bones and Diana. Here we are. See? Through this gate. There's Saxenden, they've given him the warm corner. Go round by that stile and come on him from behind. Michael will be jammed away at the end, he always gets the worst stand.'

She parted from Dinny and went on down the lane. Conscious that she had not asked Fleur what she had wanted to, Dinny crossed to the stile, and climbing over, stalked Lord Saxenden warily from the other side. The peer was moving from one hedge to the other in the corner of the field to which he had been assigned. Beside a tall stick, to a cleft in which was attached a white card with a number on it, stood a young keeper holding two guns, and at his feet a retriever dog was lying with his tongue out. The fields of roots and stubble on the far side of the lane rose rather steeply, and it was evident to Dinny – something of an expert – that birds driven off them would come high and fast. 'Unless,' she thought, 'there's fresh cover just behind,' and she turned to look. There was not. She was in a very large grass field and the nearest roots were three hundred yards away at least. 'I wonder,' she thought, 'if he shoots better or worse with a woman watching. Shouldn't think he had any nerves.' Turning again, she saw that he had noticed her.

'Do you mind me, Lord Saxenden? I'll be very quiet.'

The peer plucked at his cap, which had special peaks before and behind.

'Well, well!' he said. 'H'm!'

'That sounds as if you did. Shall I go?'

'No, no! That's all right. Can't touch a feather today, anyway. You'll bring me luck.'

Dinny seated herself on her stick alongside the retriever, and began playing with its ears.

'That American chap has wiped my eye three times.'

'What bad taste!'

'He shoots at the most impossible birds, but, dash it, he hits 'em. All the birds I miss he gets on the horizon. Got the style of a poacher; lets everything go by, then gets a right and left about seventy yards behind him. Says he can't see them when they sit on his foresight.'

'That's funny,' said Dinny, with a little burst of justice.

'Don't believe he's missed today,' added Lord Saxenden, resentfully. 'I asked him why he shot so darned well, and he said: "Why! I'm used to shoot for the pot, where I can't afford to miss."'

'The "beat's" beginning, my lord,' said the young keeper's voice.

The retriever began to pant slightly. Lord Saxenden grasped a gun; the keeper held the other ready.

'Covey to the left, my lord,' Dinny heard a creaky whirring, and saw eight birds stringing towards the lane. Bang-bang . . . bang – bang!

'God bless my soul!' said Lord Saxenden: 'What the deuce—!'

Dinny saw the same eight birds swoop over the hedge at the other end of the grass field.

The retriever uttered a little choked sound, panting horribly.

'The light,' she said, 'must be terribly puzzling!'

'It's not the light,' said Lord Saxenden, 'it's the liver!'

'Three birds coming straight, my lord.'

Bang! . . . Bang – bang! A bird jerked, crumpled, turned over and pitched four yards behind her. Something caught Dinny by the throat. That anything so alive should be so dead! Often as she had seen birds shot, she had never before had that feeling. The other two birds were crossing the far hedge; she watched them vanish, with a faint sigh. The retriever, with the dead bird in his mouth, came up to the keeper, who took it from him. Sitting on his haunches, the dog continued to gaze at the bird, with his tongue out. Dinny saw the tongue drip, and closed her eyes.

Lord Saxenden said something inaudibly.

Lord Saxenden said the same word more inaudibly, and, opening her eyes, Dinny saw him put up his gun.

'Hen pheasant, my lord!' warned the young keeper.

A hen pheasant passed over at a most reasonable height, as if aware that her time was not yet.

'H'm!' said Lord Saxenden, resting the butt on his bent knee.

'Covey to the right; too far, my lord!'

Several shots rang out, and beyond the hedge Dinny saw two birds only flying on, one of which was dropping feathers.

'That's a dead bird,' said the keeper, and Dinny saw him shade his eyes, watching its flight. 'Down!' he said; the dog panted, and looked up at him.

Shots rang out to the left.

'Damn!' said Lord Saxenden, 'nothing comes my way.'

'Hare, my lord!' said the keeper, sharply. 'Along the hedge!'

Lord Saxenden wheeled and raised his gun.

'Oh, no!' said Dinny, but her words were drowned by the report. The hare, struck behind, stopped short, then wriggled forward, crying pitifully.

'Fetch it, boy!' said the keeper.

Dinny put her hands over her ears and shut her eyes.

'Blast!' muttered Lord Saxenden. 'Tailored!' Through her eyelids Dinny felt his frosty stare. When she opened her eyes the hare was lying dead beside the bird. It looked incredibly soft.

Suddenly she rose, meaning to go, but sat down again. Until the beat was over she could go nowhere without interfering with the range of the shots. She closed her eyes again; and the shooting went on.

'That's the lot, my lord.'

Lord Saxenden was handing over his gun, and three more birds lay beside the hare.

Rather ashamed of her new sensations, she rose, closed her shooting stick, and moved towards the stile. Regardless of the old convention, she crossed it and waited for him.

'Sorry I tailored that hare,' he said. 'But I've been seeing spots all day. Do you ever see spots?'

'No. Stars once in a way. A hare's crying is dreadful, isn't it?'

'I agree – never liked it.'

'Once when we were having a picnic I saw a hare sitting up behind us like a dog – and the sun through its ears all pink. I've always liked hares since.'

'They're not a sporting shot,' admitted Lord Saxenden; 'personally I prefer 'em roast to jugged.'

Dinny stole a glance at him. He looked red and fairly satisfied.

'Now's my chance,' she thought.

'Do you ever tell Americans that they won the war, Lord Saxenden?'

He stared frostily.

'Why should I?'

'But they did, didn't they?'

'Does that Professor chap say so?'

'I've never heard him, but I feel sure he thinks so.'

Again Dinny saw that sharp look come on his face. 'What do you know about him?'

'My brother went on his expedition.'

'Your brother? Ah!' It was just as if he had said to himself out loud: 'This young woman wants something out of me.'

Dinny felt suddenly that she was on very thin ice.

'If you read Professor Hallorsen's book,' she said, 'I hope you will also read my brother's diary.'

'I never read anything,' said Lord Saxenden; 'haven't time. But I remember now. Bolivia – he shot a man, didn't he, and lost the transport?'

'He had to shoot the man to save his own life, and he had to flog two for continual cruelty to the mules; then all but three men deserted, stampeding the mules. He was the only white man there, with a lot of Indian half-castes.'

And to his frosty shrewd eyes she raised her own suddenly, remembering Sir Lawrence's: 'Give him the Botticellian eye, Dinny!'

'Might I read you a little of his diary?'

'Well, if there's time.'

'When?'

'Tonight? I have to go up after shooting tomorrow.'

'Any time that suits you,' she said, hardily.

'There won't be a chance before dinner. I've got some letters that must go.'

'I can stay up till any hour.' She saw him give her a quick, all-over glance.

'We'll see,' he said, abruptly. And at this minute they were joined by the others.

Escaping the last drive, Dinny walked home by herself. Her sense of humour was tickled, but she was in a quandary. She judged shrewdly that the diary would not produce the desired effect unless Lord Saxenden felt that he was going to get something out of listening to it; and she was perceiving more clearly than ever before how difficult it was to give anything without parting from it. A fluster of wood-pigeons rose from some stooks on her left and crossed over to the wood by the river; the light was growing level, and evening sounds fluttered in the crisper air. The gold of sinking sunlight lay on the stubbles; the leaves, hardly turned as yet, were just promising colour, and away down there the blue line of the river glinted through its bordering trees.

In the air was the damp, slightly pungent scent of early autumn with wood smoke drifting already from cottage chimneys. A lovely hour, a lovely evening!

What passages from the diary should she read? Her mind faltered. She could see Saxenden's face again when he said: 'Your brother? Ah!' Could see the hard direct calculating insensitive character behind it. She remembered Sir Lawrence's words: 'Were there not, my dear? . . . Most valuable fellows!' She had just been reading the memoirs of a man, who, all through the war, had thought in moves and numbers, and, after one preliminary gasp, had given up thinking of the sufferings behind those movements and those numbers: in his will to win the war, he seemed to have made it his business never to think of its human side, and, she was sure, could never have visualised that side if he *had* thought of it. Valuable fellow! She had heard Hubert talk, with a curling lip, of 'armchair strategists' – who had enjoyed the war, excited by the interest of combining movements and numbers and of knowing this and that before someone else did, and by the importance they had gained therefrom. Valuable fellows! In another book she had lately read, she remembered a passage about the kind of men who directed what was called progress: sat in Banks, City offices, Governmental departments, combining movements and numbers, not bothered by flesh and blood, except their own; men who started this enterprise and that, drawing them up on sheets of paper, and saying to these and those: 'Do this, and see you dam' well do it properly.' Men, silk-hatted or plus-foured, who guided the machine of tropic enterprise, of mineral getting, of great shops, of railway building, of concessions here and there and everywhere. Valuable fellows! Cheery, healthy, well-fed, indomitable fellows with frosty eyes. Always dining, always in the know, careless of the cost in human feelings and human life. 'And yet,' she thought, 'they really must be valuable, or how should we have rubber or coal, or pearls or railways or the Stock Exchange, or wars and win them!' She thought of Hallorsen; he at least worked and suffered for his ideas, led his own charges;

did not sit at home, knowing things, eating ham, tailoring hares, and ordering the movements of others. She turned into the Manor grounds and paused on the croquet lawn. Aunt Wilmet and Lady Henrietta appeared to be agreeing to differ. They appealed to her:

'Is that right, Dinny?'

'No. When the balls touch you just go on playing, but you mustn't move Lady Henrietta's ball, Auntie, in hitting your own.'

'I said so,' said Lady Henrietta.

'Of course you said so, Hen. Nice position I'm in. Well, I shall just agree to differ and go on,' and Aunt Wilmet hit her ball through a hoop, moving her opponent's several inches in so doing.

'Isn't she an unscrupulous woman?' murmured Lady Henrietta, plaintively, and Dinny saw at once the great practical advantages inherent in 'agreeing to differ'.

'You're like the Iron Duke, Auntie,' she said, 'except that you don't use the word "damn" quite so often.'

'She does,' said Lady Henrietta; 'her language is appalling.'

'Go on, Hen!' said Aunt Wilmet in a flattered voice.

Dinny left them and retired towards the house.

When she was dressed she went to Fleur's room.

Her aunt's maid was passing a minute mowing-machine over the back of Fleur's neck, while Michael, in the doorway of his dressing room, had his fingers on the tips of his white tie.

Fleur turned.

'Hallo, Dinny! Come in, and sit down. That'll do, thank you, Powers. Now, Michael.'

The maid faded out and Michael advanced to have a twist given to the ends of his tie.

'There!' said Fleur; and, looking at Dinny, added: 'Have you come about Saxenden?'

'Yes. I'm to read him bits of Hubert's diary tonight. The question is: Where will be suitable to my youth and—'

'Not innocence, Dinny; you'll never be innocent, will she, Michael?'

Michael grinned. 'Never innocent but always virtuous. You were a most sophisticated little angel as a kid, Dinny; looked as if you were wondering why you hadn't wings. Wistful is the word.'

'I expect I was wondering why you'd pulled them off.'

'You ought to have worn trouserettes and chased butterflies, like the two little Gainsborough girls in the National Gallery.'

'Cease these amenities,' said Fleur; 'the gong's gone. You can have my little sitting room next door, and, if you knock, Michael can come round with a boot, as if it were rats.'

'Perfect,' said Dinny; 'but I expect he'll behave like a lamb, really.'

'You never can tell,' said Michael; 'he's a bit of a goat.'

'That's the room,' said Fleur, as they passed out. '*Cabinet particulier*. Good luck! . . .'

Chapter Ten

Seated between Hallorsen and young Tasburgh, Dinny had a slanting view of her Aunt and Lord Saxenden at the head of the table, with Jean Tasburgh round the corner on his right. 'She was a "leopardess" oh! so fair!' The tawnied skin, oblique face, and wonderful eyes of the young woman fascinated her. They appeared also to fascinate Lord Saxenden, whose visage was redder and more genial than Dinny had seen it yet. His attentions to Jean, indeed, were throwing Lady Mont to the clipped tongue of Wilfred Bentworth. For 'the Squire', though a far more distinguished personality, too distinguished to accept a peerage, was, in accordance with the table of precedence, seated on her left. Next to him again Fleur was engaging Hallorsen; so that Dinny herself was exposed to the broadside of young Tasburgh. He talked easily, directly, frankly, like a man not yet calloused by female society, and manifested what Dinny described to herself as 'transparent admiration'; yet twice at least she went into what he described as a 'near-dream', her head turned high, and motionless, towards his sister.

'Ah!' he said. 'What do you think of her?'

'Fascinating.'

'I'll tell her that, she won't turn a hair. The earth's most matter-of-fact young woman. She seems to be vamping her neighbour all right. Who is he?'

'Lord Saxenden.'

'Oh! And who's the John Bull at the corner on our side?'

'Wilfred Bentworth, "the Squire", they call him.'

'And next to you – talking to Mrs Michael?'

'That's Professor Hallorsen from America.'

'He's a fine-looking chap.'

'So everybody says,' said Dinny, drily.

'Don't you think so?'

'Men oughtn't to be so good-looking.'

'Delighted to hear you say that.'

'Why?'

'It means that the ugly have a look in.'

'Oh! Do you often go trawling?'

'You know, I'm terribly glad I've met you at last.'

'At last? You'd never even heard of me this morning.'

'No. But that doesn't prevent you from being my ideal.'

'Goodness! Is this the way they have in the Navy?'

'Yes. The first thing they teach us is to make up our minds quickly.'

'Mr Tasburgh—'

'Alan.'

'I begin to understand the wife in every port.'

'I,' said young Tasburgh, seriously, 'haven't a single one. And you're the first I've ever wanted.'

'Oo! Or is it: Coo!'

'Fact! You see, the Navy is very strenuous. When we see what we want, we have to go for it at once. We get so few chances.'

Dinny laughed. 'How old are you?'

'Twenty-eight.'

'Then you weren't at Zeebrugge?'

'I was.'

'I see. It's become a habit to lay yourself alongside.'

'And get blown up for it.'

Her eyes rested on him kindly.

'I am now going to talk to my enemy.'

'Enemy? Can I do anything about that?'

'His demise would be of no service to me, till he's done what I want.'

'Sorry for that; he looks to me dangerous.'

'Mrs Charles is lying in wait for you,' murmured Dinny, and she turned to Hallorsen, who said deferentially: 'Miss Cherrell,' as if she had arrived from the moon.

'I hear you shot amazingly, Professor.'

'Why! I'm not accustomed to birds asking for it as they do here. I'll maybe get used to that in time. But all this is quite an experience for me.'

'Everything in the garden lovely?'

'It certainly is. To be in the same house with you is a privilege I feel very deeply, Miss Cherrell.'

'"Cannon to right of me, cannon to left of me!"' thought Dinny.

'And have you,' she asked, suddenly, 'been thinking what amend you can make to my brother?'

Hallorsen lowered his voice.

'I have a great admiration for you, Miss Cherrell, and I will do what you tell me. If you wish, I will write to your papers and withdraw the remarks in my book.'

'And what would you want for that, Professor Hallorsen?'

'Why, surely, nothing but your goodwill.'

'My brother has given me his diary to publish.'

'If that will be a relief to you – go to it.'

'I wonder if you two ever began to understand each other.'

'I judge we never did.'

'And yet you were only four white men, weren't you? May I ask exactly what annoyed you in my brother?'

'You'd have it up against me if I were to tell you.'

'Oh! no, I *can* be fair.'

'Well, first of all, I found he'd made up his mind about too many things, and he wouldn't change it. There we were in a country none of us knew anything about, amongst Indians and people that were only half civilised; but the captain wanted everything done as you might in England: he wanted rules, and he wanted 'em kept. Why, I judge he would have dressed for dinner if we'd have let him.'

'I think you should remember,' said Dinny, taken aback, 'that we English have found formality pay all over the world. We succeed in all sorts of wild out of the world places because we stay English. Reading his diary, *I* think my brother failed from not being stolid enough.'

'Well, he is not your John Bull type,' he nodded towards the end of the table, 'like Lord Saxenden and Mr Bentworth there; maybe I'd have understood him better if he were. No, he's mighty high-strung and very tight held-in; his emotions kind of eat him up from within. He's like a race-horse in a hansom cab. Yours is an old family, I should judge, Miss Cherrell.'

'Not yet in its dotage.'

She saw his eyes leave her, rest on Adrian across the table, move on to her Aunt Wilmet, and thence to Lady Mont.

'I would like to talk to your uncle the Curator about old families,' he said.

'What else was there in my brother that you didn't like?'

'Well, he gave me the feeling that I was a great husky.'

Dinny raised her brows a little.

'There we were,' went on Hallorsen, 'in the hell of a country – pardon me! – a country of raw metal. Well, I was raw metal myself, out to meet and beat raw metal; and he just wouldn't be.'

'Perhaps couldn't be. Don't you think what was really wrong was your being American and his being English? Confess, Professor, that you don't like us English.'

Hallorsen laughed.

'I like *you* terribly.'

'Thank you, but every rule—'

'Well,' his face hardened, 'I just don't like the assumption of a superiority that I don't believe in.'

'Have we a monopoly of that? What about the French?'

'If I were an orang-utang, Miss Cherrell, I wouldn't care a hoot whether a chimpanzee thought himself superior.'

'I see; too far removed. But, forgive me, Professor, what about yourselves? Are you not the chosen people? And don't you frequently say so? Would you exchange with any other people in the world?'

'I certainly would not.'

'But isn't that an assumption of a superiority that *we* don't believe in?'

He laughed. 'You have me there; but we haven't touched rock-bottom in this matter. There's a snob in every man. We're a new people; we haven't gotten your roots and your old things; we haven't gotten your habit of taking ourselves for granted; we're too multiple and various and too much in the making. We have a lot of things that you could envy us besides our dollars and our bathrooms.'

'What ought we to envy you? I should very much like it made clear to me.'

'Well, Miss Cherrell, we know that we have qualities and energy and faith and opportunities that you just ought to envy; and when you don't do it, we feel we've no use for that kind of gone-dead, bone-superior attitude. It's like a man of sixty looking down his nose at a youth of thirty; and there's no such God-darned – pardon me! – mistake as that.'

Dinny sat looking at him, silent and impressed.

'Where,' Hallorsen went on, 'you British irritate us is that you've lost the spirit of enquiry; or if you've still gotten it, you have a dandy way of hiding it up. I judge there are many ways in which we irritate you. But we irritate your epidermis and you irritate our nerve centres. That's about all there is to it, Miss Cherrell.'

'I see,' said Dinny; 'that's terribly interesting and I daresay quite true. My aunt's getting up, so I must remove my epidermis and leave your nerve centres to quiet down.' She rose, and over her shoulder smiled back at him.

Young Tasburgh was at the door. At him too she smiled, and murmured: 'Talk to my friend the enemy; he's worth it.'

In the drawing room she sought out the 'leopardess', but converse between them suffered from the inhibition of a mutual admiration which neither wished to show. Jean Tasburgh was just twenty-one, but she impressed Dinny as older than herself. Her knowledge of things and people seemed precise and decided, if not profound; her mind was made up on all the subjects they touched on; she would be a marvellous person – Dinny thought – in a crisis, or if driven to the wall; would be loyal to her own side, but want to rule whatever roost she was in. But alongside her hard efficiency Dinny could well perceive a strange, almost feline fascination that would go to any man's head, if she chose that it should. Hubert would succumb to her at once! And at that conclusion his sister was the more doubtful whether she wished him to. Here was the very girl to afford the swift distraction she was seeking for her brother. But was he strong enough and alive enough for the distractor? Suppose he fell in love with her and she would have none of him? Or suppose he fell in love with her and she had all of him! And then – money! If Hubert received no appointment or lost his commission what would they live on? He had only three hundred a year without his pay, and the girl presumably nothing. The situation was perverse. If Hubert could plunge again into soldiering, he would not need distraction. If he continued to be shelved, he would need distraction but could not afford it. And yet – was not this exactly the sort of girl who would carve out a career somehow for the man she married? So they talked of Italian pictures.

'By the way,' said Jean, suddenly, 'Lord Saxenden says you want him to do something for you.'

'Oh!'

'What is it? Because I'll make him.'

Dinny smiled.

'How?'

Jean gave her a look from under her lashes.

'It'll be quite easy. What is it you want from him?'

'I want my brother back in his regiment, or, better – some

post for him. He's under a cloud owing to that Bolivian expedition with Professor Hallorsen.'

'The big man? Is that why you had him down here?'

Dinny had a feeling that she would soon have no clothes on.

'If you want frankness, yes.'

'He's rather fine to look at.'

'So your brother said.'

'Alan's the most generous person in the world. He's taken a toss over you.'

'So he was telling me.'

'He's an ingenuous child. But, seriously, shall I go for Lord Saxenden?'

'Why should you worry?'

'I like to put my fingers into pies. Give me a free hand, and I'll bring you that appointment on a charger.'

'I am credibly informed,' said Dinny, 'that Lord Saxenden is a tough proposition.'

Jean stretched herself.

'Is your brother Hubert like you?'

'Not a scrap; he's dark, and brown-eyed.'

'You know our families intermarried a long way back. Are you interested in breeding? I breed Airedales, and I don't believe much in either the tail male or the tail female theories. Prepotency can be handed down through either male or female, and at any point of the pedigree.'

'Perhaps, but except for not being covered with yellow varnish, my father and my brother are both very like the earliest portrait we have of a male ancestor.'

'Well, we've got a Fitzherbert woman who married a Tasburgh in 1547, and she's the spit of me except for the ruff; she's even got my hands.' And the girl spread out to Dinny two long brown hands, crisping them slightly as she did so.

'A strain,' she went on, 'may crop out after generations that have seemed free from it. It's awfully interesting. I should like to see your brother, if he's so unlike you.'

Dinny smiled.

'I'll get him to drive over from Condaford and fetch me. You may not think him worth your wiles.'

And at this moment the men came in.

'They do so look,' murmured Dinny, 'as if they were saying: "Do I want to sit next to a female, and if so, why?" Men are funny after dinner.'

Sir Lawrence's voice broke the hush:

'Saxenden, you and the Squire for Bridge?'

At those words Aunt Wilmet and Lady Henrietta rose automatically from the sofa where they had been having a quiet difference, and passed towards where they would continue the motion for the rest of the evening; they were followed closely by Lord Saxenden and the Squire.

Jean Tasburgh grimaced: 'Can't you just see Bridge growing on people like a fungus?'

'Another table?' said Sir Lawrence: 'Adrian? No. Professor?'

'Why, I think not, Sir Lawrence.'

'Fleur, you and I then against Em and Charles. Come along, let's get it over.'

'You can't see it growing on Uncle Lawrence,' murmured Dinny. 'Oh! Professor! Do you know Miss Tasburgh?'

Hallorsen bowed.

'It's an amazing night,' said young Tasburgh on her other side: 'Couldn't we go out?'

'Michael,' said Jean, rising, 'we're going out.'

The night had been justly described. The foliage of holm oaks and elms clung on the dark air unstirring; stars were diamond bright, and there was no dew; the flowers had colour only when peered into; and sounds were lonely – the hooting of an owl from away towards the river, the passing drone of a chafer's flight. The air was quite warm, and through the cut cypresses the lighted house stared vaguely. Dinny and the sailor strolled in front.

'This is the sort of night,' he said, 'when you can see the

Scheme a bit. My old Governor is a dear old boy, but his Services are enough to kill all belief. Have you any left?'

'In God, do you mean?' said Dinny: 'Ye-es, without knowing anything about it.'

'Don't *you* find it impossible to think of God except in the open and alone?'

'I *have* been emotionalised in church.'

'You want something beyond emotion, I think; you want to grasp infinite invention going on in infinite stillness. Perpetual motion and perpetual quiet at the same time. That American seems a decent chap.'

'Did you talk about cousinly love?'

'I kept that for you. One of our great-great-great-great-grand-fathers was the same, under Anne; we've got his portrait, terrible, in a wig. So we're cousins – the love follows.'

'Does it? Blood cuts both ways. It certainly makes every differ-ence glare out.'

'Thinking of Americans?'

Dinny nodded.

'All the same,' said the sailor, 'there isn't a question in my mind that in a scrap I'd rather have an American with me than any other kind of foreigner. I should say we all felt like that in the Fleet.'

'Isn't that just because of language being the same?'

'No. It's some sort of grain and view of things in common.'

'But surely that can only apply to British-stock Americans?'

'That's still the American who counts, especially if you lump in the Dutch and Scandinavian-stock Americans, like this fellow Hallorsen. We're very much that stock ourselves.'

'Why not German-Americans, then?'

'To some extent. But look at the shape of the German head. By and large, the Germans are Central or Eastern Europeans.'

'You ought to be talking to my Uncle Adrian.'

'Is that the tall man with the goatee? I like his face.'

'He's a dear,' said Dinny. 'We've lost the others and I can feel dew.'

'Just one moment. I was perfectly serious in what I said at dinner. You *are* my ideal, and I hope you'll let me pursue it.'

Dinny curtsied.

'Young Sir, you are very flattering. "But –" she went on with a slight blush – "I would point out that you have a noble profession—"'

'Are you never serious?'

'Seldom, when the dew is falling.'

He seized her hand.

'Well, you will be one day; and I shall be the cause of it.'

Slightly returning the pressure of his hand, Dinny disengaged hers, and walked on.

'Pleached alley – can you stand that expression? It seems to give joy to so many people.'

'Fair cousin,' said young Tasburgh, 'I shall be thinking of you day and night. Don't trouble to answer.'

And he held open a French window.

Cicely Muskham was at the piano, and Michael standing behind her.

Dinny went up to him.

'If I go to Fleur's sitting room now, could you show Lord Saxenden where it is, Michael? If he doesn't come by twelve, I shall go to bed. I must sort out the bits I want to read to him.'

'All right, Dinny. I'll leave him on the doormat. Good luck!'

Fetching the diary, Dinny threw open the window of the little sitting room and sat down to make her selections. It was half-past-ten, and not a sound disturbed her. She selected six fairly long passages which seemed to illustrate the impossible nature of her brother's task. Then, lighting a cigarette, she waited, leaning out. The night was neither more nor less 'amazing' than it had been, but her own mood was deeper. Perpetual motion in perpetual quiet? If that, indeed, were God, He was not of much immediate use to mortals but why should He be? When Saxenden tailored the hare and it had cried, had God heard and quivered? When her hand was pressed, had He seen and smiled? When Hubert

in the Bolivian wilds had lain fever-stricken, listening to the cry
of the loon, had He sent an angel with quinine? When that star
up there went out billions of years hence, and hung cold and
lightless, would He note it on his shirt cuff? The million million
leaves and blades of grass down there that made the texture of
the deeper darkness, the million million stars that gave the light
by which she saw that darkness, all – all the result of perpetual
motion in endless quiet, all part of God. And she herself, and
the smoke of her cigarette; the jasmine under her nose, whose
colour was invisible, and the movement of her brain, deciding
that it was not yellow; that dog barking so far away that the
sound was as a thread by which the woof of silence could be
grasped; all – all endowed with the purpose remote, endless,
pervading, incomprehensible, of God!

She shivered and withdrew her head. Sitting down in an
armchair, with the diary in her lap, she gazed round the room.
Fleur's taste had remodelled it; there was fine colour in the carpet,
the light was softly shaded and fell pleasantly on her sea-green
frock and hands resting on the diary. The long day had tired her.
She lay back tilting up her face, looking drowsily at the frieze
of baked China Cupids with which some former Lady Mont had
caused the room to be encircled. Fat funny little creatures they
seemed to her – thus tied by rosy chains to the perpetual examin-
ation of each other's behinds from stated distances. Chase of the
rosy hours, of the rosy—! Dinny's eyelids drooped, her lips
opened, she slept. And the discreet light visiting her face and hair
and neck revealed their negligence in slumber, their impudent
daintiness, as of the fair Italians, so very English, whom Botticelli
painted. A tendril of short ripe hair had come apart, a smile
strayed off and on to the parted lips; eyelashes, a little darker
than the hair, winked flutteringly on cheeks which seemed to
have a sort of transparence; and in the passing of her dreams,
the nose twitched and quivered as if mocking at its slight tiptilt.
Uplifted thus, the face looked as if but a twist were needed to
pluck it from its white stalk of neck . . .

With a start her head came to the erect. He who had been 'Snubby Bantham' was standing in the middle of the room, regarding her with a hard blue unwinking stare.

'Sorry,' he said; 'sorry! You were having a nice snooze.'

'I was dreaming of mince pies,' said Dinny. 'It's terribly good of you to come at whatever time of night it is.'

'Seven bells. You won't be long, I suppose. D'you mind if I smoke a pipe?'

He sat down on a sofa opposite to her and began to fill his pipe. He had the look of a man who meant her to get it over, and was going to reserve judgment when she had. She better understood at that moment the conduct of public affairs. 'Of course,' she thought, 'he's giving his quo and he doesn't see his quid. That's the result of Jean!' And whether she felt gratitude to the 'leopardess' for having deflected his interest, or whether a sort of jealousy, neither she nor any other woman would have told. Her heart was beating, however, and in a quick, matter-of-fact voice she began. She read through three of the passages before she looked at him again. His face, but for the lips sucking at his pipe, might have been made of a well-coloured wood. His eyes still regarded her in a curious and now slightly hostile way, as if he were thinking: 'This young woman is trying to make me feel something. It's very late.'

With an increasing hatred of her task Dinny hurried on. The fourth passage was – except for the last – the most harrowing, at least to herself; and her voice quivered a little as she finished it.

'Bit thick that,' said Lord Saxenden; 'mules have no feelings, you know – most extraordinary brutes.'

Dinny's temper rose; she would not look at him again. And she read on. This time she lost herself in that tortured recital, thus put into sound for the first time. She finished, breathless, quivering all over with the effort of keeping her voice controlled. Lord Saxenden's chin was resting on his hand. He was asleep.

She stood looking at him, as he not long before had looked at her. For the moment she was on the point of jerking his hand from under his chin. Her sense of humour saved her, and gazing at him rather as Venus gazes at Mars in Botticelli's picture, she took a sheet of notepaper from Fleur's bureau, wrote the words: 'So sorry I exhausted you. Good-night,' and laid it with infinite precaution on his knee. Rolling up the diary, she stole to the door, opened it and looked back, faint sounds, that would soon be snoring, were coming from him. 'Appeal to his feelings and he sleeps,' she thought: 'That's exactly how he must have won the war.' And, turning, she found herself staring up at Professor Hallorsen.

Chapter Eleven

When Dinny saw Hallorsen's eyes fixed, over her head, on the sleeping peer, she swallowed a gasp. What was he imagining of her, stealing thus at midnight away from a man of title in a little private room? His eyes, now looking into hers, were extremely grave. And, terrified lest he should say: 'Pardon me!' and rouse the sleeper, she clutched the diary, put her finger to her lips, murmured: 'Don't wake the baby!' and glided down the passage.

In her room she laughed her fill, then sat up and reviewed her sensations. Given the reputation of the titled in democratic countries, Hallorsen probably thought the worst. But she did him some rather remarkable justice. Whatever he thought of her would not go beyond him. Whatever he was – he was a *big* dog. She could imagine him at breakfast tomorrow, saying gravely: 'Miss Cherrell, I am delighted to see you looking so well.' And, saddened by her conduct of Hubert's affairs, she got into bed. She slept badly, awoke tired and pale, and had her breakfast upstairs.

During country house parties one day is very like another. The men put on the same kind of variegated tie and the same plus fours, eat the same breakfast, tap the same barometer, smoke the same pipes and kill the same birds. The dogs wag the same tails, lurk in the same unexpected spots, utter the same agonised yelps, and chase the same pigeons on the same lawns. The ladies have the same breakfast in bed or not, put the same salts in the same bath, straggle in the same garden, say of the same friends with the same spice of animosity, 'I'm frightfully fond of them, of course'; pore over the same rock borders with the same passion for portulaca; play the same croquet or tennis with the same squeaks; write the same letters to contradict the same rumours, or match the same antiques; differ with the same agreement, and agree with the same difference. The servants have the same way of not being visible, except at the same stated moments. And the house has the same smell of pot-pourri, flowers, tobacco, books, and sofa cushions.

Dinny wrote a letter to her brother in which she said nothing of Hallorsen, Saxenden, or the Tasburghs, but discoursed in lively fashion of Aunt Em, Boswell and Johnson, Uncle Adrian, Lady Henrietta, and asked him to come over for her in the car. In the afternoon the Tasburghs came in for tennis, and not until the shooting was over did she see either Lord Saxenden or the American. But he who had been 'Snubby Bantham' gave her so long and so peculiar a stare from the corner where he was having tea, that she knew he had not forgiven her. Careful not to notice, she was at heart dismayed. So far she seemed to have done Hubert nothing but harm. 'I'll let Jean loose on him,' she thought, and went out to find 'the leopardess'. On her way she came on Hallorsen, and hastily deciding to regain her ground with him, said:

'If you had come up a little earlier last night, Professor Hallorsen, you could have heard me read some of my brother's diary to Lord Saxenden. It might have done you more good than it did him.'

Hallorsen's face cleared.

'Why,' he said, 'I've been wondering what soporific you had administered to that poor lord.'

'I was preparing him for your book. You *are* giving him a copy?'

'I judge not, Miss Cherrell; I am not that interested in his health. He may lie awake for me. I have very little use for any man that could listen to you and go to sleep on it. What does he do in life, this lord?'

'What does he do? Well, he is what I think you call a Big Noise. I don't quite know where he makes it, but my father says he is a man who counts. I hope you have been wiping his eye again today, Professor, because the more you wipe his eye the better chance my brother has of recovering the position he lost by going on your expedition.'

'Is that so? Do personal feelings decide these things over here?'

'Don't they over there?'

'Why – yes! But I thought the old countries had too much tradition for that.'

'Oh! we wouldn't *admit* the influence of personal feelings, of course.'

Hallorsen smiled.

'Isn't that just wonderful? All the world is kin. You would enjoy America, Miss Cherrell; I would like the chance to show it you some day.'

He had spoken as if America were an antique that he had in his trunk; and she did not quite know how to take a remark which might have no significance or an absurdly great one. Then by his face she saw that he meant it to have the absurdly great one; and, revealing her teeth, answered:

'Thank you, but you are still my enemy.'

Hallorsen put out his hand, but she had drawn back.

'Miss Cherrell, I am going to do all I can to remove the unpleasant impression you have of me. I am your very humble servant, and I hope some day to have a chance to be something else to you.'

He looked terribly tall, handsome, and healthy, and she resented it.

'Let us not take anything too seriously, Professor; it leads to trouble. Forgive me now, I have to find Miss Tasburgh.'

With that she skimmed away. Ridiculous! Touching! Flattering!

Odious! It was all crazy! Whatever one did would be all criss-crossed and tangled, to trust to luck was best, after all!

Jean Tasburgh, who had just finished a single with Cicely Muskham, was removing a fillet from her hair.

'Come along to tea,' said Dinny; 'Lord Saxenden is pining for you.'

At the door of the room where tea was being served, however, she herself was detached by Sir Lawrence, who, saying he had seen nothing of her yet, invited her to his study to look at his miniatures.

'My record of national characteristics, Dinny; all women, you see: French, German, Italian, Dutch, American, Spanish, Russian; and I should immensely like one of you, Dinny. Would you sit to a young man?'

'I?'

'You.'

'But why?'

'Because,' said Sir Lawrence, scrutinising her through his monocle, 'you contain the answer to the riddle of the English lady, and I collect the essential difference between national cultures.'

'That sounds terribly exciting.'

'Look at this one. Here's French culture in excelsis; quick intelligence, wit, industry, decision, intellectual but not emotional aestheticism, no humour, conventional sentiment but no other, a having tendency – mark the eye; a sense of form, no originality, very clear but limited mental vision – nothing dreamy about her; quick but controlled blood. All of a piece, with very distinct edges. Now here's an American of rare type, tip-top cultured variety. Notice chiefly a look as if she had an invisible bit in her mouth and knew it; in her eyes is a battery she'll make use of but only with propriety. She'll be very well preserved to the end of her days. Good taste, a lot of knowledge, not much learning. See this German! Emotionally more uncontrolled, and less sense of form than either of those others, but has a conscience, is a hard worker, great sense of duty, not much taste, some rather unhandy humour. If she doesn't take care she'll get fat. Plenty of sentiment, plenty of good sound sense too. More capacious in every way. She isn't perhaps a very good specimen. I can't get one. Here's my prize Italian. She's interesting. Beautifully varnished, with something feral, or let's say – natural, behind. Has a mask on, prettily shaped, prettily worn, liable to fall off. Knows her own mind, perhaps too well, gets her own way if she can, and if she can't, gets somebody else's. Poetic only in connection with her senses. Strong feelings, domestic and otherwise. Clear-eyed towards danger, plenty of courage but easily unnerved. Fine taste, subject to bad lapses. No liking for Nature, here. Intellectually decisive, but not industrious or enquiring. And here,' said Sir Lawrence, suddenly confronting Dinny, 'I shall have my prize English specimen. Do you want to hear about her?'

'Help!'

'Oh! I'll be quite impersonal. Here we have a self-consciousness, developed and controlled to the point when it becomes unself-consciousness. To this lady Self is the unforgivable intruder. We observe a sense of humour, not devoid of wit, which informs and somewhat sterilises all else. We are impressed by what I may call a look not so much of domestic as of public or social service, not to be found in our other types. We discover a sort of transparency, as if air and dew had got into the system. We decide that *pre*cision is lacking, precision of learning, action, thought, judgment, but that *de*cision is very present. The senses are not highly developed; the aesthetic emotions are excited more readily by natural than by artificial objects. There is not the capacity of the German; the clarity of the French woman; the duality or colour of the Italian; the disciplined neatness of the American; but there is a peculiar something – for which, my dear, I will leave you to discover the word – that makes me very anxious to have you in my collection of cultures.'

'But I am not in the least cultured, Uncle Lawrence.'

'I use the infernal word for want of a better, and by it I don't mean learning. I mean the stamp left by blood plus bringing-up, the two taken strictly together. If that French woman had had your bringing-up, she yet wouldn't have had your stamp, Dinny; nor would you with her bringing-up have had her stamp. Now look at this pre-war Russian; more fluid and more fluent than any of the others. I found her in the Caledonian Market. That woman must have wanted to go deep into everything, and never wanted to stay there long. I'll wager she ran through life at a great pace, and, if alive, is still running; and it's taking much less out of her than it would take out of you. The face gives you the feeling that she's experienced more emotions, and been less exhausted by them than any of the others. Here's my Spaniard; perhaps the most interesting of the lot. That's woman brought up apart from man; I suspect she's getting rare. There's a sweetness here, a touch of the convent; not much curiosity, not much energy, a lot of pride, very little conceit; might be devastating in her affections, don't you think, and rather difficult to talk to? Well, Dinny, will you sit to my young man?'

'If you really want me to, of course.'

'I do. This is my hobby. I'll arrange it. He can come down to you at Condaford. I must get back now and see "Snubby" off. Have you proposed to him yet?'

'I read him to sleep last night with Hubert's diary. He dislikes me intensely. I daren't ask him anything. Is he really "a big noise", Uncle Lawrence?'

Sir Lawrence nodded mysteriously. 'Snubby,' he said, 'is the ideal public man. He has practically no feelers, and his feelings are always connected with Snubby. You can't keep a man like him down; he will always be there or thereabouts. India-rubber. Well, well, the State needs him. If we were all thin-skinned, who would sit in the seats of the mighty? They are hard, Dinny, and full of brass tacks. So you've wasted your time?'

'I think I've tied a second string to my bow.'

'Excellent. Hallorsen's off too. I like that chap. Very American, but sound wood.'

He left her, and, unwilling to encounter again either the india-rubber or the sound wood, Dinny went up to her room.

Next morning by ten o'clock, with the rapidity peculiar to the break-up of house-parties, Fleur and Michael were bearing Adrian and Diana off to Town in their car; the Muskhams had departed by train, and the Squire and Lady Henrietta were motoring across country to their Northamptonshire abode; Aunt Wilmet and Dinny alone were left, but the Tasburghs were coming to lunch and bringing their father.

'He's amiable, Dinny,' said Lady Mont: 'Old School, very courtly, says "Nevah", "Evah", like that. It's a pity they've no money. Jean is strikin', don't you think?'

'She scares me a little, Aunt Em; knows her own mind so completely.'

'Match-makin',' replied her aunt, 'is rather amusin'. I haven't done any for a long time. I wonder what Con and your mother will say to me. I shall wake up o' nights.'

'First catch your Hubert, Auntie.'

'I was always fond of Hubert; he has the family face – you haven't, Dinny, I don't know where you get your colourin' – and he looks so well on a horse. Where does he get his breeches?'

'I don't believe he's had a new pair since the war, Auntie.'

'And he wears nice long waistcoats. Those short waistcoats straight across are so abbreviatin'. I shall send him out with Jean to see the rock borders. There's nothin' like portulaca for bringin' people together. Ah! There's Boswell-and-Johnson – I must catch him.'

Hubert arrived soon after noon, and almost the first thing he said was:

'I've changed my mind about having my diary published, Dinny. Exhibiting one's sore finger is too revolting.'

Thankful that as yet she had taken no steps, she answered meekly:

'Very well, dear.'

'I've been thinking: If they're not going to employ me here, I might get attached to a Soudan regiment; or I believe they're short of men for the Indian Police. I shall be jolly glad to get out of the country again. Who's here?'

'Only Uncle Lawrence, Aunt Em, and Aunt Wilmet. The Rector and his family are coming to lunch – the Tasburghs, they're distant cousins.'

'Oh!' said Hubert, glumly.

She watched the advent of the Tasburghs almost maliciously. Hubert and young Tasburgh at once discovered mutual service in Mesopotamia and the Persian Gulf. They were talking about it when Hubert became conscious of Jean. Dinny saw him give her a long look, enquiring and detached, as of a man watching a new kind of bird; saw him avert his eyes, speak and laugh, then gaze back at her.

Her aunt's voice said: 'Hubert looks thin.'

The Rector spread his hands, as if to draw attention to his present courtly bulk. 'Dear Lady, at his age I was thinnah.'

'So was I,' said Lady Mont; 'thin as you, Dinny.'

'We gathah unearned increment, ah-ha! Look at Jean – lithe is the word; in forty years – but perhaps the young of today will nevah grow fat. They do slimming – ah-ha!'

At lunch the Rector faced Sir Lawrence across the shortened table, and the two elder ladies sat one on each side of him. Alan faced Hubert and Dinny faced Jean.

'For what we are about to receive the Lord make us truly thankful.'

'Rum thing – grace!' said young Tasburgh in Dinny's ear. 'Benediction on murder, um?'

'There'll be hare,' said Dinny, 'and I saw it killed. It cried.'

'I'd as soon eat dog as hare.'

Dinny gave him a grateful look.

'Will you and your sister come and see us at Condaford?'

'Give me a chance!'

'When do you go back to your ship?'

'I've got a month.'

'I suppose you are devoted to your profession?'

'Yes,' he said, simply. 'It's bred in the bone, we've always had a sailor in the family.'

'And we've always had a soldier.'

'Your brother's deathly keen. I'm awfully glad to have met him.'

'No, Blore,' said Dinny to the butler, 'cold partridge, please. Mr Tasburgh too will eat something cold.'

'Beef, Sir; lamb, partridge.'

'Partridge, thank you.'

'I've seen a hare wash its ears,' added Dinny.

'When you look like that,' said young Tasburgh, 'I simply—'

'Like what?'

'As if you weren't there, you know.'

'Thank you.'

'Dinny,' said Sir Lawrence, 'who was it said the world was an oyster? I say it's a clam. What's your view?'

'I don't know the clam, Uncle Lawrence.'

'You're fortunate. That travesty of the self-respecting bivalve is the only tangible proof of American idealism. They've put it on a pedestal, and go so far as to eat it. When the Americans renounce the clam, they will have become realists and joined the League of Nations. We shall be dead.'

But Dinny was watching Hubert's face. The brooding look was gone: his eyes seemed glued to Jean's deep luring eyes. She uttered a sigh.

'Quite right,' said Sir Lawrence, 'it will be a pity not to live to see the Americans abandon the clam, and embrace the League of Nations. For, after all,' he continued, pursing up his left eye, 'it *was* founded by an American and is about the only sensible product of our time. It remains, however, the pet aversion of another American called Monroe who died in 1831, and is never alluded to without a scoff by people like "Snubby".

> A scoff, a sneer, a kick or two,
> With few, but with how splendid jeers—

D'you know that thing by Elroy Flecker?'

'Yes,' said Dinny, startled, 'it's in Hubert's diary; I read it out
to Lord Saxenden. It was just then he went to sleep.'

'He would. But don't forget, Dinny, that Snubby's a deuced
clever fellow, and knows his world to a T. It may be a world
you wouldn't be seen dead in, but it's the world where ten million
more-or-less-young men were recently seen dead. I wonder,'
concluded Sir Lawrence, more thoughtfully, 'when I have been
so well fed at my own table as these last days; something has
come over your aunt.'

Organising after lunch a game of croquet between herself and
Alan Tasburgh against his father and Aunt Wilmet, Dinny watched
the departure of Jean and her brother towards the rock borders.
They stretched from the sunken garden down to an old orchard,
beyond which rose a swell of meadow-land.

'*They* won't stop at the portulaca,' she thought.

Two games, indeed, were over before she saw them again
coming from a different direction, deep in talk. 'This,' she thought,
hitting the Rector's ball with all her force, 'is about the quickest
thing ever known.'

'God bless me!' murmured the smitten clergyman, and Aunt
Wilmet, straight as a grenadier, uttered a loud: 'Damn it, Dinny,
you're impossible! . . .'

Later, beside her brother in the open car, she was silent, making
up her mind, as it were, to second place. Though what she had
hoped for had come to pass, she was depressed. She had been
first with Hubert until now. She needed all her philosophy
watching the smile coming and going on his lips.

'Well, what do you think of our cousins?'

'He's a good chap. I thought he seemed rather gone on you.'

'Did you now? When would you like them to come over?'

'Any time.'

'Next week?'

'Yes.'

Seeing that he did not mean to be drawn, she lapsed into

savouring the day's slowly sinking light and beauty. The high land, Wantage, and Faringdon way, was glamoured by level sunlight; and Wittenham Clumps bastioned-up the rise ahead. Rounding to the right, they came on the bridge. In the middle of it she touched his arm:

'That stretch up there is where we saw the kingfishers, Hubert; d'you remember?'

Halted, they gazed up the quiet river, deserted and fit for the bright birds. Falling light sprinkled it through willows on the southern bank. The quietest river, it seemed, in the world, most subdued to the moods of men, flowing with an even clear stream among bright fields and those drooping shapely trees; having, as it were, a bland intensity of being, a presence of its own, gracious and apart.

'Three thousand years ago,' said Hubert suddenly, 'this old river used to be like those I've seen in the wilds, an unshaped flow of water in matted jungle.'

He drove on. They had their backs to the sunlight now, and it was like driving into what had been painted for them.

And so they sped on, while into the sky crept the sunset glow, and the cleaned-up fields darkened a little, and gathered loneliness under the evening flight of birds.

At the door of Condaford Grange Dinny got out, humming: '"She was a shepherdess oh! so fair,"' and looking into her brother's face. He was, however, busy with the car and did not appear to see the connection.

Chapter Twelve

The outline of a young Englishman of the inarticulate variety is difficult to grasp. The vocal variety is easily enough apprehended. Its manners and habits bulk large to the eye and have but little importance in the national life. Vociferous, critical, ingenious, knowing and advertising only its own kind, it forms an iridescence shimmering over the surface of the bog, and disguising the peat below. It constantly and brilliantly expresses almost nothing; while those whose lives are spent in the application of trained energy remain invisible, but none the less solid; for feelings continually voiced cease to be feelings, and feelings never voiced deepen with their dumbness. Hubert did not look solid, nor was he stolid; even those normal aids to the outline of the inarticulate were absent. Trained, sensitive, and no fool, he was capable of passing quiet judgment on people and events that would have surprised the vocal, but, except to himself, he never passed it. Till quite recently, indeed, he had lacked time and opportunity; but seeing him in a smoking room, at a dinner-table, or wherever the expressive scintillate, you would know at once that neither time nor opportunity was going to make him vociferous. Going into the war, so early, as a professional, he had missed the expanding influences of the 'Varsity and London. Eight years in Mesopotamia, Egypt and India, a year of illness and the Hallorsen expedition, had given him a remote, drawn, rather embittered look. He was of the temperament that, in idleness, eats its heart out. With dog and gun or on a horse, he found it bearable, but only just; and without those adventitious aids he wilted. Three days after the return to Condaford he came to Dinny on the terrace, with *The Times* in his hand.

'Look at this!'

Dinny read:

SIR,

You will pardon me, I trust, this intrusion on your space. It has come to my knowledge that certain passages in my book, 'Bolivia and Its Secrets', published last July, have grievously annoyed my second-in-command, Captain Hubert Charwell, D.S.O., who had charge of the transport of the expedition. On re-reading these passages I certainly believe that in the vexation caused me by the partial failure of the expedition, and owing to the over-strained state in which I returned from the adventure, I have passed undue criticism on Captain Charwell's conduct; and I wish, pending the issue of the second and amended edition which I trust will not be long delayed, to take this opportunity of publicly withdrawing in your great journal the gravamen of my written words. It is my duty and pleasure to express to Captain Charwell and the British Army of which he is a member, my sincere apology, and my regret for any pain I may have caused him.

Sir, Your obedient servant,

EDWARD HALLORSEN (Professor)
Piedmont Hotel
London

'Very handsome!' said Dinny, trembling a little.

'Hallorsen in London! What the devil does he mean by this all of a sudden?'

She began pulling yellowed leaves out of an Agapanthus. The danger of doing things for other people was being disclosed to her.

'It almost looks like repentance, dear.'

'That fellow repent! Not he! There's something behind it.'

'Yes, I am.'

'You!'

Dinny quailed behind her smile.

'I met Hallorsen at Diana's in London; he was at Lippinghall, too. So I – er – got at him.'

Hubert's sallowed face went red.

'You asked – you begged—?'

'Oh! no!'

'What then?'

'He seemed to take rather a fancy to me. It's odd, but I couldn't help it, Hubert.'

'He's done this to curry favour with you?'

'You put it like a man and a brother.'

'Dinny!'

Dinny flushed too, angry now behind her smile.

'I didn't lead him on. He took this highly unreasonable fancy, in spite of plenty of cold water. But, if you ask me, Hubert, he has quite a decent side to him.'

'You would naturally think so,' said Hubert, coldly. His face had resumed its sallow hue and was even a little ashened.

Dinny caught impulsively at his sleeve.

'Don't be silly, dear! If he chooses to make a public apology for any reason, even such a bad one, isn't it all to the good?'

'Not when my own sister comes into it. In this thing I'm like – I'm like a—' he put his hands to his head: 'I'm in Chancery. Anyone can punch my head, and I can't move.'

Dinny's coolness had come back to her.

'You needn't be afraid that I shall compromise you. This letter is very good news; it takes the wind out of the whole thing. In face of this apology, who can say anything?'

But Hubert, leaving the paper in her hand, went back into the house.

Dinny had practically no 'small' pride. Her sense of humour prevented her from attaching value to her own performances. She felt that she ought to have provided against this contingency, though she did not see how.

Hubert's resentment was natural enough. If Hallorsen's apology had been dictated by conviction, it would have soothed him; arising from a desire to please his sister, it was only the more galling; and he clearly abhorred the Professor's fancy for her. Still, there was the letter – an open and direct admission of false criticism, which changed the whole position! At once she began to consider what use could be made of it. Should she send it to Lord Saxenden? Having meddled so far, she decided that she would, and went in to write the covering letter.

Condaford Grange. Sept. 21.

DEAR LORD SAXENDEN,

I am venturing to send you the enclosed cutting from today's 'Times', for I feel it excuses me to some extent for my effrontery the other evening. I really ought not to have bored you at the end of a long day with those passages of my brother's diary. It was unpardonable, and I don't wonder that you sought refuge. But the enclosed will show you the injustice from which my brother has suffered; and I hope you will forgive me.

Sincerely yours,

ELIZABETH CHARWELL

Enclosing the cutting, she looked up Lord Saxenden in *Who's Who*, and addressed the envelope to his London abode, marking it 'Personal'.

A little later, trying to find Hubert, she was told that he had taken the car and gone up to London . . .

Hubert drove fast. Dinny's explanation of the letter had disturbed him greatly. He covered the fifty odd miles in a little under two hours and reached the Piedmont Hotel at one o'clock. Since he had parted from Hallorsen nearly six months ago, no word had passed between them. He sent his card in and waited in the hall with no precise knowledge of what he wanted to say. When the American's tall figure approached behind the buttoned boy, a cold stillness possessed his every limb.

'Captain Cherrell,' said Hallorsen, and held out his hand.

With a horror of 'scenes' deeper than his more natural self, Hubert took it, but without pressure in his fingers.

'I saw you were here, from *The Times*. Is there anywhere we could go and talk for a few minutes?'

Hallorsen led towards an alcove. 'Bring some cocktails,' he said to a waiter.

'Not for me, thank you. But may I smoke?'

'I trust this is the pipe of peace, Captain.'

'I don't know. An apology that does not come from conviction means less than nothing to me.'

'Who says it doesn't come from conviction?'

'My sister.'

'Your sister, Captain Cherrell, is a very rare and charming young lady, and I would not wish to contradict her.'

'Do you mind my speaking plainly?'

'Why, surely no!'

'Then I would much rather have had no apology from you than know I owed it to any feeling of yours for one of my family.'

'Well,' said Hallorsen, after a pause, 'I can't write to *The Times* and say I was in error when I made that apology. I judge they wouldn't stand for that. I had a sore head when I wrote that book. I told your sister so, and I tell you so now. I lost all sense of charity, and I have come to regret it.'

'I don't want charity. I want justice. Did I or did I not let you down?'

'Why, there's no question but that your failure to hold that pack together did in fact finish my chance.'

'I admit that. Did I fail you from my fault, or from yours in giving me an impossible job?'

For a full minute the two men stood with their eyes on each other, and without a word. Then Hallorsen again held out his hand.

'Put it there,' he said; 'my fault.'

Hubert's hand went out impulsively, but stopped half way.

'One moment. Do you say that because it would please my sister?'

'No, Sir; I mean it.'

Hubert took his hand.

'That's great,' said Hallorsen. 'We didn't get on, Captain; but since I've stayed in one of your old homes here, I think I've grasped the reason why. I expected from you what you class Englishmen seemingly will never give – that's the frank expression of your feelings. I judge one has to translate you, and I just couldn't do it, so we went on in the dark about each other. And that's the way to get raw.'

'I don't know why, but we got raw all right.'

'Well, I wish it could come all over again.'

Hubert shivered. 'I don't.'

'Now, Captain, will you lunch with me, and tell me how I can serve you? I will do anything you say to wipe out my mistake.'

For a moment Hubert did not speak, his face was unmoved, but his hands shook a little.

'That's all right,' he said. 'It's nothing.'

And they moved towards the grill room.

Chapter Thirteen

*O*f one thing is more certain than another – which is extremely doubtful – it is that nothing connected with a Public Department will run as a private individual expects.

A more experienced and less simply faithful sister than Dinny would have let sleeping dogs lie. But she had as yet no experience of the fact that the usual effect of letters to those in high places is the precise opposite of what was intended by the sender. Arousing his *amour-propre*, which in the case of public men should be avoided, it caused Lord Saxenden to look no further into the matter. Did that young woman suppose for a moment that he didn't see how this American chap was feeding out of her hand? In accordance, indeed, with the irony latent in human affairs, Hallorsen's withdrawal of the charge had promoted in the authorities a more suspicious and judgmatic attitude, and Hubert received, two days before his year of leave was up, an intimation to the effect that it was extended indefinitely and he was to go on half-pay, pending an enquiry into the matter raised in the House of Commons by Major Motley, MP. A letter from that military civilian had appeared in reply to Hallorsen's asking whether he was to assume that the shooting and flogging mentioned in his book had not really taken place, and if so, what explanation could this American gentleman afford of such an amazing discrepancy? This, in turn, had elicited from Hallorsen the answer that the facts were as stated in his book, but that his deductions from them had been erroneous, and that Captain Charwell had been perfectly justified in his actions.

On receiving intimation that his leave was extended, Hubert went up to the War Office. He obtained no comfort, beyond the non-official saying of an acquaintance that the Bolivian Authorities were 'butting in'. This news created little less than consternation at Condaford. None of the four young people, indeed, for the Tasburghs were still there, and Clare away in Scotland, appreciated the report at its full value, for none of them had as yet much knowledge of the extent to which officialdom can go when it starts out to do its duty; but to the General it had so sinister a significance that he went up to stay at his Club.

After tea that day in the billiard room, Jean Tasburgh, chalking her cue, said quietly:

'What does that Bolivian news mean, Hubert?'

'It may mean anything. I shot a Bolivian, you know.'

'But he tried to kill you first.'

'He did.'

She leaned her cue against the table; her hands brown, slim, and strong, gripped the cushion; suddenly she went up to him and put her hand through his arm. 'Kiss me,' she said; 'I am going to belong to you.'

'Jean!'

'No, Hubert; no chivalry and that sort of nonsense. You shan't have all this beastliness alone. I'm going to share it. Kiss me.'

The kiss was given. It was long, and soothing to them both; but, when it was over, he said:

'Jean, it's quite impossible, until things dry straight.'

'Of course they'll dry straight, but I want to help dry them. Let's be married quickly, Hubert. Father can spare me a hundred a year; what can you manage?'

'I've three hundred a year of my own, and half pay, which may be cut off.'

'That's four hundred a year certain; people have married on

lots less, and that's only for the moment. Of course we can be married. Where?'

Hubert stood breathless.

'When the war was on,' said Jean, 'people married at once; they didn't wait because the man was going to be killed. Kiss me again.'

And Hubert stood more breathless than ever, with her arms round his neck. It was so that Dinny found them.

Without moving her arms, Jean said:

'We're going to be married, Dinny. Where do you think best? A Registry Office? Banns take so much time.'

Dinny gasped.

'I didn't think you'd propose quite so soon, Jean.'

'I had to. Hubert is full of stuffy chivalry. Dad won't like a Registry Office; why not a special licence?'

Hubert's hands on her shoulders held her away from him.

'Be serious, Jean.'

'I am. With a special licence, nobody need know till it's over. So nobody will mind.'

'Well,' said Dinny, quietly, 'I believe you're right. When a thing has to be, it had better be quickly. I daresay Uncle Hilary would tie you up.'

Hubert dropped his hands. 'You're both cracked.'

'Polite!' said Jean. 'Men are absurd. They want a thing, and when it's offered they carry on like old women. Who is Uncle Hilary?'

'Vicar of St Augustine's-in-the-Meads; he has no sense of propriety to speak of.'

'Good! You go up tomorrow, Hubert, and get the licence. We'll come after you. Where can we stay, Dinny?'

'Diana would have us, I think.'

'That settles it. We'll have to go round by Lippinghall, for me to get some clothes, and see Dad. I can cut his hair while I'm talking to him; there won't be any trouble. Alan can come too; we shall want a best man. Dinny, you talk to Hubert.' Left alone with her brother, Dinny said:

'She's a wonderful girl, Hubert, and far from cracked, really. It's breathless, but terribly good sense. She's always been poor, so it won't make any difference to her in that way.'

'It isn't that. It's the feeling of something hanging over me, that'll hang over her too.'

'It'll hang over her worse, if you don't. I really should, dear boy. Father won't mind. He likes her, and he'd rather you married a girl of breeding and spirit than any amount of money.'

'It doesn't seem decent – a special licence,' muttered Hubert.

'It's romantic, and people won't have a chance to discuss whether you ought to or not; when it's done they'll accept it, as they always do.'

'What about Mother?'

'I'll tell Mother, if you like. I'm sure she won't really mind – you're not being fashionable, marrying a chorus girl or anything of that sort. She admires Jean. So do Aunt Em and Uncle Lawrence.'

Hubert's face cleared.

'I'll do it. It's too wonderful. After all, I've nothing to be ashamed of.'

He walked up to Dinny, kissed her almost violently, and hurried out. Dinny stayed in the billiard-room practising the spot stroke. Behind her matter-of-fact attitude, she was extremely stirred. The embrace she had surprised had been so passionate; the girl was so strange a mixture of feeling and control, of lava and of steel, so masterful and yet so amusingly young. It might be a risk; but Hubert was already a different man because of it. All the same she was fully conscious of inconsistency; for to herself such a sensational departure would not be possible. The giving of her heart would be no rushing affair. As her old Scotch nurse used to say: 'Miss Dinny aye knows on hoo many toes a pussy-cat goes.' She was not proud of that 'sense of humour not devoid of wit which informed and somewhat sterilised all else'. Indeed, she envied Jean her colourful decision, Alan his direct conviction, Hallorsen's robust adventurousness. But she had her compensations, and, with a smile breaking her lips apart, went to find her mother.

Lady Cherrell was in her sanctum next to her bedroom, making muslin bags for the leaves of the scented verbena which grew against the house.

'Darling,' said Dinny, 'prepare for slight concussion. You remember my saying I wished we could find the perfect girl for Hubert. Well, she's found; Jean has just proposed to him.'

'Dinny!'

'They're going to be married offhand by special licence.'

'But—'

'Exactly, darling. So we go up tomorrow, and Jean and I stay with Diana till it's over. Hubert will tell Father.'

'But, Dinny, really—!'

Dinny came through the barrage of muslin, knelt down and put her arm round her mother.

'I feel exactly like you,' she said, 'only different, because after all I didn't produce him; but, Mother darling, it is all right. Jean is a marvellous creature, and Hubert's head over ears. It's done him a lot of good already, and she'll see to it that he goes ahead, you know.'

'But, Dinny – money?'

'They're not expecting Dad to do anything. They'll just be able to manage, and they needn't have children, you know, till later.'

'I suppose not. It's terribly sudden. Why a special licence?'

'Intuition,' and, with a squeeze of her mother's slender body, she added: 'Jean has them. Hubert's position *is* awkward, Mother.'

'Yes; I'm scared about it, and I know your father is, though he's not said much.'

This was as far as either of them would go in disclosure of their uneasiness, and they went into committee on the question of a perch for the adventuring couple.

'But why shouldn't they live here until things are settled?' said Lady Cherrell.

'They'll find it more exciting if they have to do their own washing up. The great thing is to keep Hubert's mind active just now.'

Lady Cherrell sighed. Correspondence, gardening, giving household orders, and sitting on village committees were certainly not exciting, and Condaford would be even less exciting if, like the young, one had none of these distractions.

'Things *are* quiet here,' she admitted.

'And thank God for it,' murmured Dinny; 'but I feel Hubert wants the strenuous life just now, and he'll get it with Jean in London. They might take a workman's flat. It can't be for long, you know. So, Mother dear, you'll not seem to know anything about it this evening, and we shall all know you do. That'll be so restful for everybody.' And, kissing the rueful smile on her mother's face, she went away.

Next morning the conspirators were early afoot, Hubert looking, so Jean put it, as though he were 'riding at a bullfinch'; Dinny resolutely whimsical. Alan had the handy air of a best man in embryo; Jean alone appeared unmoved. They set forth in the Tasburghs' brown roadster, dropping Hubert at the station and proceeding towards Lippinghall. Jean drove. The other two sat behind.

'Dinny,' said young Tasburgh, 'couldn't *we* have a special licence, too?'

'Reduction on taking a quantity. Behave yourself. You will go to sea and forget all about me in a month.'

'Do I look like that?'

Dinny regarded his brown face.

'Well, in spots.'

'Do be serious!'

'I can't; I keep seeing Jean snipping a lock and saying: "Now Dad, bless me or I'll tonsure you!" and the Rector answering "I – er – nevah—!" and Jean snipping another lock and saying: "That's all right then, and I must have a hundred a year or off go your eyebrows!"'

'Jean's a holy terror. Promise me anyway, Dinny, not to marry anyone else?'

'But suppose I met someone I liked terribly, would you wish to blight my young life?'

'Yes.'

'Not so do they answer on the "screen".'

'You'd make a saint swear.'

'But not a naval lieutenant. Which reminds me: Those texts at the head of the fourth column of *The Times*. It struck me this morning what a splendid secret code could be made out of "The Song of Solomon", or that Psalm about the Leviathan. "My beloved is like a young roe" might mean "Eight German battleships in Dover harbour. Come quickly." "And there is that Leviathan that takes his pastime therein" could be "Tirpirz in command", and so on. No one could possibly decipher it unless they had a copy of the code.'

'I'm going to speed,' said Jean, looking back. The speedometer rose rapidly: Forty – forty-five – fifty – fifty-five—! The sailor's hand slipped under Dinny's arm.

'This can't last, the car will bust. But it's a tempting bit of road.'

Dinny sat with a fixed smile; she hated being driven really fast, and, when Jean had dropped again to her normal thirty-five, said plaintively:

'Jean, I have a nineteenth century inside.'

At Folwell she leaned forward again: 'I don't want them to see me at Lippinghall. Please go straight to the Rectory and hide me somewhere while you deal with your parent.'

Refuged in the dining-room opposite the portrait of which Jean had spoken, Dinny studied it curiously. Underneath were the words: '1553, Catherine Tastburgh, neé Fitzherbert, aetate 35; wife of Sir Walter Tastburgh.'

Above the ruff encircling the long neck, that time-yellowed face might truly have been Jean fifteen years hence, the same tapering from the broad cheek-bones to the chin, the same long dark-lashed luring eyes; even the hands, crossed on the stomacher, were the very spit of Jean's. What had been the history of that strange prototype; did they know it, and would it be repeated by her descendant?

'Awfully like Jean, isn't she?' said young Tasburgh: 'She was a corker, from all accounts; they say she staged her own funeral, and got out of the country when Elizabeth set about the Catholics in the fifteen-sixties. D'you know what was the fate of anyone who celebrated Mass just then? Ripping up was a mere incident in it. The Christian religion! What oh! That lady had a hand in most pies, I fancy. I bet she speeded when she could.'

'Any news from the front?'

'Jean went into the study with an old *Times*, a towel, and a pair of scissors. The rest is silence.'

'Isn't there anywhere from which we can see them when they come out?'

'We could sit on the stairs. They wouldn't notice us, there, unless they happen to go up.'

They went out and sat in a dark corner of the stairway, whence through the bannisters they could see the study door. With some of the thrill of childhood Dinny watched for it to open. Suddenly Jean came forth, with a sheet of newspaper folded as a receptacle in one hand, and in the other a pair of scissors. They heard her say:

'Remember, dear, you're not to go out without a hat today.'

An inarticulate answer was shut off by the closing of the door. Dinny rose above the bannisters: 'Well?'

'It's all right. He's a bit grumpy – doesn't know who'll cut his hair and that; thinks a special licence a waste of money; but he's going to give me the hundred a year. I left him filling his pipe.' She stood still, looking into the sheet of newspaper. 'There was an awful lot to come away. We'll have lunch in a minute, Dinny, and then be off again.'

The Rector's manner at lunch was still courtly, and Dinny observed him with admiring attention. Here was a widower well on in years, about to be deprived of his only daughter, who did everything about the house and parish, even to the cutting of his hair, yet he was apparently unmoved. Not a murmur escaped his lips. Was it breeding, benevolence, or unholy relief? She could not be sure; and her heart quailed a little. Hubert would soon be in his shoes. She stared at Jean. Little doubt but that she could stage her own funeral, if not other people's; still, there would be nothing ungraceful or raucous about her dominations; no vulgar domesticity in the way she stirred her pies. If only she and Hubert had enough sense of humour!

After lunch the Rector took her apart.

'My deah Dinny – if I may call you that – how do you feel about it? And how does your Mothah feel?'

'We both feel it's a little bit like "The Owl and the Pussycat went to sea!"'

'"In a beautiful pea-green boat." Yes, indeed, but not "with plenty of money" I feah. Still,' he added, dreamily, 'Jean is a good girl; very – ah – capable. I am glad our families are to be – er – reunited. I shall miss her, but one must not be – ah – selfish.'

'"What we lose on the swings we gain on the roundabouts,"' murmured Dinny.

The Rector's blue eyes twinkled.

'Ah!' he said, 'yes, indeed; the rough with the smooth. Jean refuses to let me give her away. Here is her birth certificate in case of – ah – questions. She is of age.'

He produced a long yellowed slip. 'Deah me!' he added, sincerely: 'Deah me!'

Dinny continued to feel doubtful whether she was sorry for him: and, directly after, they resumed their journey.

Chapter Fourteen

Dropping Alan Tasburgh at his Club, the two girls headed the car for Chelsea. Dinny had sent no telegram, trusting to luck. On reaching the house in Oakley Street she got out and rang the bell. An elderly maid, with a frightened expression on her face, opened the door.

'Mrs Ferse in?'

'No, Miss; Captain Ferse.'

'Captain Ferse?'

The maid, looking to right and left, spoke in a low and hurried voice.

'Yes, Miss; we're dreadfully put about, we don't know what to do. Captain Ferse came in sudden at lunch time, and we never knew nothing of it, beforehand. The Mistress was out. There's been a telegram for her, but Captain Ferse took it; and someone's been on the 'phone for her twice but wouldn't give a message.' Dinny sought for words in which to discover the worst.

'How – how does he seem?'

'Well, Miss, I couldn't say. He never said nothing but "Where's your mistress?" He *looks* all right, but not having heard anything, we're afraid; the children are in and we don't know where the Mistress is.'

'Wait a minute,' and Dinny went back to the car.

'What's the matter?' asked Jean, getting out.

The two girls stood consulting on the pavement, while from the doorway the maid watched them.

'I ought to get hold of Uncle Adrian,' said Dinny. 'There are the children.'

'You do that, and I'll go in and wait for you. That maid looks scared.'

'I believe he used to be violent, Jean; he may have escaped, you know.'

'Take the car. I shall be all right.' Dinny squeezed her hand.

'I'll take a taxi; then you'll have the car if you want to get away.'

'Right! Tell the maid who I am, and then buzz off. It's four o'clock.'

Dinny looked up at the house; and, suddenly, saw a face in the window of the dining room. Though she had only twice seen Ferse, she recognised him at once. His face was not to be forgotten, it gave the impression of fire behind bars: A cut, hard face with a toothbrush moustache, broad cheek-bones, strong-growing dark slightly-grizzled hair, and those steel-bright flickering eyes. They stared out at her now with a kind of dancing intensity that was painful, and she looked away.

'Don't look up! He's in there!' she said to Jean: 'But for his eyes he looks quite normal – well-dressed and that. Let's both go, Jean, or both stay.'

'No; I shall be quite all right; you go,' and she went into the house.

Dinny hurried away. This sudden reappearance of one whom all had assumed to be hopelessly unhinged was staggering. Ignorant of the circumstances of Ferse's incarceration, ignorant of everything except that he had given Diana a terrible time before his break-down, she thought of Adrian as the only person likely to know enough. It was a long anxious drive. She found her uncle on the point of leaving the Museum, and told him hurriedly, while he stood looking at her with horror.

'Do you know where Diana is?' she finished.

'She was dining tonight with Fleur and Michael. I was going too, but till then I don't know. Let's get on back to Oakley Street. This is a thunderbolt.'

They got into the cab.

'Couldn't you telephone to that Mental Home, Uncle?'

'Without seeing Diana, I daren't. You say he looked normal?'

'Yes. Only his eyes – but they always were like that, I remember.'

Adrian put his hands up to his head. 'It's too horrible! My poor girl!'

Dinny's heart began to ache – as much for him as for Diana.

'Horrible too,' said Adrian, 'to be feeling like this because that poor devil has come back. Ah, me! This is a bad business, Dinny; a bad business.' Dinny squeezed his arm.

'What is the law about it, Uncle?'

'God knows! He never was certified. Diana wouldn't have that. They took him as a private patient.'

'But surely he couldn't come away just when he liked, without any notice being given?'

'Who knows what's happened? He may be as crazy as ever and have got away in a flash of sanity. But whatever we do,' and Dinny felt moved by the expression on his face, 'we must think of him as well as of ourselves. We mustn't make it harder for him. Poor Ferse! Talk about trouble, Dinny – illness, poverty, vice, crime – none of them can touch mental derangement for sheer tragedy to all concerned.'

'Uncle,' said Dinny, 'the night?'

Adrian groaned. 'That we must save her from somehow.'

At the end of Oakley Street they dismissed the cab and walked to the door . . .

On going in Jean had said to the maid: 'I'm Miss Tasburgh. Miss Dinny has gone for Mr Cherrell. Drawing room upstairs? I'll wait there. Has he seen the children?'

'No, Miss. He's only been here half an hour. The children are up in the schoolroom with Mam'selle.'

'Then I shall be between them,' said Jean. 'Take me up.'

'Shall I wait with you, Miss?'

'No. Keep a look-out for Mrs Ferse and tell her at once.'

The maid gazed at her admiringly and left her in the drawing room. Setting the door ajar Jean stood listening. There was no sound. And she began to move silently up and down from door to window. If she saw Diana approaching she meant to run down to her; if Ferse came up she meant to go out to him. Her heart beat a little faster than usual, but she felt no real nervousness. She had been patrolling thus for a quarter of an hour when she heard a sound behind her, and, turning, saw Ferse just within the room.

'Oh!' she said: 'I'm waiting for Mrs Ferse; are you Captain Ferse?'

The figure bowed. 'And you?'

'Jean Tasburgh. I'm afraid you wouldn't know me.'

'Who was that with you?'

'Dinny Cherrell.'

'Where has she gone?'

'To see one of her uncles, I believe.'

Ferse uttered a queer sound – not quite a laugh.

'Adrian?'

'I think so.'

He stood turning those bright flickering eyes on the pretty room.

'Prettier than ever,' he said, 'I've been away some time. Do you know my wife?'

'I met her staying at Lady Mont's.'

'Lippinghall? Is Diana well?'

The words came out with a sort of hungry harshness.

'Yes. Quite.'

'And beautiful?'

'Very.'

'Thank you.'

Looking at him from under her long lashes Jean could see nothing in him from top to toe that gave the impression of derangement. He looked what he was – a soldier in mufti, very neat and self-contained, all – all but those eyes.

'I haven't seen my wife for four years,' he said, 'I shall want to see her alone.'

Jean moved towards the door.

'I'll go,' she said.

'No!' The word came out with startling suddenness: 'Stay there!' And he blocked the doorway.

'Why?'

'I wish to be the first to tell her that I'm back.'

'Naturally.'

'Stay there, then!'

Jean moved back to the window. 'Just as you like,' she said. There was a silence.

'Have you heard about me?' he asked, suddenly.

'Very little. I know you haven't been well.'

He came from the door. 'Do you see anything the matter with me?'

Jean looked up, her eyes held his till they went flickering away.

'Nothing. You look very fit.'

'I am. Sit down, won't you?'

'Thank you.' Jean sat down.

'That's right,' he said. 'Keep your eyes on me.'

Jean looked at her feet. Again Ferse uttered that travesty of a laugh.

'You've never been mentally sick, I take it. If you had you'd know that everybody keeps their eyes on you; and you keep your eyes on everybody. I must go down now. *Au revoir!*'

He turned quickly and went out, shutting the door. Jean continued to sit quite still, expecting him to open it again. She had a feeling of having been worsted, and a curious tingling all over, as if she had been too close to a fire. He did not open the door again, and she got up to do so herself. It was locked. She stood looking at it. Ring the bell? Hammer on it and attract the maid? She decided to do neither, but went to the window and stood watching the street. Dinny would be back soon and she could call to her. Very coolly she reviewed the scene she had been through. He had locked her in because he meant no one to interfere before he saw his wife – suspicious of everyone – very natural! A dim sense of what it meant to be looked on as deranged penetrated her young hard intelligence. Poor man! She wondered if she could get out of the window without being noticed, and, deciding that she couldn't, continued to stand watching the end of the street for the appearance of relief. And, suddenly, without anything to cause it, a shiver ran through her, the aftermath of that encounter. His eyes! It must be terrible to be his wife. She threw the window wider, and leaned out . . .

Chapter Fifteen

The sight of Jean at the window stayed Dinny and her uncle on the doorstep.

'I'm locked in the drawing room,' said Jean, quietly; 'you might let me out.'

Adrian took his niece to the car.

'Stay here, Dinny. I'll send her out to you. We mustn't make a show of this.'

'Take care, Uncle! I feel as if you were Daniel going into—'

With a wan smile Adrian rang the bell. Ferse himself opened the door.

'Ah! Cherrell? Come in.'

Adrian held out his hand; but it was not taken.

'I can hardly expect a welcome,' said Ferse.

'My dear fellow!'

'No, I can hardly expect a welcome, but I'm going to see Diana. Don't try and prevent me, Cherrell – you or anyone.'

'Of course not! Do you mind if I fetch young Jean Tasburgh? Dinny is waiting for her in the car.'

'I locked her in,' said Ferse, sombrely. 'Here's the key. Send her away.'

He went into the dining room.

Jean was standing just inside the door.

'Go out to Dinny,' said Adrian, 'and take her away. I'll manage. No trouble, I hope?'

'Only being locked in.'

'Tell Dinny,' said Adrian, 'that Hilary is almost sure to be able to put you both up; if you go on there now I shall know where you are if I want you. You have pluck, young lady.'

'Oh, not specially!' said Jean: 'Good-bye!' and ran downstairs. Adrian heard the front door close and went slowly down to the dining room. Ferse was at the window watching the girls start the car. He turned round sharply. The movement was that of a man used to being spied on. There was little change in him, less thin, less haggard, and his hair greyer – that was all. His dress as neat as ever, his manner composed; his eyes – but then – his eyes!

'Yes,' said Ferse, uncannily, 'you can't help pitying me, but you'd like to see me dead. Who wouldn't? A fellow has no business to go off his chump. But I'm sane enough now, Cherrell, don't make any mistake.'

Sane? Yes, he seemed sane. But what strain could he stand?

Ferse spoke again: 'You all thought I was gone for good. About three months ago I began to mend. As soon as I realised that – I kept dark. Those who look after us' – he spoke with concentrated bitterness – 'must be so certain of our sanity that if it were left to them we should never be sane again. It's to their interest, you see.' And his eyes, burning into Adrian's seemed to add: 'And to yours, and to hers?' 'So I kept dark. I had the will-power to keep dark in that place for three months, in my right mind. It's only this last week or so that I've shown them I'm responsible. They want much more than a week before they'll write home about it. I didn't want them writing home. I wanted to come straight here and show myself as I am. I didn't want Diana or anybody warned. And I wanted to make sure of myself, and I have.'

'Terrible!' said Adrian below his breath.

Ferse's eyes seemed to burn into him again.

'You used to be in love with my wife, Cherrell; you still are. Well?'

'We are just as we were,' said Adrian, 'friends.'

'You'd say that anyway.'

'Perhaps. But there is no more to say, except that I'm bound to think of her first, as I always have.'

'That's why you're here, then?'

'Gracious, man! Haven't you realised the shock it will be to her? Perhaps you can't remember the life you led her before you went in there? But do you think she's forgotten? Wouldn't it be fairer to her and to yourself if you came to my room, say, at the Museum, and saw her there for the first time?'

'No; I'll see her here in my own house.'

'This is where she went through hell, Ferse. You may have been right to keep dark, as you call it, so far as the doctors are concerned, but you're certainly not right to spring your recovery on her like this.'

Ferse made a violent gesture.

'You want her kept from me.'

Adrian bowed his head.

'That may be,' he said, gently. 'But look here, Ferse, you're just as well able to gauge this situation as myself. Put yourself in her place. Imagine her coming in, as she may at any minute, seeing you without warning, knowing nothing of your recovery, needing time to believe in it – with all her memories of you as you were. What chance are you giving yourself?'

Ferse groaned. 'What chance shall I be given, if I don't take any chance I can? Do you think I trust anyone now? Try it – try four years of it, and see!' and his eyes went swiftly round: 'Try being watched, try being treated like a dangerous child. I've looked on at my own treatment, as a perfectly sane man, for the last three months. If my own wife can't take me for what I am – clothed and in my right mind, who will or can?'

Adrian went up to him.

'Gently!' he said: 'That's where you're wrong. Only *she* knew you at the worst. It should be more difficult for her than for anyone.'

Ferse covered his face.

Adrian waited, grey with anxiety; but when Ferse uncovered his face again he could not bear the look on it, and turned his eyes away.

'Talk of loneliness!' said Ferse. 'Go off your chump, Cherrell, then you'll know what it means to be lonely for the rest of your days.'

Adrian put a hand on his shoulder.

'Look here, my dear fellow, I've got a spare room at my digs, come and put up with me till we get things straightened out.' Sudden suspicion grinned from Ferse's face, an intense searching look came into his eyes; it softened as if with gratitude, grew bitter, softened again.

'You were always a white man, Cherrell; but no, thanks – I couldn't. I must be here. Foxes have holes, and I've still got this.'

Adrian sighed.

'Very well; then we must wait for her. Have you seen the children?'

'No. Do they remember me?'

'I don't think so.'

'Do they know I'm alive?'

'Yes. They know that you're away, ill.'

'Not—?' Ferse touched his forehead.

'No. Shall we go up to them?'

Ferse shook his head, and at that moment through the window Adrian saw Diana coming. He moved quietly towards the door. What was he to do or say? His hand was on the knob when Ferse pushed by him into the hall. Diana had come in with her latchkey. Adrian could see her face grow deadly pale below the casque of her close hat. She recoiled against the wall.

'It's all right, Diana,' he said quickly, and held open the dining-room door. She came from the wall, passed them both into the room, and Ferse followed.

'If you want to consult me I shall be here,' said Adrian, and closed the door . . .

Husband and wife stood breathing as if they had run a hundred yards instead of walking three.

'Diana!' said Ferse: 'Diana!'

It seemed as if she couldn't speak, and his voice rose:

'I'm all right. Don't you believe me?'

She bent her head, and still didn't speak.

'Not a word to throw to a dog?'

'It's – it's the shock.'

'I have come back sane, I have been sane for three months now.'

'I am so glad, so glad.'

'My God! You're as beautiful as ever.'

And suddenly he gripped her, pressed her hard against him, and began kissing her hungrily. When he let her go, she sank breathless into a chair, gazing at him with an expression of such terror that he put his hands over his face.

'Ronald – I couldn't – I couldn't let it be as it was before. I couldn't – I couldn't!'

He dropped on his knees at her feet. 'I didn't mean to be violent. Forgive me!'

And then, from sheer exhaustion of the power of feeling, both rose and moved apart.

'We had better talk it over quietly,' said Ferse.

'Yes.'

'Am I not to live here?'

'It's your house. You must do whatever's best for you.'

He uttered the sound that was so like a laugh.

'It would be best for me if you and everyone would treat me exactly as if nothing had happened to me.'

Diana was silent. She was silent so long that again he made that sound.

'Don't!' she said. 'I will try. But I must – I must have a separate room.'

Ferse bowed. Suddenly his eyes darted at her. 'Are you in love with Cherrell?'

'No.'

'With anyone?'

'No.'

'Scared then?'

'Yes.'

'I see. Naturally. Well, it's not for God's playthings to make terms. We take what we can get. Will you wire for them to send my things from that place? That will save any fuss they might want to make. I came away without saying good-bye. There is probably something owing too.'

'Of course. I will see to all that.'

'Can we let Cherrell go now?'

'I will tell him.'

'Let me!'

'No, Ronald, I will,' and she moved resolutely past him.

Adrian was leaning against the wall opposite the door. He looked up at her and tried to smile; he had divined the upshot.

'He is to stay here, but apart. My dear, thank you so much for all. Will you see to that Home for me? I will let you know everything. I'll take him up to the children now. Good-bye!' He kissed her hand and went out.

Chapter Sixteen

Hubert Cherrell stood outside his father's club in Pall Mall, a senior affair of which he was not yet a member. He was feeling concerned, for he had a respect for his father somewhat odd in days when fathers were commonly treated as younger brethren, or alluded to as 'that old man'. Nervously therefore he entered an edifice wherein more people had held more firmly to the prides and prejudices of a lifetime than possibly anywhere else on earth. There was little however, either of pride or prejudice, about the denizens of the room into which he was now shown. A short alert man with a pale face and a tooth-brush moustache was biting the end of a pen, and trying to compose a letter to *The Times* on the condition of Iraq; a modest-looking little Brigadier General with a bald forehead and grey moustache was discussing with a tall modest-looking Lieutenant Colonel the flora of the island of Cyprus; a man of square build, square cheek-bones and lion-like eyes, was sitting in the window as still as if he had just buried an aunt and were thinking whether or not he would try and swim the Channel next year; and Sir Conway himself was reading *Whitaker's Almanac*.

'Hallo, Hubert! This room's too small. Come into the hall.' Hubert had the instant feeling not only that he wanted to say something to his father, but that his father wanted to say something to him. They sat down in a recess.

'What's brought you up?'

'I want to get married, Sir.'

'Married?'

'To Jean Tasburgh.'

'Oh!'

'We thought of getting a special licence and having no fuss.'

The General shook his head. 'She's a fine girl, and I'm glad you feel like that, but the fact is your position's queer, Hubert. I've just been hearing.'

Hubert noticed suddenly how worn-looking was his father's face. 'That fellow you shot. They're pressing for your extradition on a charge of murder.'

'What?'

'It's a monstrous business, and I can't believe they'll go on with it in the face of what you say about his going for you – luckily you've still got his scar on your arm; but it seems there's the deuce of a fuss in the Bolivian papers; and those half-castes are sticking together about it.'

'I must see Hallorsen at once.'

'The authorities won't be in a hurry, I expect.'

After this, the two sat silent in the big hall, staring in front of them with very much the same expression on their faces. At the back of both their minds the fear of this development had lurked, but neither had ever permitted it to take definite shape; and its wretchedness was therefore the more potent. To the General it was even more searing than to Hubert. The idea that his only son could be haled half across the world on a charge of murder was as horrible as a nightmare.

'No good to let it prey on our minds, Hubert,' he said at last; 'if there's any sense in the country at all we'll get this stopped. I was trying to think of someone who knows how to get at people. I'm helpless in these matters – some fellows seem to know everybody and exactly how to work them. I think we'd better go to Lawrence Mont; he knows Saxenden anyway, and probably the people at the Foreign Office. It was Topsham who told me, but he can do nothing. Let's walk, shall we? Do us good.'

Much touched by the way his father was identifying himself with his trouble, Hubert squeezed his arm, and they left the Club. In Piccadilly the General said, with a transparent effort: 'I don't much like all these changes.'

'Well, Sir, except for Devonshire House, I don't believe I notice them.'

'No, it's queer; the spirit of Piccadilly is stronger than the street itself, you can't destroy its atmosphere. You never see a top hat now, and yet it doesn't seem to make any difference. I felt the same walking down Piccadilly after the war as I did as a youngster back from India. One just had the feeling of having got there at last.'

'Yes; you get a queer sort of homesickness for it. I did in Mespot and Bolivia. If one closed one's eyes the whole thing would start up.'

'Core of English life,' began the General, and stopped, as if surprised at having delivered a summary.

'Even the Americans feel it,' remarked Hubert, as they turned into Half-Moon Street. 'Hallorsen was saying to me they had nothing like it over there; "no focus for their national influence" was the way he put it.'

'And yet they *have* influence,' said the General.

'No doubt about that, Sir, but can you define it? Is it their speed that gives it them?'

'Where does their speed get them? Everywhere in general; nowhere in particular. No, it's their money, I think.'

'Well, I've noticed about Americans, and it's where most people go wrong, that they care very little for money as money. They like to get it fast; but they'd rather lose it fast than get it slow.'

'Queer thing having no core,' said the General.

'The country's too big, Sir. But they have a sort of core, all the same – pride of country.'

The General nodded.

'Queer little old streets these. I remember walking with my Dad from Curzon Street to the St James' Club in '82 – day I first went to Harrow – hardly a stick changed.' And so, concerned in talk that touched not on the feelings within them, they reached Mount Street.

'There's your Aunt Em, don't tell her.'

A few paces in front of them Lady Mont was, as it were, swimming home. They overtook her some hundred yards from the door.

'Con,' she said, 'you're lookin' thin.'

'My dear girl, I never was anything else.'

'No. Hubert, there was somethin' I wanted to ask you. Oh! I know! But Dinny said you hadn't had any breeches since the war. How do you like Jean? Rather attractive?'

'Yes, Aunt Em.'

'She wasn't expelled.'

'Why should she have been?'

'Oh! well, you never know. She's never terrorised me. D'you want Lawrence? It's Voltaire now and Dean Swift. So unnecessary – they've been awfully done; but he likes doin' them because they bite. About those mules, Hubert?'

'What about them?'

'I never can remember if the donkey is the sire or the dam.'

'The donkey is the sire and the dam a mare, Aunt Em.'

'Yes, and they don't have children – such a blessin'. Where's Dinny?'

'She's in town, somewhere.'

'She ought to marry.'

'Why?' said the General.

'Well, there she is! Hen was saying she'd make a good lady-in-waitin' – unselfish. That's the danger.' And, taking a latchkey out of her bag, Lady Mont applied it to the door.

'I can't get Lawrence to drink tea – would you like some?'

'No thank you, Em.'

'You'll find him stewin' in the library.' She kissed her brother and her nephew, and swam towards the stairs. 'Puzzlin',' they heard her say as they entered the library. They found Sir Lawrence surrounded by the works of Voltaire and Swift, for he was engaged on an imaginary dialogue between those two serious men. He listened gravely to the General's tale.

'I saw,' he said, when his brother-in-law had finished, 'that Hallorsen had repented him of the evil – that will be Dinny. I think we'd better see him – not here, there's no cook, Em's still slimming – but we can all dine at the Coffee House.' And he took up the telephone.

Professor Hallorsen was expected in at five and should at once be given the message.

'This seems to be more of an F.O. business than a Police matter,' went on Sir Lawrence. 'Let's go over and see old Shropshire. He must have known your father well, Con; and his nephew, Bobbie Ferrar, is about as fixed a star as there is at the F.O. Old Shropshire's always in!'

Arrived at Shropshire House Sir Lawrence said:

'Can we see the Marquess, Pommett?'

'I rather think he's having his lesson, Sir Lawrence.'

'Lesson – in what?'

'Heinstein, is it, Sir Lawrence?'

'Then the blind is leading the blind, and it will be well to save him. The moment there's a chance, Pommett, let us in.'

'Yes, Sir Lawrence.'

'Eighty-four and learning Einstein. Who said the aristocracy was decadent? I should like to see the bloke who's teaching it, though; he must have singular powers of persuasion – there are no flies on old Shropshire.'

At this moment a man of ascetic aspect, with a cold deep eye and not much hair, entered, took hat and umbrella from a chair, and went out.

'Behold the man!' said Sir Lawrence. 'I wonder what he charges? Einstein is like the electron or the vitamin – inapprehensible; it's as clear a case of money under false pretences as I've ever come across. Come along.'

The Marquess of Shropshire was walking up and down his study, nodding his quick and sanguine grey-bearded head as if to himself.

'Ah! young Mont,' he said, 'did you meet that man – if he offers to teach you Einstein, don't let him. He can no more explain space bounded yet infinite, than I can.'

'But even Einstein can't, Marquess.'

'I am not old enough,' said the Marquess, 'for anything but the exact sciences. I told him not to come again. Whom have I the pleasure of seeing?'

'My brother-in-law General Sir Conway Cherrell, and his son Captain Hubert Cherrell, D.S.O. You'll remember Conway's father, Marquess – he was Ambassador at Madrid.'

'Yes, yes, dear me, yes! I know your brother Hilary, too; a live wire. Sit down! Sit down, young man! Is it anything to do with electricity?'

'Not wholly, Marquess; more a matter of extradition.'

'Indeed!' The Marquess, raising his foot to the seat of a chair, leaned his elbow on his knee and his bearded chin on his hand. And, while the General was explaining, he continued to stand in this attitude, gazing at Hubert, who was sitting with compressed lips, and lowered eyes. When the General had finished the Marquess said:

'D.S.O., I think your uncle said. In the war?'

'Yes, Sir.'

'I shall do what I can. Could I see that scar?'

Hubert drew up his left sleeve, unlinked his shirt cuff and exposed an arm up which a long glancing scar stretched almost from wrist to elbow.

The Marquess whistled softly through teeth still his own. 'Narrow escape that, young man.'

'Yes, Sir. I put up my arm just as he struck.'

'And then?'

'Jumped back and shot him as he came on again. Then I fainted.'

'This man was flogged for ill-treating his mules, you say?'

'Continually ill-treating them.'

'Continually?' repeated the Marquess. 'Some think the meat-trade and Zoological Society continually ill-treat animals, but I never heard of their being flogged. Tastes differ. Now, let me see, what can I do? Is Bobbie in town, young Mont?'

'Yes, Marquess. I saw him at the Coffee House yesterday.'

'I will get him to breakfast. If I remember he does not allow his children to keep rabbits, and has a dog that bites everybody. That should be to the good. A man who is fond of animals would always like to flog a man who isn't. Before you go, young Mont, will you tell me what you think of this?' And replacing his foot on the ground, the Marquess went to the corner, took up a canvas that was leaning against the wall, and brought it to the light. It represented with a moderate degree of certainty a young woman without clothes.

'By Steinvitch,' said the Marquess; 'she could corrupt no morals, could she – if hung?'

Sir Lawrence screwed in his monocle: 'The oblong school. This comes of living with women of a certain shape, Marquess. No, she couldn't corrupt morals, but she might spoil digestions – flesh sea-green, hair tomato, style blobby. Did you buy her?'

'Hardly,' said the Marquess; 'she is worth a good deal of money, I am told. You – you wouldn't take her away, I suppose?'

'For you, Sir, I would do most things, but not that; no,' repeated Sir Lawrence, moving backwards, 'not that.'

'I was afraid of it,' said the Marquess, 'and yet I am told that she has a certain dynamic force. Well, that is that! I liked your father, General,' he said, more earnestly, 'and if the word of his grandson is not to be taken against that of half-caste muleteers, we shall have reached a stage of altruism in this country so complete that I do not think we can survive. I will let you know what my nephew says. Good-bye, General; good-bye, my dear young man – that is a very nasty scar. Good-bye, young Mont – you are incorrigible.'

On the stairs Sir Lawrence looked at his watch. 'So far,' he said, 'the matter has taken twenty minutes – say twenty-five from door to door. They can't do it at that pace in America – and we very nearly had an oblong young woman thrown in. Now for the Coffee House, and Hallorsen.' And they turned their faces towards St James's Street. 'This street,' he said, 'is the Mecca of Western man, as the Rue de la Paix is the Mecca of Western woman.' And he regarded his companions whimsically. What good specimens they were of a product at once the envy and mock of every other country! All over the British Empire men made more or less in their image were doing the work and playing the games of the British world. The sun never set on the type; history had looked on it and decided that it would survive. Satire darted at its joints, and rebounded from an unseen armour. 'It walks quietly down the days of Time,' he thought, 'the streets and places of the world, without manner to speak of, without parade of learning, strength, or anything, endowed with the conviction, invisible, impermeable, of being IT.'

'Yes,' he said on the doorstep of 'The Coffee House', 'I look on this as the plumb centre of the universe. Others may claim the North Pole, Rome, Montmartre – I claim the Coffee House, oldest Club in the world, and I suppose, by plumbing standards, the worst. Shall we wash, or postpone it to a more joyful opportunity? Agreed. Let's sit down here, then, and await the apostle of plumbing. I take him for a hustler. Pity we can't arrange a match between him and the Marquess. I'd back the old boy.'

The American looked very big coming into the low hall of the oldest Club in the world.

'Sir Lawrence Mont,' he said; 'Ah! Captain! General Sir Conway Cherrell? Proud to meet you, General. And what can I do for you, gentlemen?'

He listened to Sir Lawrence's recital with a deepening gravity. 'Isn't that too bad? I can't take this sitting. I'm going right along now to see the Bolivian Minister. And, Captain, I've kept the address of your boy Manuel, I'll cable our Consul at La Paz to get a statement from him right away, confirming your story. Who ever heard of such darned foolishness? Forgive me, gentlemen, but I'll have no peace till I've set the wires going.' And with a circular movement of his head he was gone. The three Englishmen sat down again.

'Old Shropshire must look to his heels,' Sir Lawrence said.

'So that's Hallorsen,' said the General. 'Fine-looking chap.'

Hubert said nothing. He was moved.

Chapter Seventeen

*U*neasy and silent, the two girls drove towards St Augustine's-in-the-Meads.

'I don't know which I'm most sorry for,' said Dinny, suddenly: 'I never thought about insanity before. People either make a joke of it or hide it away. But it seems to me more pitiful than anything in the world; especially when it's partial like this.'

Jean turned on her a surprised look – Dinny with the mask of humour off was new.

'Which way now?'

'Up here; we have to cross the Euston Road. Personally, I don't believe Aunt May can put us up. She's sure to have people learning to slum. Well, if she can't, we'll telephone to Fleur. I wish I'd thought of that before.'

Her prediction was verified – the Vicarage was full, her aunt out, her uncle at home.

'While we're here, we'd better find out whether Uncle Hilary will do you in,' whispered Dinny.

Hilary was spending the first free hour of three days in his shirtsleeves, carving the model of a Viking ship. For the production of obsolete ships in miniature was the favourite recreation now of one who had no longer leisure or muscle for mountain climbing. The fact that they took more time to complete than anything else, and that he had perhaps less time than anybody else to give to their completion, had not yet weighed with him.

After shaking hands with Jean, he excused himself for proceeding with his job.

'Uncle Hilary,' began Dinny, abruptly, 'Jean is going to marry Hubert, and they want it to be by special licence; so we've come to ask if you would marry them.'

Hilary halted his gouging instrument, narrowed his eyes till they were just shrewd slits, and said:

'Afraid of changing your minds?'

'Not at all,' said Jean.

Hilary regarded her attentively. In three words and one look she had made it clear to him that she was a young woman of character.

'I've met your father,' he said, 'he always takes plenty of time.'

'Dad is perfectly docile about this.'

'That's true,' said Dinny; 'I've seen him.'

'And *your* father, my dear?'

'He *will* be.'

'If he is,' said Hilary, again gouging at the stern of his ship, 'I'll do it. No point in delay if you really know your minds.' He turned to Jean. 'You ought to be good at mountains; the season's over, or I'd recommend that to you for your honeymoon. But why not a trawler in the North Sea?'

'Uncle Hilary,' said Dinny, 'refused a Deanship. He is noted for his asceticism.'

'The hat ropes did it, Dinny, and let me tell you that the grapes have been sour ever since. I cannot think why I declined a life of some ease with time to model all the ships in the world, the run of the newspapers, and the charms of an increasing stomach. Your Aunt never ceases to throw them in my teeth. When I think of what Uncle Cuffs did with his dignity, and how he looked when he came to the end, I see my wasted life roll out behind me, and visions of falling down when they take me out of the shafts. How strenuous is your father, Miss Tasburgh?'

'Oh, he just marks time,' said Jean; 'but that's the country.'

'Not entirely! To mark time and to think you're not – there never was a more universal title than "The Man who was".'

'Unless,' said Dinny, 'it's "The Man who never was". Oh! Uncle, Captain Ferse suddenly turned up today at Diana's.'

Hilary's face became very grave.

'Ferse! That's either most terrible, or most merciful. Does your Uncle Adrian know?'

'Yes; I fetched him. He's there now with Captain Ferse. Diana wasn't in.'

'Did you see Ferse?'

'*I* went in and had a talk with him,' said Jean; 'he seemed perfectly sane except that he locked me in.'

Hilary continued to stand very still.

'We'll say good-bye now, Uncle; we're going to Michael's.'

'Good-bye; and thank you very much, Mr Cherrell.'

'Yes,' said Hilary, absently, 'we must hope for the best.'

The two girls, mounting the car, set out for Westminster.

'He evidently expects the worst,' said Jean.

'Not difficult, when both alternatives are so horrible.'

'Thank you!'

'No, no!' murmured Dinny: 'I wasn't thinking of you.' And she thought how remarkably Jean could keep to a track when she was on it!

Outside Michael's house in Westminster they encountered Adrian, who had telephoned to Hilary and been informed of their changed destination. Having ascertained that Fleur could put the girls up, he left them; but Dinny, smitten by the look on his face, ran after him. He was walking towards the river, and she joined him at the corner of the Square.

'Would you rather be alone, Uncle?'

'I'm glad of *you*, Dinny. Come along.'

They went at a good pace westward along the Embankment, Dinny slipping her hand within his arm. She did not talk, however, leaving him to begin if he wished.

'You know I've been down to that Home several times,' he said, presently, 'to see how things were with Ferse, and make sure they were treating him properly. It serves me right for not having been these last months. But I always dreaded it. I've been talking to them now on the 'phone. They wanted to come up, but I've told them not to. What good can it do? They admit he's been quite normal for the last two weeks. In such cases it seems they wait a month at least before reporting. Ferse himself says he's been normal for three months.'

'What sort of place is it?'

'A largish country house – only about ten patients; each has his own rooms and his own attendant. It's as good a place, I suppose, as you could find. But it always gave me the horrors with its spikey wall round the grounds and general air of something hidden away. Either I'm over-sensitive, Dinny, or this particular affliction does seem to me too dreadful.'

Dinny squeezed his arm. 'So it does to me. How did he get away?'

'He'd been so normal that they weren't at all on their guard – he seems to have said he was going to lie down, and slipped out during lunch time. He must have noticed that some tradesman came at a certain time every day, for he slid out when the lodge-keeper was taking in parcels; he walked to the station and took the first train. It's only twenty miles. He'll have been in town before they found out he was gone. I'm going down there tomorrow.'

'Poor Uncle!' said Dinny, softly.

'Well, my dear, so things go in this life. But to be torn between two horrors is not my dream.'

'Was it in his family?'

Adrian nodded. 'His grandfather died raving. But for the war it might never have developed in Ferse, but you can't tell. Hereditary madness? Is it fair? No, Dinny, I'm not a believer in divine mercy in any form that we humans can understand, or in any way that we would exercise it ourselves. An all-embracing creativity and power of design without beginning and without end – obviously. But – tie it to our apron-strings we can't. Think of a mad-house! One simply daren't. And see what the fact that one daren't means for those poor creatures. The sensitive recoil and that leaves them mainly to the insensitive, and God help them!'

'According to you, God won't.'

'God is the helping of man by man, somebody once said; at all events that's all the working version we can make of Him.'

'And the Devil?'

'The harming of man by man, only I'd throw in animals.'

'Pure Shelley, Uncle.'

'Might be a lot worse. But I become a wicked Uncle, corrupting the orthodoxy of Youth.'

'You can't corrupt what is not, dear. Here's Oakley Street. Would you like me to go and ask Diana if she wants anything?'

'Wouldn't I? I'll wait for you at this corner, Dinny; and thank you ever so.'

Dinny walked swiftly, looking neither to right nor left, and rang the bell. The same maid answered it.

'I don't want to come in, but could you find out for me quietly from Mrs Ferse whether she's all right, or whether she wants anything. And will you tell her that I'm at Mrs Michael Mont's, and am ready to come at any moment, and to stay if she'd like me.'

While the maid was gone upstairs she strained her ears, but no sound reached them till the maid came back.

'Mrs Ferse says, Miss, to thank you very heartily, and to say she won't fail to send for you if she needs you. She's all right at present, Miss; but, oh dear! we *are* put about, hoping for the best. And she sends her love, Miss; and Mr Cherrell's not to worry.'

'Thank you,' said Dinny: 'Give her our love and say there we are – all ready.'

Then, swiftly, looking neither to left nor right, she returned to Adrian. The message repeated, they walked on.

'Hanging in the wind,' said Adrian, 'is there anything more dreadful? And how long – oh, Lord! How long? But as she says, we mustn't worry,' and he uttered an unhappy little laugh. It began to grow dusk, and in that comfortless light, neither day nor night, the ragged ends of the streets and bridges seemed bleak and unmeaning. Twilight passed, and with the lamps form began again and contours softened.

'Dinny, my dear,' said Adrian, 'I'm not fit to walk with; we'd better get back.'

'Come and dine at Michael's then, Uncle – do!'

Adrian shook his head.

'Skeletons should not be at feasts. I don't know how to abide myself, as your Nurse used to say, I'm sure.'

'She did not; she was Scotch. Is Ferse a Scottish name?'

'May have been originally. But Ferse came from West Sussex, somewhere in the Downs – an old family.'

'Do you think old families are queer?'

'I don't see why. When there's a case of queerness in an old family, it's conspicuous of course, instead of just passing without notice. Old families are not inbred like village folk.' By instinct for what might distract him, Dinny went on:

'Do you think age in families has any points to it at all, Uncle?'

'What is age? All families are equally old, in one sense. But if you're thinking of quality due to mating for generations within a certain caste, well, I don't know – there's certainly "good breeding" in the sense that you'd apply it to dogs or horses, but you can get that in any favourable physical circumstances – in the dales, by the sea; wherever conditions are good. Sound stock breeds sound stock – that's obvious. I know villages in the very North of Italy where there isn't a person of rank, and yet not one without beauty and a look of breeding. But when you come to breeding from people with genius or those exceptional qualities which bring men to the front, I'm very doubtful whether you don't get distortion rather than symmetry. Families with military or naval origin and tradition have the best chance, perhaps – good physique and not too much brain; but Science and the Law and Business are very distorting. No! where I think "old" families may have a pull is in the more definite sense of direction their children get in growing up, a set tradition, a set objective; also perhaps to a better chance in the marriage market; and in most cases to more country life, and more encouragement to taking their own line and more practice in taking it. What's talked of as "breeding" in humans is an attribute of mind rather than of body. What one thinks and feels is mainly due to tradition, habit and education. But I'm boring you, my dear.'

'No, no, Uncle; I'm terribly interested. You believe then in the passing on of an attitude to life rather than in blood.'

'Yes, but the two are very mixed.'

'And do you think "oldness" is going out and soon nothing will be handed on?'

'I wonder. Tradition is extraordinarily strong, and in this country there's a lot of machinery to keep it alive. You see, there are such a tremendous lot of directive jobs to be done; and the people most fit for such jobs are those who, as children, have had most practice in taking their own line, been taught not to gas about themselves, and to do things because it's their duty. It's they, for instance, who run the Services, and they'll go on running them, I expect. But privilege is only justified nowadays by running till you drop.'

'A good many,' said Dinny, 'seem to drop first, and then do the running. Well, here we are again, at Fleur's. Now do come in, Uncle! If Diana did want anything you'd be on the spot.'

'Very well, my dear, and bless you – you got me on a subject I often think about. Serpent!'

Chapter Eighteen

By pertinacious use of the telephone, Jean had discovered Hubert at 'The Coffee House' and learned his news. She passed Dinny and Adrian as they were coming in.

'Whither away?'

'Shan't be long,' said Jean, and walked round the corner.

Her knowledge of London was small, and she hailed the first cab. Arriving in Eaton Square before a mansion of large and dreary appearance, she dismissed the cab and rang the bell.

'Lord Saxenden in Town?'

'Yes, my lady, but he's not in.'

'When will he be in?'

'His lordship will be in to dinner, but—'

'Then I'll wait.'

'Excuse me – my lady—'

'Not my lady,' said Jean, handing him a card; 'but he'll see me, all the same.'

The man struggled a moment, received a look straight between the eyes, and said:

'Will you come in here, my – Miss?'

Jean went. The little room was barren except for gilt-edged chairs of the Empire period, a chandelier, and two marble-topped console tables.

'Please give him my card the moment he comes in.'

The man seemed to rally.

'His Lordship will be pressed for time, Miss.'

'Not more than I am, don't worry about that.' And on a gilt-edged chair she sat down. The man withdrew. With her eyes now on the darkening Square, now on a marble and gilt clock, she sat slim, trim, vigorous, interlacing the long fingers of browned hands from which she had removed her gloves. The man came in again and drew the curtains.

'You wouldn't,' he said, 'like to leave a message, Miss, or write a note?'

'Thank you, no.'

He stood a moment, looking at her as if debating whether she was armed.

'Miss Tas*burgh*?' he said.

'Tas*borough*,' answered Jean. 'Lord Saxenden knows me,' and raised her eyes.

'Quite so, Miss,' said the man, hastily, and again withdrew.

The clock's hands crept on to seven before she heard voices in the hall. A moment later the door was opened and Lord Saxenden came in with her card in his hand, and a face on which his past, present, and future seemed to agree.

'Pleasure!' he said: 'A pleasure.'

Jean raised her eyes, and the thought went through her: 'Purring stockfish.' She extended her hand.

'It's terribly nice of you to see me.'

'Not at all.'

'I wanted to tell you of my engagement to Hubert Cherrell – you remember his sister at the Monts'. Have you heard of this absurd request for his extradition? It's too silly for words – the shooting was in pure self-defence – he's got a most terrible scar he could show you at any time.'

Lord Saxenden murmured something inaudible. His eyes had become somewhat frosted.

'So you see, I wanted to ask you to put a stop to it. I know you have the power.'

'Power? Not a bit – none at all.'

Jean smiled.

'Of course you have the power. Everybody knows that. This means such a lot to me.'

'But you weren't engaged, were you, the other night?'

'No.'

'Very sudden!'

'Aren't all engagements sudden?' She could not perhaps realise the impact of her news on a man over fifty who had entered the room with at all events vague hopes of having made an impression on Youth; but she did realise that she was not all that he had thought her, and that he was not all that she had thought him. A wary and polite look had come over his face.

'More hard-boiled than I imagined,' was her reflection. And changing her tone, she said coldly: 'After all, Captain Cherrell is a D.S.O. and one of you. Englishmen don't let each other down, do they? Especially when they've been to the same school.'

This remarkably astute utterance, at that disillusioned moment, impressed him who had been 'Snubby Bantham'.

'Oh!' he said: 'Was he there, too?'

'Yes. And you know what a time he had on that expedition. Dinny read you some of his diary.'

The colour deepened in his face, and he said with sudden exasperation: 'You young ladies seem to think I've nothing to do but meddle in things that don't concern me. Extradition is a legal job.'

Jean looked up through her lashes, and the unhappy peer moved as if to duck his head.

'What can I do?' he said, gruffly. 'They wouldn't listen to me.'

'Try,' said Jean. 'Some men are always listened to.'

Lord Saxenden's eyes bulged slightly.

'You say he's got a scar. Where?'

Jean pushed up the sleeve on her left arm.

'From here to here. He shot as the man came on again.'

'H'm!'

Looking intently at the arm, he repeated that profound remark, and there was silence, till Jean said suddenly: 'Would *you* like to be extradited, Lord Saxenden?'

He made an impatient movement.

'But this is an official matter, young lady.'

Jean looked at him again.

'Is it really true that no influence is ever brought to bear on anybody about anything?'

He laughed.

'Come and lunch with me at the Piedmont Grill the day after tomorrow – no, the day after that, and I'll let you know if I've been able to do anything.'

Jean knew well when to stop; never in parish meetings did she talk on. She held out her hand: 'Thank you ever so. One-thirty?'

Lord Saxenden gave her an astonished nod. This young woman had a directness which appealed to one whose life was passed among public matters conspicuous for the lack of it.

'Good-bye!' she said.

'Good-bye, Miss Tasburgh; congratulations.'

'Thank you. That will depend on you, won't it?' And before he could answer she was through the door. She walked back, her mind not in a whirl. She thought clearly and quickly, with a natural distrust of leaving things to others. She must see Hubert that very night; and, on getting in, she went at once to the tele-phone again and rang up 'The Coffee House'.

'Is that you, Hubert? Jean speaking.'

'Yes, darling.'

'Come here after dinner. I must see you.'

'About nine?'

'Yes. My love to you. That's all.' And she cut off.

She stood for a moment before going up to dress, as if to endorse that simile of 'leopardess'. She looked, indeed, like Youth stalking its own future – lithe, intent, not to be deviated, in Fleur's finished and stylistic drawing room as much at home and yet as foreign to its atmosphere as a cat might be.

Dinner, when any of the diners have cause for really serious anxiety and the others know of it, is conspicuous for avoidance of all but quick-fire conversation. Nobody touched on the Ferse topic, and Adrian left as soon as he had drunk his coffee. Dinny saw him out.

'Good-night, Uncle dear. I shall sleep with my emergency suit-case; one can always get a taxi here at a moment's notice. Promise me not to worry.'

Adrian smiled, but he looked haggard. Jean met her coming from the door and told her the fresh news of Hubert. Her first feeling, of complete dismay, was succeeded by burning indignation.

'What utter ruffianism!'

'Yes,' said Jean. 'Hubert's coming in a minute or two and I want him to myself.'

'Take him up to Michael's study, then. I'll go and tell Michael. Parliament ought to know; only,' she added, 'it's not sitting. It only seems to sit when it oughtn't to.'

Jean waited in the hall to let Hubert in. When he had gone up with her to that room whose walls were covered with the graven witticisms of the last three generations, she put him into Michael's most comfortable chair, and sat down on his knee. Thus, with her arm round his neck, and her lips more or less to his, she stayed for some minutes.

'That'll do,' she said, rising, and lighting cigarettes. 'This extradition business isn't going to come to anything, Hubert.'

'But suppose it does.'

'It won't. But if it does – all the more reason for our being married at once.'

'My darling girl, I can't possibly.'

'You must. You don't suppose that if you *were* extradited – which is absurd – I shouldn't go too. Of course I should, and by the same boat – married or not.'

Hubert looked at her.

'You're a marvel,' he said, 'but—'

'Oh! yes, I know. Your father, and your chivalry, and your desire to make me unhappy for my own good, and all that. I've seen your uncle Hilary. He's ready to do it; he's a padre and a man of real experience. Now, look here – we'll tell him of this development, and if he'll still do it, we'll be done. We'll go to him together tomorrow morning.'

'But—'

'But! Surely you can trust him; he strikes me as a real person.'

'He is,' said Hubert; 'no one more so.'

'Very well then; that's settled. Now you can kiss me again.' And she resumed her position on his knee. So, but for her acute sense of hearing, they would have been surprised. She was, however, examining the White Monkey on the wall, and Hubert was taking out his cigarette case, when Dinny opened the door.

'This monkey is frightfully good,' said Jean. 'We're going to be married, Dinny, in spite of this new nonsense – that is, if your Uncle Hilary still will. You can come with us to him again tomorrow morning, if you like.'

Dinny looked at Hubert, who had risen.

'She's hopeless,' he said: 'I can't do anything with her.'

'And you can't do anything without her. Imagine! He thought, if the worst came to the worst and he was sent out to be tried, that I shouldn't be going too. Men really are terribly like babies. Well, Dinny?'

'I'm glad.'

'It depends on Uncle Hilary,' said Hubert; 'you understand that, Jean.'

'Yes. He's in touch with real life, and what he says shall go. Come for us at ten tomorrow. Turn your back, Dinny. I'll give him one kiss, and then he must be off.'

Dinny turned her back.

'Now,' said Jean. They went down; and soon after, the girls went up to bed. Their rooms were next each other, and furnished with all Fleur's taste. They talked a little, embraced and parted. Dinny dawdled over her undressing.

The quiet Square, inhabited for the most part by Members of Parliament away on holiday, had few lights in the windows of its houses; no wind stirred the dark branches of the trees; through her open window came air that had no night sweetness; and rumbling noises of the Town kept alive in her the tingling sensations of that long day.

'I couldn't live with Jean,' she thought, 'but,' she added with the greater justice, 'Hubert could. He needs that sort of thing.' And she smiled wryly, mocking her sense of having been supplanted. Once in bed she lay, thinking of Adrian's fear and dismay, of Diana, and that poor wretch, her husband – longing for her – shut off from her – shut off from everyone. In the darkness she seemed to see his eyes flickering, burning and intense; the eyes of a being that yearned to be at home, at rest, and could not be. She drew the bedclothes up to her own eyes, and over and over, for comfort, repeated to herself the nursery rhyme:

> Mary, Mary, quite contrary,
> How does your garden grow?
> Silver bells and cockle shells
> And pretty girls all of a row!

Chapter Nineteen

If you had examined Hilary Cherrell, Vicar of St Augustine's-in-the-Meads, in the privacy that lies behind all appearance, all spoken words, even all human gesture, you would have found that he did not really believe his faithful activity was leading anywhere. But to 'serve' was bred into his blood and bone, as they serve, that is, who lead and direct. As a setter dog, untrained, taken for a walk, will instantly begin to range, as a Dalmatian dog, taken out riding, will follow from the first under the heels of the horse, so was it bred into Hilary, coming of families who for generations had manned the Services, to wear himself out, leading, directing and doing things for the people round him, without conviction that in his leadership or ministrations he was more than marking the time of his own duty. In an age when doubt obscured everything and the temptation to sneer at caste and tradition was irresistible, he illustrated an 'order' bred to go on doing its job, not because it saw benefit to others, not because it sighted advantage to self, but because to turn tail on the job was equivalent to desertion. Hilary never dreamed of justifying his 'order' or explaining the servitude to which his father the diplomat, his uncle the Bishop, his brothers the soldier, the 'curator', and the judge (for Lionel had just been appointed) were, in their different ways, committed. He thought of them and himself as just 'plugging along'. Besides, each of his activities had some specious advantage which he could point to, but which, in his heart, he suspected of being graven on paper rather than on stone.

He had dealt with a manifold correspondence when, at nine-thirty on the morning after the reappearance of Ferse, Adrian entered his somewhat threadbare study. Among Adrian's numerous male friends Hilary alone understood and appreciated his brother's feelings and position. There were but two years between them in age, they had been fast chums as boys; were both mountaineers, accustomed in pre-war days to each other's company in awkward ascents and descents still more awkward; had both been to the war, Hilary as Padre in France, Adrian, who spoke Arabic, on liaison work in the East; and they had very different temperaments, always an advantage to abiding comradeship. There was no need of spiritual discovery between them, and they went at once into Committee of Ways and Means.

'Any news this morning?' asked Hilary.

'Dinny reports all quiet; but sooner or later the strain of being in the same house is bound to break down his control. For the moment the feeling of being home and free may be enough; but I don't give that more than a week. I'm going down to the Home, but they'll know no more than we.'

'Forgive me, old man, but normal life with her would be best.'

Adrian's face quivered.

'It's beyond human power, Hilary. There's something about such a relationship too cruel for words. It shouldn't be asked of a woman.'

'Unless the poor fellow's going to stay sane.'

'The decision's not for you, or me, or him – it's for her; it's more than anyone ought to have to bear. Don't forget what she went through before he went into the Home. He ought to be got out of the house, Hilary.'

'It would be simpler if she took asylum.'

'Who would give it her, except myself, and that would send him over the edge again for a certainty.'

'If she could put up with the conditions here, we could take her,' said Hilary.

'But the children?'

'We could squeeze them in. But to leave him alone and idle wouldn't help him to stay sane. Could he do any work?'

'I don't suppose he could. Four years of that would rot any man. And who'd give him a job? If I could get him to come to me!'

'Dinny and that other young woman said that he looks and talks all right.'

'In a way he does. Those people down there may have some suggestion.'

Hilary took his brother's arm.

'Old boy, it's ghastly for you. But ten to one it won't be so bad as we think. I'll talk to May, and if, after you've seen those people, you think asylum here is the best thing for Diana – offer it.'

Adrian pressed the hand within his arm.

'I'll get off now and catch my train.'

Left to himself Hilary stood frowning. He had seen in his time so much of the inscrutability of Providence that he had given up classing it as benevolent even in his sermons. On the other hand he had seen many people by sheer tenacity defeat many misfortunes, and many other people, defeated by their misfortunes, live well enough on them afterwards; he was convinced, therefore, that misery was over-rated, and that what was lost was usually won. The thing was to keep going and not worry. At this moment he received his second visitor, the girl Millicent Pole, who, though acquitted, had lost her job at Petter and Poplin's; notoriety not being dispelled by legal innocence.

She came, by appointment, in a neat blue dress, and all her money, as it were, in her stockings, and stood waiting to be catechised.

'Well, Millie, how's your sister?'

'She went back yesterday, Mr Cherrell.'

'Was she fit to go?'

'I don't think so, but she said if she didn't, she'd likely lose her job, too.'

'I don't see that.'

'She said if she stayed away any longer they'd think we was in *that* together.'

'Well, and what about *you*? Would you like to go into the country?'

'Oh, no.'

Hilary contemplated her. A pretty girl, with a pretty figure and ankles, and an easy-going mouth; it looked to him, frankly, as if she ought to be married.

'Got a young man, Millie?'

The girl smiled.

'Not very special, Sir.'

'Not special enough to get married?'

'He don't want to, so far as I can see.'

'Do you?'

'I'm not in a hurry.'

'Well, have you any views?'

'I'd like – well, I'd like to be a mannykin.'

'I daresay. Have Petters given you a reference?'

'Yes, and they said they were sorry I had to go; but being so much in the papers the other girls—'

'Yes. Millie, you got yourself into that scrape, you know. I stood up for you because you were hard pressed, but I'm not blind. You've got to promise me that you won't do that again; it's the first step to blue ruin.'

The girl made just the answer he expected – none.

'I'm going to turn you over to my wife now. Consult with her, and if you can't get a job like your old one, we might give you some quick training, and get you a post as a waitress. How would that suit you?'

'I wouldn't mind that.'

She gave him a look half-shy, half-smiling; and Hilary thought: 'Faces like that ought to be endowed by the State; there's no other way to keep them safe.'

'Shake hands, Millie, and remember what I said. Your mother

and father were friends of mine, and you're going to remain a credit to them.'

'Yes, Mr Cherrell.'

'You bet!' thought Hilary, and led her into the dining room opposite, where his wife was working a typing machine. Back in his study he pulled out a drawer of his bureau and prepared to wrestle with accounts, for if there were a place where money was of more importance than in this slum centre of a Christendom whose religion scorns money, Hilary had yet to meet with it.

'The lilies of the field,' he thought, 'toil not, neither do they spin, but they beg all right. How the deuce am I going to get enough to keep the Institute going over the year?' The problem had not been solved when the maid said:

'Captain and Miss Cherrell, and Miss Tasburgh.'

'Phew!' he thought: '*They* don't let grass grow.'

He had not seen his nephew since his return from the Hallorsen Expedition, and was struck by the darkened and aged look of his face.

'Congratulations, old man,' he said. 'I heard something of your aspiration, yesterday.'

'Uncle,' said Dinny, 'prepare for the role of Solomon.'

'Solomon's reputation for wisdom, my irreverent niece, is perhaps the thinnest in history. Consider the number of his wives. Well?'

'Uncle Hilary,' said Hubert: 'I've had news that a warrant may be issued for my extradition, over that muleteer I shot. Jean wants the marriage at once in spite of that—'

'Because of that,' put in Jean.

'I say it's too chancey altogether; and not fair to her. But we agreed to put it to you, and abide by your judgment.'

'Thank you,' murmured Hilary; 'and why to me?'

'Because,' said Dinny, 'you have to make more decisions-while-they-wait than anybody, except police magistrates.'

Hilary grimaced. 'With your knowledge of Scripture, Dinny,

you might have remembered the camel and the last straw. However—!' And he looked from Jean to Hubert and back again.

'Nothing can possibly be gained by waiting,' said Jean; 'because if they took him I should go out too, anyway.'

'You would?'

'Of course.'

'Could you prevent that, Hubert?'

'No, I don't suppose I could.'

'Am I dealing, young people, with a case of love at first sight?' Neither of them answered, but Dinny said:

'Very much so; I could see it from the croquet lawn at Lippinghall.'

Hilary nodded. 'Well, that's not against you; it happened to me and I've never regretted it. Is your extradition really likely, Hubert?'

'No,' said Jean.

'Hubert?'

'I don't know; Father's worried, but various people are doing their best. I've got this scar, you know,' and he drew up his sleeve.

Hilary nodded. 'That's a mercy.'

Hubert grinned. 'It wasn't at the time, in that climate, I can tell you.'

'Have you got the licence?'

'Not yet.'

'Get it, then. I'll turn you off.'

'Really?'

'Yes, I may be wrong, but I don't think so.'

'You aren't.' And Jean seized his hand. 'Will tomorrow at two o'clock be all right for you, Mr Cherrell?'

'Let me look at my book.' He looked at it and nodded.

'Splendid!' cried Jean. 'Now Hubert, you and I will go and get it.'

'I'm frightfully obliged to you, Uncle,' said Hubert; 'if you really think it's not rotten of me.'

'My dear boy,' said Hilary, 'when you take up with a young

woman like Jean here, you must expect this sort of thing. *Au revoir*, and God bless you both!'

When they had gone out, he turned to Dinny: 'I'm much touched, Dinny. That was a charming compliment. Who thought of it?'

'Jean.'

'Then she's either a very good or a very bad judge of character. I wonder which. That was quick work. It was ten five when you came in, it's now ten fourteen; I don't know when I've disposed of two lives in a shorter time. There's nothing wrong about the Tasburghs, is there?'

'No, they seem rather sudden, that's all.'

'On the whole,' said Hilary, 'I like them sudden. It generally means sand.'

'The Zeebrugge touch.'

'Ah! Yes, there's a sailor brother, isn't there?'

Dinny's eyelids fluttered.

'Has he laid himself alongside yet?'

'Several times.'

'And?'

'*I'm* not sudden, Uncle.'

'Backer and filler?'

'Especially backer.'

Hilary smiled affectionately at his favourite niece: 'Blue eye true eye. I'll marry you off yet, Dinny. Excuse me now, I have to see a man who's in trouble with the hire-purchase system. He's got in and he can't get out – goes swimming about like a dog in a pond with a high bank. By the way, the girl you saw in Court the other day is in there with your Aunt. Like another look at her? She is, I fear, what we call an insoluble problem, which being interpreted means a bit of human nature. Have a shot at solving her.'

'I should love to, but she wouldn't.'

'I don't know that. As young woman to young woman you might get quite a lot of change out of her, and most of it bad,

I shouldn't wonder. That,' he added, 'is cynical. Cynicism's a relief.'

'It must be, Uncle.'

'It's where the Roman Catholics have a pull over us. Well, good-bye, my dear. See you tomorrow at the execution.'

Locking up his accounts, Hilary followed her into the hall; opening the door of the dining room, he said: 'My Love, here's Dinny! I'll be back to lunch,' and went out, hatless.

Chapter Twenty

owards South Square, where Fleur was to be asked to give another reference, the girls left the Vicarage together.

'I'm afraid,' said Dinny, overcoming her shyness, 'that I should want to take it out of somebody, if I were you. I can't see why you should have lost your place.' She could see the girl scrutinising her askance, as if trying to make up her mind whether or no to say what was in it.

'I got meself talked about,' she said, at last.

'Yes, I happened to come into the Court the day you were acquitted. I thought it brutal to make you stand there.'

'I reely did speak to a man,' said the girl, surprisingly, 'I wouldn't tell Mr Cherrell, but I did. I was just fed-up with wanting money. D'you think it was bad of me?'

'Well, personally, I should have to want more than money before I did it.'

'You never have wanted money – not reely.'

'I suppose you're right, although I've never had much.'

'It's better than stealin',' said the girl, grimly: 'after all, what is it? You can forget about it. At least, that's what I thought. Nobody thinks the worse of a man or does anything to him for it. But you won't tell Mrs Mont what I'm telling you?'

'Of course not. Had things been going very badly?'

'Shockin'. Me and my sister make just enough when we're in full work. But she was ill five weeks, and on the top of that I lost my purse one day, with thirty bob in it. That wasn't my fault, anyway.'

'Wretched luck.'

'Rotten! If I'd been a reel one d'you think they'd have spotted me – it was just my being green. I bet girls in high life have no trouble that way when they're hard up.'

'Well,' said Dinny, 'I suppose there are girls not above helping out their incomes in all sorts of ways. All the same, I think that kind of thing ought only to go with affection; but I expect I'm old-fashioned.'

The girl turned another long and this time almost admiring look on her.

'You're a lady, Miss. I must say I should like to be one meself, but what you're born you stay.'

Dinny wriggled. 'Oh! Bother that word! The best ladies I've known are old cottage women in the country.'

'Reely?'

'Yes. And I think some of the girls in London shops are the equal of anyone.'

'Well, there is some awful nice girls, I must say. My sister is much better than me. She'd never 'ave done a thing like that. Your uncle said something I shall remember, but I can't never depend on meself. I'm one to like pleasure if I can get it; and why not?'

'The point is rather: What is pleasure? A casual man can't possibly be pleasure. He'd be the very opposite.'

The girl nodded.

'That's true enough. But when you're bein' chivied about for want of money you're willin' to put up with things you wouldn't otherwise. You take my word for that.'

It was Dinny's turn to nod.

'My uncle's a nice man, don't you think?'

'He's a gentleman – never comes religion over you. And he'll always put his hand in his pocket, if there's anything there.'

'That's not often, I should think,' said Dinny; 'my family is pretty poor.'

'It isn't money makes the gentleman.'

Dinny heard the remark without enthusiasm; she seemed, indeed, to have heard it before. 'We'd better take a bus now,' she said.

The day was sunny, and they got on the top. 'D'you like this new Regent Street?' asked Dinny.

'Oh yes! I think it's fine.'

'Didn't you like the old street better?'

'No. It was so dull and yellow, and all the same.'

'But unlike any other street, and the regularity suited the curve.'

The girl seemed to perceive that a question of taste was concerned; she hesitated, then said assertively:

'It's much brighter now, I think. Things seem to move more – not so formal-like.'

'Ah!'

'I do like the top of a bus,' continued the girl; 'you can see such a lot. Life does go on, don't it?'

In the girl's cockney-fied voice, those words hit Dinny a sort of blow. What was her own life but a cut-and-dried affair? What risks or adventure did it contain? Life for people who depended on their jobs was vastly more adventurous. Her own job so far had been to have no job. And, thinking of Jean, she said: 'I'm afraid I live a very humdrum life. I always seem to be waiting for things.'

The girl again stole a sideway look.

'Why, you must have lots of fun, pretty like you are!'

'Pretty? My nose turns up.'

'Ah! but you've got style. Style's everything. I always think you may have looks, but it's style that gets you there.'

'I'd rather have looks.'

'Oh! no. Anyone can be a good-looker.'

'But not many are,' and with a glance at the girl's profile Dinny added: 'You're lucky, yourself.'

The girl bridled.

'I told Mr Cherrell I'd like to be a mannykin, but he didn't seem to fall for it.'

'I'm afraid I think that of all inane pursuits that's the worst. Dressing up for a lot of disgruntled women!'

'Someone's got to do it,' said the girl, defiantly; 'I like wearing clothes meself. But you need interest to get a thing like that. Perhaps Mrs Mont'll speak for me. My! Wouldn't you make a mannykin, with your style, Miss, and slim.'

Dinny laughed. The bus had halted at the Westminster end of Whitehall.

'We get off here. Ever been in Westminster Abbey?'

'No.'

'Perhaps you'd like a look before they pull it down and put up flats or a Cinema.'

'Are they reely goin' to?'

'I fancy it's only in the back of their minds so far. At present they talk about restoring it.'

'It's a big place,' said the girl, but under the walls a silence fell on her, which remained unbroken when they passed within. Dinny watched her, as with chin uplifted she contemplated the statue to Chatham and its neighbour.

'Who's the old beaver with no clothes on?'

'Neptune. He's a symbol. Britannia rules the waves, you know.'

'Oh!' And they moved on till the full proportions of the old Museum were better disclosed.

'My! Isn't it full of things?'

'It *is* rather an Old Curiosity Shop. They've got all English history here, you know.'

'It's awful dark. The pillars look dirty, don't they?'

'Shall we just have a look at the Poets' Corner?' said Dinny.

'What's that?'

'Where they bury great writers.'

'Because they wrote rhymes?' said the girl. 'Isn't that funny?'

Dinny did not answer. She knew some of the rhymes and was uncertain. Having scrutinised a number of effigies and names which had for her a certain limited interest, and for the girl apparently none, they moved slowly down the aisle to where between two red wreaths lay the black and gold tablet to the Unknown Warrior.

'I wonder whether 'e knows,' said the girl, 'but I shouldn't think 'e cares, anyway; nobody knows 'is name, so 'e gets nothin' out of it.'

'No. It's we who get something out of it,' said Dinny, feeling the sensation in her throat with which the world rewards the Unknown Warrior.

Out in the street again the girl asked suddenly:

'Are you religious, Miss?'

'In a sort of way, I think,' said Dinny, doubtingly.

'I never was taught any – Dad and Mother liked Mr Cherrell, but they thought it was a mistake; my Dad was a Socialist, you see, and he used to say religion was part of the capitalist system. Of course we don't go to Church, in our class. We haven't time, for one thing. You've got to keep so still in Church, too. I must say I like more movement. And then, if there's a God, why is he called He? It puts me against Him, I know. Callin' God He gets girls treated as they are, I think. Since my case I've thought about that a good deal after what the Court missionary said. A he can't get on with creation without a she, anyway.'

Dinny stared.

'You should have said that to my uncle. It's quite a thought.'

'They say women are the equal of men now,' the girl went on, 'but they aren't, you know. There wasn't a girl at my place that wasn't scared of the boss. Where the money is, there's the power. And all the magistrates and judges and clergy are he's, and all the generals. They've got the whip, you see, and yet they can't do nothin' without us; and if I was Woman as a whole, I'd show 'em.'

Dinny was silent. This girl was bitter from her experience, no doubt, but there was truth behind what she was saying. The Creator was bi-sexual, or the whole process would have ended at the start. In that was a primal equality, which she had never before quite realised. If the girl had been of her own order she

would have answered, but it was impossible to be unreserved
with her; and feeling herself snobbish, she fell back on irony.

'Some rebel! – as the Americans would say!'

'Of course I'm a rebel,' said the girl, 'after that.'

'Well, here we are at Mrs Mont's. I've got one or two things
to see to, so I'll leave you with her. I hope we shall meet again.'
She held out her hand, the girl took it and said simply: 'I've
enjoyed it.'

'So have I. Good luck!'

Leaving her in the hall, Dinny walked towards Oakley Street,
and her mood was that of one who has failed to go as far as
she has wished. She had touched on the uncharted, and recoiled.
Her thoughts and feelings were like the twittering of Spring birds
who have not yet shaped out their songs. That girl had roused
in her some queer desire to be at grips with Life, without supplying
the slightest notion of how to do it. It would be a relief even to
be in love. How nice to know one's mind, as Jean and Hubert
seemed at once to have known it; as Hallorsen and Alan Tasburgh
had declared they knew it. Existence seemed like a Shadow Show
rather than Reality. And, greatly dissatisfied, she leaned her elbows
on the river parapet, above the tide that was flowing up. Religious?
In a sort of way. But what way? A passage in Hubert's diary
came back to her. 'Anyone who believes he's going to Heaven
has a pull on chaps like me. He's got a pension dangled.' Was
religion belief in reward? If so, it seemed vulgar. Belief in goodness for the sake of goodness, because goodness was beautiful,
like a perfect flower, a starry night, a lovely tune! Uncle Hilary
did a difficult job well for the sake of doing it well. Was he religious? She must ask him. A voice at her side said:

'Dinny!'

She turned with a start, to see Alan Tasburgh standing there
with a broad grin on his face.

'I went to Oakley Street to ask for you and Jean; they told
me you were at the Monts'. I was on my way there, and here
you are, stupendous luck!'

'I was wondering,' said Dinny, 'whether I'm religious.'

'How queer! So was I!'

'D'you mean whether *you* were or whether *I* was?'

'As a matter of fact I look on us as one person.'

'Do you? Well, is one religious?'

'At a pinch.'

'Did you hear the news at Oakley Street?'

'No.'

'Captain Ferse is back there.'

'Cripes!'

'Precisely what everybody is saying! Did you see Diana?'

'No; only the maid – seemed a bit flustered. Is the poor chap still cracked?'

'No; but it's awful for Diana.'

'She ought to be got away.'

'I'm going to stay there,' said Dinny, suddenly, 'if she'll have me.'

'I don't like the idea of that.'

'I daresay not; but I'm going to.'

'Why? You don't know her so very well.'

'I'm sick of scrimshanking.'

Young Tasburgh stared.

'I don't understand.'

'The sheltered life has not come your way. I want to begin to earn my corn.'

'Then marry me.'

'Really, Alan, I never met anyone with so few ideas.'

'Better to have good ideas than many.'

Dinny walked on. 'I'm going to Oakley Street now.'

They went along in silence till young Tasburgh said gravely:

'What's biting you, my very dear?'

'My own nature; it doesn't seem able to make trouble enough for me.'

'I could do that for you perfectly.'

'I am serious, Alan.'

'That's good. Until you are serious you will never marry me. But why do you want to be bitten?'

Dinny shrugged. 'I seem to have an attack of Longfellow: "Life is real, life is earnest"; I suppose you can't realise that being a daughter in the country doesn't amount to very much.'

'I won't say what I was going to say.'

'Oh, do!'

'That's easily cured. Become a mother in a town.'

'This is where they used to blush,' sighed Dinny. 'I don't want to turn everything into a joke, but it seems I do.'

Young Tasburgh slipped his hand through her arm.

'If you can turn being the wife of a sailor into a joke, you will be the first.'

Dinny smiled. 'I'm not going to marry anyone till it hurts not to. I know myself well enough for that.'

'All right, Dinny; I won't worry you.'

They moved on in silence; at the corner of Oakley Street she stopped.

'Now, Alan, don't come any further.'

'I shall turn up at the Monts' this evening and discover what's happened to you. And if you want anything done – mind, anything – about Ferse, you've only to 'phone me at the Club. Here's the number.' He pencilled it on a card and handed it to her.

'Shall you be at Jean's wedding tomorrow?'

'Sure thing! I give her away. I only wish—'

'Good-bye!' said Dinny.

Chapter Twenty-one

She had parted from the young man lightly, but she stood on the doorstep with nerves taut as fiddlestrings. Never having come into contact with mental trouble, her thought of it was the more scaring. The same elderly maid admitted her. Mrs Ferse was with Captain Ferse, and would Miss Cherrell come up to the drawing room? Where Jean had been locked in Dinny waited some time. Sheila came in, said: 'Hallo! Are you waiting for Muvver?' and went out again. When Diana did appear her face wore an expression as if she were trying to collect the evidence of her own feelings.

'Forgive me, my dear, I was going through papers. I'm trying my best to treat him as if nothing had happened.' Dinny went up to her and stood stroking her arm.

'But it can't last, Dinny; it won't last. I can see it won't last.'

'Let me come and stay. You can put it that it was arranged before.'

'But, Dinny, it may be rather horrible. I don't know what to do with him. He dreads going out, or meeting people. And yet he won't hear of going away where nobody knows; and he won't see a doctor, or take any advice. He won't see anyone.'

'He'll see me, and that'll accustom him. I expect it's only the first few days. Shall I go off now and get my things?'

'If you *are* going to be an angel, do!'

'I'll let Uncle Adrian know before I come back; he went down to the Home this morning.'

Diana crossed to the window and stood there with her back to Dinny. Suddenly she turned:

'I've made up my mind, Dinny: I won't let him down in any way. If there's anything I can do to give him a chance, I'm going to do it.'

'Bless you!' said Dinny. 'I'll help!' And, not trusting either Diana or herself further, she went out and down the stairs. Outside, in passing the dining room window, she was again conscious of a face with eyes, burningly alive, watching her go by. A feeling of tragic unfairness was with her all the way back to South Square.

Fleur said at lunch:

'It's no good fashing yourself till something happens, Dinny. It's lucky that Adrian's been such a saint. But this is a very good instance of how little the Law can help. Suppose Diana could have got free, it wouldn't have prevented Ferse coming straight back to her, or her feeling about him as she does. The Law can't touch the human side of anything. Is Diana in love with Adrian?'

'I don't think so.'

'Are you sure?'

'No, I'm not. I find it difficult enough to know what goes on inside myself.'

'Which reminds me that your American rang up. He wants to call.'

'Well, he can. But I shall be at Oakley Street.'

Fleur gave her a shrewd look.

'Am I to back the sailor, then?'

'No. Put your money on Old Maid.'

'My dear! Unthinkable!'

'I don't see what one gains by marriage.'

Fleur answered with a little hard smile:

'We can't stand still, you know, Dinny. At least, we don't; it's too dull.'

'You're modern, Fleur; I'm medieval.'

'Well, you *are* rather early Italian in face. But the early Italians never escaped. Entertain no flattering hopes. Sooner or later you'll be fed up with yourself, and then!'

Dinny looked at her, startled by this flash of discernment in her disillusioned cousin-in-law.

'What have *you* gained, Fleur?'

'I at least am the complete woman, my dear,' Fleur answered, drily.

'Children, you mean?'

'They are possible without marriage, or so I am told, but improbable. For you, Dinny, impossible; you're controlled by an ancestral complex, really old families have an inherited tendency towards legitimacy. Without it they can't be really old, you see.'

Dinny wrinkled her forehead.

'I never thought of it before, but I *should* strongly object to having an illegitimate child. By the way, did you give that girl a reference?'

'Yes. I don't see at all why she shouldn't be a mannequin. She's narrow enough. I give the boyish figure another year, at least. After that, mark my words, skirts will lengthen, and we shall go in for curves again.'

'Rather degrading, isn't it?'

'How?'

'Chopping and changing shape and hair and all that.'

'Good for trade. We consent to be in the hands of men in order that they may be in ours. Philosophy of vamping.'

'That girl won't have much chance of keeping straight as a mannequin, will she?'

'More, I should say. She might even marry. But I always refuse to worry about my neighbour's morals. I suppose you have to keep up the pretence at Condaford, having been there since the Conquest. By the way, has your father made provision against Death Duties?'

'He's not old, Fleur.'

'No, but people do die. Has he got anything besides the estate?'

'Only his pension.'

'Is there plenty of timber?'

'I loathe the idea of cutting down trees. Two hundred years of shape and energy all gone in half an hour. It's revolting.'

'My dear, there's generally nothing else for it, except selling, and clearing out.'

'We shall manage somehow,' said Dinny shortly; 'we'd never let Condaford go.'

'Don't forget Jean.'

Dinny sat up very straight.

'She'd never, either. The Tasburghs are just as old as we are.'

'Admitted; but that's a young woman of infinite variety and go. She'll never vegetate.'

'Condaford is not vegetation.'

'Don't get ruffled, Dinny; I'm only thinking for the best. I don't want to see you outed, any more than I want Kit to lose Lippinghall. Michael is thoroughly unsound. He says that if he's one of the country's roots he's sorry for the country, which is silly of course. No one,' added Fleur, with a sudden queer depth, 'will ever know from me what pure gold Michael is.' Then, seeming to notice Dinny's surprised eyes, she added: 'So, I can wash out the American?'

'You can. Three thousand miles between me and Condaford – no, Ma'am!'

'Then I think you should put the poor brute out of his misery, for he confided to me that you were what he called his "ideal".'

'Not that again!' cried Dinny.

'Yes, indeed; and he further said that he was crazy about you.'

'That means nothing.'

'From a man who goes to the ends of the earth to discover the roots of civilisation it probably does. Most people would go to the ends of the earth to avoid discovering them.'

'The moment this thing of Hubert's is over,' said Dinny, 'I will put an end to him.'

'I think you'll have to take the veil to do it. You'll look very nice in the veil, Dinny, walking down the village aisle with the sailor, in a feudal atmosphere, to a German tune. May I be there to see!'

'I'm not going to marry anyone.'

'Well, in the meantime shall we ring up Adrian?'

From Adrian's rooms came the message that he was expected back at four o'clock. He was asked to come on to South Square, and Dinny went up to put her things together. Coming down again at half-past three, she saw on the coat 'sarcophagus' a hat whose brim she seemed to recognise. She was slinking back towards the stairs when a voice said:

'Why! This is fine! I was scared I'd missed you.'

Dinny gave him her hand, and together they entered Fleur's 'parlour'; where, among the Louis Quinze furniture, he seemed absurdly male.

'I wanted to tell you, Miss Cherrell, what I've done about your brother. I've fixed it for our Consul in La Paz to get that boy Manuel to cable his sworn testimony that the Captain was attacked with a knife. If your folk here are anyway sensible, that should clear him. This fool game's got to stop if I have to go back to Bolivia myself.'

'Thank you ever so, Professor.'

'Why! There's nothing I wouldn't do for your brother, now. I've come to like him as if he were my own.'

Those ominous words had a large simplicity, a generous warmth, which caused her to feel small and thin.

'You aren't looking all that well,' he said, suddenly. 'If there's anything worrying you, tell me and I'll fix it.'

Dinny told him of Ferse's return.

'That lovely lady! Too bad! But maybe she's fond of him, so it'll be a relief to her mind after a time.'

'I am going to stay with her.'

'That's bully of you! Is this Captain Ferse dangerous?'

'We don't know yet.'

He put his hand into a hip pocket and brought out a tiny automatic.

'Put that in your bag. It's the smallest made. I bought it for this country, seeing you don't go about with guns here.'

Dinny laughed.

'Thank you, Professor, but it would only go off in the wrong place. And, even if there were danger, it wouldn't be fair.'

'That's so! It didn't occur to me, but that's so. A man afflicted that way has every consideration due to him. But I don't like to think of you going into danger.'

Remembering Fleur's exhortation, Dinny said hardily:

'Why not?'

'Because you are very precious to me.'

'That's frightfully nice of you; but I think you ought to know, Professor, that I'm not in the market.'

'Surely every woman's in the market till she marries.'

'Some think that's when she begins to be.'

'Well,' said Hallorsen gravely, 'I've no use for adultery myself. I want a straight deal in sex as in everything else.'

'I hope you will get it.'

He drew himself up. 'And I want it from you. I have the honour to ask you to become Mrs Hallorsen, and please don't say "No" right away.'

'If you want a straight deal, Professor, I must.'

She saw his blue eyes film as if with pain, and felt sorry. He came a little closer, looking, as it seemed to her, enormous, and she gave a shiver.

'Is it my nationality?'

'I don't know what it is.'

'Or the grouch you had against me over your brother?'

'I don't know.'

'Can't I hope?'

'No. I am flattered, and grateful, believe me. But no.'

'Pardon me! Is there another man?'

Dinny shook her head.

Hallorsen stood very still; his face wore a puzzled expression, then cleared suddenly.

'I judge,' he said, 'I haven't done enough for you. I'll have to serve a bit.'

'I'm not worth service. It's simply that I don't feel like that towards you.'

'I have clean hands and a clean heart.'

'I'm sure you have; I admire you, Professor, but I should never love you.'

Hallorsen drew back again to his original distance, as if distrusting his impulses. He gave her a grave bow. He looked really splendid standing there, full of simple dignity. There was a long silence, then he said:

'Well, I judge there's no use crying over spilt milk. Command me in any way. I am your very faithful servant.' And, turning round, he went out.

Dinny heard the front door close with a slight choke in her throat. She felt pain at having caused him pain, but relief, too, the relief one feels when something very large, simple, primitive – the sea, a thunderstorm, a bull – is no longer imminent. In front of one of Fleur's mirrors she stood despitefully, as though she had just discovered the over-refinement of her nerves. How could that great handsome, healthy creature care for one so spindly and rarefied as she looked reflected there? He could snap her off with his hands. Was that why she recoiled? The great open spaces of which he seemed a part, with his height, strength, colour, and the boom of his voice! Funny, silly perhaps – but very real recoil! She belonged where she belonged – not to such as them, to such as him. About such juxtapositions there was even something comic. She was still standing there with a wry smile when Adrian was ushered in.

She turned to him impulsively. Sallow and worn and lined, subtle, gentle, harassed, no greater contrast could have appeared, not any that could have better soothed her jangled nerves. Kissing him, she said:

'I waited to see you before going to stay at Diana's!'

'You *are* going, Dinny?'

'Yes. I don't believe you've had lunch or tea or anything,' and she rang the bell. 'Coaker, Mr Adrian would like—'

'A brandy and soda, Coaker, thank you!'

'Now, Uncle?' she said, when he had drunk it.

'I'm afraid, Dinny, one can't set much store by what they say down there. According to them Ferse ought to go back. But why he should, so long as he acts sanely, I don't know. They query the idea of his recovery, but they can bring nothing abnormal against him for some weeks past. I got hold of his personal attendant and questioned him. He seems a decent chap, and he thinks Ferse at the moment is as sane as himself. But – and the whole trouble lies there – he says he was like this once before for three weeks, and suddenly lapsed again. If anything really upsets him – opposition or whatnot – he thinks Ferse will be just as bad again as ever, perhaps worse. It's a really terrible position.'

'When he's in mania is he violent?'

'Yes; a kind of gloomy violence, more against himself than anyone else.'

'They're not going to do anything to get him back?'

'They can't. He went there voluntarily; I told you he hasn't been certified. How is Diana?'

'She looks tired, but lovely. She says she is going to do everything she can to give him a chance.'

Adrian nodded.

'That's like her; she has wonderful pluck. And so have you, my dear. It's a great comfort to know you'll be with her. Hilary is ready to take Diana and the children if she'd go, but she won't, you say.'

'Not at present, I'm sure.'

Adrian sighed.

'Well, we must chance it.'

'Oh! Uncle,' said Dinny. 'I *am* so sorry for you.'

'My dear, what happens to the fifth wheel doesn't matter so long as the car runs. Don't let me keep you. You can get at me any time either at the Museum or my rooms. Good-bye and bless you! My love to her, and tell her all I've told you.'

Dinny kissed him again, and soon after in a cab set forth with her things to Oakley Street.

Chapter Twenty-two

Bobbie Ferrar had one of those faces which look on tempests and are never shaken; in other words, he was an ideal permanent official – so permanent that one could not conceive of the Foreign Office functioning without him. Secretaries of State might come, might go, Bobbie Ferrar remained, bland, inscrutable, and with lovely teeth. Nobody knew whether there was anything in him except an incalculable number of secrets. Of an age which refused to declare itself, short and square, with a deep soft voice, he had an appearance of complete detachment. In a dark suit with a little light line, and wearing a flower, he existed in a large ante-room wherein was almost nothing except those who came to see the Foreign Minister and instead saw Bobbie Ferrar. In fact the perfect buffer. His weakness was criminology. No murder trial of importance ever took place without the appearance, if only for half-an-hour, of Bobbie Ferrar in a seat more or less kept for him. And he preserved the records of all those trials in a specially bound edition. Perhaps the greatest testimony to his character, whatever that might be, lay in the fact that no one ever threw his acquaintanceship with nearly everybody up against him. People came to Bobbie Ferrar, not he to them. Yet why? What had he ever done that he should be 'Bobbie' Ferrar to all and sundry? Not even 'the honourable', merely the son of a courtesy lord, affable, unfathomable, always about, he was unquestionably a last word. Without him, his flower, and his faint grin,

Whitehall would have been shorn of something that made it almost human. He had been there since before the war, from which he had been retrieved just in time, some said, to prevent the whole place from losing its character, just in time, too, to stand, as it were, between England and herself. She could not become the shrill edgy hurried harridan the war had tried to make her while his square, leisurely, beflowered, inscrutable figure passed daily up and down between those pale considerable buildings.

He was turning over a Bulb Catalogue, on the morning of Hubert's wedding day, when the card of Sir Lawrence Mont was brought to him, followed by its owner, who said at once:

'You know what I've come about, Bobbie?'

'Completely,' said Bobbie Ferrar, his eyes round, his head thrown back, his voice deep.

'Has the Marquess seen you?'

'I had breakfast with him yesterday. Isn't he amazing?'

'Our finest old boy,' said Sir Lawrence. 'What are you going to do about it? Old Sir Conway Cherrell was the best Ambassador to Spain you ever turned out of the shop, and this is his grandson.'

'Has he really got a scar?' asked Bobbie Ferrar, through a faint grin.

'Of course he has.'

'Did he really get it over that?'

'Sceptical image! Of course he did.'

'Amazing!'

'Why?'

Bobbie Ferrar showed his teeth. 'Who can prove it?'

'Hallorsen is getting evidence.'

'It's not in our department, you know.'

'No? But you can get at the Home Secretary.'

'Um!' said Bobbie Ferrar, deeply.

'You can see the Bolivians about it, anyway.'

'Um!' said Bobbie Ferrar still more deeply, and handed him the catalogue. 'Do you know this new tulip? Complete, isn't it?'

'Now, look you, Bobbie,' said Sir Lawrence, 'this is my nephew; emphatically a "good egg", as you say, and it won't do! See!'

'The age is democratic,' said Bobbie Ferrar cryptically; 'it came up in the House, didn't it – flogging?'

'We can pull out the national stop if there's any more fuss there. Hallorsen has taken back his criticism. Well, I'll leave it to you; you won't commit yourself if I stay here all the morning. But you'll do your best because it really is a scandalous charge.'

'Completely,' said Bobbie Ferrar. 'Would you like to see the Croydon murder trial? It's amazing. I've got two seats; I offered one to my Uncle. But he won't go to any trial until they bring in electrocution.'

'Did the fellow do it?'

Bobbie Ferrar nodded.

'The evidence is very shaky,' he added.

'Well, good-bye, Bobbie; I rely on you.'

Bobbie Ferrar grinned faintly, and held out his hand.

'Good-bye,' he said, through his teeth.

Sir Lawrence went westward to the Coffee House where the porter handed him a telegram: 'Am marrying Jean Tasburgh two o'clock today St Augustine's-in-the-Meads delighted to see you and Aunt Em Hubert.'

Passing into the coffee room, Sir Lawrence said to the Chief Steward: 'Butts, I am about to see a nephew turned off. Fortify me quickly.'

Twenty minutes later he was on his way to St Augustine's, in a cab. He arrived a few minutes before two o'clock and met Dinny going up the steps.

'You look pale and interesting, Dinny.'

'I *am* pale and interesting, Uncle Lawrence.'

'This proceeding appears to be somewhat sudden.'

'That's Jean. I'm feeling terribly responsible. I found her for him, you see.'

They entered the church and moved up to the front pews. Apart from the General, Lady Cherrell, Mrs Hilary and Hubert there was no one except two sightseers and a verger. Someone's fingers were wandering on the organ. Sir Lawrence and Dinny took a pew to themselves.

'I'm not sorry Em isn't here,' he whispered; 'she still gives way. When you marry, Dinny, have "No tears by request" on your invitation cards. What is it produces moisture at weddings? Even bailiffs weep.'

'It's the veil,' said Dinny; 'nobody will cry today because there is none. Look! Fleur and Michael!'

Sir Lawrence turned his monocle on them as they came up the aisle.

'Eight years since we saw them married. Take it all round, they haven't done so badly.'

'No,' whispered Dinny; 'Fleur told me yesterday that Michael was pure gold.'

'Did she? That's good. There have been times, Dinny, when I've had my doubts.'

'Not about Michael.'

'No, no; he's a first-rate fellow. But Fleur has fluttered their dovecote once or twice; since her father's death, however, she's been exemplary. Here they come!'

The organ had broken into annunciation. Alan Tasburgh with Jean on his arm was coming up the aisle. Dinny admired his square and steady look. As for Jean, she seemed the very image of colour and vitality. Hubert, standing, hands behind him, as if at ease, turned as she came up, and Dinny saw his face, lined and dark, brighten as if the sun had shone on it. A choky feeling gripped her throat. Then she saw that Hilary in his surplice had come quietly and was standing on the step.

'I do like Uncle Hilary,' she thought.

Hilary had begun to speak.

Contrary to her habit in church, Dinny listened. She waited for the word "obey" – it did not come; she waited for the sexual allusions – they were omitted. Now Hilary was asking for the ring. Now it was on. Now he was praying. Now it was the

Lord's Prayer, and they were going to the vestry. How strangely short!

She rose from her knees.

'Amazingly complete,' whispered Sir Lawrence, 'as Bobbie Ferrar would say. Where are they going after?'

'To the theatre. Jean wants to stay in Town. She's found a workman's flat.'

'Calm before the storm. I wish that affair of Hubert's were over, Dinny.'

They were coming back from the vestry now, and the organ had begun to play the Mendelssohn march. Looking at those two passing down the aisle Dinny had feelings of elation and of loss, of jealousy and of satisfaction. Then, seeing that Alan looked as if he, too, had feelings, she moved out of her pew to join Fleur and Michael; but, catching sight of Adrian near the entrance, went to him instead.

'What news, Dinny?'

'All right so far, Uncle. I am going straight back now.'

With the popular instinct for experiencing emotion at second-hand a little crowd of Hilary's parishioners had gathered outside, and a squeaky cheer rose from them as Jean and Hubert got into the brown roadster, and drove away.

'Come in this cab with me, Uncle,' said Dinny.

'Does Ferse seem to mind your being there?' asked Adrian, in the cab.

'He's quite polite, just silent; his eyes are always on Diana. I'm terribly sorry for him.'

Adrian nodded. 'And she?'

'Wonderful; as if nothing were out of the ordinary. He won't go out, though; just stays in the dining room – watches from there all the time.'

'The world must seem to him a conspiracy. If he remains sane long enough he'll lose that feeling.'

'Need he ever become insane again? Surely there are cases of complete recovery?'

'So far as I can gather, my dear, his case is not likely to be one of them. Heredity is against him, and temperament.'

'I could have liked him, it's such a daring face; but his eyes *are* frightening.'

'Have you seen him with the children?'

'Not yet; but they speak quite nicely and naturally about him; so he hasn't scared them, you see.'

'At the Home they talked jargon to me about complexes, obsessions, repressions, dissociation – all that sort of thing, but I gathered that his case is one where fits of great gloom alternate with fits of great excitement. Lately, both have grown so much milder that he has become practically normal. What has to be watched for is the recrudescence of one or of the other. He always had a streak of revolt in him; he was up against the leadership in the war, up against democracy after the war. He'll almost certainly get up against something now he's back. If he does it will ungear him again in no time. If there's any weapon in the house, Dinny, it ought to be removed.'

'I'll tell Diana.'

The cab turned into the King's Road.

'I suppose I'd better not come to the house,' said Adrian, sadly.

Dinny got out, too. She stood a moment watching him, tall and rather stooping, walk away, then turned down Oakley Street, and let herself in. Ferse was in the dining-room doorway.

'Come in here,' he said; 'I want a talk.'

In that panelled room, painted a greenish-gold, lunch had been cleared away, and on the narrow refectory table were a newspaper, a tobacco jar, and several books. Ferse drew up a chair for her and stood with his back to a fire which simulated flames. He was not looking at her, so she was able to study him as she had not yet had the chance of doing. His handsome face was uncomfortable to look on. The high cheek-bones, stiff jaw, and crisp grizzled hair set off those thirsty burning steel-blue eyes. Even his attitude, square and a-kimbo, with head thrust forward, set off those eyes. Dinny leaned back, scared and faintly smiling. He turned to her and said:

'What are people saying about me?'

'I've not heard anything; I've only been to my brother's wedding.'

'Your brother Hubert? Whom has he married?'

'A girl called Jean Tasburgh. You saw her the day before yesterday.'

'Oh! Ah! I locked her in.'

'Yes, why?'

'She looked dangerous to me. I consented to go into that place, you know. I wasn't put there.'

'Oh! I know; I knew you were there of your own accord.'

'It wasn't such a bad place, but – well! How do I look?'

Dinny said softly: 'You see, I never saw you before, except at a distance, but I think you look very well.'

'I am well. I kept my muscles up. The fellow that looked after me saw to that.'

'Did you read much?'

'Lately – yes. What do they think about me?'

At the repetition of this question Dinny looked up into his face.

'How can they think about you without having seen you?'

'You mean I ought to see people?'

'I don't know anything about it, Captain Ferse. But I don't see why not. You're seeing me.'

'I like *you*.'

Dinny put out her hand.

'Don't say you're sorry for me,' Ferse said, quickly.

'Why should I? You're perfectly all right, I'm sure.'

He covered his eyes with his hand.

'I am, but how long shall I be?'

'Why not always?'

Ferse turned to the fire.

Dinny said, timidly: 'If you don't worry, nothing will happen again.'

Ferse spun round to her. 'Have you seen much of my children?'

'Not very much.'

'Any likeness to me in them?'

'No; they take after Diana.'

'Thank God for that! What does Diana think about me?' This time his eyes searched hers, and Dinny realised that on her answer everything might depend.

'Diana is just glad.'

He shook his head violently. 'Not possible.'

'The truth is often not possible.'

'She doesn't hate me?'

'Why should she?'

'Your Uncle Adrian – what's between them? Don't just say: Nothing.'

'My uncle worships her,' said Dinny, quietly, 'that's why they are just friends.'

'Just friends?'

'Just friends.'

'That's all you know, I suppose.'

'I know for certain.'

Ferse sighed, 'You're a good sort. What would you do if you were me?'

Again Dinny felt her ruthless responsibility.

'I think I should do what Diana wanted.'

'What is that?'

'I don't know. I don't think she does yet.'

Ferse strode to the window and back.

'I've got to do something for poor devils like myself.'

'Oh!' said Dinny, dismayed.

'I've had luck. Most people like me would have been certified, and stuck away against their will. If I'd been poor we couldn't have afforded that place. To be there was bad enough, but it was miles better than the usual run of places. I used to make my man talk. He'd seen two or three of them.'

He stood silent, and Dinny thought of her uncle's words: 'He'll get up against something, and that will ungear him again in no time.'

Ferse went on suddenly: 'If you had any other kind of job possible, would *you* take on the care of the insane? Not you, nor anyone with nerves or sensibility. A saint might, here and there, but there aren't saints enough to go round by a long chalk. No! To look after us you've got to shed the bowels of compassion, you must be made of iron, you must have a hide like leather; and no nerves. With nerves you'd be worse than the thick-skinned because you'd be jumpy, and that falls on us. It's an impasse. My God! Haven't I thought about it? And – money. No one with money ought to be sent to one of those places. Never, never! Give him his prison at home somehow – somewhere. If I hadn't known that I could come away at any time – if I hadn't hung on to that knowledge even at my worst, I wouldn't be here now – I'd be raving. God! I'd be raving! Money! And how many have money? Perhaps five in a hundred! And the other ninety-five poor devils are stuck away, willy-nilly, stuck away! I don't care how scientific, how good those places may be, as asylums go – they mean death in life. They must. People outside think we're as good as dead already – so who cares? Behind all the pretence of scientific treatment that's what they really feel. We're obscene – no longer human – the old idea of madness clings, Miss Cherrell; we're a disgrace, we've failed. Hide us away, put us underground. Do it humanely – twentieth century! Humanely! Try! You can't! Cover it all up with varnish then – varnish – that's all it is. What else can it be? Take my word for that. Take my man's word for it. He knew.'

Dinny was listening, without movement. Suddenly Ferse laughed. 'But we're not dead; that's the misfortune, we're not dead. If only we were! All those poor brutes – not dead – as capable of suffering in their own way as anyone else – more capable. Don't I know? And what's the remedy?' He put his hands to his head.

'To find a remedy,' said Dinny, softly, 'wouldn't it be wonderful?'

He stared at her.

'Thicken the varnish – that's all we do, all we shall do.'

'Then why worry yourself?' sprang to Dinny's lips, but she held the words back.

'Perhaps,' she said, 'you will find the remedy, only that will need patience and calm.'

Ferse laughed.

'You must be bored to death.' And he turned away to the window.

Dinny slipped quietly out.

Chapter Twenty-three

In that resort of those who know – the Piedmont Grill – the knowing were in various stages of repletion, bending towards each other as if in food they had found the link between their souls. They sat, two by two, and here and there four by five, and here and there a hermit, moody or observant over a cigar, and between the tables moved trippingly the lean and nimble waiters with faces unlike their own, because they were harassed by their memories. Lord Saxenden and Jean, in a corner at the near end, had already consumed a lobster, drunk half a bottle of hock, and talked of nothing in particular, before she raised her eyes slowly from an empty claw and said:

'Well, Lord Saxenden?'

His blue stare goggled slightly at that thick-lashed glance.

'Good lobster?' he said.

'Amazing.'

'I always come here when I want to be well fed. Is that partridge coming, waiter?'

'Yes, milord.'

'Well, hurry with it. Try this hock, Miss Tasburgh; you're not drinking.'

Jean raised her greenish glass. 'I became Mrs Hubert Cherrell yesterday. It's in the paper.'

Lord Saxenden's cheeks expanded slightly with the thought:

'Now, how does that affect me? Is this young lady more amusing single or more amusing married?'

'You don't waste time,' he said, his eyes exploring her, as though seeking confirmation of her changed condition. 'If I'd known, I shouldn't have had the cheek to ask you to lunch without him.'

'Thank you,' said Jean; 'he's coming along presently.' And, through her lashes, she looked at him draining his glass thoughtfully.

'Have you any news for me?'

'I've seen Walter.'

'Walter?'

'The Home Secretary.'

'How terribly nice of you!'

'It was. Can't bear the fellow. Got a head like an egg, except for his hair.'

'What did he say?'

'Young lady, nobody in any official department ever *says* anything. He always "thinks it over". Administration has to be like that.'

'But of course he'll pay attention to what *you* said. What *did* you say?'

Lord Saxenden's iced eyes seemed to answer: 'Really, you know, really!'

But Jean smiled; and the eyes thawed gradually.

'You're the most direct young woman I've ever come across. As a matter of fact I said: "Stop it, Walter."'

'How splendid!'

'He didn't like it. He's a "just beast".'

'Could I see him?'

Lord Saxenden began to laugh. He laughed like a man who has come across the priceless.

Jean waited for him to finish, and said:

'Then I shall.'

The partridge filled the ensuing gap.

'Look here!' said Lord Saxenden, suddenly: 'If you really mean that, there's one man who might wangle you an interview – Bobbie Ferrar. He used to be with Walter when he was Foreign Secretary. I'll give you a chit to Bobbie. Have a sweet?'

'No, thank you. But I *should* like some coffee, please. There's Hubert!'

Just free of the revolving cage, which formed the door, was Hubert, evidently in search of his wife.

'Bring him over here!'

Jean looked intently at her husband. His face cleared, and he came towards them.

'You've got the eye all right,' murmured Lord Saxenden, rising. 'How de do? You've married a remarkable wife. Have some coffee? The brandy's good here.' And taking out a card he wrote on it in a hand both neat and clear:

'Robert Ferrar, Esq., F.O., Whitehall. Dear Bobbie, do see my young friend Mrs Hubert Charwell and get her an interview with Walter if at all possible. Saxenden.'

Then, handing it to Jean, he asked the waiter for his bill.

'Hubert,' said Jean, 'show Lord Saxenden your scar,' and, undoing the link of his cuff, she pushed up his sleeve. That livid streak stared queer and sinister above the tablecloth.

'H'm!' said Lord Saxenden: 'useful wipe, that.'

Hubert wriggled his arm back under cover. 'She still takes liberties,' he said.

Lord Saxenden paid his bill and handed Hubert a cigar.

'Forgive me if I run off now. Stay and finish your coffee. Goodbye and good luck to you both!' And, shaking their hands, he threaded his way out among the tables. The two young people gazed after him.

'Such delicacy,' said Hubert, 'is not his known weakness, I believe. Well, Jean?'

Jean looked up.

'What does F.O. mean?'

'Foreign Office, my country girl.'

'Finish your brandy, and we'll go and see this man.'

But in the courtyard a voice behind them said:

'Why! Captain! Miss Tasburgh!'

'My wife, Professor.'

Hallorsen seized their hands.

'Isn't that just wonderful? I've a cablegram in my pocket, Captain, that's as good as a wedding present.'

Over Hubert's shoulder, Jean read out: '"Exonerating statement sworn by Manuel mailed stop American Consulate La Paz." That's splendid, Professor. Will you come with us and see a man at the Foreign Office about this?'

'Surely. I don't want any grass to grow. Let's take an automobile.'

Opposite to them in the cab he radiated surprised benevolence.

'You were mighty quick off the mark, Captain.'

'That was Jean.'

'Yes,' said Hallorsen, as if she were not present, 'when I met her at Lippinghall I thought she could move. Is your sister pleased?'

'Is she, Jean?'

'Rather!'

'A wonderful young lady. There's something good in low buildings. This Whitehall of yours makes me feel fine. The more sun and stars you can see from a street the more moral sense there is to the people. Were you married in a stovepipe hat, Captain?'

'No; just as I am now.'

'I'm sorry about that. They seem to me so cunning; like carrying a lost cause about on your head. I believe you are of an old family, too, Mrs Cherrell. Your habit over here of families that serve their country from father to son is inspiring, Captain.'

'I hadn't thought about that.'

'I had a talk with your brother, Ma'am, at Lippinghall, he informed me you'd had a sailor in your family for centuries. And I'm told that in yours, Captain, there's always been a soldier.

I believe in heredity. Is this the Foreign Office?' He looked at his watch. 'I'm just wondering whether that guy will be in? I've a kind of impression they do most of their business over food. We should do well to go and look at the ducks in the Park till three o'clock.'

'I'll leave this card for him,' said Jean.

She rejoined them quickly. 'He's expected in at any minute.'

'That'll be half an hour,' said Hallorsen. 'There's one duck here I'd like your opinion of, Captain.'

Crossing the wide road to the water they were nearly run down by the sudden convergence of two cars embarrassed by unwonted space. Hubert clutched Jean convulsively. He had gone livid under his tan. The cars cleared away to right and left. Hallorsen, who had taken Jean's other arm, said with an exaggeration of his drawl:

'That just about took our paint off.'

Jean said nothing.

'I sometimes wonder,' continued Hallorsen, as they reached the ducks, 'whether we get our money's worth out of speed. What do you say, Captain?'

Hubert shrugged. 'The hours lost in going by car instead of by train are just about as many as the hours saved, anyway.'

'That is so,' said Hallorsen. 'But flying's a real saver of time.'

'Better wait for the full bill before we boast about flying.'

'You're right, Captain. We're surely headed for hell. The next war will mean a pretty thin time for those who take part in it. Suppose France and Italy came to blows, there'd be no Rome, no Paris, no Florence, no Venice, no Lyons, no Milan, no Marseilles within a fortnight. They'd just be poisoned deserts. And the ships and armies maybe wouldn't have fired a shot.'

'Yes. And all governments know it. I'm a soldier, but I can't see why they go on spending hundreds of millions on soldiers and sailors who'll probably never be used. You can't run armies and navies when the nerve centres have been destroyed. How long could France and Italy function if their big towns were gassed? England or Germany certainly couldn't function a week.'

'Your Uncle the Curator was saying to me that at the rate Man was going he would soon be back in the fish state.'

'How?'

'Why! Surely! Reversing the process of evolution – fishes, reptiles, birds, mammals. We're becoming birds again, and the result of that will soon be that we shall creep and crawl, and end up in the sea when land's uninhabitable.'

'Why can't we all bar the air for war?'

'How can we bar the air?' said Jean. 'Countries never trust each other. Besides, America and Russia are outside the League of Nations.'

'We Americans would agree. But maybe not our Senate.'

'That Senate of yours,' muttered Hubert, 'seems to be a pretty hard proposition.'

'Why! It's like your House of Lords before a whip was taken to it in 1910. That's the duck,' and Hallorsen pointed to a peculiar bird. Hubert stared at it.

'I've shot that chap in India. It's a – I've forgotten the name. We can get it from one of these boards – I shall remember if I see.'

'No!' said Jean; 'it's a quarter past three. He must be in by now.' And, without allocating the duck, they returned to the Foreign Office.

Bobbie Ferrar's handshake was renowned. It pulled his adversary's hand up and left it there. When Jean had restored her hand, she came at once to the point. 'You know about this extradition business, Mr Ferrar?'

Bobbie Ferrar nodded.

'This is Professor Hallorsen, who was head of the expedition. Would you like to see the scar my husband has?'

'Very much,' murmured Bobbie Ferrar, through his teeth.

'Show him, Hubert.'

Unhappily Hubert bared his arm again.

'Amazing!' said Bobbie Ferrar: 'I told Walter.'

'You've seen him?'

'Sir Lawrence asked me to.'

'What did Wal— the Home Secretary say?'

'Nothing. He'd seen Snubby; he doesn't like Snubby, so he's issued the order to Bow Street.'

'Oh! Does that mean there will be a warrant?'

Bobbie Ferrar nodded, examining his nails.

The two young people stared at each other.

Hallorsen said, gravely:

'Can no one stop this gang?'

Bobbie Ferrar shook his head, his eyes looked very round.

Hubert rose.

'I'm sorry that I let anyone bother himself in the matter. Come along, Jean!' and with a slight bow he turned and went out. Jean followed him.

Hallorsen and Bobbie Ferrar were left confronted.

'I don't understand this country,' said Hallorsen. 'What ought to have been done?'

'Nothing,' answered Bobbie Ferrar. 'When it comes before the magistrate, bring all the evidence you can.'

'We surely will. Mr Ferrar, I am glad to have met you!'

Bobbie Ferrar grinned. His eyes looked even rounder.

Chapter Twenty-four

*I*n the due course of justice, Hubert was brought up at Bow Street on a warrant issued by one of its magistrates. Attending, in common with other members of the family, Dinny sat through the proceedings in a state of passive protest. The sworn evidence of six Bolivian muleteers, testifying to the shooting and to its being unprovoked; Hubert's countering statement, the exhibition of his scar, his record, and the evidence of Hallorsen, formed the material on which the magistrate was invited to come to his decision. He came to it. 'Remanded' till the arrival of the defendant's supporting evidence. That principle of British law, 'A prisoner is presumed innocent till he is proved guilty,' so constantly refuted by its practice, was then debated in regard to bail, and Dinny held her breath. The idea of Hubert, just married, being presumed innocent in a cell, while his evidence crossed the Atlantic, was unbearable. The considerable bail offered by Sir Conway and Sir Lawrence, however, was finally accepted, and with a sigh of relief she walked out, her head held high. Sir Lawrence joined her outside.

'It's lucky,' he said, 'that Hubert looks so unaccustomed to lying.'

'I suppose,' murmured Dinny, 'this will be in the papers.'

'On that, my nymph, you may bet the buttoned boots you haven't got.'

'How will it affect Hubert's career?'

'I think it will be good for him. The House of Commons

questions were damaging. But "British Officer *versus* Bolivian Half-Castes" will rally the prejudice we all have for our kith and kin.'

'I'm more sorry for Dad than for anybody. His hair is distinctly greyer since this began.'

'There's nothing dishonourable about it, Dinny.'

Dinny's head tilted up.

'No, indeed!'

'You remind me of a two-year-old, Dinny – one of those whip-cordy chestnuts that kick up their heels in the paddock, get left at the post, and come in first after all. Here's your American bearing down on us. Shall we wait for him? He gave very useful evidence.'

Dinny shrugged her shoulders, and almost instantly Hallorsen's voice said:

'Miss Cherrell!'

Dinny turned.

'Thank you very much. Professor, for what you said.'

'I wish I could have lied for you, but I had no occasion. How is that sick gentleman?'

'All right so far.'

'I am glad to hear that. I have been worried thinking of you.'

'What you said, Professor,' put in Sir Lawrence, 'about not being seen dead with any of those muleteers hit the magistrate plumb centre.'

'To be seen alive with them was bad enough. I've an auto-mobile here, can I take you and Miss Cherrell anywhere?'

'You might take us to the borders of civilisation, if you're going West.'

'Well, Professor,' continued Sir Lawrence, when they were seated, 'what do you think of London? Is it the most barbarous or the most civilised town on earth?'

'I just love it,' said Hallorsen, without ever taking his eyes off Dinny.

'I don't,' murmured Dinny; 'I hate the contrasts and the smell of petrol.'

'Well, a stranger can't tell why he loves London, unless it's the variety and the way you've gotten freedom and order all mixed up; or maybe it's because it's so different from our towns over there. New York is more wonderful and more exciting, but not so homey.'

'New York,' said Sir Lawrence, 'is like strychnine. It perks you up until it lays you out.'

'I certainly couldn't live in New York. The West for me.'

'The great open spaces,' murmured Dinny.

'Why yes, Miss Cherrell; you would love them.'

Dinny smiled wanly. 'No one can be pulled up by the roots, Professor.'

'Ah!' said Sir Lawrence, 'my son once took up the question of Emigration in Parliament. He found that people's roots were so strong that he had to drop it like a hot potato.'

'Is that so?' said Hallorsen. 'When I look at your town folk, undersized and pale and kind of disillusioned, I can't help wondering what roots they can have.'

'The townier the type, the more stubborn its roots – no open spaces for them; the streets, fried fish, and the pictures. Would you put me down here, Professor? Dinny, where are you bound for?'

'Oakley Street.'

Hallorsen stopped the car and Sir Lawrence got out.

'Miss Cherrell, may I have the great pleasure of taking you as far as Oakley Street?'

Dinny bowed.

Seated thus side by side with him in the closed car, she wondered uneasily what use he would make of his opportunity. Presently, without looking at her, he said:

'As soon as your brother is fixed up I shall be sailing. I'm going to take an expedition to New Mexico. I shall always count it a privilege to have known you, Miss Cherrell.'

His ungloved hands were gripping each other between his knees; and the sight moved her.

'I am very sorry for misjudging you at first, Professor, just as my brother did.'

'It was natural. I shall be glad to think I have your goodwill when all's been said and done.'

Dinny put out her hand impulsively.

'You have.'

He took the hand with gravity, raised it to his lips, and returned it to her gently. Dinny felt extremely unhappy. She said, timidly: 'You've made me think quite differently about Americans, Professor.'

Hallorsen smiled.

'That is something, anyway.'

'I'm afraid I was very crude in my ideas. You see, I haven't really known any.'

'That is the little trouble between us; we don't really know each other. We get on each other's nerves, with little things, and there it ends. But I shall always remember you as the smile on the face of this country.'

'That,' said Dinny, 'is very pretty, and I wish it were true.'

'If I could have a picture of you, I should treasure it.'

'Of course you shall! I don't know if I have a decent one, but I'll send you the best.'

'I thank you. I think if you will allow me I will get out here; I am just not too sure of myself. The car will take you on.' He tapped on the glass and spoke to the chauffeur.

'Good-bye!' he said, and took her hand again, looked at it rather long, pressed it hard, and slid his long frame through the doorway.

'Good-bye!' murmured Dinny, sitting back, with rather a choky feeling in her throat.

Five minutes later the car pulled up before Diana's house, and, very subdued, she went in.

Diana, whom she had not seen that morning, opened the door of her room as she was passing.

'Come in here, Dinny.' Her voice was stealthy, and a little

shudder went through Dinny. They sat down side by side on the
four-poster bed, and Diana spoke low and hurriedly:

'He came in here last night and insisted on staying. I didn't
dare refuse. There's a change; I have a feeling that it's the beginning of the end, again. His self-control is weakening, all round.
I think I ought to send the children somewhere. Would Hilary
take them?'

'I'm sure he would; or Mother would certainly.'

'Perhaps that would be better.'

'Don't you think you ought to go, yourself?'

Diana sighed and shook her head.

'That would only precipitate things. Could you take the children down for me?'

'Of course. But do you really think he—?'

'Yes. I'm sure he's working up again. I know the signs so well.
Haven't you noticed, Dinny, he's been drinking more each evening?
It's all of a piece.'

'If he'd get over his horror of going out.'

'I don't believe that would help. Here at all events we know
what there is to know, and the worst at once if it comes. I dread
something happening with strangers, and our hands being forced.'

Dinny squeezed her arm.

'When would you like the children taken down?'

'As soon as possible. I can't say anything to him. You must
just go off as quietly as you can. Mademoiselle can go down
separately, if your mother will have her too.'

'I shall come back at once, of course.'

'Dinny, it isn't fair on you. I've got the maids. It's really too
bad to bother you with my troubles.'

'But of course I shall come back. I'll borrow Fleur's car. Will
he mind the children going?'

'Only if he connects it with our feeling about his state. I can
say it's an old invitation.'

'Diana,' said Dinny, suddenly, 'have you any love for him left?'

'Love? No!'

'Just pity?'

Diana shook her head.

'I can't explain; it's the past and a feeling that if I desert him I help the fates against him. That's a horrible thought!'

'I understand. I'm so sorry for you both, and for Uncle Adrian.'

Diana smoothed her face with her hands, as if wiping off the marks of trouble.

'I don't know what's coming, but it's no good going to meet it. As to you, my dear, don't for God's sake let me spoil your time.'

'That's all right. I'm wanting something to take me out of myself. Spinsters, you know, should be well shaken before being taken.'

'Ah! When *are* you going to be taken, Dinny?'

'I have just rejected the great open spaces, and I feel a beast.'

'Between the great open spaces and the deep sea – are you?'

'And likely to remain so. The love of a good man – and all that, seems to leave me frost-bitten.'

'Wait! Your hair is the wrong colour for the cloister.'

'I'll have it dyed and sail in my true colours. Icebergs are sea-green.'

'As I said before – wait!'

'I will,' said Dinny. . . .

Fleur herself drove the South Square car to the door two days later. The children and some luggage were placed in it without incident, and they started.

That somewhat hectic drive, for the children were little used to cars, to Dinny was pure relief. She had not realised how much the tragic atmosphere of Oakley Street was on her nerves; and yet it was but ten days since she had come up from Condaford. The colours of 'the fall' were deepening already on the trees. The day had the soft and sober glow of fine October; the air, as the country deepened and grew remote, had again its beloved tang; wood smoke rose from cottage chimneys, and rooks from the bared fields.

They arrived in time for lunch, and, leaving the children with
Mademoiselle, who had come down by train, Dinny went forth
with the dogs alone. She stopped at an old cottage high above
the sunken road. The door opened straight into the living room,
where an old woman was sitting by a thin fire of wood.

'Oh! Miss Dinny,' she said, 'I am that glad. I haven't seen you
not all this month.'

'No, Betty; I've been away. How are you?'

The little old woman, for she was of pocket size, crossed her
hands solemnly on her middle.

'My stummick's bad again. I 'aven't nothin' else the matter –
the doctor says I'm wonderful. Just my stummick. 'E says I ought
to eat more; and I've such an appetite, Miss Dinny. But I can't
eat 'ardly nothin' without I'm sick, and that's the truth.'

'Dear Betty, I'm so sorry. Tummies are a dreadful nuisance.
Tummies and teeth. I can't think why we have them. If you haven't
teeth you can't digest; and if you have teeth you can't digest either.'

The old lady cackled thinly.

''E du say I ought to 'ave the rest of my teeth out, but I don't
like to part with 'em, Miss Dinny. Father 'e's got none, and 'e
can bite an apple, 'e can. But at my age I can't expect to live to
'arden up like that.'

'But you could have some lovely false ones, Betty.'

'Oh! I don't want to 'ave no false teeth – so pretenshus. You
wouldn't never wear false teeth, would you, Miss Dinny?'

'Of course I would, Betty. Nearly all the best people have them
nowadays.'

'You will 'ave your joke. No, I shouldn't like it. I'd as soon
wear a wig. But my 'air's as thick as ever. I'm wonderful for my
age. I've got a lot to be thankful for; it's only my stummick, an'
that's like as if there was somethin' there.'

Dinny saw the pain and darkness in her eyes.

'How is Benjamin, Betty?'

The eyes changed, became amused and yet judgmatic, as if
she were considering a child.

'Oh! Father's all right, Miss; 'e never 'as anything the matter except 'is rheumatiz; 'e's out now doin' a bit o' diggin'.'

'And how's Goldie?' said Dinny, looking lugubriously at a goldfinch in a cage. She hated to see birds in cages, but had never been able to bring herself to say so to these old people with their small bright imprisoned pet. Besides, didn't they say that if you released a tame goldfinch, it would soon be pecked to death?

'Oh!' said the old lady, ''e thinks 'e's someone since you give him that bigger cage.' Her eyes brightened. 'Fancy the Captain married, Miss Dinny, and that dreadful case against him an' all – whatever are they thinkin' about? I never 'eard of such a thing in all my life. One of the Cherrells to be put in Court like that. It's out of all knowledge.'

'It is, Betty.'

'I'm told she's a fine young lady. And where'll they be goin' to live?'

'Nobody knows yet; we have to wait for this case to be over. Perhaps down here, or perhaps he'll get a post abroad. They'll be very poor, of course.'

'Dreadful; it never was like that in old days. The way they put upon the gentry now – oh, dear! I remember your great-grandfather, Miss Dinny, drivin' four-in-hand when I was a little bit of a thing. Such a nice old gentleman – curtly, as you might say.'

Such references to the gentry never ceased to make Dinny feel uneasy, only too well aware that this old lady had been one of eight children brought up by a farm worker whose wages had been eleven shillings a week, and that she and her husband now existed on their Old Age pensions, after bringing up a family of seven.

'Well, Betty dear, what *can* you digest, so that I can tell cook?'

'Thank you kindly, Miss Dinny; a nice bit of lean pork do seem to lie quiet sometimes.' Again her eyes grew dark and troubled. 'I 'ave such dreadful pain; really sometimes I feel I'd be glad to go 'ome.'

'Oh! no, Betty dear. With a little proper feeding I know you're going to feel better.'

The old lady smiled below her eyes.

'I'm wonderful for my age, so it'd never do to complain. And when are the bells goin' to ring for you, Miss Dinny?'

'Don't mention them, Betty. They won't ring of their own accord – that's certain.'

'Ah! People don't marry young, and 'ave the families they did in my young days. My old Aunt 'ad eighteen an' reared eleven.'

'There doesn't seem room or work for them now, does there?'

'Aye! The country's changed.'

'Less down here than in most places, thank goodness.' And Dinny's eyes wandered over the room where these two old people had spent some fifty years of life; from brick floor to raftered ceiling it was scrupulously clean and had a look of homely habit.

'Well, Betty, I must go. I'm staying in London just now with a friend, and have to get back there this evening. I'll tell cook to send some little things that'll be better for you than pork even. Don't get up!'

But the little old woman was on her feet, her eyes looking out from her very soul.

'I am that glad to 'ave seen you, Miss Dinny. God bless you! And I do 'ope the Captain won't 'ave any trouble with those dreadful people.'

'Good-bye, Betty dear, and remember me to Benjamin,' and pressing the old lady's hand Dinny went out to where the dogs were waiting for her on the flagged pathway. As always after such visits she felt humble and inclined to cry. Roots! That was what she missed in London, what she would miss in the 'great open spaces'. She walked to the bottom of a narrow straggling beechwood, and entered it through a tattered gate that she did not even have to open. She mounted over the damp beech mast which smelled sweetly as of husks; to the left a grey-blue sky was rifted by the turning beeches, and to her right stretched fallow ground where a squatting hare turned and raced for the hedgerow; a pheasant rose squawking before one of the dogs and rocketed over the wood. She emerged from the trees at the top, and stood looking down at the house, long and stone-coloured, broken by magnolias and the trees on the lawn; smoke was rising from two chimneys, and the fantails speckled with white one gable. She breathed deeply, and for full ten minutes stood there, like a watered plant drawing up the food of its vitality. The scent was of leaves and turned earth and of rain not far away; the last time she had stood there had been at the end of May, and she had inhaled that scent of summer which is at once a memory and a promise, an aching and a draught of delight. . . .

After an early tea she started back, in the now closed car, sitting beside Fleur.

'I must say,' said that shrewd young woman, 'Condaford is the most peaceful place I was ever in. I should die of it, Dinny. The rurality of Lippinghall is nothing thereto.'

'Old and mouldering, um?'

'Well, I always tell Michael that your side of his family is one of the least expressed and most interesting phenomena left in England. You're wholly unvocal, utterly out of the limelight. Too unsensational for the novelists, and yet you're there, and go on being there, and I don't quite know how. Every mortal thing's against you, from Death Duties down to gramophones. But you persist generally at the ends of the earth, doing things that nobody knows or cares anything about. Most of your sort haven't even got Condafords now to come home and die in; and yet you still have roots, and a sense of duty. I've got neither, you know; I suppose that comes of being half French. My father's family – the Forsytes – may have roots, but they haven't a sense of duty – not in the same way; or perhaps it's a sense of service that I mean. I admire it, you know, Dinny, but it bores me stiff. It's making you go and blight your young life over this Ferse business. Duty's a disease, Dinny; an admirable disease.'

'What do you think I ought to do about it?'

'Have your instincts out. I can't imagine anything more ageing than what you're doing now. As for Diana, she's of the same sort – the Montjoys have a kind of Condaford up in Dumfriesshire – I admire her for sticking to Ferse, but I think it's quite crazy of her. It can only end one way, and that'll be the more unpleasant the longer it's put off.'

'Yes; I feel she's riding for a bad fall, but I hope I should do the same.'

'I know I shouldn't,' said Fleur, cheerfully.

'I don't believe that anybody knows what they'll do about anything until it comes to the point.'

'The thing is never to let anything come to a point.'

Fleur spoke with a tang in her voice, and Dinny saw her lips harden. She always found Fleur attractive, because she was mystifying.

'You haven't seen Ferse,' she said, 'and without seeing him you can't appreciate how pathetic he is.'

'That's sentiment, my dear. I'm not sentimental.'

'I'm sure you've had a past, Fleur; and you can't have had that without being sentimental.'

Fleur gave her a quick look, and trod on the accelerator.

'Time I turned on my lights,' she said.

For the rest of the journey she talked on Art, Letters, and other unimportant themes. It was nearly eight o'clock when she dropped Dinny at Oakley Street.

Diana was in, already dressed for dinner.

'Dinny,' she said, 'he's out.'

Chapter Twenty-five

*P*ortentous – those simple words!

'After you'd gone this morning he was in a great state – seemed to think we were all in a conspiracy to keep things from him.'

'As we were,' murmured Dinny.

'Mademoiselle's going to upset him again. Soon after, I heard the front door bang – he hasn't been back since. I didn't tell you, but last night was dreadful. Suppose he doesn't come back?'

'Oh! Diana, I wish he wouldn't.'

'But where has he gone? What can he do? Whom can he go to? O God! It's awful!'

Dinny looked at her in silent distress.

'Sorry, Dinny! You must be tired and hungry. We won't wait dinner.'

In Ferse's 'lair', that charming room panelled in green shot with a golden look, they sat through an anxious meal. The shaded light fell pleasantly on their bare necks and arms, on the fruit, the flowers, the silver; and until the maid was gone they spoke of indifferent things.

'Has he a key?' asked Dinny.

'Yes.'

'Shall I ring up Uncle Adrian?'

'What can he do? If Ronald does come in, it will be more dangerous if Adrian is here.'

'Alan Tasburgh told me he would come any time if anyone was wanted.'

'No, let's keep it to ourselves tonight. Tomorrow we can see.'

Dinny nodded. She was scared, and more scared of showing it, for she was there to strengthen Diana by keeping cool and steady.

'Come upstairs and sing to me,' she said, at last.

Up in the drawing-room Diana sang 'The Sprig of Thyme', 'Waley, Waley', 'The Bens of Jura', 'Mowing the Barley', 'The Castle of Dromore', and the beauty of the room, of the songs, of the singer, brought to Dinny a sense of unreality. She had gone into a drowsy dream, when, suddenly, Diana stopped.

'I heard the front door.'

Dinny got up and stood beside the piano.

'Go on, don't say anything, don't show anything.'

Diana began again to play, and sing the Irish song 'Must I go bound and you go free'. Then the door was opened, and, in a mirror at the end of the room, Dinny saw Ferse come in and stand listening.

'Sing on,' she whispered.

'Must I go bound, and you go free?
Must I love a lass that couldn't love me?
Oh! was I taught so poor a wit
As love a lass would break my heart.'

And Ferse stood there listening. He looked like a man excessively tired or overcome with drink; his hair was disordered and his lips drawn back so that his teeth showed. Then he moved. He seemed trying to make no noise. He passed round to a sofa on the far side and sank down on it. Diana stopped singing. Dinny, whose hand was on her shoulder, felt her trembling with the effort to control her voice.

'Have you had dinner, Ronald?'

Ferse did not answer, staring across the room with that queer and ghostly grin.

'Play on,' whispered Dinny.

Diana played the Red Sarafan; she played the fine simple tune over and over, as if making hypnotic passes towards that mute figure. When, at last, she stopped, there followed the strangest silence. Then Dinny's nerve snapped and she said, almost sharply:

'Is it raining, Captain Ferse?'

Ferse passed his hand down his trousers, and nodded.

'Hadn't you better go up and change them, Ronald?'

He put his elbows on his knees, and rested his head on his hands.

'You must be tired, dear; won't you go to bed? Shall I bring you something up?'

And still he did not move. The grin had faded off his lips; his eyes were closed. He looked like a man suddenly asleep, as some overdriven beast of burden might drop off between the shafts.

'Shut the piano,' whispered Dinny; 'let's go up.'

Diana closed the piano without noise and rose. With their arms linked they waited, but he did not stir.

'Is he really asleep?' whispered Dinny.

Ferse started up. 'Sleep! I'm for it. I'm for it again. And I won't stand it. By God! I won't stand it!'

He stood a moment transfigured with a sort of fury; then, seeing them shrink, sank back on the sofa and buried his face in his hands. Impulsively Diana moved towards him.

Ferse looked up. His eyes were wild.

'Don't!' he growled out. 'Leave me alone! Go away!'

At the door Diana turned and said:

'Ronald, won't you see someone? Just to make you sleep – just for that.'

Ferse sprang up again. 'I'll see no one. Go away!'

They shrank out of the room, and up in Dinny's bedroom stood with their arms round each other, quivering.

'Have the maids gone to bed?'

'They always go early, unless one of them is out.'

'I think I ought to go down and telephone, Diana.'

'No, Dinny, I will. Only to whom?'

That was, indeed, the question. They debated it in whispers. Diana thought her doctor; Dinny thought Adrian or Michael should be asked to go round to the doctor and bring him.

'Was it like this before the last attack?'

'No. He didn't know then what was before him. I feel he might kill himself, Dinny.'

'Has he a weapon?'

'I gave his Service revolver to Adrian to keep for me.'

'Razors?'

'Only safety ones; and there's nothing poisonous in the house.'

Dinny moved to the door.

'I *must* go and telephone.'

'Dinny, I can't have you—'

'He wouldn't touch *me*. It's you that are in danger. Lock the door while I'm gone.'

And before Diana could stop her, she slid out. The lights still burned, and she stood a moment. Her room was on the second floor, facing the street. Diana's bedroom and that of Ferse were on the drawing-room floor below. She must pass them to reach the hall and the little study where the telephone was kept. No sound came up. Diana had opened the door again and was standing there; and, conscious that at any moment she might slip past her and go down, Dinny ran forward and began descending the stairs. They creaked and she stopped to take off her shoes. Holding them in her hand she crept on past the drawing-room door. No sound came thence; and she sped down to the hall. She noticed Ferse's hat and coat thrown across a chair, and, passing into the study, closed the door behind her. She stood a moment to recover breath, then, turning on the light, took up the directory. She found Adrian's number and was stretching out her hand for the receiver when her wrist was seized, and with a gasp she turned to face Ferse. He twisted her round and stood pointing to the shoes still in her hand.

'Going to give me away,' he said, and, still holding her, took a knife out of his side pocket. Back, at the full length of her arm, Dinny looked him in the face. Somehow she was not so scared as she had been; her chief feeling was a sort of shame at having her shoes in her hand.

'That's silly, Captain Ferse,' she said, icily. 'You know we'd neither of us do you any harm.'

Ferse flung her hand from him, opened the knife, and with a violent effort severed the telephone wire. The receiver dropped on the floor. He closed the knife and put it back into his pocket. Dinny had the impression that with action he had become less unbalanced.

'Put on your shoes,' he said.

She did so.

'Understand me, I'm not going to be interfered with, or messed about. I shall do what I like with myself.'

Dinny remained silent. Her heart was beating furiously, and she did not want her voice to betray it.

'Did you hear?'

'Yes. No one wants to interfere with you, or do anything you don't like. We only want your good.'

'I know that good,' said Ferse. 'No more of that for me.' He went across to the window, tore a curtain aside, and looked out. 'It's raining like hell,' he said, then turned and stood looking at her. His face began to twitch, his hands to clench. He moved his head from side to side. Suddenly he shouted: 'Get out of this room, quick! Get out, get out!'

As swiftly as she could without running Dinny slid to the door, closed it behind her and flew upstairs. Diana was still standing in the bedroom doorway. Dinny pushed her in, locked the door, and sank down breathless.

'He came out after me,' she gasped, 'and cut the wire. He's got a knife; I'm afraid there's mania coming on. Will that door hold if he tries to break it down? Shall we put the bed against it?'

'If we do we should never sleep.'

'We shall never sleep, anyway,' and she began dragging at the bed. They moved it square against the door.

'Do the maids lock their doors?'

'They have, since he's been back.'

Dinny sighed with relief. The idea of going out again to warn them made her shudder. She sat on the bed looking at Diana, who was standing by the window.

'What are you thinking of, Diana?'

'I was thinking what I should be feeling if the children were still here.'

'Yes, thank heaven, they're not.'

Diana came back to the bed and took Dinny's hand. Grip and answering grip tightened till they were almost painful.

'Is there nothing we can do, Dinny?'

'Perhaps he'll sleep, and be much better in the morning. Now there's danger I don't feel half so sorry for him.'

Diana said stonily: 'I'm past feeling. I wonder if he knows yet that I'm not in my own room? Perhaps I ought to go down and face it.'

'You shan't!' And taking the key from the lock Dinny thrust it into the top of her stocking: its cold hardness rallied her nerves.

'Now,' she said, 'we'll lie down with our feet to the door. It's no good getting worn out for nothing.'

A sort of apathy had come over both of them, and they lay a long time thus, close together under the eiderdown, neither of them sleeping, neither of them quite awake. Dinny had dozed off at last when a stealthy sound awakened her. She looked at Diana. She was asleep, really asleep, dead asleep. A streak of light from outside showed at the top of the door, which fitted loosely. Leaning on her elbow she strained her ears. The handle of the door was turned, and softly shaken. There was a gentle knocking.

'Yes,' said Dinny, very low, 'what is it?'

'Diana,' said Ferse's voice, but quite subdued: 'I want her.'

Dinny crouched forward close to the keyhole.

'Diana's not well,' she said. 'She's asleep now, don't disturb her.'

There was silence. And then to her horror she heard a long moaning sigh; a sound so miserable, and as it were so final that she was on the point of taking out the key. The sight of Diana's face, white and worn, stopped her. No good! Whatever that sound meant – no good! And crouching back on the bed, she listened. No more sound! Diana slept on, but Dinny could not get to sleep again. 'If he kills himself,' she thought, 'shall I be to blame?' Would that not be best for everyone, for Diana and his children, for himself? But that long sighing moan went on echoing through her nerves. Poor man, poor man! She felt nothing now but a dreadful sore pity, a sort of resentment at the inexorability of Nature that did such things to human creatures. Accept the mysterious ways of Providence? Who could? Insensate and cruel! Beside the worn-out sleeper she lay, quivering. What had they done that they ought not to have done? Could they have helped him more than they had tried to? What could they do when morning came? Diana stirred. Was she going to wake? But she just turned and sank back into her heavy slumber. And slowly a drowsy feeling stole on Dinny herself and she slept.

A knocking on the door awakened her. It was daylight. Diana was still sleeping. She looked at her wrist watch. Eight o'clock. She was being called.

'All right, Mary!' she answered, softly: 'Mrs Ferse is here.'

Diana sat up, her eyes on Dinny's half-clothed figure.

'What is it?'

'It's all right, Diana. Eight o'clock! We'd better get up and put the bed back. You've had a real good sleep. The maids are up.'

They put on wrappers, and pulled the bed into place. Dinny took the key from its queer hiding nook, and unlocked the door.

'No good craning at it. Let's go down!'

They stood a moment at the top of the stairs listening, and then descended. Diana's room was untouched. The maid had evidently been in and pulled aside the curtains. They stood at the door that led from it to Ferse's room. No sound came from there. They went out to the other door. Still no sound!

'We'd better go down,' whispered Dinny. 'What shall you say to Mary?'

'Nothing. She'll understand.'

The dining room and study doors were open. The telephone receiver still lay severed on the floor; there was no other sign of last night's terrors.

Suddenly, Dinny said: 'Diana, his hat and coat are gone. They were on that chair.'

Diana went into the dining room and rang the bell. The elderly maid, coming from the basement stairs, had a scared and anxious look.

'Have you seen Captain Ferse's hat and coat this morning Mary?'

'No, Ma'am.'

'What time did you come down?'

'Seven o'clock.'

'You haven't been to his room?'

'Not yet, Ma'am.'

'I was not well last night; I slept upstairs with Miss Dinny.'

'Yes, Ma'am.'

They all three went upstairs.

'Knock on his door.'

The maid knocked. Dinny and Diana stood close by. There was no answer.

'Knock again, Mary, louder.'

Again and again the maid knocked. No answer. Diana put her aside and turned the handle. The door came open. Ferse was not there. The room was in disorder, as if someone had tramped and wrestled in it. The water bottle was empty, and tobacco ash was strewn about. The bed had been lain on, but not slept in. There was no sign of packing or of anything having been taken from the drawers. The three women looked at each other. Then Diana said:

'Get breakfast quick, Mary. We must go out.'

'Yes, Ma'am – I saw the telephone.'

'Hide that up, and get it mended; and don't tell the others anything. Just say: "He's away for a night or two." Make things here look like that. We'll dress quickly, Dinny.'

The maid went downstairs again.

Dinny said: 'Has he any money?'

'I don't know. I can see if his cheque book has gone.'

She ran down again, and Dinny waited. Diana came back into the hall.

'No; it's on the bureau in the dining room. Quick, Dinny, dress!'

That meant . . . What did it mean? A strange conflict of hopes and fears raged within Dinny. She flew upstairs.

Chapter Twenty-six

*O*ver a hasty breakfast they consulted. To whom should they go?

'Not to the police,' said Dinny.

'No, indeed.'

'I think we should go to Uncle Adrian first.'

They sent the maid for a taxi, and set out for Adrian's rooms. It was not quite nine o'clock. They found him over tea and one of those fishes which cover the more ground when eaten, and explain the miracle of the seven baskets full.

Seeming to have grown greyer in these few days he listened to them, filling his pipe, and at last said:

'You must leave it to me now. Dinny, can you take Diana down to Condaford?'

'Of course.'

'Before you go, could you get young Alan Tasburgh to go down to that Home and ask if Ferse is there, without letting them know that he's gone off on his own? Here's the address.'

Dinny nodded.

Adrian raised Diana's hand to his lips.

'My dear, you look worn out. Don't worry; just rest down there with the children. We'll keep in touch with you.'

'Will there be publicity, Adrian?'

'Not if we can prevent it. I shall consult Hilary; we'll try everything first. Do you know how much money he had?'

'The last cheque cashed was for five pounds two days ago, but all yesterday he was out.'

'How was he dressed?'

'Blue overcoat, blue suit, bowler hat.'

'And you don't know where he went yesterday?'

'No. Until yesterday he was never out at all.'

'Does he still belong to any Club?'

'No.'

'Has any old friend been told of his return?'

'No.'

'And he took no cheque book? How soon can you get hold of that young man, Dinny?'

'Now, if I could telephone, Uncle; he's sleeping at his Club.'

'Try, then.'

Dinny went out to the telephone. She soon reported that Alan would go down at once, and let Adrian know. He would ask as an old friend, with no knowledge that Ferse had ever left. He would beg them to let him know if Ferse came back, so that he might come and see him.

'Good,' said Adrian; 'you have a head, my child. And now go off and look after Diana. Give me your number at Condaford.'

Having jotted it down, he saw them back into their cab.

'Uncle Adrian is the best man in the world,' said Dinny.

'No one should know that better than I, Dinny.'

Back in Oakley Street, they went upstairs to pack. Dinny was afraid that at the last minute Diana might refuse to go. But she had given her word to Adrian, and they were soon on the way to the station. They spent a very silent hour and a half on the journey, leaning back in their corners, tired out. Dinny, indeed, was only now realising the strain she had been through. And yet, what had it amounted to? No violence, no attack, not even a great scene. How uncannily disturbing was insanity! What fear it inspired; what nerve-racking emotions! Now that she was free from chance of contact with Ferse he again seemed to her just pitiful. She pictured him wandering and distraught, with nowhere to lay his head and no one to take him by the hand; on the edge, perhaps already over that edge! The worst tragedies were always connected with fear. Criminality, leprosy, insanity, anything that inspired fear in other people – the victims of such were hopelessly alone in a frightened world. Since last night she understood far better Ferse's outburst about the vicious circle in which insanity moved. She knew now that her own nerves were not strong enough, her own skin not thick enough, to bear contact with the insane; she understood the terrible treatment of the insane in old days. It was like the way dogs had, of setting on an hysterical dog, their own nerves jolted beyond bearing. The contempt lavished on the imbecile, the cruelty and contempt had been defensive – defensive revenge on something which outraged the nerves. All the more pitiable, all the more horrible to think about. And, while the train bore her nearer to her peaceful home, she was more and more torn between the wish to shut away all thought of the unhappy outcast and feelings of pity for him. She looked across at Diana lying back in the corner opposite with closed eyes. What must she be feeling, bound to Ferse by memory, by law, by children of whom he was the father? The face under the close casque hat had the chiselling of prolonged trial – fine-lined and rather hard. By the faint movement of the lips she was not asleep. 'What keeps her going?' thought Dinny. 'She's not religious; she doesn't believe much in anything. If I were she I should throw everything up and rush to the ends of the earth – or should I?' Was there perhaps something inside one, some sense of what was due to oneself, that kept one unyielding and unbroken?

There was nothing to meet them at the station, so, leaving their things, they set forth for the Grange on foot, taking a path across the fields.

'I wonder,' said Dinny, suddenly, 'how little excitement one could do with in these days? Should I be happy if I lived down here all my time, like the old cottage folk? Clare is never happy here. She has to be on the go all the time. There *is* a kind of jack-in-the-box inside one.'

'I've never seen it popping out of you, Dinny.'

'I wish I'd been older during the war. I was only fourteen when it stopped.'

'You were lucky.'

'I don't know. You must have had a terribly exciting time, Diana.'

'I was your present age when the war began.'

'Married?'

'Just.'

'I suppose he was right through it?'

'Yes.'

'Was that the cause?'

'An aggravation, perhaps.'

'Uncle Adrian spoke of heredity.'

'Yes.'

Dinny pointed to a thatched cottage.

'In that cottage an old pet couple of mine have lived fifty years. Could you do that, Diana?'

'I could now; I want peace, Dinny.'

They reached the house in silence. A message had come through from Adrian: Ferse was not back at the Home: but he and Hilary believed they were on the right track.

After seeing the children Diana went to her bedroom to lie down, and Dinny to her mother's sitting room.

'Mother, I must say it to someone – I am praying for his death.'

'Dinny!'

'For his own sake, for Diana's, for the children's, for every-body's; even my own.'

'Of course, if it's hopeless—'

'Hopeless or not, I don't care. It's too dreadful. Providence is a wash-out, Mother.'

'My dear!'

'It's too remote. I suppose there is an eternal Plan – but we're like gnats for all the care it has for us as individuals.'

'You want a good sleep, darling.'

'Yes. But that won't make any difference.'

'Don't encourage such feelings, Dinny; they affect one's character.'

'I don't see the connection between beliefs and character. I'm not going to behave any worse because I cease to believe in Providence or an after life.'

'Surely, Dinny—'

'No; I'm going to behave *better*; if I'm decent it's because decency's the decent thing; and not because I'm going to get anything by it.'

'But why is decency the decent thing, Dinny, if there's no God?'

'O subtle and dear mother, I didn't say there wasn't God. I only said his Plan was too remote. Can't you hear God saying: "By the way, is that ball the Earth still rolling?" And an angel answering: "Oh! Yes, Sir, quite nicely." "Let's see, it must be fungused over by now. Wasn't there some particularly busy little parasite—"'

'Dinny!'

'"Oh! Yes, Sir, you mean man!" "Quite! I remember we called it that."'

'Dinny, how dreadful!'

'No, Mother, if I'm decent, it will be because decency is devised by humans for the benefit of humans; just as beauty is devised by humans for the delight of humans. Am I looking awful, darling? I feel as if I had no eyes. I think I'll go and lie down. I don't know why I've got so worked up about this, Mother. I think it must be looking at his face.' And with suspicious swiftness Dinny turned and went away.

Chapter Twenty-seven

Ferse's disappearance was a holiday to the feelings of one who had suffered greatly since his return. That he had engaged to end that holiday by finding him was not enough to spoil Adrian's relief. Almost with zest he set out for Hilary's in a taxi, applying his wits to the problem. Fear of publicity cut him off from those normal and direct resorts – Police, Radio, and Press. Such agencies would bring on Ferse too fierce a light. And in considering what means were left he felt as when confronted with a crossword puzzle, many of which he had solved in his time, like other men of noted intellect. From Dinny's account he could not tell within several hours at what time Ferse had gone out, and the longer he left enquiry in the neighbourhood of the house, the less chance one would have of stumbling on anyone who had seen him. Should he, then, stop the cab and go back to Chelsea? In holding on towards the Meads, he yielded to instinct rather than to reason. To turn to Hilary was second nature with him – and, surely, in such a task two heads were better than one! He reached the Vicarage without forming any plan save that of enquiring vaguely along the Embankment and the King's Road. It was not yet half-past nine, and Hilary was still at his correspondence. On hearing the news, he called his wife into the study.

'Let's think for three minutes,' he said, 'and pool the result.'

The three stood in a triangle before the fire, the two men smoking, and the woman sniffing at an October rose.

'Well?' said Hilary at last: 'Any light, May?'

'Only,' said Mrs Hilary, wrinkling her forehead, 'if the poor man was as Dinny describes, you can't leave out the hospitals. I could telephone to the three or four where there was most chance of his having been taken in, if he's made an accident for himself. It's so early still, they can hardly have had anybody in.'

'Very sweet of you, my dear; and we can trust your wits to keep his name out of it.'

Mrs Hilary went out.

'Adrian?'

'I've got a hunch, but I'd rather hear you first.'

'Well,' said Hilary, 'two things occur to me: It's obvious we must find out from the Police if anyone's been taken from the river. The other contingency, and I think it's the more likely, is drink.'

'But he couldn't get drink so early.'

'Hotels. He had money.'

'I agree, we must try them, unless you think my idea any good.'

'Well?'

'I've been trying to put myself in poor Ferse's shoes. I think, Hilary, if I had a doom over me, I might run for Condaford; not the place itself, perhaps, but round about, where we haunted as boys; where I'd been, in fact, before Fate got hold of me at all. A wounded animal goes home.'

Hilary nodded.

'Where *was* his home?'

'West Sussex – just under the Downs to the north. Petworth was the station.'

'Oh! I know that country. Before the war May and I used to stay a lot at Bignor and walk. We could have a shot at Victoria station, and see if anyone like him has taken a train. But I think I'll try the Police about the river first. I can say a parishioner is missing. What height is Ferse?'

'About five feet ten, square, broad head and cheek-bones,

strong jaw, darkish hair, steel-blue eyes, a blue suit and over-coat.'

'Right!' said Hilary: 'I'll get on to them as soon as May is through.'

Left to himself before the fire, Adrian brooded. A reader of detective novels, he knew that he was following the French, induc-tive method of a psychological shot in the blue, Hilary and May following the English model of narrowing the issue by elimination – excellent, but was there time for excellence? One vanished in London as a needle vanishes in hay; and they were so handi-capped by the need for avoiding publicity. He waited in anxiety for Hilary's report. Curiously ironical that he – *he* – should dread to hear of poor Ferse being found drowned or run over, and Diana free!

From Hilary's table he took up an A.B.C. There had been a train to Petworth at 8.50, another went at 9.56. A near thing! And he waited again, his eyes on the door. Useless to hurry Hilary, a past-master in saving time.

'Well?' he said when the door was opened.

Hilary shook his head.

'No go! Neither hospitals nor Police. No one received or heard of anywhere.'

'Then,' said Adrian, 'let's try Victoria – there's a train in twenty minutes. Can you come rightaway?'

Hilary glanced at his table. 'I oughtn't to, but I will. There's something unholy in the way a search gets hold of you. Hold on, old man, I'll tell May and nick my hat. You might look for a taxi. Go St Pancras way and wait for me.'

Adrian strode along looking for a taxi. He found one issuing from the Euston Road, turned it round, and stood waiting. Soon Hilary's thin dark figure came hurrying into view.

'Not in the training I was,' he said, and got in.

Adrian leaned through the window.

'Victoria, quick as you can!'

Hilary's hand slipped through his arm.

'I haven't had a jaunt with you, old man, since we went up the Carmarthen Van in that fog the year after the war. Remember?'

Adrian had taken out his watch.

'We just shan't do it, I'm afraid. The traffic's awful.' And they sat, silent, jerked back and forth by the spasmodic efforts of the taxi.

'I'll never forget,' said Adrian, suddenly, 'in France once, passing a "*maison d'aliénes*", as they call it – a great place back from the railway with a long iron grille in front. There was a poor devil standing upright with his arms raised and his legs apart, clutching at the grille, like an orang-utang. What's death compared with that? Good clean earth, and the sky over you. I wish now they'd found him in the river.'

'They may still; this is a bit of a wild-goose chase.'

'Three minutes more,' muttered Adrian; 'we shan't do it.'

But as if animated by its national character the taxi gathered unnatural speed, and the traffic seemed to melt before it. They pulled up at the station with a jerk.

'You ask at the first class, I'll go for the third,' said Hilary as they ran. 'A parson gets more show.'

'No,' said Adrian; 'if he's gone, he'll have gone first class; *you* ask there. If there's any doubt – *his eyes*.'

He watched Hilary's lean face thrust into the opening and quickly drawn back.

'He *has*!' he said; 'this train. Petworth! Rush!'

The brothers ran, but as they reached the barrier the train began to move. Adrian would have run on, but Hilary grabbed his arm.

'Steady, old man, we shall never get in; he'll only see us, and that'll spill it.'

They walked back to the entrance with their heads down.

'That was an amazing shot of yours, old boy,' said Hilary: 'What time does that train get down?'

'Twelve twenty-three.'

'Then we can do it in a car. Have you any money?'

Adrian felt in his pockets. 'Only eight and six,' he said ruefully.

'I've got just eleven bob. Awkward! I know! We'll take a cab to young Fleur's: if her car's not out, she'd let us have it, and she or Michael would drive us. We must both be free of the car at the other end.'

Adrian nodded, rather dazed at the success of his induction.

At South Square Michael was out, but Fleur in. Adrian, who did not know her so well as Hilary, was surprised by the quickness with which she grasped the situation and produced the car. Within ten minutes, indeed, they were on the road with Fleur at the wheel.

'I shall go through Dorking and Pulborough,' she said, leaning back. 'I can speed all the way after Dorking on that road. But, Uncle Hilary, what are you going to do if you get him?'

At that simple but necessary question the brothers looked at each other. Fleur seemed to feel their indecision through the back of her head, for she stopped with a jerk in front of an imperilled dog, and, turning, said:

'Would you like to think it over before we start?'

Gazing from her short clear-cut face, the very spit of hard, calm, confident youth, to his brother's long, shrewd face, wrinkled, and worn by the experiences of others and yet not hard, Adrian left it to Hilary to answer.

'Let's get on,' said Hilary; 'it's a case of making the best of what turns up.'

'When we pass a post-office,' added Adrian, 'please stop. I want to send a wire to Dinny.'

Fleur nodded. 'There's one in the King's Road, I must fill up, too, somewhere.'

And the car slid on among the traffic.

'What shall I say in the wire?' asked Adrian. 'Anything about Petworth?'

Hilary shook his head.

'Just that we think we're on the right track.'

When they had sent the wire there were only two hours left before the train arrived.

'It's fifty miles to Pulborough,' said Fleur, 'and I suppose about five on. I wonder if I can risk my petrol. I'll see at Dorking.' From that moment on she was lost to them, though the car was a closed saloon, giving all her attention to her driving.

The two brothers sat silent with their eyes on the clock and speedometer.

'I don't often go joy-riding,' said Hilary, softly: 'What are you thinking of, old man?'

'Of what on earth we're going to do.'

'If I were to think of that beforehand, in my job, I should be dead in a month. In a slum parish one lives, as in a jungle, surrounded by wild cats; one grows a sort of instinct and has to trust to it.'

'Oh!' said Adrian, 'I live among the dead, and get no practice.'

'Our niece drives well,' said Hilary in a low voice. 'Look at her neck. Isn't that capability personified?'

The neck, white, round and shingled, was held beautifully erect and gave a remarkable impression of quick close control of the body by the brain.

For several miles after that they drove in silence.

'Box Hill,' said Hilary: 'a thing once happened to me hereabouts I've never told you and never forgotten, it shows how awfully near the edge of mania we live.' He sunk his voice and went on: 'Remember that jolly parson Durcott we used to know? When I was at Beaker's before I went to Harrow, he was a master there; he took me on a walk one Sunday over Box Hill. Coming back in the train we were alone. We were ragging a little, when all of a sudden he seemed to go into a sort of frenzy, his eyes all greedy and wild. I hadn't the least notion what he was after and was awfully scared. Then, suddenly, he seemed to get hold of himself again. Right out of the blue! Repressed sex, of course – regular mania for the moment – pretty horrible. A very nice fellow, too. There are forces, Adrian.'

'Daemonic. And when they break the shell for good . . . Poor Ferse!'

Fleur's voice came back to them.

'She's beginning to go a bit wonky; I must fill up, Uncle Hilary. There's a station close here.'

'Right-o!'

The car drew up before the filling station.

'It's always slow work to Dorking,' said Fleur, stretching: 'we can get along now. Only thirty-two miles, and a good hour still. Have you thought?'

'No,' said Hilary, 'we've avoided it like poison.'

Fleur's eyes, whose whites were so clear, flashed on him one of those direct glances which so convinced people of her intelligence.

'Are you going to take him back in this? I wouldn't, if I were you.' And, taking out her case, she repaired her lips slightly, and powdered her short straight nose.

Adrian watched her with a sort of awe. Youth, up to date, did not come very much his way. Not her few words, but the implications in them impressed him. What she meant was crudely this: Let him dree his weird – you can do nothing. Was she right? Were he and Hilary just pandering to the human instinct for interference; attempting to lay a blasphemous hand on Nature? And yet for Diana's sake they must know what Ferse did, what he was going to do. For Ferse's sake they must see, at least, that he did not fall into the wrong hands. On his brother's face was a faint smile. He at least, thought Adrian, knew youth, had a brood of his own, and could tell how far the clear hard philosophy of youth would carry.

They started again, trailing through the traffic of Dorking's long and busy street.

'Clear at last,' said Fleur, turning her head, 'if you really want to catch him, you shall;' and she opened out to full speed. For the next quarter of an hour they flew along, past yellowing spinneys, fields and bits of furzy common dotted with geese and old horses, past village greens and village streets, and all the other evidences of a country life trying to retain its soul. And then the car, which had been travelling very smoothly, began to grate and bump.

'Tyre gone!' said Fleur, turning her head: 'That's torn it.'

She brought the car to a standstill, and they all got out. The off hind tyre was right down.

'Pipe to!' said Hilary, taking his coat off. 'Jack her up, Adrian. I'll get the spare wheel off.'

Fleur's head was lost in the tool-box, but her voice was heard saying: 'Too many cooks, better let me!'

Adrian's knowledge of cars was nil, his attitude to machinery helpless; he stood willingly aside, and watched them with admiration. They were cool, quick, efficient, but something was wrong with the jack.

'Always like that,' said Fleur, 'when you're in a hurry.'

Twenty minutes was lost before they were again in motion.

'I can't possibly do it now,' she said, 'but you'll be able to pick up his tracks easily, if you really want to. The station's right out beyond the town.'

Through Billingshurst and Pulborough and over Stopham bridge, they travelled at full speed.

'Better go for Petworth itself,' said Hilary, 'if he's heading back for the town, we shall meet him.'

'Am I to stop if we meet him?'

'No, carry straight on past and then turn.'

But they passed through Petworth and on for the mile and a half to the station without meeting him.

'The train's been in a good twenty minutes,' said Adrian, 'let's ask.'

A porter had taken the ticket of a gentleman in a blue overcoat and black hat. No! He had no luggage. He had gone off, towards the Downs. How long ago? Half an hour, maybe.

Regaining the car hastily they made towards the Downs.

'I remember,' said Hilary, 'a little further on there's a turn to Sutton. The point will be whether he's taken that or gone on up. There are some houses there somewhere. We'll ask, they may have seen him.'

Just beyond the turning was a little post-office, and a postman was cycling towards it from the Sutton road.

Fleur pulled the car to a walk alongside.

'Have you seen a gentleman in a blue coat and bowler hat making towards Sutton?'

'No, Miss, 'aven't passed a soul.'

'Thank you. Shall I carry on for the Downs, Uncle Hilary?'

Hilary consulted his watch.

'If I remember, it's a mile about to the top of the Down close to Duncton Beacon. We've come a mile and a half from the station; and he had, say, twenty-five minutes' start, so by the time we get to the top we should have about caught him. From the top we shall see the road ahead and be able to make sure. If we don't come on him, it'll mean he's taken to the Down – but which way?'

Adrian said under his breath: 'Homewards.'

'To the East?' said Hilary. 'On then, Fleur, not too fast.'

Fleur headed the car up the Downs road.

'Feel in my coat, you'll find three apples,' she said. 'I caught them up.'

'What a head!' said Hilary. 'But you'll want them yourself.'

'No. I'm slimming. You can leave me one.'

The brothers, munching each an apple, kept their eyes fixed on the woods on either side of the car.

'Too thick,' said Hilary; 'he'll be carrying on to the open. If you sight him, Fleur, stop dead.'

But they did not sight him, and, mounting slower and slower, reached the top. To their right was the round beech tree clump of Duncton, to the left the open Down; no figure was on the road in front.

'Not ahead,' said Hilary. 'We've got to decide, old man.'

'Take my advice, and let me drive you home, Uncle Hilary.'

'Shall we, Adrian?'

Adrian shook his head.

'I shall go on.'

'All right, I'm with you.'

'Look!' said Fleur suddenly, and pointed.

Some fifty yards in, along a rough track leaving the road to the left, lay a dark object.

'It's a coat, I think.'

Adrian jumped out and ran towards it. He returned with a blue overcoat over his arm.

'No doubt now,' he said. 'Either he was sitting there and left it by mistake, or he tired of carrying it. It's a bad sign, whichever it was. Come along, Hilary!'

He dropped the coat in the car.

'What orders for me, Uncle Hilary?'

'You've been a brick, my dear. Would you be still more of a brick and wait here another hour? If we're not back by then, go down and keep close along under the Downs slowly by way of Sutton Bignor and West Burton, then if there's no sign of us anywhere along that way, take the main road through Pulborough back to London. If you've any money to spare, you might lend us some.'

Fleur took out her bag.

'Three pounds. Shall I give you two?'

'Gratefully received,' said Hilary. 'Adrian and I never have any money. We're the poorest family in England, I do believe. Good-bye, my dear, and thank you! Now, old man!'

Chapter Twenty-eight

Waving their hands to where Fleur stood by her car with the remaining apple raised to her lips, the two brothers took the track on to the Down.

'You lead,' said Hilary; 'you've got the best eyes, and your clothes are less conspicuous. If you sight him, we'll consult.'

They came almost at once on a long stretch of high wire fence running across the Down.

'It ends there to the left,' said Adrian; 'we'll go round it above the woods; the lower we keep the better.'

They kept round it on the hillside over grass rougher and more uneven, falling into a climber's loping stride as if once more they were off on some long and difficult ascent. The doubt whether they would catch up with Ferse, what they could do if they did, and the knowledge that it might be a maniac with whom they had to deal, brought to both their faces a look that soldiers have, and sailors, and men climbing mountains, of out-staring what was before them.

They had crossed an old and shallow chalk working and were mounting the few feet to the level on its far side, when Adrian dropped back and pulled Hilary down.

'He's there,' he whispered; 'about seventy yards ahead!'

'See you?'

'No. He looks wild. His hat's gone, and he's gesticulating. What shall we do?'

'Put your head up through that bush.'

Adrian knelt, watching. Ferse had ceased to gesticulate, he was standing with arms crossed and his bare head bent. His back was to Adrian, and, but for that still, square, wrapped-in attitude, there was nothing to judge from. He suddenly uncrossed his arms, shook his head from side to side and began to walk rapidly on. Adrian waited till he had disappeared among the bushes on the slope, and beckoned Hilary to follow.

'We mustn't let him get too far ahead,' muttered Hilary, 'or we shan't know whether he's taken to the wood.'

'He'll keep to the open, he wants air, poor devil. Look out!' He pulled Hilary down again. The ground had suddenly begun to dip. It sloped right down to a grassy hollow, and halfway down the slope they could see Ferse plainly. He was walking slowly, clearly unconscious of pursuit. Every now and then his hands would go up to his bare head, as if to clear away something that entangled it.

'God!' murmured Adrian: 'I hate to see him.'

Hilary nodded.

They lay watching. Part of the weald was visible, rich with colour on that sunny autumn day. The grass, after heavy morning dew, was scented still; the sky of the dim spiritual blue that runs almost to white above the chalky downs. And the day was silent well-nigh to breathlessness. The brothers waited without speaking.

Ferse had reached the level at the bottom; they could see him dejectedly moving across a rough field towards a spinney. A pheasant rose just in front of him; they saw him start, as if wakened from a dream, and stand watching its rising flight.

'I expect he knows every foot round here,' said Adrian: 'he was a keen sportsman.' And just then Ferse threw up his hands as if they held a gun. There was something oddly reassuring in that action.

'Now,' said Hilary, as Ferse disappeared in the spinney, 'run!' They dashed down the hill, and hurried along over rough ground.

'Suppose,' gasped Adrian, 'that he's stopped in the spinney.'

'Risk it! Gently now, till we can see the rise.'

About a hundred yards beyond the spinney, Ferse was plodding slowly up the hill.

'All right so far,' murmured Hilary, 'we must wait till that rise flattens out and we lose sight of him. This is a queer business, old boy, for you and me. And at the end of it, as Fleur said: What?'

'We *must know*,' said Adrian.

'We're just losing him now. Let's give him five minutes. I'll time it.'

That five minutes seemed interminable. A jay squawked from the wooded hillside, a rabbit stole out and squatted in front of them; faint shiverings of air passed through the spinney.

'Now!' said Hilary. They rose, and breasted the grass rise at a good pace. 'If he comes back on his tracks, here—'

'The sooner it's face to face the better,' said Adrian, 'but if he sees us following he'll run, and we shall lose him.'

'Go slow, old man. It's beginning to flatten.'

Cautiously they topped the rise. The Down now dipped a little to where a chalky track ran above a beech wood to their left. There was no sign of Ferse.

'Either he's gone into the wood or he's through that next thicket, and on the rise again. We'd better hurry and make sure.'

They ran along the track between deep banks, and were turning into the brush, when the sound of a voice not twenty yards ahead jerked them to a standstill. They dropped back behind the bank and lay breathless. Somewhere in the thicket Ferse was muttering to himself. They could hear no words, but the voice gave them both a miserable feeling.

'Poor chap!' whispered Hilary: 'shall we go on, and try to comfort him?'

'Listen!'

There was the sound as of a branch cracking underfoot, a muttered oath, and then with appalling suddenness a huntsman's scream. It had a quality that froze the blood. Adrian said:

'Pretty ghastly! But he's broken covert.'

Cautiously they moved into the thicket; Ferse was running for the Down that rose from the end of it.

'He didn't see us, did he?'

'No, or he'd be looking back. Wait till we lose sight of him again.'

'This is poor work,' said Hilary, suddenly, 'but I agree with you it's got to be done. That was a horrible sound! But we must know exactly what we're going to do, old man.'

'I was thinking,' said Adrian, 'if we could induce him to come back to Chelsea, we'd keep Diana and the children away, dismiss the maids, and get him special attendants. I'd stay there with him till it was properly fixed. It seems to me that his own house is the only chance.'

'I don't believe he'll come of his free will.'

'In that case, God knows! I won't have a hand in caging him.'

'What if he tries to kill himself?'

'That's up to you, Hilary.'

Hilary was silent.

'Don't bet on my cloth,' he said, suddenly; 'a slum parson is pretty hard-boiled.'

Adrian gripped his hand. 'He's out of sight now.'

'Come on, then!'

They crossed the level at a sharp pace and began mounting the rise. Up there the character of the ground changed, the hill was covered sparsely by hawthorn bushes, and yew trees, and bramble, with here and there a young beech. It gave good cover, and they moved more freely.

'We're coming to the crossroads above Bignor,' murmured Hilary. 'He might take the track down from there. We could easily lose him!'

They ran, but suddenly stood still behind a yew tree.

'He's not going down,' said Hilary: 'Look!'

On the grassy open rise beyond the cross tracks, where a sign-post stood, Ferse was running towards the north side of the hill.

'A second track goes down there, I remember.'

'It's all chance, but we can't stop now.'

Ferse had ceased to run, he was walking slowly with stooped head up the rise. They watched him from behind their yew tree till he vanished over the hill's shoulder.

'Now!' said Hilary.

It was a full half mile, and both of them were over fifty.

'Not too fast, old man,' panted Hilary; 'we mustn't bust our bellows.'

They kept to a dogged jog, reached the shoulder, over which Ferse had vanished, and found a grass track trailing down.

'Slowly does it now,' gasped Hilary.

Here too the hillside was dotted with bushes and young trees, and they made good use of them till they came to a shallow chalk pit.

'Let's lie up here a minute, and get our wind. He's not going off the Down or we'd have seen him. Listen!'

From below them came a chanting sound. Adrian raised his head above the pit side and looked over. A little way down by the side of the track lay Ferse on his back. The words of the song he was droning out came up quite clearly:

> 'Must I go bound, and you go free?
> Must I love a lass that couldn't love me?
> Was e'er I taught so poor a wit
> As love a lass, would break my heart.'

He ceased and lay perfectly still; then, to Adrian's horror, his face became distorted; he flung his fists up in the air, cried out: 'I won't – I won't be mad!' and rolled over on his face.

Adrian dropped back.

'It's terrible! I must go down and speak to him.'

'We'll both go – round by the track – slow – don't startle him.'

They took the track which wound round the chalk pit. Ferse was no longer there.

'Quietly on, old son,' said Hilary.

They walked on in a curious calm, as if they had abandoned the chase.

'Who can believe in God?' said Adrian.

A wry smile contorted Hilary's long face.

'In God I believe, but not a merciful one as we understand the word. On this hillside, I remember, they trap. Hundreds of rabbits suffer the tortures of the damned. We used to let them out and knock them on the head. If my beliefs were known, I should be unfrocked. That wouldn't help. My job's a concrete one. Look! A fox!'

They stood a moment watching his low fulvous body steal across the track.

'Marvellous beast, a fox! Great places for wild life, these wooded chines; so steep, you can't disturb them – pigeons, jays, woodpeckers, rabbits, foxes, hares, pheasants – every mortal thing.'

The track had begun to drop, and Hilary pointed.

Ahead, beyond the dip into the chine they could see Ferse walking along a wire fence.

They watched till he vanished then reappeared on the side of the hill, having rounded the corner of the fence.

'What now?'

'He can't see us from there. To speak to him, we must somehow get near before we try, otherwise he'll just run.'

They crossed the dip and went up along and round the corner of the fence under cover of the hawthorns. On the uneven hillside Ferse had again vanished.

'This is wired for sheep,' said Hilary. 'Look! they're all over the hill – Southdowns.'

They reached a top. There was no sign of him.

They kept along the wire, and reaching the crest of the next rise, stood looking. Away to the left the hill dropped steeply into another chine; in front of them was open grass dipping to a wood. On their right was still the wire fencing and rough pasture.

Suddenly Adrian gripped his brother's arm. Not seventy yards away on the other side of the wire Ferse was lying face to the grass, with sheep grazing close to him. The brothers crawled to the shelter of a bush. From there, unseen, they could see him quite well, and they watched him in silence. He lay so still that the sheep were paying him no attention. Round-bodied, short-legged, snub-nosed, of a greyish white, and with the essential cosiness of the Southdown breed, they grazed on, undisturbed.

'Is he asleep, d'you think?'

Adrian shook his head. 'Peaceful, though.'

There was something in his attitude that went straight to the heart; something that recalled a small boy hiding his head in his mother's lap; it was as if the feel of the grass beneath his body, his face, his outstretched hands, were bringing him comfort; as if he were groping his way back into the quiet security of Mother Earth. While he lay like that it was impossible to disturb him.

The sun, in the west, fell on their backs, and Adrian turned his face to receive it on his cheek. All the nature-lover and country man in him responded to that warmth, to the scent of the grass, the song of the larks, the blue of the sky; and he noticed that Hilary too had turned his face to the sun. It was so still that, but for the larks' song and the muffled sound of the sheep cropping, one might have said Nature was dumb. No voice of man or beast, no whirr of traffic came up from the weald.

'Three o'clock. Have a nap, old man,' he whispered to Hilary; 'I'll watch.'

Ferse seemed asleep now. Surely his brain would rest from its disorder here. If there were healing in air, in form, in colour, it was upon this green cool hill for a thousand years and more undwelt on and freed from the restlessness of men. The men of old, indeed, had lived up there; but since then nothing had touched it but the winds and the shadows of the clouds. And today there was no wind, no cloud to throw soft and moving darkness on the grass.

So profound a pity for the poor devil, lying there as if he

would never move again, stirred Adrian that he could not think of himself, nor even feel for Diana. Ferse, so lying, awakened in him a sensation quite impersonal, the deep herding kinship men have for each other in the face of Fortune's strokes which seem to them unfair. Yes! He was sleeping now, grasping at the earth for refuge; to grasp for eternal refuge in the earth was all that was left him. And for those two quiet hours of watching that prostrate figure among the sheep, Adrian was filled not with futile rebellion and bitterness but with a strange unhappy wonder. The old Greek dramatists had understood the tragic plaything which the gods make of man; such understanding had been overlaid by the Christian doctrine of a merciful God. Merciful? – No! Hilary was right! Faced by Ferse's fate – what would one do? What – while the gleam of sanity remained? When a man's life was so spun that no longer he could do his job, be no more to his fellows than a poor distraught and frightening devil, the hour of eternal rest in quiet earth had surely come. Hilary had seemed to think so too; yet he was not sure what his brother would do if it came to the point. His job was with the living, a man who died was lost to him, so much chance of service gone! And Adrian felt a sort of thankfulness that his own job was with the dead, classifying the bones of men – the only part of men that did not suffer, and endured, age on age, to afford evidence of a marvellous animal. So he lay, and watched, plucking blade after blade of grass and rubbing the sweetness of them out between his palms.

The sun wore on due west, till it was almost level with his eyes; the sheep had ceased cropping and were moving slowly together over the hill, as if waiting to be folded. Rabbits had stolen out and were nibbling the grass; and the larks, one by one, had dropped from the sky. A chill was creeping on the air; the trees down in the weald had darkened and solidified; and the whitening sky seemed waiting for the sunset glow. The grass too had lost its scent; there was no dew as yet.

Adrian shivered. In ten minutes now the sun would be off the hill, and then it would be cold. When Ferse awoke, would he be better or worse? They must risk it. He touched Hilary, who lay with his knees drawn up, still sleeping. He woke instantly.

'Hallo, old man!'

'Hssh! He's still asleep. What are we to do when he wakes? Shall we go up to him now and wait for it?'

Hilary jerked his brother's sleeve. Ferse was on his feet. From behind their bush they could see him wildly looking round, as some animal warned of danger might stand gazing before he takes to flight. It was clear that he could not see them, but that he had heard or sensed some presence. He began walking towards the wire, crawled through and stood upright, turned towards the reddening sun balanced now like a fiery globe on the far wooded hill. With the glow from it on his face, bareheaded and so still that he might have been dead on his feet, he stood till the sun vanished.

'Now,' whispered Hilary, and stood up. Adrian saw Ferse come suddenly to life, fling out his arm with a wild defiance, and turn to run.

Hilary said, aghast: 'He's desperate. There's a chalk pit just above the main road. Come on, old man, come on!'

They ran, but stiffened as they were, had no chance with Ferse, who gained with every stride. He ran like a maniac, flinging his arms out, and they could hear him shout. Hilary gasped out:

'Stop! He's not going for that pit after all. It's away to the right. He's making for the wood down there. Better let him think we've given up.'

They watched him running down the slope, and lost him as, still running, he entered the wood.

'Now!' said Hilary.

They laboured on down to the wood and entered it as near to the point of his disappearance as they could. It was of beech and except at the edge there was no undergrowth. They stopped to listen, but there was no sound. The light in there was already dim, but the wood was narrow and they were soon at its far edge. Below they could see some cottages and farm buildings.

'Let's get down to the road.'

They hurried on, came suddenly to the edge of a high chalk pit, and stopped aghast.

'I didn't know of this,' said Hilary. 'Go that way and I'll go this along the edge.'

Adrian went upwards till he reached the top. Below, at the bottom some sixty steep feet down, he could see a dark thing lying. Whatever it was, it did not move, and no sound came up. Was this the end then, a headlong dive into the half dark? A choking sensation seized him by the throat, and for a moment he stood unable to call out or move. Then hastily he ran along the edge till he came to where Hilary was standing.

'Well?'

Adrian pointed back into the pit. They went on along the edge through undergrowth till they could scramble down, and make their way over the grassed floor of the old pit to the farther corner below the highest point.

The dark thing was Ferse. Adrian knelt and raised his head. His neck was broken; he was dead.

Whether he had dived deliberately to that end, or in his mad rush fallen over, they could not tell. Neither of them spoke, but Hilary put his hand on his brother's shoulder.

At last he said: 'There's a cart shed a little way along the road, but perhaps we ought not to move him. Stay with him, while I go on to the village and 'phone. It's a matter for the police, I suppose.'

Adrian nodded, still on his knees beside the broken figure.

'There's a post office quite near, I shan't be long.' Hilary hurried away.

Alone in the silent darkening pit Adrian sat cross-legged, with the dead man's head resting against him. He had closed the eyes and covered the face with his handkerchief. In the wood above birds rustled and chirped, on their way to bed. The dew had begun to fall, and into the blue twilight the ground mist of autumn was creeping. Shape was all softened, but the tall chalk pit face still showed white. Though not fifty yards from a road on which cars were passing, this spot where Ferse had leapt to his rest seemed to Adrian desolate, remote, and full of ghostliness. Though he knew that he ought to be thankful for Ferse, for Diana, for himself, he could feel nothing but that profound pity for a fellow man so tortured and broken in his prime – profound pity, and a sort of creeping identification with the mystery of Nature enwrapping the dead man and this his resting-place.

A voice roused him from that strange coma. An old whiskered countryman was standing there with a glass in his hand.

'So there been an accident, I year,' he was saying; 'a parson gentleman sent me with this. 'Tis brandy, sir.' He handed the glass to Adrian. 'Did 'e fall over yere, or what?'

'Yes, he fell over.'

'I allus said as they should put a fence up there. The gentleman said I was to tell you as the doctor and the police was comin'.'

'Thank you,' said Adrian, handing back the emptied glass.

'There be a nice cosy cart shed a little ways along the road maybe we could carry 'im along there.'

'We mustn't move him till they come.'

'Ah!' said the old countryman: 'I've read as there was a law about that, in case as 'twas murder or sooicide.' He peered down. 'He do look quiet, don't 'e? D'e know 'oo 'e is, Sir?'

'Yes. A Captain Ferse. He came from round here.'

'What, one of the Ferses o' Burton Rise? Why, I worked there as a boy; born in that parish I were.' He peered closer: 'This'd never be Mr Ronald, would it?'

Adrian nodded.

'Yeou don' say! There's none of 'em there neow. His grandfather died mad, so 'e did. Yeou don' say! Mr Ronald! I knew 'im as a young lad.' He stooped to look at the face in the last of the light, then stood, moving his whiskered head mournfully from side to side. To him – Adrian could see – it made all the difference that here was no 'foreigner'.

The sudden sputtering of a motorcycle broke the stillness; it came with a gleaming headlight down the cart track into the pit, and two figures got off. A young man and a girl. They came gingerly towards the group disclosed by the beam from the headlight, and stood, peering down.

'We heard there's been an accident.'

'Ah!' said the old countryman.

'Can we do anything?'

'No, thank you,' said Adrian; 'the doctor and the police are coming. We must just wait.'

He could see the young man open his mouth as if to ask more, close it without speaking, and put his arm round the girl, then, like the old countryman, they stood silent with their eyes fixed on the figure with the broken neck lying against Adrian's knee. The cycle's engine, still running, throbbed in the silence, and its light made even more ghostly the old pit and the little group of the living around the dead.

Chapter Twenty-nine

t Condaford, the telegram came just before dinner. It ran: 'Poor F dead down chalk pit here Removed to Chichester Adrian and I going with him Inquest will be there. Hilary.'

Dinny was in her room when it was brought to her, and she sat down on her bed with that feeling of constriction in the chest which comes when relief and sorrow struggle together for expression. Here was what she had prayed for, and all she could think of was the last sound she had heard him utter, and the look on his face, when he was standing in the doorway listening to Diana singing. She said to the maid who had brought in the telegram:

'Amy, find Scaramouch.'

When the Scotch terrier came with his bright eyes and his air of knowing that he was of value, she clasped him so tight that he became uneasy. With that warm and stiffly hairy body in her arms, she regained the power of feeling; relief covered the background of her being, but pity forced tears into her eyes. It was a curious state, and beyond the comprehension of her dog. He licked her nose and wriggled till she set him down. She finished dressing hurriedly and went to her mother's room.

Lady Cherrell, dressed for dinner, was moving between open wardrobe and open chest of drawers, considering what she could best part with for the approaching jumble sale which must keep the village nursing fund going over the year's end. Dinny put the telegram into her hand without a word. Having read it, she said quietly:

'That's what you prayed for, dear.'

'Does it mean suicide?'

'I think so.'

'Ought I to tell Diana now, or wait till she's had a night's sleep?'

'Now, I think. *I* will, if you like.'

'No, no, darling. It's up to me. She'll like dinner upstairs, I expect. Tomorrow, I suppose, we shall have to go to Chichester.'

'This is all very dreadful for you, Dinny.'

'It's good for me.' She took back the telegram and went out.

Diana was with the children, who were giving as long as possible to the process of going to bed, not having reached the age when to do such a thing has become desirable. Dinny beckoned her out into her own room, and, once more without a word, handed over the telegram. Though she had been so close to Diana these last days, there were sixteen years between them, and she made no consoling gesture as she might have to one of her own age. She had, indeed, a feeling of never quite knowing how Diana would take things. She took this stonily. It might have been no news at all. Her beautiful face, fine and worn as that on a coin, expressed nothing. Her eyes fixed on Dinny's, remained dry and clear. All she said was: 'I won't come down. Tomorrow – Chichester?'

Checking all impulse, Dinny nodded and went out. Alone with her mother after dinner, she said:

'I wish I had Diana's self-control.'

'Self-control like hers is the result of all she's been through.'

'There's the Vere de Vere touch about it, too.'

'That's no bad thing, Dinny.'

'What will this inquest mean?'

'She'll need all her self-control there, I'm afraid.'

'Mother, shall I have to give evidence?'

'You were the last person who spoke to him so far as is known, weren't you?'

'Yes. Must I speak of his coming to the door last night?'

'I suppose you ought to tell everything you know, if you're asked.'

A flush stained Dinny's cheeks.

'I don't think I will. I never even told Diana that. And I don't see what it has to do with outsiders.'

'No, I don't see either; but we're not supposed to exercise our own judgments as to that.'

'Well, I shall; I'm not going to pander to people's beastly curiosity, and give Diana pain.'

'Suppose one of the maids heard him?'

'They can't prove that *I* did.'

Lady Cherrell smiled. 'I wish your father were here.'

'You are not to tell Dad what I told you, Mother. I can't have the male conscience fussing around; the female's is bad enough, but one has it in hand.'

'Very well.'

'I shan't have the faintest scruple,' said Dinny, fresh from her recollection of London Police Courts, 'about keeping a thing dark, if I can safely. What do they want an inquest for, anyway? He's dead. It's just morbidity.'

'I oughtn't to aid and abet you, Dinny.'

'Yes, you ought, Mother. You know you agree at heart.'

Lady Cherrell said no more. She did . . .

The General and Alan Tasburgh came down next morning by the first train, and half an hour later they all started in the open car; Alan driving, the General beside him, and in the back seat Lady Cherrell, Dinny and Diana wedged together. It was a long and gloomy drive. Leaning back with her nose just visible above her fur, Dinny pondered. It was dawning on her gradually that she was in some sort the hub of the approaching inquest. She it was to whom Ferse had opened his heart; she who had taken the children away; she who had gone down in the night to telephone; she who had heard what she did not mean to tell; and, lastly but much the most importantly, it must be she who had called in Adrian and Hilary. Only behind her, their niece, who had caused Diana to turn to them for assistance when Ferse vanished, could Adrian's friendship for Diana be masked. Like everybody else, Dinny read, and even enjoyed, the troubles and scandals of others, retailed in the papers; like everybody else, she revolted against the papers having anything that could be made into scandal to retail about her family or her friends. If it came out crudely that her uncle had been applied to as an old and intimate friend of Diana's, he and she would be asked all sorts of questions, leading to all sorts of suspicions in the sex-ridden minds of the Public. Her roused imagination roamed freely. If Adrian's long and close friendship with Diana became known, what would there be to prevent the Public from suspecting even that her uncle had pushed Ferse over the edge of that chalk pit, unless, of course, Hilary were with him – for as yet they knew no details. Her mind, in fact, began running before the hounds. A lurid explanation of anything was so much more acceptable than a dull and true one! And there hardened within her an almost vicious determination to cheat the Public of the thrills it would be seeking.

Adrian met them in the hall of the hotel at Chichester, and she took her chance to say: 'Uncle, can I speak to you and Uncle Hilary privately?'

'Hilary had to go back to Town, my dear, but he'll be down the last thing this evening; we can have a talk then. The inquest's tomorrow.'

With that she had to be content.

When he had finished his story, determined that Adrian should not take Diana to see Ferse, she said: 'If you'll tell us where to go, Uncle, *I'll* go with Diana.'

Adrian nodded. He had understood.

When they reached the mortuary, Diana went in alone, and Dinny waited in a corridor which smelled of disinfectant and looked out on to a back street. A fly, disenchanted by the approach of winter, was crawling dejectedly up the pane. Gazing out into that colourless back alley, under a sky drained of all warmth and light, she felt very miserable. Life seemed exceptionally bleak, and heavy with sinister issues. This inquest, Hubert's impending fate – no light or sweetness anywhere! Not even the thought of Alan's palpable devotion gave her comfort.

She turned to see Diana again beside her, and, suddenly forgetting her own woe, threw an arm round her and kissed her cold cheek. They went back to the hotel without speaking, except for Diana's: 'He looked marvellously calm.'

She went early to her room after dinner, and sat there with a book, waiting for her uncles. It was ten o'clock before Hilary's cab drew up, and a few minutes later they came. She noted how shadowy and worn they both looked; but there was something reassuring in their faces. They were the sort who ran till they dropped, anyway. They both kissed her with unexpected warmth, and sat down sideways, one on each side of her bed. Dinny stood between them at the foot and addressed Hilary.

'It's about Uncle Adrian, Uncle. I've been thinking. This inquest is going to be horrid if we don't take care.'

'It is, Dinny. I came down with a couple of journalists who didn't suspect my connection. They've got hold of the Mental Home, and are all agog. I've a great respect for journalists, they do their job very thoroughly.'

Dinny addressed Adrian.

'You won't mind my talking freely, will you, Uncle?'

Adrian smiled. 'No, Dinny. You're a loyal baggage; go ahead!'

'It seems to me, then,' she went on, plaiting her fingers on the bed-rail, 'that the chief point is to keep Uncle Adrian's friendship for Diana out of it, and I thought that the asking of you two to find him ought to be put entirely on to me. You see, I was the last person known to speak to him, when he cut the telephone wire, you know, so, when I'm called, I could get it into their minds that you were entirely my suggestion, as a couple of Uncles who were clever and good at crossword puzzles. Otherwise, why did we go to Uncle Adrian? Because he was *such a friend*, and then you'd get at once all that they may think that means, especially when they hear that Captain Ferse was away four years.'

There was silence before Hilary said:

'She's wise, old boy. Four years' friendship with a beautiful woman in a husband's absence means only one thing with a jury, and many things with the Public.'

Adrian nodded. 'But I don't see how the fact that I've known them both so long can be concealed.'

'First impressions,' said Dinny eagerly, 'will be everything. I can say that Diana suggested going to her doctor and Michael, but that I overruled her, knowing that you were marvellous at tracing things out because of your job, and could get at Uncle Hilary, who was so good at human nature. If we *start* them right, I don't believe the mere fact that you knew both of them would matter. It seems to me awfully important that I should be called as early as possible.'

'It's putting a lot on you, my dear.'

'Oh! no. If I'm not called before you and Uncle Hilary, will you both say that it was I who came and asked you, and I can rub it in afterwards?'

'After the doctor and the police, Diana will be the first witness.'

'Yes, but I can speak to her, so that we shall all be saying the same thing.'

Hilary smiled. 'I don't see why not, it's very white lying. I can put in that I've known them as long as you, Adrian. We both met Diana first at that picnic Lawrence gave near the Land's End, when she was a flapper, and we both met Ferse first at her wedding. Family friendship, um?'

'My visits to the Mental Home will come out,' said Adrian, 'the Doctor's been summoned as witness.'

'Oh! well,' said Dinny, 'you went there as his friend, and specially interested in mental derangement. After all, you're supposed to be scientific, Uncle.'

Both smiled, and Hilary said: 'All right, Dinny, we'll speak to the Sergeant, he's a very decent chap, and get you called early, if possible.' He went to the door.

'Good-night, little serpent,' said Adrian.

'Good-night, dear Uncle; you look terribly tired. Have you got a hot water-bottle?'

Adrian shook his head. 'I've nothing but a toothbrush which I bought today.'

Dinny hauled her bottle out of her bed, and forced it on him. 'Shall I speak to Diana, then, about what we've been saying?'

'If you will, Dinny.'

'After tomorrow the sun will shine.'

'Will it?' said Adrian.

As the door closed, Dinny sighed. Would it? Diana seemed as if dead to feeling. And – there was Hubert's business!

Chapter Thirty

The reflections of Adrian and his niece, when together they entered the Coroner's Court on the following day, might have been pooled as follows:

A coroner's inquest was like roast beef and Yorkshire pudding on Sundays, devised for other times. When Sunday afternoons were devoted to games, murders infrequent, and suicides no longer buried at crossroads, neither custom had its initial wisdom. In old days, Justice and its emissaries were regarded as the foes of mankind, so it was natural to interpose a civilian arbiter between death and the Law. In an age in which one called the police 'a splendid force' was there not something unnatural in supposing them incapable of judging when it was necessary for them to take action? Their incompetence, therefore, could not well be considered the reason for the preservation of these rites. The cause was, surely, in one's dread of being deprived of knowledge. Every reader of a newspaper felt that the more he or she heard about what was doubtful, sensational, and unsavoury, the better for his or her soul. One knew that, without coroners' inquests, there would often be no published enquiry at all into sensational death; and never two enquiries. If, then, in place of no enquiry one could always have one enquiry, and in place of one enquiry sometimes have two enquiries, how much pleasanter! The dislike which one had for being nosy disappeared the moment one got into a crowd. The nosier one could be in a crowd the happier one felt. And the oftener one could find room in a Coroner's Court, the greater the thankfulness to Heaven. 'Praise God from whom all blessings flow' could never go up more fervently than from the hearts of such as had been privileged to find seats at an enquiry about death. For an enquiry about death nearly always meant the torture of the living, and than that was anything more calculated to give pleasure?

The fact that the Court was full confirmed these reflections and they passed on into a little room to wait. Adrian saying: 'You go in fifth wicket down, Dinny, both Hilary and I are taken before you. If we keep out of Court till we're wanted they can't say we copied each other.'

They sat very silent in the little bare room. The police, the doctor, Diana and Hilary had all to be examined first.

'It's like the ten little nigger boys,' murmured Dinny. Her eyes were fixed on a calendar on the wall opposite; she could not read it, but it seemed necessary.

'See, my dear,' said Adrian, and drew a little bottle from his breast pocket, 'take a sip or two of this – not more – it's fifty-fifty sal volatile and water; it'll steady you no end. Be careful!'

Dinny took a little gulp. It burned her throat, but not too badly.

'You too, Uncle.'

Adrian also took a cautious gulp.

'No finer dope,' he said, 'before going in to bat, or anything like that.'

And they again sat silent, assimilating the fumes. Presently Adrian said:

'If spirits survive, as I don't believe, what is poor Ferse thinking of this farce? We're still barbarians. There's a story of Maupassant's about a Suicide Club that provided a pleasant form of death to those who felt they had to go. I don't believe in suicide for the sane, except in very rare cases. We've got to stick things out; but for the insane, or those threatened with it, I wish we had that Club, Dinny. Has that stuff steadied you?'

Dinny nodded.

'It'll last pretty well an hour.' He got up. 'My turn, I see. Good-bye, my dear, good luck! Stick in a "Sir", to the Coroner, now and then.'

Watching him straighten himself as he passed through the door, Dinny felt a sort of inspiration. Uncle Adrian was the man she admired most of any she had ever seen. And she sent up a little illogical prayer for him. Certainly that stuff had steadied her; the sinking, fluttering feeling she had been having was all gone. She took out her pocket mirror and powder-puff. She could go to the stake, anyway, with a nose that did not shine.

Another quarter of an hour, however, passed before she was called, and she spent it, with her eyes still fixed on that calendar, thinking of Condaford and recalling all her pleasantest times there. The old days of its unrestored state, when she was very small, hayfield days, and picnics in the woods; pulling lavender, riding on the retriever, promotion to the pony when Hubert was at school; days of pure delight in a new, fixed home, for, though she had been born there, she had been nomadic till she was four – at Aldershot, and Gibraltar. She remembered with special pleasure winding the golden silk off the cocoons of her silk-worms, how they had made her think of creeping, crawling elephants, and how peculiar had been their smell.

'Elizabeth Charwell.'

Nuisance to have a name that everyone pronounced wrong as a matter of course! And she rose, murmuring to herself:

'One little nigger, walking all alone,
Up came a coroner, and then there was none.'

Someone took charge of her on her entry, and, taking her across the Court, placed her in a sort of pen. It was fortunate that she had been in such places lately, for it all felt rather familiar, and even faintly comic. The jury in front of her looked as it were disused, the coroner had a funny importance. Down there, not far to her left, were the other little niggers; and, behind them, stretching to the blank wall, dozens and dozens and dozens of faces in rows, as of sardines set up on their tails in a huge sardine box. Then aware that she was being addressed, she concentrated on the coroner's face.

'Your name is Elizabeth Cherrell. You are the daughter, I believe, of Lieutenant-General Sir Conway Cherrell, K.C.B., C.M.G., and Lady Charwell?'

Dinny bowed. 'I believe he likes me for that,' she thought.

'And you live with them at Condaford Grange in Oxfordshire?'

'Yes.'

'I believe, Miss Cherrell, that you were staying with Captain and Mrs Ferse up to the morning on which Captain Ferse left his house?'

'I was.'

'Are you a close friend of theirs?'

'Of Mrs Ferse. I had seen Captain Ferse only once, I think, before his return.'

'Ah! his return. Were you staying with Mrs Ferse when he returned?'

'I had come up to stay with her on that very afternoon.'

'The afternoon of his return from the Mental Home?'

'Yes, I actually went to stay at their house the following day.'

'And were you there until Captain Ferse left his house?'

'I was.'

'During that time what was his demeanour?'

At this question for the first time Dinny realised the full disadvantage of not knowing what has been said already. It almost looked as if she must say what she really knew and felt.

'He seemed to me quite normal, except that he would not go

out or see anybody. He looked quite healthy, only his eyes made one feel unhappy.'

'How do you mean exactly?'

'They – they looked like a fire behind bars, they seemed to flicker.'

And, at those words, she noticed that the jury for a moment looked a trifle less disused.

'He would not go out, you say? Was that during the whole time you were there?'

'No; he went out on the day before he left his home. He was out all that day, I believe.'

'You believe? Were you not there?'

'No; that morning I took the two children down to my mother's at Condaford Grange, and returned in the evening just before dinner. Captain Ferse was not in then.'

'What made you take the children down?'

'Mrs Ferse asked me to. She had noticed some change in Captain Ferse, and she thought the children would be better away.'

'Could you say that you had noticed a change?'

'Yes. I thought he seemed more restless, and, perhaps, suspicious; and he was drinking more at dinner.'

'Nothing very striking?'

'No. I—'

'Yes, Miss Cherrell?'

'I was going to say something that I don't know of my own knowledge.'

'Something that Mrs Ferse had told you?'

'Yes.'

'Well, you needn't tell us that.'

'Thank you, Sir.'

'Coming back to when you returned from taking the children to your home, Captain Ferse was not in, you say; was Mrs Ferse in?'

'Yes, she was dressed for dinner. I dressed quickly and we dined alone together. We were very anxious about him.'

'And then?'

'After dinner we went up to the drawing room, and to distract her I made Mrs Ferse sing, she was so nervous and anxious. After a little we heard the front door, and Captain Ferse came in and sat down.'

'Did he say anything?'

'No.'

'How was he looking?'

'Dreadful, I thought. Very strange and strained, as if under the power of some terrible thought.'

'Yes?'

'Mrs Ferse asked him if he had had dinner, and if he would like to go to bed; and if he would see a doctor; but he wouldn't speak – he sat with his eyes closed, almost as if he might be asleep, until at last I whispered: "Is he asleep, d'you think?" Then suddenly he cried out: "Sleep! I'm for it again, and I won't stand it. By God! I won't stand it."'

When she had repeated those words of Ferse, Dinny understood better than hitherto what is meant by the expression 'sensation in Court'; in some mysterious way she had supplied what had been lacking to the conviction carried by the witnesses who had preceded her. Whether she had been wise in this, she was utterly unable to decide; and her eyes sought Adrian's face. He gave her an almost imperceptible nod.

'Yes, Miss Cherrell?'

'Mrs Ferse went towards him, and he cried out: "Leave me alone. Go away!" I think she said: "Ronald, won't you see someone just to give you something to make you sleep?" but he sprang up and cried out violently: "Go away! I'll see no one – no one!"'

'Yes, Miss Cherrell, what then?'

'We were frightened. We went up to my room and consulted, and I said we ought to telephone.'

'To whom?'

'To Mrs Ferse's doctor. She wanted to go, but I prevented her and ran down. The telephone was in the little study on the ground floor, and I was just getting the number when I felt my hand seized, and there was Captain Ferse behind me. He cut the wire with a knife. Then he stood holding my arm, and I said: "That's silly, Captain Ferse; you know we wouldn't hurt you." He let me go, and put his knife away, and told me to put on my shoes, because I had them in my other hand.'

'You mean you had taken them off?'

'Yes, to run down quietly. I put them on. He said: "I'm not going to be messed about. I shall do what I like with myself." I said: "You know we only want your good." And he said: "I know that good – no more of that for me." And then he looked out of the window and said: "It's raining like hell," and turned to me and cried: "Get out of this room, quick. Get out!" and I flew back upstairs again.'

Dinny paused and took a long breath. This second living through those moments was making her heart beat. She closed her eyes.

'Yes, Miss Cherrell, what then?'

She opened her eyes. There was the coroner still, and there the jury with their mouths a little open, as it seemed.

'I told Mrs Ferse. We didn't know what to do or what was coming – we didn't see what we could do, and I suggested that we should drag the bed against the door and try to sleep.'

'And did you?'

'Yes; but we were awake a long time. Mrs Ferse was so exhausted that she did sleep at last, and I think I did towards morning. Anyway the maid woke me by knocking.'

'Did you hear nothing further of Captain Ferse during the night?'

The old school-boy saying 'If you tell a lie, tell a good 'un,' shot through her mind, and she said firmly: 'No, nothing.'

'What time was it when you were called?'

'Eight o'clock. I woke Mrs Ferse and we went down at once. Captain Ferse's dressing room was in disorder, and he seemed to have lain upon the bed; but he was nowhere in the house; and his hat and overcoat were gone from the chair where he had thrown them down in the hall.'

'What did you do then?'

'We consulted, and Mrs Ferse wanted to go to her doctor and to her cousin and mine, Mr Michael Mont, the Member of Parliament; but I thought if I could get my uncles they would be better able to trace Captain Ferse; so I persuaded her to come with me to my Uncle Adrian and ask him to get my Uncle Hilary and see if they could find Captain Ferse. I knew they were both very clever men and very tactful,' Dinny saw the coroner bow slightly towards her uncles, and hurried on, 'and they were old family friends; I thought if they couldn't manage to find him without publicity, nobody could. So we went to my Uncle Adrian, and he agreed to get my Uncle Hilary to help him and try; then I took Mrs Ferse down with me to the children at Condaford, and that's all I know, Sir.'

The coroner bowed quite low towards her and said: 'Thank you, Miss Cherrell. You have given your evidence admirably.' The jury moved uneasily as if trying to bow too, and Dinny, with an effort, stepped down from the pen and took her seat beside Hilary, who put his hand on hers. She sat very still, and then was conscious that a tear, as it were the last of the sal volatile, was moving slowly down her cheek. Listening dully to what followed, the evidence of the Doctor in charge of the Mental Home, and the coroner's address, then waiting dumbly for the jury's verdict, she suffered from the feeling that in her loyalty to the living she had been disloyal to the dead. It was a horrid sensation, that: of having borne evidence of mania against one who could not defend or explain himself; and it was with a fearful interest that she watched the jury file back into their seats, and the foreman stand up in answer to the demand for their verdict.

'We find that the deceased died from falling down a chalk pit.'

'That,' said the coroner, 'is death from misadventure.'

'We wish to express our sympathy with the widow.'

Dinny almost clapped her hands. So! They had given him the benefit of the doubt – those disused men! And with a sudden, almost personal, warmth she tilted her head up and smiled at them.

Chapter Thirty-one

*W*hen she had come to from smiling, Dinny perceived that her uncle was looking at her quizzically.

'Can we go now, Uncle Hilary?'

'It would be as well, Dinny, before you've quite vamped the foreman.'

Outside, in the damp October air, for the day was English autumn personified, she said:

'Let's go for a little breather, Uncle, and get the smell of that Court out of us.'

They turned down towards the distant sea, walking at a good pace.

'I'm frightfully anxious to know what went before me, Uncle; did I say anything contradictory?'

'No. It came out at once in Diana's evidence that Ferse had come back from the Home, and the coroner treated her tenderly. It was lucky they called me before Adrian, so that his evidence was only a repetition of mine, and he was in no way conspicuous. I feel quite sorry for the journalists. Juries avoid suicide and unsound mind when they can, and, after all, we don't know what happened to poor Ferse at that last minute. He may quite easily have run on over the edge, it was pretty blind there and the light was failing.'

'Do you really think that, Uncle?'

Hilary shook his head. 'No, Dinny. I think he meant to do it all along, and that was the nearest place to his old home. And, though I say it that shouldn't, thank God he did, and is at rest.'

'Yes, oh! yes! What will happen to Diana and Uncle Adrian, now?'

Hilary filled his pipe and stopped to light it. 'Well, my dear, I've given Adrian some advice. I don't know whether he'll take it, but you might back it up if you get a chance. He's waited all these years. He'd better wait another.'

'Uncle, I agree terribly.'

'Oh!' said Hilary, surprised.

'Yes. Diana is simply not fit to think even of him. She ought to be left to herself and the children.'

'I'm wondering,' said Hilary, 'whether one couldn't wangle some "bones" expedition that would take him out of England for a year.'

'Hallorsen!' said Dinny, clasping her hands: 'He's going again. And he loves Uncle Adrian.'

'Good! But would he take him?'

'If *I* asked him,' said Dinny, simply.

Hilary again gave her a quizzical look. 'What a dangerous young woman you are! I daresay the Trustees would give Adrian leave. I can set old Shropshire and Lawrence on to it. We must go back now, Dinny. I've got to catch a train. It's distressing, because this air smells good; but the Meads are pining for me.'

Dinny slipped her hand through his arm.

'I do admire you, Uncle Hilary.'

Hilary stared. 'I doubt if I follow you, my dear.'

'Oh! you know what I mean: you've got all the old "I serve" tradition, and that kind of thing; and yet you're so frightfully up-to-date, and tolerant, and free-thinking.'

'H'm!' said Hilary, emitting a cloud of smoke.

'I'm sure you believe in birth control?'

'Well,' said Hilary, 'the position there is ironical for us parsons. It used to be considered unpatriotic to believe in limiting our population. But now that flying and poison gas have made food for powder unnecessary, and unemployment is rampant, I'm afraid there's no question but that it's unpatriotic *not* to believe in limiting our population. As for our Christian principles; being patriots, we didn't apply the Christian principle "Thou shalt not kill" during the war, so, being patriots, we can't logically apply the Christian principle "Thou shalt not limit" now. Birth control is essential for the slums anyway.'

'And you don't believe in hell.'

'I do, they've got it.'

'You support games on Sundays, don't you?' Hilary nodded. 'And sun bathing with nothing on?'

'I might, if there were any sun.'

'And pyjamas and smoking for women.'

'Not stinkers; emphatically not stinkers.'

'I call that undemocratic.'

'I can't help it, Dinny. Sniff!' And he puffed some smoke at her.

Dinny sniffed. 'There's latakia in that, it does smell good; but women can't smoke pipes. I suppose we all have a blind spot somewhere, and yours is: "No stinkers." Apart from that you're amazingly modern, Uncle. When I was in that Court looking at all those people, it seemed to me that yours was the only really modern face.'

'It's a Cathedral town, my dear.'

'Well, I think the amount of modernity is awfully overestimated.'

'You don't live in London, Dinny. All the same, you're right in a way. Frankness about things is not change. The difference between the days of my youth and today is only the difference of expression. We had doubts, we had curiosity, we had desires; but we didn't express them. Now they do. I see a lot of young 'Varsity men – they come and work in the Meads, you know. Well, from their cradles they've been brought up to say whatever comes into their heads, and just don't they? We didn't, you know; but the same things came into our heads. That's all the difference. That and cars.'

'Then I'm still old-fashioned. I'm not a bit good at expressing things.'

'That's your sense of humour, Dinny. It acts as a restraint, and keeps you self-conscious. Few young people nowadays seem to have much sense of humour; they often have wit – it isn't the same thing. Our young writers, and painters and musicians, could they carry on as they do if they could see a joke against themselves? Because that's the real test of humour.'

'I'll think that over.'

'Yes, but don't lose your sense of humour, Dinny. It's the scent to the rose. Are you going back to Condaford now?'

'I expect so, Hubert's remand won't be till after that mail boat comes in, and that's not for ten days yet.'

'Well, give my love to Condaford. I don't suppose I'll ever have days again quite so good as when we were children there.'

'That's what I was thinking, Uncle, when I was waiting to be the last little nigger boy.'

'You're a bit young for that conclusion, Dinny. Wait till you're in love.'

'I am.'

'What, in love?'

'No, in waiting.'

'Fearsome process, being in love,' said Hilary. 'Still, I never regretted it.'

Dinny gazed at him sideways, and her teeth showed.

'What if you took it again, Uncle?'

'Ah! there,' said Hilary, knocking his pipe out on a pillar box, 'I'm definitely out of it. In my profession we can't run to it. Besides, I've never really got over my first attack.'

'No,' said Dinny, with compunction, 'Aunt May's such a duck.'

'You've said a mouthful. Here's the station. Good-bye, and bless you! I sent my bag down this morning.' He waved his hand and was gone.

On reaching the hotel Dinny sought Adrian. He was not in,

and, rather disconsolate, she wandered out again into the Cathedral. She was just about to sit down and take its restful beauty in, when she saw her Uncle standing against a column with his eyes fixed on the rose window. Going up she slid her arm through his. He squeezed it, but said nothing.

'Fond of glass, Uncle?'

'Terribly fond of good glass, Dinny. Ever see York Minster?'

Dinny shook her head: then, conscious that nothing she could say would lead up to what she wanted to say, she asked directly: 'What are you going to do now, Uncle dear?'

'Have you been talking to Hilary?'

'Yes.'

'He wants me to keep away for a year.'

'So do I.'

'It's a long time, Dinny; I'm getting on.'

'Would you go on Professor Hallorsen's expedition if he wanted you?'

'He wouldn't want me.'

'Yes, he would.'

'I could only go if I were certain that Diana wished it.'

'She would never say so, but I'm quite sure she wants complete rest for a long time.'

'When you worship the sun,' said Adrian, very low, 'it is hard to go where the sun never shines.'

Dinny squeezed his arm. 'I know; but you'd have it to look forward to. And it's a nice healthy expedition this time, only to New Mexico. You'd come back very young, with hair all down the outsides of your legs. They do in the films. You'd be irresistible, Uncle; and I do want you to be irresistible. All that's wanted is to let the tumult and the shouting die.'

'And my job?'

'Oh! that can be wangled all right. If Diana doesn't have to think of anything for a year, she'll be a different creature, and you will seem like the promised land. I do feel I know what I'm talking about.'

'You're an endearing little serpent,' said Adrian, with his shadowy smile.

'Diana is pretty badly wounded.'

'I sometimes think it's a mortal wound, Dinny.'

'No, no!'

'Why should she think of me again, if I once go away?'

'Because women are like that.'

'What do you know about women, at your age? I went away long ago, and she thought of Ferse. I fancy I'm made of the wrong stuff.'

'If you are, New Mexico's the very place. You'll come back a "he-man". Think of that! I promise to watch over her, and the children will keep you to the fore. They're always talking of you. And I'll see that they go on doing it.'

'It's certainly curious,' said Adrian, impersonally, 'but I feel she's further from me now than when Ferse was alive.'

'For the moment, and it'll be a long moment. But I know it'll dry straight in the long run. Really, Uncle.'

Adrian was silent a long time. Then he said:

'I'll go, Dinny, if Hallorsen will take me.'

'He shall. Bend down, Uncle. I *must* kiss you.'

Adrian bent down. The kiss lighted on his nose. A verger coughed . . .

The return to Condaford was made by car that afternoon in precisely the same order, young Tasburgh driving. He had been extremely tactful during these twenty-four hours, had not proposed at all, and Dinny was proportionately grateful. If Diana wanted peace, so did she. Alan left that same evening, Diana and the children the following day, and Clare came back from her long stay in Scotland, so that none but her own family were at the Grange. Yet had she no peace. For now that the preoccupation with poor Ferse was gone, she was oppressed and worried by the thought of Hubert. Extraordinary what power of disturbance was in that overhanging issue! He and Jean wrote cheerfully from the East Coast. According to themselves they were not worrying. Dinny was. And she knew that her mother, and even more her father, were. Clare was more angry than worried, and the effect of anger on her was to stimulate her energy, so that she went out 'cubbing' with her father; and in the afternoons would disappear with the car to neighbouring houses, where she would often stay till after dinner. The festive member of the family, she was always in great request. Dinny had her anxiety to herself. She had written to Hallorsen about her uncle, sending him the promised photograph, which depicted her in her presentation frock of two years back, when she and Clare had been economically presented together. Hallorsen answered promptly: 'The picture is just too lovely. Nothing will please me more than to take your uncle. I am getting in touch with him rightaway': he signed himself 'Always your devoted servant.'

She read the letter gratefully, but without a tremor, and called herself a hard-hearted beast. Her mind thus set at rest about Adrian, for she knew his year of leave could be safely left to Hilary, she thought all the time of Hubert with a growing presentiment of evil. She tried to persuade herself that this came from having nothing particular to do, from the reaction after Ferse, and the habit of nerves into which he had thrown her; but such excuses were unconvincing. If they did not believe Hubert sufficiently here to refuse his extradition, what chance would he have out there? She spent surreptitious minutes staring at the map of Bolivia, as if its conformation could give her insight into the psychology of its people. She had never loved Condaford more passionately than during these uneasy days. The place was entailed, and if Hubert were sent out there and condemned, or died in prison, or was murdered by one of those muleteers, and if Jean had no son, it would pass away to Hilary's eldest boy – a cousin she had barely seen, a boy at school; in the family, yes, but as good as lost. With Hubert's fate was wrapped up the fate of her beloved home. And, though astonished that she could think of herself at all, when it meant so terribly much more to Hubert, she never quite lost the thought.

One morning she got Clare to run her over to Lippinghall. Dinny hated driving, and not without reason, for her peculiar way of seeing the humours of what she was passing had often nearly brought her to grief. They arrived at lunch time. Lady Mont was just sitting down, and greeted them with:

'My dears, but how provokin'! Unless you can eat carrots – your Uncle's away – so purifyin'. Blore, see if Augustine has a cooked bird somewhere. Oh! and, Blore, ask her to make those nice pancakes with jam, that I can't eat.'

'Oh! but, Aunt Em, nothing that you can't eat, please.'

'I can't eat anythin' just now. Your Uncle's fattin', so I'm slimmin'. And, Blore, cheese ramequins, and a nice wine – and coffee.'

'But this is awful, Aunt Em.'

'Grapes, Blore. And those cigarettes up in Mr Michael's room. Your Uncle doesn't smoke them, and I smoke gaspers, so we run low. And, Blore.'

'Yes, my lady?'

'Cocktails, Blore.'

'Aunt Em, we never drink cocktails.'

'You do; I've seen you. Clare, you're lookin' thin; are you slimmin' too?'

'No. I've been in Scotland, Aunt Em.'

'Followin' the guns, and fishin'. Now run about the house. I'll wait for you.'

When they were running about the house, Clare said to Dinny: 'Where on earth did Aunt Em learn to drop her g's?'

'Father told me once that she was at a school where an undropped "g" was worse than a dropped "h". They were bringin' in a county fashion then, huntin' people, you know. Isn't she a dear?'

Clare nodded, slightly brightening her lips.

Re-entering the dining room, they heard Lady Mont say: 'James's trousers, Blore.'

'Yes, my lady.'

'They look as if they were comin' down. Can somethin' be done about it?'

'Yes, my lady.'

'Here you are! Your Aunt Wilmet's gone to stay with Hen, Dinny. They'll be differin' all over the place. You've got a cold bird each. Dinny, what have you been doin' with Alan? He's lookin' so interestin', and his leave's up tomorrow.'

'I've not been doing anything with him, Aunt Em.'

'That's it, then. No. Give me my carrots, Blore. Aren't you goin' to marry him? I know he has prospects in Chancery – somewhere – Wiltshire, is it? He comes and puts his head in my hand about you.'

Under Clare's gaze Dinny sat with fork suspended.

'If you don't take care, he'll be gettin' transferred to China and marryin' a purser's daughter. They say Hong Kong's full of them. Oh! And my portulaca's dead, Dinny. Boswell and Johnson went and watered it with liquid manure. They've no sense of smell. D'you know what they did once?'

'No, Aunt Em.'

'Had hay fever all over my pedigree rabbit – sneezin' about the hutch, and the poor thing died. I gave them notice, but they didn't go. They don't, you know. Your Uncle pets them. Are you to wed, Clare?'

'To "wed"! Aunt Em!'

'I think it's rather sweet, the uneducated papers use it. But are you?'

'Of course not.'

'Why? Haven't you the time? I don't like carrots really – so depressin'. But your Uncle's gettin' to a time of life – I have to be careful. I don't know why men have a time of life. By rights he ought to be over it.'

'He is, Aunt Em. Uncle Lawrence is sixty-nine; didn't you know?'

'Well, he's never shown any signs yet. Blore!'

'Yes, my lady.'

'Go away!'

'Yes, my lady.'

'There are some things,' said Lady Mont, as the door closed, 'that you can't talk about before Blore – birth control, and your uncle, and that. Poor Pussy!'

She rose, went to the window, and dropped a cat into a flower bed.

'How perfectly sweet Blore is with her!' murmured Dinny.

'They stray,' she said, as she came back, 'at forty-five, and they stray at sixty-five, and I don't know when after that. I never strayed. But I'm thinkin' of it with the Rector.'

'Is he very lonely now, Auntie?'

'No,' said Lady Mont, 'he's enjoyin' himself. He comes up here a lot.'

'It would be delicious if you could work up a scandal.'

'Dinny!'

'Uncle Lawrence would love it.'

Lady Mont seemed to go into a sort of coma.

'Where's Blore?' she said: 'I want one of those pancakes after all.'

'You sent him away.'

'Oh! yes.'

'Shall I tread on the gas, Aunt Em?' said Clare: 'it's under my chair.'

'I had it put there for your Uncle. He's been readin' me Gulliver's Travels, Dinny. The man was coarse, you know.'

'Not so coarse as Rabelais, or even as Voltaire.'

'Do you read coarse books?'

'Oh! well, those are classics.'

'They say there was a book – Achilles, or something; your Uncle bought it in Paris; and they took it away from him at Dover. Have you read that?'

'No,' said Dinny.

'I have,' said Clare.

'From what your Uncle tells me, you oughtn't to.'

'Oh! one reads anything now. Auntie, it never makes any difference.'

Lady Mont looked from one niece to the other.

'Well,' she said, cryptically, 'there's the Bible. Blore!'

'Yes, my lady.'

'Coffee in the hall on the tiger. And put a sniff on the fire, Blore. My Vichy.'

When she had drunk her glass of Vichy they all rose.

'Marvellous!' whispered Clare in Dinny's ear.

'What are you doin' about Hubert?' said Lady Mont, in front of the hall fire.

'Sweating in our shoes, Auntie.'

'I told Wilmet to speak to Hen. She sees Royalty, you know. Then there's flyin'. Couldn't he fly somewhere?'

'Uncle Lawrence went bail for him.'

'He wouldn't mind. We could do without James, he's got adenoids; and we could have one man instead of Boswell and Johnson.'

'Hubert would mind, though.'

'I'm fond of Hubert,' said Lady Mont: 'and bein' married – it's too soon. Here's the sniff.'

Blore, bearing coffee and cigarettes, was followed by James bearing a cedar log; and a religious silence ensued while Lady Mont made coffee.

'Sugar, Dinny?'

'Two spoonfuls, please.'

'Three for me. I know it's fattenin'. Clare?'

'One, please.'

The girls sipped, and Clare sighed out:

'Amazing!'

'Yes. Why is your coffee so much better than anybody else's, Aunt Em?'

'I agree,' said her aunt. 'About that poor man, Dinny: I was so relieved that he didn't bite either of you after all. Adrian will get her now. Such a comfort.'

'Not for some time, Aunt Em: Uncle Adrian's going to America.'

'But why?'

'We all thought it best. Even he did.'

'When he goes to Heaven,' said Lady Mont, 'someone will have to go with him, or he won't get in.'

'Surely he'll have a seat reserved!'

'You never know. The Rector was preachin' on that last Sunday.'

'Does he preach well?'

'Well, cosy.'

'I expect Jean wrote his sermons.'

'Yes, they used to have more zip. Where did I get that word, Dinny?'

'From Michael, I expect.'

'He always caught everythin'. The rector said we were to deny ourselves; he came here to lunch.'

'And had a whacking good feed.'

'Yes.'

'What does he weigh, Aunt Em?'

'Without his clothes – I don't know.'

'But with?'

'Oh! quite a lot. He's goin' to write a book.'

'What about?'

'The Tasburghs. There was that one that was buried, and lived in France afterwards, only she was a Fitzherbert by birth. Then there was the one that fought the battle of – not Spaghetti – the other word, Augustine gives it us sometimes.'

'Navarino? But did he?'

'Yes, but they said he didn't. The rector's goin' to put that right. Then there was the Tasburgh that got beheaded, and forgot to put it down anywhere. The rector's nosed that out.'

'In what reign?'

'I never can be bothered with reigns, Dinny. Edward the Sixth – or Fourth, was it? He was a red rose. Then there was the one that married into us. Roland his name was – or was it? But he did somethin' strikin' – and they took away his land. Recusancy – what is that?'

'It means he was a Catholic, Auntie, in a Protestant reign.'

'They burnt his house first. He's in Mercurius Rusticus, or some book. The rector says he was greatly beloved. They burnt his house twice, I think, and then robbed it – or was it the other way? It had a moat. And there's a list of what they took.'

'How entrancing!'

'Jam, and silver, and chickens, and linen, and I think his umbrella, or something funny.'

'When was all this, Auntie?'

'In the Civil War. He was a Royalist. Now I remember his name wasn't Roland, and she was Elizabeth after you, Dinny. History repeatin' itself.'

Dinny looked at the log.

'Then there was the last Admiral – under William the Fourth – he died drunk, not William. The Rector says he didn't, so he's writin' to prove it. He says he caught cold and took rum for it; and it didn't click – where did I get *that* word?'

'I sometimes use it, Auntie.'

'Yes. So there's quite a lot, you see, besides all the dull ones, right away back to Edward the Confessor or somebody. He's tryin' to make out they're older than we are. So unreasonable.'

'My Aunt!' murmured Clare. 'Who would read a book like that?'

'I shouldn't think so. But he'll simply love snobbin' into it: and it'll keep him awake. Here's Alan! Clare, you haven't seen where my portulaca was. Shall we take a turn?'

'Aunt Em, you're shameless,' said Dinny in her ear; 'and it's no good.'

'"If at first you don't succeed" – d'you remember every mornin' when we were little? Wait till I get my hat, Clare.'

They passed away.

'So your leave's up, Alan?' said Dinny, alone with the young man. 'Where shall you be?'

'Portsmouth.'

'Is that nice?'

'Might be worse. Dinny, I want to talk to you about Hubert. If things go wrong at the Court next time, what's going to happen?'

All 'bubble and squeak' left Dinny, she sank down on a fireside cushion, and gazed up with troubled eyes.

'I've been enquiring,' said young Tasburgh; 'they leave it two or three weeks for the Home Secretary to go into, and then, if he confirms, cart them off as soon as they can. From Southampton it would be, I expect.'

'You don't really think it will come to that, do you?'

He said gloomily: 'I don't know. Suppose a Bolivian had killed somebody, here, and gone back, we should want him rather badly, shouldn't we, and put the screw on to get him?'

'But it's fantastic!'

The young man looked at her with an extremely resolute compassion.

'We'll hope for the best; but if it goes wrong something's got to be done about it. I'm not going to stand for it, nor is Jean.'

'But what could be done?'

Young Tasburgh walked round the hall looking at the doors; then, leaning above her, he said:

'Hubert can fly, and I've been up every day since Chichester. Jean and I are working the thing out – in case.'

Dinny caught his hand.

'My dear boy, that's crazy!'

'No crazier than thousands of things done in the war.'

'But it would ruin your career.'

'Blast my career! Look on and see you and Jean miserable for years, perhaps, and a man like Hubert broken rottenly like that – what d'you think?'

Dinny squeezed his hand convulsively and let it go.

'It can't, it shan't come to that. Besides, how could you get Hubert? He'd be under arrest.'

'I don't know, but I shall know all right if and when the time comes. What's certain is that if they once get him over there, he'll have a damned thin chance.'

'Have you spoken to Hubert?'

'No. It's all perfectly vague as yet.'

'I'm sure he wouldn't consent.'

'Jean will see to that.'

Dinny shook her head. 'You don't know Hubert; he would never let you.'

Alan grinned, and she suddenly recognised that in him there was something formidably determined.

'Does Professor Hallorsen know?'

'No, and he won't, unless it's absolutely necessary. But he's a good egg, I admit.'

She smiled faintly. 'Yes, he's a good egg; but an outsize.'

'Dinny, you're not gone on him, are you?'

'No, my dear.'

'Well, thank God for that! You see,' he went on, 'they're not likely to treat Hubert as an ordinary criminal. That will make things easier perhaps.'

Dinny gazed at him, thrilled to her very marrow. Somehow that last remark convinced her of the reality of his purpose. 'I'm beginning to understand Zeebrugge. But—'

'No buts, and buck up! That boat arrives the day after tomorrow, and then the case will be on again. I shall see you in Court, Dinny. I must go now – got my daily flight. I just thought I'd like you to know that if the worst comes to the worst, we aren't going to take it lying down. Give my love to Lady Mont; shan't be seeing her again. Good-bye, and bless you!' And, kissing her hand, he was out of the hall before she could speak.

Dinny sat on beside the cedar log, very still, and strangely moved. The idea of defiance had not before occurred to her, mainly perhaps because she had never really believed that Hubert would be committed for trial. She did not really believe it now, and that made this 'crazy' idea the more thrilling; for it has often been noticed that the less actual a risk, the more thrilling it seems. And to the thrill was joined a warmer feeling for Alan. The fact that he had not even proposed added to the conviction that he was in dead earnest. And on that tiger-skin, which had provided very little thrill to the eighth baronet, who from an elephant had shot its owner while it was trying to avoid notice, Dinny sat, warming her body in the glow from the cedar log, and her spirit in the sense of being closer to the fires of life than she had ever yet been. Her Uncle's old black and white spaniel dog, Quince, who in his master's absences, which were frequent, took little interest in human beings, came slowly across the hall and, lying down four-square, put his head on his fore-paws and looked up at her with eyes that showed red rims beneath them. 'It may be all that, and it may not,' he seemed to say. The log hissed faintly, and a grandfather clock on the far side of the hall struck three with its special slowness.

Chapter Thirty-two

Over any impending issue, whether test match, ultimatum, the Cambridgeshire, or the hanging of a man, excitement beats up in the last few hours, and the feeling of suspense in the Cherrell family became painful when the day of Hubert's remand was reached. As some Highland clan of old, without summons issued, assembled when one of its number was threatened, so were Hubert's relatives collected in the Police Court. Except Lionel, who was in session, and his and Hilary's children, who were at school, they were all there. It might have been a wedding or a funeral, but for the grimness of their faces, and the sense of unmerited persecution at the back of every mind. Dinny and Clare sat between their father and mother, with Jean, Alan, Hallorsen and Adrian next to them; just behind them were Hilary and his wife, Fleur and Michael and Aunt Wilmet; behind them again sat Sir Lawrence and Lady Mont, and in the extreme rear the Rector formed the spear tail of an inverted phalanx.

Coming in with his lawyer, Hubert gave them a clansman's smile.

Now that she was actually in Court, Dinny felt almost apathetic. Her brother was innocent of all save self-defence. If they committed him, he would still be innocent. And, after she had answered Hubert's smile, her attention was given to Jean's face. If ever the girl looked like a leopardess, it was now; her strange, deep-set eyes kept sliding from her 'cub' to him who threatened to deprive her of it.

The evidence from the first hearing having been read over, the new evidence – Manuel's affidavit – was produced by Hubert's lawyer. But then Dinny's apathy gave way, for this affidavit was countered by the prosecution with another, sworn by four muleteers, to the effect that Manuel had not been present at the shooting.

That was a moment of real horror.

Four half-castes against one!

Dinny saw a disconcerted look flit across the magistrate's face.

'Who procured this second affidavit, Mr Buttall?'

'The lawyer in charge of the case in La Paz, Your Honour. It became known to him that the boy Manuel was being asked to give evidence.'

'I see. What do you say now on the question of the scar shown us by the accused?'

'Beyond the accused's own statement there is no evidence whatever before you, Sir, or before me, as to how or when that scar was inflicted.'

'That is so. You are not suggesting that this scar could have been inflicted by the dead man after he was shot?'

'If Castro, having drawn a knife, had fallen forward after he was shot, it is conceivable, I suppose.'

'Not likely, I think, Mr Buttall.'

'No. But my evidence, of course, is that the shooting was deliberate, cold-blooded, and at a distance of some yards. I know nothing of Castro's having drawn a knife.'

'It comes to this, then: Either your six witnesses are lying, or the accused and the boy Manuel are.'

'That would appear to be the position, Your Honour. It is for you to judge whether the sworn words of six citizens are to be taken, or the sworn words of two.'

Dinny saw the magistrate wriggle.

'I am perfectly aware of that, Mr Buttall. What do you say, Captain Cherrell, to this affidavit that has been put in as to the absence of the boy Manuel?'

Dinny's eyes leaped to her brother's face. It was impassive, even slightly ironic.

'Nothing, Sir. I don't know where Manuel was. I was too occupied in saving my life. All I know is that he came up to me almost immediately afterwards.'

'Almost? How long afterwards?'

'I really don't know, Sir – perhaps a minute. I was trying to stop the bleeding; I fainted just as he came.'

During the speeches of the two lawyers which followed, Dinny's apathy returned. It fled again during the five minutes of silence which succeeded them. In all the Court the magistrate alone seemed occupied; and it was as if he would never be done. Through her lowered lashes she could see him consulting this paper, consulting that; he had a red face, a long nose, a pointed chin, and eyes which she liked whenever she could see them. Instinctively she knew that he was not at ease. At last he spoke.

'In this case,' he said, 'I have to ask myself not whether a crime has been committed, or whether the accused has committed it; I have only to ask myself whether the evidence brought before me is such as to satisfy me that the alleged crime is an extraditable offence, that the foreign warrant is duly authenticated, and that such evidence has been produced as would in this country justify me in committing the accused to take his trial.' He paused a moment and then added: 'There is no question but that the crime alleged is an extraditable offence, and that the foreign warrant is duly authenticated.' He paused again, and in the dead silence Dinny heard a long sigh, as if from a spirit, so lonely and disembodied was the sound. The Magistrate's eyes passed to Hubert's face, and he resumed:

'I have come to the conclusion reluctantly that it is my duty on the evidence adduced to commit the accused to prison to await surrender to the foreign State on a warrant from the Secretary of State, if he sees fit to issue it. I have heard the accused's evidence to the effect that he had an antecedent justification removing the act complained of from the category of crime, supported by the affidavit of a witness which is contradicted by the affidavit of four others. I have no means of judging between the conflicting evidence of these two affidavits except in so far that it is in the proportion of four to one, and I must therefore dismiss it from my mind. In face of the sworn testimony of six witnesses that the shooting was deliberate, I do not think that the unsupported word of the accused to the contrary would justify me in the case of an offence committed in this country in refusing to commit for trial; and I am therefore unable to accept it as justification for a refusal to commit for trial in respect of an offence committed in another country. I make no hesitation in confessing my reluctance to come to this conclusion, but I consider that I have no other course open to me. The question, I repeat, is not whether the accused is guilty or innocent, it is a question of whether or not there should be a trial. I am not able to take on myself the responsibility of saying that there should not. The final word in cases of this nature rests with the Secretary of State, who issues the surrender warrant. I commit you, therefore, to prison to await the issue of such a warrant. You will not be surrendered until after fifteen days, and you have the right to apply for a writ of *habeas corpus* in regard to the lawfulness of your custody. I have not the power to grant you any further bail; but it may be that you may secure it, if you so desire, by application to the King's Bench Division.'

Dinny's horrified eyes saw Hubert, standing very straight, make the magistrate a little bow, and leave the dock, walking slowly and without a look back. Behind him his lawyer, too, passed out of Court.

She herself sat as if stunned, and her only impression of those next minutes was the sight of Jean's stony face, and of Alan's brown hands gripping each other on the handle of his stick.

She came to herself conscious that tears were stealing down her mother's face, and that her father was standing up.

'Come!' he said: 'Let's get out of here!'

At that moment she was more sorry for her father than for

any other of them all. Since this thing began he had said so little and had felt so much. It was ghastly for him! Dinny understood very well his simple feelings. To him, in the refusal of Hubert's word, an insult had been flung not merely in his son's face, and his own as Hubert's father, but in the face of what they stood for and believed in; in the face of all soldiers and all gentlemen! Whatever happened now, he would never quite get over this. Between justice and what was just, what inexorable incompatibility! Were there men more honourable than her father and her brother, or than that magistrate, perhaps? Following him out into that dishevelled backwater of life and traffic, Bow Street, she noted that they were all there except Jean, Alan and Hallorsen. Sir Lawrence said:

'We must just "take cabs and go about!" Better come to Mount Street and consult what we can each best do.'

When half an hour later they assembled in Aunt Em's drawing-room, those three were still absent.

'What's happened to them?' asked Sir Lawrence.

'I expect they went after Hubert's lawyer,' answered Dinny; but she knew better. Some desperate plan was being hatched, and she brought but a distracted mind to council.

In Sir Lawrence's opinion Bobbie Ferrar was still their man. If he could do nothing with 'Walter', nothing could be done. He proposed to go again to him and to the Marquess.

The General said nothing. He stood a little apart, staring at one of his brother-in-law's pictures, evidently without seeing it. Dinny realised that he did not join in because he could not. She wondered of what he was thinking. Of when he was young like his son, just married; of long field-days under burning sun among the sands and stones of India and South Africa; of longer days of administrative routine; of strenuous poring over maps with his eyes on the clock and his ear to the telephone; of his wounds and his son's long sickness; of two lives given to service and this strange reward at the end?

She herself stood close to Fleur, with the instinctive feeling that from that clear, quick brain might come a suggestion of real value.

'The Squire carries weight with the Government; I might go to Bentworth,' she heard Hilary say, and the Rector add:

'Ah! I knew him at Eton, I'll come with you.'

She heard her Aunt Wilmet's gruff: 'I'll go to Hen again about Royalty.' And Michael's:

'In a fortnight the House will be sitting'; and Fleur's impatient:

'No good, Michael. The Press is no use either. I've got a hunch.'

'Ah!' she thought, and moved closer.

'We haven't gone deep enough. What's at the back of it? Why should the Bolivian Government care about a half-caste Indian? It's not the actual shooting, it's the slur on their country. Floggings and shootings by foreigners! What's wanted is something done to the Bolivian Minister that will make him tell "Walter" that they don't really care.'

'We can't kidnap him,' muttered Michael; 'it's not done in the best circles.'

A faint smile came on Dinny's lips; she was not so sure.

'I'll see,' said Fleur, as if to herself. 'Dinny, you must come to us. They'll get no further here.' And her eyes roved swiftly over the nine elders. 'I shall go to Uncle Lionel and Alison. He won't dare move, being a new judge, but she will, and she knows all the Legation people. Will you come, Dinny?'

'I ought to be with Mother and Father.'

'They'll be here, Em's just asked them. Well, if you stay here too, come round as much as you can; you might help.'

Dinny nodded, relieved at staying in town; for the thought of Condaford during this suspense oppressed her.

'We'll go now,' said Fleur, 'and I'll get on to Alison at once.'

Michael lingered to squeeze Dinny's arm.

'Buck up, Dinny! We'll get him out of it somehow. If only it wasn't "Walter"! He's the worst kind of egg. To fancy yourself "just" is simply to addle.'

When all except her own people had gone, Dinny went up to her father. He was still standing before a picture, but not the same one. Slipping her hand under his arm, she said:

'It's going to be all right, Dad dear. You could see the magistrate was really sorry. He hadn't the power, but the Home Secretary must have.'

'I was thinking,' said the General, 'what the people of this country would do if we didn't sweat and risk our lives for them.' He spoke without bitterness, or even emphasis: 'I was thinking why we should go on doing our jobs, if our words aren't to be believed. I was wondering where that magistrate would be – oh! I dare say he's all right according to his lights – if boys like Hubert hadn't gone off before their time. I was wondering why we've chosen lives that have landed me on the verge of bankruptcy, and Hubert in this mess, when we might have been snug and comfortable in the City or the Law. Isn't a man's whole career to weigh a snap when a thing like this happens? I feel the insult to the Service, Dinny.'

She watched the convulsive movement of his thin brown hands, clasped as if he were standing at ease, and her whole heart went out to him, though she could perfectly well see the unreason of the exemption he was claiming. 'It is easier for Heaven and Earth to pass than for one tittle of the Law to fail.' Wasn't that the text she had just read in what she had suggested might be made into a secret naval code?

'Well,' he said, 'I must go out now with Lawrence. See to your mother, Dinny, her head's bad.'

When she had darkened her mother's bedroom, applied the usual remedies, and left her to try and sleep, she went downstairs again. Clare had gone out, and the drawing room, just now so full, seemed deserted. She passed down its length and opened the piano. A voice said:

'No, Polly, you must go to bed, I feel too sad'; and she became aware of her aunt in the alcove at the end placing her parakeet in its cage.

'Can we be sad together, Aunt Em?'

Lady Mont turned round.

'Put your cheek against mine, Dinny.'

Dinny did so. The cheek was pink and round and smooth and gave her a sense of relaxation.

'From the first I knew what he would say,' said Lady Mont, 'his nose was so long. In ten years' time it'll touch his chin. Why they allow them, I don't know. You can do nothing with a man like that. Let's cry, Dinny. You sit there, and I'll sit here.'

'Do you cry high or low, Aunt Em?'

'Either. You begin. A man who can't take a responsibility. I could have taken that responsibility perfectly, Dinny. Why didn't he just say to Hubert "Go and sin no more"?'

'But Hubert hasn't sinned.'

'It makes it all the worse. Payin' attention to foreigners! The other day I was sittin' in the window at Lippin'hall, and there were three starlin's on the terrace, and I sneezed twice. D'you think they paid any attention? Where is Bolivia?'

'In South America, Aunt Em.'

'I never could learn geography. My maps were the worst ever made at my school, Dinny. Once they asked me where Livin'stone kissed Stanley, and I answered? "Niagara Falls." And it wasn't.'

'You were only a continent wrong there, Auntie.'

'Yes. I've never seen anybody laugh as my schoolmistress laughed when I said that. Excessive – she was fat. I thought Hubert lookin' thin.'

'He's always thin, but he's looking much less "tucked up" since his marriage.'

'Jean's fatter, that's natural. You ought, Dinny, you know.'

'You never used to be so keen on people getting married, Auntie.'

'What happened on the tiger the other day?'

'I can't possibly tell you that, Aunt Em.'

'It must have been pretty bad, then.'

'Or do you mean good?'

'You're laughin' at me.'

'Did you ever know me disrespectful, Auntie?'

'Yes. I perfectly well remember you writin' a poem about me:

> I do not care for Auntie Em,
> She says I cannot sew or hem.
> Does she? Well! I can sew a dem
> Sight better than my Auntie Em.

I kept it. I thought it showed character.'

'Was I such a little demon?'

'Yes. There's no way, is there, of shortenin' dogs?' And she pointed to the golden retriever lying on a rug. 'Bonzo's middle is really too long.'

'I told you that, Aunt Em, when he was a puppy.'

'Yes, but I didn't notice it till he began to scratch for rabbits. He can't get over the hole properly. It makes him look so weak. Well! If we're not goin' to cry, Dinny, what shall we do?'

'Laugh?' murmured Dinny.

Chapter Thirty-three

Her father and Sir Lawrence not coming back to dinner, and her mother remaining in bed, Dinny dined alone with her aunt, for Clare was staying with friends.

'Aunt Em,' she said, when they had finished, 'do you mind if I go round to Michael's? Fleur has had a hunch.'

'Why?' said Lady Mont: 'It's too early for that – not till March.'

'You're thinking of the hump, Auntie. A "hunch" means an idea.'

'Then why didn't she say so?' And, with that simple dismissal of the more fashionable forms of speech, Lady Mont rang the bell.

'Blore, a taxi for Miss Dinny. And, Blore, when Sir Lawrence comes in, let me know; I'm goin' to have a hot bath, and wash my hair.'

'Yes, my lady.'

'Do you wash your hair when you're sad, Dinny?'

Driving through the misty dark evening to South Square, Dinny experienced melancholy beyond all she had felt yet. The thought of Hubert actually in a prison cell, torn from a wife not more than three weeks married, facing separation that might be permanent, and a fate that would not bear thinking of; and all because they were too scrupulous to stretch a point and take his word, caused fear and rage to bank up in her spirit, as unspent heat before a storm.

She found Fleur and her Aunt Lady Alison discussing ways and means. The Bolivian Minister, it appeared, was away convalescing after an illness, and a subordinate was in charge. This in Lady Alison's opinion made it more difficult, for he would probably not take any responsibility. She would, however, arrange a luncheon to which Fleur and Michael should be bidden, and Dinny, too, if she wished; but Dinny shook her head – she had lost faith in her power of manipulating public men.

'If you and Fleur can't manage it, Aunt Alison, I certainly can't. But Jean is singularly attractive when she likes.'

'Jean telephoned just now, Dinny. If you came in tonight, would you go round and see her at their flat; otherwise she was writing to you.'

Dinny stood up. 'I'll go at once.'

She hurried through the mist along the Embankment and turned down towards the block of workmen's flats where Jean had found her lodgment. At the corner boys were crying the more sanguinary tidings of the day; she bought a paper to see if Hubert's case was mentioned, and opened it beneath a lamp. Yes! There it was! 'British officer committed. Extradition on shooting charge.' How little attention she would have given to that, if it had not concerned her! This, that was agony to her and hers, was to the Public just a little pleasurable excitement. The misfortunes of others were a distraction; and the papers made their living out of it! The man who had sold the paper to her had a thin face, dirty clothes, and was lame; and, throwing a libationary drop out of her bitter cup, she gave him back the paper and a shilling. His eyes widened in a puzzled stare, his mouth remained a little open. Had she backed the winner – that one?

Dinny went up the bricked stairs. The flat was on the second floor. Outside its door a grown black cat was spinning round after its own tail. It flew round six times on the same spot, then sat down, lifted one of its back legs high into the air, and licked it.

Jean herself opened the door. She was evidently in the throes of packing, having a pair of combinations over her arm. Dinny kissed her and looked round. She had not been here before. The doors of the small sitting room, bedroom, kitchen and bathroom were open; the walls were distempered apple green, the floors covered with dark-green linoleum. For furniture there was a double bed, and some suitcases in the bedroom, two armchairs and a small table in the sitting room; a kitchen table and some bath salts in a glass jar; no rugs, no pictures, no books, but some printed linen curtains to the windows and a hanging cupboard along one whole side of the bedroom, from which Jean had been taking the clothes piled on the bed. A scent of coffee and lavender bags distinguished the atmosphere from that on the stairs.

Jean put down the combinations.

'Have some coffee, Dinny? I've just made it.'

She poured out two cups, sweetened them, handed Dinny one and a paper packet of cigarettes, then pointed to one of the armchairs and sat down in the other.

'You got my message, then? I'm glad you've come – saves my making up a parcel. I hate making parcels, don't you?'

Her coolness and unharassed expression seemed to Dinny miraculous.

'Have you seen Hubert since?'

'Yes. He's fairly comfortable. It's not a bad cell, he says, and they've given him books and writing paper. He can have food in, too; but he's not allowed to smoke. Someone ought to move about that. According to English law Hubert's still as innocent as the Home Secretary; there's no law to prevent the Home Secretary smoking, is there? I shan't be seeing him again, but you'll be going, Dinny – so give him my special love, and take him some cigarettes in case they let him.'

Dinny stared at her.

'What are you going to do, then?'

'Well, I wanted to see you about that. This is all strictly for your ear only. Promise to lie absolutely doggo, Dinny, or I shan't say anything.'

Dinny said, resolutely: 'Cross my heart as they say. Go on.'

'I'm going to Brussels tomorrow. Alan went today; he's got extension of leave for urgent family affairs. We're simply going to prepare for the worst, that's all. I'm to learn flying in double quick time. If I go up three times a day, three weeks will be quite enough. Our lawyer has guaranteed us three weeks, at least. Of course, he knows nothing. Nobody is to know anything, except you. I want you to do something for me.' She reached forward and took out of her vanity bag a tissue-papered packet.

'I've got to have five hundred pounds. We can get a good second-hand machine over there for very little, they say, but we shall want all the rest. Now, look here Dinny, this is an old family thing. It's worth a lot. I want you to pop it for five hundred; if you can't get as much as that by popping, you'll have to sell it. Pop, or sell, in your name, and change the English notes into Belgian money and send it to me registered to the G.P.O. Brussels. You ought to be able to send me the money within three days.' She undid the paper, and disclosed an old-fashioned but very beautiful emerald pendant.

'Oh!'

'Yes,' said Jean, 'it really is good. You can afford to take a high line. Somebody will give you five hundred on it, I'm sure. Emeralds are up.'

'But why don't you "pop" it yourself before you go?'

Jean shook her head.

'No, nothing whatever that awakens suspicion. It doesn't matter what you do, Dinny, because you're not going to break the law. We possibly are, but we're not going to be copped.'

'I think,' said Dinny, 'you ought to tell me more.'

Again Jean shook her head.

'Not necessary, and not possible; we don't know enough yet ourselves. But make your mind easy, they're not going to get away with Hubert. You'll take this, then?' And she wrapped up the pendant.

Dinny took the little packet, and, having brought no bag, slipped it down her dress. She leaned forward and said earnestly:

'Promise you won't do anything, Jean, till everything else has failed.'

Jean nodded. 'Nothing till the very last minute. It wouldn't be good enough.'

Dinny grasped her hand. 'I oughtn't to have let you in for this, Jean, it was I who brought the young things together, you know.'

'My dear, I'd never have forgiven you if you hadn't. I'm in love.'

'But it's so ghastly for you.'

Jean looked into the distance so that Dinny could almost feel the cub coming round the corner.

'No! I like to think it's up to me to pull him out of it. I've never felt so alive as I feel now.'

'Is there much risk for Alan?'

'Not if we work things properly. We've several schemes, according as things shape.'

Dinny sighed.

'I hope to God they'll none of them be necessary.'

'So do I, but it's impossible to leave things to chance, with a "just beast" like "Walter".'

'Well, good-bye, Jean, and good luck!'

They kissed, and Dinny went down into the street with the emerald pendant weighing like lead on her heart. It was drizzling now and she took a cab back to Mount Street. Her father and Sir Lawrence had just come in. Their news was inconsiderable. Hubert, it seemed, did not wish for bail again. 'Jean,' thought Dinny, 'has to do with that.' The Home Secretary was in Scotland and would not be back till Parliament sat, in about a fortnight's time. The warrant could not be issued till after that. In expert opinion they had three weeks at least in which to move heaven and earth. Ah! but it was easier for heaven and earth to pass than for one tittle of the Law to fail. And yet was it quite nonsense when people talked of 'interest' and 'influence' and 'wangling' and 'getting things through'? Was there not some talismanic way of which they were all ignorant?

Her father kissed her and went dejectedly up to bed, and Dinny was left alone with Sir Lawrence. Even he was in heavy mood.

'No bubble and squeak in the pair of us,' he said. 'I sometimes think, Dinny, that the Law is overrated. It's really a rough-and-ready system, with about as much accuracy in adjusting penalty to performance as there is to a doctor's diagnosis of a patient he sees for the first time; and yet for some mysterious reason we give it the sanctity of the Holy Grail and treat its dicta as if they were the broadcastings of God. If ever there was a case where a Home Secretary might let himself go and be human, this is one. And yet I don't see him doing it. I don't, Dinny, and Bobbie Ferrar doesn't. It seems that some wrongly-inspired idiot, not long ago, called Walter "the very spirit of integrity", and Bobbie says that instead of turning up his stomach, it went to his head, and he hasn't reprieved anybody since. I've been wondering whether I couldn't write to *The Times* and say: "This pose of inexorable incorruptibility in certain quarters is more dangerous to justice than the methods of Chicago." Chicago ought to fetch him. He's been there, I believe. It's an awful thing for a man to cease to be human.'

'Is he married?'

'Not even that, now,' said Sir Lawrence.

'But some men don't even begin to be human, do they?'

'That's not so bad; you know where you are, and can take a fire-shovel to them. No, it's the blokes who get a swelled head that make the trouble. By the way, I told my young man that you would sit for your miniature.'

'Oh! Uncle, I simply couldn't sit with Hubert on my mind!'

'No, no! Of course not! But something must turn up.' He looked at her shrewdly and added: 'By the way, Dinny, young Jean?'

Dinny lifted a wide and simple gaze:

'What about her?'

'She doesn't look to me too easy to bite.'

'No, but what can she do, poor dear?'

'I wonder,' said Sir Lawrence, raising one eyebrow, 'I just wonder. "They're dear little innocent things, they are, they're angels without any wings, they are." That's "Punch" before your time, Dinny. And it will continue to be "Punch" after your time, except that wings are growing on you all so fast.'

Dinny, still looking at him innocently, thought: 'He's rather uncanny, Uncle Lawrence!' And soon after she went up to bed.

To go to bed with one's whole soul in a state of upheaval! And yet how many other upheaved souls lay, cheek to pillow, unsleeping! The room seemed full of the world's unreasoning misery. If one were talented, one would get up and relieve oneself in a poem about Azrael, or something! Alas! It was not so easy as all that. One lay, and was sore – sore and anxious and angry. She could remember still how she had felt, being thirteen, when Hubert, not quite eighteen, had gone off to the war. That had been horrid, but this was much worse; and she wondered why. Then he might have been killed at any minute; now he was safer than anybody who was not in prison. He would be preserved meticulously even while they sent him across the world and put him up for trial in a country not his own, before some judge of alien blood. He was safe enough for some months yet. Why, then, did this seem so much worse than all the risks through which he had passed since he first went soldiering, even than that long, bad time on the Hallorsen expedition? Why? If not that those old risks and hardships had been endured of his free will; while the present trouble was imposed on him. He was being held down, deprived of the two great boons of human existence, independence and private life, boons to secure which human beings in communities had directed all their efforts for thousands of years, until – until they went Bolshy! Boons to every human being, but especially to people like themselves, brought up under no kind of whip except that of their own consciences. And she lay there as if she were lying in his cell, gazing into his future, longing for Jean, hating the locked-in feeling, cramped and miserable and bitter. For what had he done, what in God's name had he done that any other man of sensibility and spirit would not do!

The mutter of the traffic from Park Lane formed a sort of ground base to her rebellious misery. She became so restless that she could not lie in bed, and, putting on her dressing gown, stole noiselessly about her room till she was chilled by the late October air coming through the opened window. Perhaps there was something in being married, after all; you had a chest to snuggle against and if need be weep on; you had an ear to pour complaint into; and lips that would make the mooing sounds of sympathy. But worse than being single during this time of trial was being inactive. She envied those who, like her father and Sir Lawrence, were at least taking cabs and going about; greatly she envied Jean and Alan. Whatever they were up to was better than being up to nothing, like herself! She took out the emerald pendant and looked at it. That at least was something to do on the morrow, and she pictured herself with this in her hand forcing large sums of money out of some flinty person with a tendency towards the art of lending.

Placing the pendant beneath her pillow, as though its proximity were an insurance against her sense of helplessness, she fell asleep at last.

Next morning she was down early. It had occurred to her that she could perhaps pawn the pendant, get the money, and take it to Jean before she left. And she decided to consult the butler, Blore. After all, she had known him since she was five; he was an institution and had never divulged any of the iniquities she had confided in him in her childhood.

She went up to him, therefore, when he appeared with her Aunt's special coffee machine.

'Blore.'

'Yes, Miss Dinny.'

'Will you be frightfully nice and tell me, *in confidence*, who is supposed to be the best pawnbroker in London?'

Surprised but impassive – for, after all, anybody might have to 'pop' anything in these days – the butler placed the coffee machine at the head of the table and stood reflecting.

'Well, Miss Dinny, of course there's Attenborough's, but I'm told the best people go to a man called Frewen in South Molton Street. I can get you the number from the telephone book. They say he's reliable and very fair.'

'Splendid, Blore! It's just a little matter.'

'Quite so, Miss.'

'Oh! And, Blore, would you – should I give my own name?'

'No, Miss Dinny; if I might suggest: give my wife's name and this address. Then, if there has to be any communication, I could get it to you by telephone, and no one the wiser.'

'Oh! that's a great relief. But wouldn't Mrs Blore mind?'

'Oh! no, Miss, only too glad to oblige you. I could do the matter for you if you wish.'

'Thank you, Blore, but I'm afraid I must do it myself.'

The butler caressed his chin and regarded her; his eye seemed to Dinny benevolent but faintly quizzical.

'Well, Miss, if I may say so, a little nonchalance goes a long way even with the best of them. There are others if he doesn't offer value.'

'Thank you frightfully, Blore; I'll let you know if he doesn't. Would half-past nine be too early?'

'From what I hear, Miss, that is the best hour; you get him fresh and hearty.'

'Dear Blore!'

'I'm told he's an understanding gent, who can tell a lady when he sees one. He won't confuse you with some of those Tottie madams.'

Dinny laid her finger to her lips.

'Cross your heart, Blore.'

'Oh! absolutely, Miss. After Mr Michael you were always my favourite.'

'And so were you, Blore.' She took up *The Times* as her father entered, and Blore withdrew.

'Sleep well, Dad?'

The General nodded.

'And Mother's head?'

'Better. She's coming down. We've decided that it's no use to worry, Dinny.'

'No, darling, it isn't, of course. D'you think we could begin breakfast?'

'Em won't be down, and Lawrence has his at eight. You make the coffee.'

Dinny, who shared her aunt's passion for good coffee went reverentially to work.

'What about Jean?' asked the General, suddenly. 'Is she coming to us?'

Dinny did not raise her eyes.

'I don't think so, Dad; she'll be too restless; I expect she'll just make out by herself. I should want to, if I were her.'

'I daresay, poor girl. She's got pluck, anyway. I'm glad Hubert married a girl of spirit. Those Tasburghs have got their hearts in the right place. I remember an uncle of hers in India – daring chap, a Goorkha regiment, they swore by him. Let me see, where was he killed?'

Dinny bent lower over the coffee.

It was barely half-past nine when she went out with the pendant in her vanity bag, and her best hat on. At half-past nine precisely she was going up to the first floor above a shop in South Molton Street. Within a large room, at a mahogany table, were two seated gentlemen, who might have seemed to her like high-class bookmakers if she had known what such were like. She looked at them anxiously, seeking for signs of heartiness. They appeared, at least, to be fresh, and one of them came towards her.

Dinny passed an invisible tongue over her lips.

'I'm told that you are so good as to lend money on valuable jewellery?'

'Quite, Madam.' He was grey, and rather bald, and rather red, with light eyes, and he stood regarding her through a pair of pince-nez which he held in his hand. Placing them on his nose, he drew a chair up to the table, made a motion with one hand, and resumed his seat. Dinny sat down.

'I want rather a lot, five hundred,' and she smiled: 'It was an heirloom, quite nice.'

Both the seated gentlemen bowed slightly.

'And I want it at once, because I have to make a payment. Here it is!' And out of her bag she drew the pendant, unwrapped it and pushed it forward on the table. Then, remembering the needed touch of nonchalance, she leaned back and crossed her knees.

Both of them looked at the pendant for a full minute without movement or speech. Then the second gentleman opened a drawer and took out a magnifying glass. While he was examining the pendant, Dinny was conscious that the first gentleman was examining herself. That – she supposed – was the way they divided labour. Which would they decide was the more genuine piece? She felt rather breathless, but kept her eyebrows slightly raised and her eyelids half closed.

'Your own property, Madam?' said the first gentleman.

Remembering once more the old proverb, Dinny uttered an emphatic: 'Yes.'

The second gentleman lowered his glass, and seemed to weigh the pendant in his hand.

'Very nice,' he said. 'Old-fashioned, but very nice. And for how long would you want the money?'

Dinny, who had no idea, said boldly: 'Six months; but I suppose I could redeem it before?'

'Oh! yes. Five hundred, did you say?'

'Please.'

'If you are satisfied, Mr Bondy,' said the second gentleman, 'I am.'

Dinny raised her eyes to Mr Bondy's face. Was he going to say, 'No, she's just told me a lie?' Instead, he pushed his underlip up over his upper lip, bowed to her and said:

'Quite!'

'I wonder,' she thought, 'if they always believe what they hear, or never? I suppose it's the same thing, really – *they* get the pendant and it's I who have to trust them or, rather, it's Jean.'

The second gentleman now swept up the pendant, and, producing a book, began to write in it. Mr Bondy, on the other hand, went towards a safe.

'Did you wish for notes, Madam?'

'Please.'

The second gentleman, who had a moustache and white spats, and whose eyes goggled slightly, passed her the book.

'Your name and address, Madam.'

As she wrote: 'Mrs Blore' and her aunt's number in Mount Street, the word 'Help!' came into her mind, and she cramped her left hand as to hide what should have been the ringed finger. Her gloves fitted dreadfully well and there was no desirable circular protuberance.

'Should you require the article, we shall want £550 on the 29th of April next. After that, unless we hear from you, it will be for sale.'

'Yes, of course. But if I redeem it before?'

'Then the amount will be according. The interest is at 20 per cent., so in a month, say, from now, we should only require £508 6s. 8d.'

'I see.'

The first gentleman detached a slip of paper and gave it to her.

'That is the receipt.'

'Could the pendant be redeemed on payment by anyone with this receipt, in case I can't come myself?'

'Yes, Madam.'

Dinny placed the receipt in her vanity bag, together with as much of her left hand as would go in, and listened to Mr Bondy counting notes on the table. He counted beautifully; the notes, too, made a fine crackle, and seemed to be new. She took them with her right hand, inserted them into the bag, and still holding it with her concealed left hand, arose.

'Thank you very much.'

'Not at all, Madam, the pleasure is ours. Delighted to be of service. Good-bye!'

Dinny bowed, and made slowly for the door. There, from under her lashes she distinctly saw the first gentleman close one eye.

She went down the stairs rather dreamily, shutting her bag.

'I wonder if they think I'm going to have a baby,' she thought; 'or it may be only the Cambridgeshire.' Anyway she had the money, and it was just a quarter to ten. Thomas Cook's would change it, perhaps, or at least tell her where to get Belgian money.

It took an hour and visits to several places before she had most of it in Belgian money, and she was hot when she passed the barrier at Victoria with a platform ticket. She moved slowly down the train, looking into each carriage. She had gone about two-thirds down when a voice behind had called:

'Dinny!' And, looking round, she saw Jean in the doorway of a compartment.

'Oh! there you are, Jean! I've had such a rush. Is my nose shiny?'

'You never look hot, Dinny.'

'Well! I've done it; here's the result, five hundred nearly all in Belgian.'

'Splendid!'

'And the receipt. Anyone can get it on this. The interest's at 20 per cent, calculated from day to day, but after April 28th, unless redeemed, it'll be for sale.'

'You keep that, Dinny.' Jean lowered her voice. 'If we have to do things, it will mean we shan't be on hand. There are several places that have no treaties with Bolivia, and that's where we shall be till things have been put straight somehow.'

'Oh!' said Dinny, blankly, 'I could have got more. They lapped it up.'

'Never mind! I must get in. G.P.O. Brussels. Good-bye! Give

my dear love to Hubert and tell him all's well.' She flung her arms round Dinny, gave her a hug, and sprang back into the train. It moved off almost at once, and Dinny stood waving to that brilliant browned face turned back towards her.

Chapter Thirty-four

his active and successful opening to her day had the most acute drawbacks, for it meant that she was now the more loose-ended.

The absence of the Home Secretary and the Bolivian Minister seemed likely to hold up all activity even if she could have been of use in those directions, which was improbable. Nothing for it but to wait, eating one's heart out! She spent the rest of the morning wandering about, looking at shop windows, looking at the people who looked at shop windows. She lunched off poached eggs at an A.B.C. and went into a cinema, with a vague idea that whatever Jean and Alan were preparing would seem more natural if she could see something of the sort on the screen. She had no luck. In the film she saw there were no aeroplanes, no open spaces, no detectives, no escaping from justice whatever; it was the starkest record of a French gentleman, not quite in his first youth, going into wrong bedrooms for an hour and more on end, without anyone actually losing her virtue. Dinny could not help enjoying it – he was a dear, and perhaps the most accomplished liar she had ever watched.

After this warmth and comfort, she set her face again towards Mount Street.

She found that her mother and father had taken the afternoon train back to Condaford, and this plunged her into uncertainty. Ought she to go back, too, and 'be a daughter' to them? Or ought she to remain 'on the spot' in case anything turned up for her to do?

She went up to her room undecided, and began half-heartedly to pack. Pulling open a drawer, she came on Hubert's diary, which still accompanied her. Turning the pages idly, she lighted on a passage which seemed to her unfamiliar, having nothing to do with his hardships:

'Here's a sentence in a book I'm reading: "We belong, of course, to a generation that's seen through things, seen how futile everything is, and had the courage to accept futility, and say to ourselves: There's nothing for it but to enjoy ourselves as best we can." Well, I suppose that's my generation, the one that's seen the war and its aftermath; and, of course, it *is* the attitude of quite a crowd; but when you come to think of it, it might have been said by any rather unthinking person in any generation; certainly might have been said by the last generation after religion had got the knock that Darwin gave it. For what does it come to? Suppose you admit having seen through religion and marriage and treaties, and commercial honesty and freedom and ideals of every kind, seen that there's nothing absolute about them, that they lead of themselves to no definite reward, either in this world or a next which doesn't exist perhaps, and that the only thing absolute is pleasure and that you mean to have it – are you any farther towards getting pleasure? No! you're a long way farther off. If everybody's creed is consciously and crudely "grab a good time at all costs", everybody is going to grab it at the expense of everybody else, and the devil will take the hindmost, and that'll be nearly everybody, especially the sort of slackers who naturally hold that creed, so that *they*, most certainly, aren't going to get a good time. All those things they've so cleverly seen through are only rules of the road devised by men throughout the ages to keep people within bounds, so that we may all have a reasonable chance of getting a good time, instead of the good time going only to the violent, callous, dangerous and able few. All our institutions, religion, marriage, treaties, the law, and the rest, are simply forms of consideration for others necessary to secure consideration for self. Without them we should be a society of feeble motor-bandits and streetwalkers in slavery to a few super-crooks. You can't, therefore, disbelieve in consideration for others without making an idiot of yourself and spoiling your own chances of a good time. The funny thing is that no matter how we all talk, we recognise that perfectly. People who prate like the fellow in that book don't act up to their creed when it comes to the point. Even a motor-bandit doesn't turn King's evidence. In fact, this new philosophy of "having the courage to accept futility and grab a good time" is simply a shallow bit of thinking; all the same, it seemed quite plausible when I read it.'

Dinny dropped the page as if it had stung her, and stood with a transfigured look on her face. Not the words she had been reading caused this change – she was hardly conscious of what they were. No! She had got an inspiration, and she could not think why she had not had it before! She ran downstairs to the telephone and rang up Fleur's house.

'Yes?' came Fleur's voice.

'I want Michael, Fleur; is he in?'

'Yes. Michael – Dinny.'

'Michael? Could you by any chance come round at once? It's about Hubert's diary. I've had a "hunch", but I'd rather not discuss it on the 'phone. Or could I come to you? – You *can* come? Good! Fleur too, if she likes; or, if not, bring her wits.'

Ten minutes later Michael arrived alone. Something in the quality of Dinny's voice seemed to have infected him, for he wore an air of businesslike excitement. She took him into the alcove and sat down with him on a sofa under the parakeet's cage.

'Michael dear, it came to me suddenly: if we could get Hubert's diary – about 15,000 words – printed at once, ready for publication, with a good title like "Betrayed" – or something—'

'"Deserted,"' said Michael.

'Yes, "Deserted", and it could be shown to the Home Secretary as about to come out with a fighting preface, it might stop him from issuing a warrant. With that title and preface and a shove from the Press, it would make a real sensation, and be very nasty for him. We could get the Preface to pitch it strong about desertion of one's kith and kin, and pusillanimity and truckling to the foreigner and all that. The Press would surely take it up on those lines.'

Michael ruffled his hair.

'It *is* a hunch, Dinny; but there are several points: first, how to do it without making it blackmailish. If we can't avoid that, then it's no go. If Walter sniffs blackmail, he can't possibly rise.'

'But the whole point is to make him feel that if he issues the warrant he's going to regret it.'

'My child,' said Michael, blowing smoke at the parakeet, 'it's got to be much more subtle than that. You don't know public men. The thing is to make them do of their own accord out of high motives what is for their own good. We must get Walter to do this from a low motive, and feel it to be a high one. That's indispensable.'

'Won't it do if he says it's a high one? I mean need he feel it?'

'He must, at least by daylight. What he feels at three in the morning doesn't matter. He's no fool, you know. I believe,' and Michael rumpled his hair again, 'that the only man who can work it after all is Bobbie Ferrar. He knows Walter upside down.'

'Is he a nice man? Would he?'

'Bobbie's a sphinx, but he's a perfectly good sphinx. And he's in the know all round. He's a sort of receiving station, hears everything naturally, so that we shouldn't have to appear directly in any way.'

'Isn't the first thing, Michael, to get the diary printed, so that it looks ready to come out on the nail?'

'Yes, but the Preface is the hub.'

'How?'

'What we want is that Walter should read the printed diary, and come to the conclusion from it that to issue the warrant will be damned hard luck on Hubert – as, of course, it will. In other words, we want to sop his private mind. After that, what I see Walter saying to himself is this: "Yes, hard luck on young Cherrell, hard luck, but the magistrate committed him, and the Bolivians are pressing, and he belongs to the classes; one must be careful not to give an impression of favouring privilege—"'

'I think that's so unfair,' interrupted Dinny, hotly. 'Why should it be made harder for people just because they happen not to be Tom, Dick and Harry? I call it cowardly.'

'Ah! Dinny, but we are cowardly in that sort of way. But as Walter was saying when you broke out: "One must not lightly stretch points. The little Countries look to us to treat them with special consideration."'

'But why?' began Dinny again: 'That seems—'

Michael held up his hand.

'I know, Dinny, I know. And this seems to me the psychological moment when Bobbie, out of the blue as it were, might say: "By the way, there's to be a preface. Someone showed it me. It takes the line that England is always being generous and just at the expense of her own subjects. It's pretty hot stuff, Sir. The Press will love it. That lay: We can't stand by our own people, is always popular. And you know" — Bobbie would continue – "it has often seemed to me, Sir, that a strong man, like you, ought perhaps to do something about this impression that we can't stand by our own people. It oughtn't to be true, perhaps it isn't true, but it exists and very strongly; and you, Sir, perhaps better than anyone, could redress the balance there. This particular case wouldn't afford a bad chance at all of restoring confidence on that point. In itself it would be right, I think" – Bobbie would say – "not to issue a warrant, because that scar, you know, was genuine, the shooting really *was* an act of self-defence; and it would certainly do the country good to feel that it could rely again on the authorities not to let our own people down." And there he would leave it. And Walter would feel, not that he was avoiding attack, but that he was boldly going to do what was good for the Country – indispensable, that, Dinny, in the case of public men.' And Michael rolled his eyes. 'You see,' he went on, 'Walter is quite up to realising, without admitting it, that the preface won't appear if he doesn't issue the warrant. And I daresay he'll be frank with himself in the middle of the night; but if in his 6 p.m. mind he feels he's doing the courageous thing in not issuing the warrant, then what he feels in his 3 a.m. mind won't matter. See?'

'You put it marvellously, Michael. But won't he have to read the preface?'

'I hope not, but I think it ought to be in Bobbie's pocket, in case he has to fortify his line of approach. There are no flies on Bobbie, you know.'

'But will Mr Ferrar care enough to do all this?'

'Yes,' said Michael, 'on the whole, yes. My Dad once did him a good turn, and old Shropshire's his uncle.'

'And who could write that preface?'

'I believe I could get old Blythe. They're still afraid of him in our party, and when he likes he can make livers creep all right.'

Dinny clasped her hands.

'Do you think he will like?'

'It depends on the diary.'

'Then I think he will.'

'May I read it before I turn it over to the printers?'

'Of course! Only, Michael, Hubert doesn't want the diary to come out.'

'Well, that's O.K. If it works with Walter and he doesn't issue the warrant, it won't be necessary; and if it doesn't work, it won't be necessary either, because the "fat will be in the fire", as old Forsyte used to say.'

'Will the cost of printing be much?'

'A few pounds – say twenty.'

'I can manage that,' said Dinny; and her mind flew to the two gentlemen, for she was habitually hard up.

'Oh! that'll be all right, don't worry!'

'It's my hunch, Michael, and I should like to pay for it. You've no idea how horrible it is to sit and do nothing, with Hubert in this danger! I have the feeling that if he's once given up, he won't have a dog's chance.'

'It's ill prophesying,' said Michael, 'where public men are concerned. People underrate them. They're a lot more complicated than they're supposed to be, and perhaps better principled; they're certainly a lot shrewder. All the same, I believe this will click, if we can work old Blythe and Bobbie Ferrar properly. I'll go for Blythe, and set Bart on to Bobbie. In the meantime this shall be printed,' and he took up the diary. 'Good-bye, Dinny dear, and don't worry more than you can help.'

Dinny kissed him, and he went.

That evening about ten he rang her up.

'I've read it, Dinny. Walter must be pretty hard-boiled if it doesn't fetch him. He won't go to sleep over it, anyway, like the other bloke; he's a conscientious card, whatever else he is. After all this is a sort of reprieve case, and he's bound to recognise its seriousness. Once in his hands, he's got to go through with this diary, and it's moving stuff, apart from the light on the incident itself. So buck up!'

Dinny said: 'Bless you!' fervently, and went to bed lighter at heart than she had been for two days.

Chapter Thirty-five

In the slow long days, and they seemed many, which followed, Dinny remained at Mount Street, to be in command of any situation that might arise. Her chief difficulty lay in keeping people ignorant of Jean's machinations. She seemed to succeed with all except Sir Lawrence, who, raising his eyebrow, said cryptically:

'*Pour une gaillarde, c'est une gaillarde!*'

And, at Dinny's limpid glance, added: 'Quite the Botticellian virgin! Would you like to meet Bobbie Ferrar? We're lunching together underground at Dumourieux's in Drury Lane, mainly on mushrooms.'

Dinny had been building so on Bobbie Ferrar that the sight of him gave her a shock, he had so complete an air of caring for none of those things. With his carnation, bass drawl, broad bland face, and slight drop of the underjaw, he did not inspire her.

'Have you a passion for mushrooms, Miss Cherrell?' he said.

'Not French mushrooms.'

'No?'

'Bobbie,' said Sir Lawrence, looking from one to the other, 'no one would take you for one of the deepest cards in Europe. You are going to tell us that you won't guarantee to call Walter a strong man, when you talk about the preface?'

Several of Bobbie Ferrar's even teeth became visible.

'I have no influence with Walter.'

'Then who has?'

'No one. Except—'

'Yes?'

'Walter.'

Before she could check herself, Dinny said:

'You do understand, Mr Ferrar, that this is practically death for my brother and frightful for all of us?'

Bobbie Ferrar looked at her flushed face without speaking. He seemed, indeed, to admit or promise nothing all through that lunch, but when they got up and Sir Lawrence was paying his bill, he said to her:

'Miss Cherrell, when I go to see Walter about this, would you like to go with me? I could arrange for you to be in the background.'

'I should like it terribly.'

'Between ourselves, then. I'll let you know.'

Dinny clasped her hands and smiled at him.

'Rum chap!' said Sir Lawrence, as they walked away: 'Lots of heart, really. Simply can't bear people being hanged. Goes to all the murder trials. Hates prisons like poison. You'd never think it.'

'No,' said Dinny, dreamily.

'Bobbie,' continued Sir Lawrence, 'is capable of being Private Secretary to a Cheka, without their ever suspecting that he's itching to boil them in oil the whole time. He's unique. The diary's in print, Dinny, and old Blythe's writing that preface. Walter will be back on Thursday. Have you seen Hubert yet?'

'No, but I'm to go with Dad tomorrow.'

'I've refrained from pumping you, but those young Tasburghs are up to something, aren't they? I happen to know young Tasburgh isn't with his ship.'

'Not?'

'Perfect innocence!' murmured Sir Lawrence. 'Well, my dear, neither nods nor winks are necessary; but I hope to goodness they won't strike before peaceful measures have been exhausted.'

'Oh! surely they wouldn't!'

'They're the kind of young person who still make one believe in history. Has it ever struck you, Dinny, that history is nothing but the story of how people have taken things into their own hands, and got themselves or others into and out of trouble over it? They can cook at that place, can't they? I shall take your aunt there some day when she's thin enough.'

And Dinny perceived that the dangers of cross-examination were over.

Her father called for her and they set out for the prison the following afternoon of a windy day charged with the rough melancholy of November. The sight of the building made her feel like a dog about to howl. The Governor, who was an army man, received them with great courtesy and the special deference of one to another of higher rank in his own profession. He made no secret of his sympathy with them over Hubert's position, and gave them more than the time limit allowed by the regulations.

Hubert came in smiling. Dinny felt that if she had been alone he might have shown some of his real feelings, but that in front of his father he was determined to treat the whole thing as just a bad joke. The General, who had been grim and silent all the way there, became at once matter-of-fact and as if ironically amused. Dinny could not help thinking how almost absurdly alike, allowing for age, they were in looks and in manner. There was that in both of them which would never quite grow up, or rather which had grown up in early youth and would never again budge. Neither, from beginning to end of that half-hour, touched on feeling. The whole interview was a great strain, and so far as intimate talk was concerned, might never have taken place. According to Hubert, everything in his life there was perfectly all right, and he wasn't worrying at all; according to the General, it was only a matter of days now, and the coverts were waiting to be shot. He had a good deal to say about India, and the unrest on the frontier. Only when they were shaking hands at the end did their faces change at all, and then only to the simple gravity of a very straight look into each other's eyes. Dinny followed with a hand-clasp and a kiss behind her father's back.

'Jean?' asked Hubert, very low.

'Quite all right, sent her dear love. Nothing to worry about, she says.'

The quiver of his lips hardened into a little smile, he squeezed her hand, and turned away.

In the gateway the doorkeeper and two warders saluted them respectfully. They got into their cab, and not one word did they say the whole way home. The thing was a nightmare from which they would awaken some day, perhaps.

Practically the only comfort of those days of waiting was derived by Dinny from Aunt Em, whose inherent incoherence continually diverted thought from logical direction. The antiseptic value, indeed, of incoherence became increasingly apparent as day by day anxiety increased. Her aunt was genuinely worried by Hubert's position, but her mind was too plural to dwell on it to the point of actual suffering. On the fifth of November she called Dinny to the drawing-room window to look at some boys dragging a guy down a Mount Street desolate in wind and lamplight.

'The rector's workin' on that,' she said; 'there was a Tasburgh who wasn't hanged, or beheaded, or whatever they did with them, and he's tryin' to prove that he ought to have been; he sold some plate or somethin' to buy the gunpowder, and his sister married Catesby, or one of the others. Your father and I and Wilmet, Dinny, used to make a guy of our governess; she had very large feet, Robbins. Children are so unfeelin'. Did you?'

'Did I what, Aunt Em?'

'Make guys?'

'No.'

'We used to go out singin' carols, too, with our faces blacked. Wilmet was the corker. Such a tall child, with legs that went down straight like sticks wide apart from the beginning, you know – angels have them. It's all rather gone out. I do think there ought to be somethin' done about it. Gibbets, too. We had one. We hung a kitten from it. We drowned it first – not we – the staff.'

'Horrible, Aunt Em!'

'Yes; but not really. Your father brought us up as Red Indians. It was nice for him, then he could do things to us and we couldn't cry. Did Hubert?'

'Oh! no. Hubert only brought himself up as a Red Indian.'

'That was your mother; she's a gentle creature, Dinny. Our mother was a Hungerford. You must have noticed.'

'I don't remember Grandmother.'

'She died before you were born. That was Spain. The germs there are extra special. So did your grandfather. I was thirty-five. He had very good manners. They did, you know, then. Only sixty. Claret and piquet, and a funny little beard thing. You've seen them, Dinny?'

'Imperials?'

'Yes, diplomatic. They wear them now when they write those articles on foreign affairs. I like goats myself, though they butt you rather.'

'Their smell, Aunt Em!'

'Penetratin'. Has Jean written to you lately?'

In Dinny's bag was a letter just received. 'No,' she said. The habit was growing on her.

'This hidin' away is weak-minded. Still, it *was* her honeymoon.'

Her aunt had evidently not been made a recipient of Sir Lawrence's suspicions.

Upstairs she read the letter again before tearing it up.

Poste restante, Brussels.

DEAR DINNY,

All goes on for the best here and I'm enjoying it quite a lot. They say I take to it like a duck to water. There's nothing much to choose now between Alan and me, except that I have the better hands. Thanks awfully for your letters. Terribly glad of the diary stunt, I think it may quite possibly work the oracle. Still we can't afford not to be ready for the worst. You don't say whether Fleur's having any luck. By the way, could you get me a Turkish conversation book, the pronouncing kind? I expect your Uncle Adrian could tell you where to get it. I can't lay hands on one here. Alan sends you his love. Same from me. Keep us informed by wire if necessary.

Your affte

JEAN

A Turkish conversation book! This first indication of how their minds were working set Dinny's working too. She remembered Hubert having told her that he had saved the life of a Turkish officer at the end of the war, and had kept up with him ever since. So Turkey was to be the asylum if—! But the whole plan was desperate. Surely it would not, must not come to that! But she went down to the Museum the next morning.

Adrian, whom she had not seen since Hubert's committal, received her with his usual quiet alacrity, and she was sorely tempted to confide in him. Jean must know that to ask his advice about a Turkish conversation book would surely stimulate his curiosity. She restrained herself, however, and said:

'Uncle, you haven't a Turkish conversation book? Hubert thought he'd like to kill time in prison brushing up his Turkish.'

Adrian regarded her, and closed one eye.

'He hasn't any Turkish to brush. But here you are—'

And, fishing a small book from a shelf, he added: 'Serpent!' Dinny smiled.

'Deception,' he continued, 'is wasted on me, Dinny, I am in whatever know there is.'

'Tell me, Uncle!'

'You see,' said Adrian, 'Hallorsen is in it.'

'Oh!'

'And I, whose movements are dependent on Hallorsen's, have had to put two and two together. They make five, Dinny, and I sincerely trust the addition won't be needed. But Hallorsen's a fine chap.'

'I know that,' said Dinny, ruefully. 'Uncle, do tell me exactly what's in the wind.'

Adrian shook his head.

'They obviously can't tell themselves till they hear how Hubert is to be exported. All I know is that Hallorsen's Bolivians are going back to Bolivia instead of to the States, and that a very queer padded, well-ventilated case is being made to hold them.'

'You mean his Bolivian bones?'

'Or possibly replicas. They're being made, too.'

Thrilled, Dinny stood gazing at him.

'And,' added Adrian, 'the replicas are being made by a man who believes he is repeating Siberians, and not for Hallorsen, and they've been very carefully weighed – one hundred and fifty-two pounds, perilously near the weight of a man. How much is Hubert?'

'About eleven stone.'

'Exactly.'

'Go on, Uncle.'

'Having got so far, Dinny, I'll give you my theory, for what it's worth. Hallorsen and his case full of replicas will travel by the ship that Hubert travels by. At any port of call in Spain or Portugal, Hallorsen will get off with his case, containing Hubert. He will contrive to have extracted and dropped the replicas over-board. The real bones will be waiting there for him, and he will fill up when Hubert has been switched off to a plane: that's where Jean and Alan come in. They'll fly to, well – Turkey, judging from your request just now. I was wondering where before you came. Hallorsen will pop his genuine bones into the case to satisfy the authorities, and Hubert's disappearance will be put down to a jump overboard – the splash of the replicas, I shouldn't wonder – or anyway will remain mysterious. It looks to me pretty forlorn.'

'But suppose there's no port of call?'

'They're pretty certain to stop somewhere; but, if not, they'll have some alternative, which will happen on the way down to the ship. Or possibly they may elect to try the case dodge on the arrival in South America. That would really be safest, I think, though it lets out the flying.'

'But why is Professor Hallorsen going to run such a risk?'

'*You* ask me that, Dinny?'

'It's too much – I – I don't want him to.'

'Well, my dear, he also has the feeling, I know, that he got Hubert into this, and must get him out. And you must remember that he belongs to a nation that is nothing if not energetic and believes in taking the law into its own hands. But he's the last man to trade on a service. Besides, it's a three-legged race he's running with young Tasburgh, who's just as deep in it, so you're no worse off.'

'But I don't want to owe anything to either of them. It simply mustn't come to that. Besides, there's Hubert – do you think he'll ever consent?'

Adrian said gravely:

'I think he has consented, Dinny; otherwise he'd have asked for bail. Probably he'll be in charge of Bolivians and won't feel he's breaking English law. I fancy they've convinced him between them that they won't run much risk. No doubt he feels fed up with the whole thing and ready for anything. Don't forget that he's really being very unjustly treated, and is just married.'

'Yes,' said Dinny, in a hushed voice. 'And you, Uncle? How are things?'

Adrian's answer was no less quiet:

'Your advice was right; and I'm fixed up to go, subject to this business.'

Chapter Thirty-six

The feeling that such things did not happen persisted with Dinny even after her interview with Adrian; she had too often read of them in books. And yet, there was history, and there were the Sunday papers! Thought of the Sunday papers calmed her curiously and fortified her resolution to keep Hubert's affair out of them. But she conscientiously posted to Jean the Turkish primer, and took to poring over maps in Sir Lawrence's study when he was out. She also studied the sailing dates of the South American lines.

Two days later Sir Lawrence announced at dinner that 'Walter' was back; but after a holiday it would no doubt take him some time to reach a little thing like Hubert's.

'A little thing!' cried Dinny: 'merely his life and our happiness.'

'My dear, people's lives and happiness are the daily business of a Home Secretary.'

'It must be an awful post. I should hate it.'

'That,' said Sir Lawrence, 'is where your difference from a public man comes in, Dinny. What a public man hates is *not* dealing with the lives and happiness of his fellow-beings. Is our bluff ready, in case he comes early to Hubert?'

'The diary's printed – I've passed the proof; and the preface is written. I haven't seen that, but Michael says it's a "corker".'

'Good! Mr Blythe's corkers give no mean pause. Bobbie will let us know when Walter reaches the case.'

'What is Bobbie?' asked Lady Mont.

'An institution, my dear.'

'Blore, remind me to write about that sheep-dog puppy.'

'Yes, my lady.'

'When their faces are mostly white they have a kind of divine madness, have you noticed, Dinny? They're all called Bobbie.'

'Anything less divinely mad than our Bobbie – eh, Dinny?'

'Does he always do what he says he will, Uncle?'

'Yes; you may bet on Bobbie.'

'I do want to see some sheep-dog trials,' said Lady Mont: 'Clever creatures. People say they know exactly what sheep not to bite; and so thin, really. All hair and intelligence. Hen has two. About your hair, Dinny?'

'Yes, Aunt Em?'

'Did you keep what you cut off?'

'I did.'

'Well, don't let it go out of the family; you may want it. They say we're goin' to be old-fashioned again. Ancient but modern, you know.'

Sir Lawrence cocked his eye. 'Have you ever been anything else, Dinny? That's why I want you to sit. Permanence of the type.'

'What type?' said Lady Mont. 'Don't be a type, Dinny; they're so dull. There was a man said Michael was a type; I never could see it.'

'Why don't you get Aunt Em to sit instead, Uncle? She's younger than I am any day, aren't you, Auntie?'

'Don't be disrespectful. Blore, my Vichy.'

'Uncle, how old is Bobbie?'

'No one really knows. Rising sixty, perhaps. Some day, I suppose, his date will be discovered; but they'll have to cut a section and tell it from his rings. You're not thinking of marrying him, are you, Dinny? By the way, Walter's a widower. Quaker blood somewhere, converted Liberal – inflammable stuff.'

'Dinny takes a lot of wooin',' said Lady Mont.

'Can I get down, Aunt Em? I want to go to Michael's.'

'Tell her I'm comin' to see Kit tomorrow mornin'. I've got him a new game called Parliament – they're animals divided into Parties; they all squeak and roar differently, and behave in the wrong places. The Prime Minister's a zebra, and the Chancellor of the Exchequer's a tiger – striped. Blore, a taxi for Miss Dinny.'

Michael was at the House, but Fleur was in. She reported that Mr Blythe's preface had already been sent to Bobbie Ferrar. As for the Bolivians – the Minister was not back, but the Attaché in charge had promised to have an informal talk with Bobbie. He had been so polite that Fleur was unable to say what was in his mind. She doubted if there was anything.

Dinny returned on as many tenterhooks as ever. It all seemed to hinge on Bobbie Ferrar, and he 'rising' sixty, so used to everything that he must surely have lost all persuasive flame. But perhaps that was for the best. Emotional appeal might be wrong. Coolness, calculation, the power of hinting at unpleasant consequences, of subtly suggesting advantage, might be what was wanted. She felt, indeed, completely at sea as to what really moved the mind of Authority. Michael, Fleur, Sir Lawrence had spoken from time to time as if they knew, and yet she felt that none of them were really wiser than herself. It all seemed to balance on the knife-edge of mood and temper. She went to bed and had practically no sleep.

One more day like that, and then, as a sailor, whose ship has been in the doldrums, wakes to movement under him, so felt Dinny when at breakfast she opened an unstamped envelope with 'Foreign Office' imprinted on it.

DEAR MISS CHERRELL,

I handed your brother's diary to the Home Secretary yesterday afternoon. He promised to read it last night, and I am to see him today at six o'clock. If you will come

to the Foreign Office at ten minutes to six, we might go
round together.
Sincerely yours,

R. FERRAR

So! A whole day to get through first! By now 'Walter' must
have read the diary; had perhaps already made up his mind
on the case! With the receipt of that formal note, a feeling of
being in conspiracy and pledged to secrecy had come to her.
Instinctively she said nothing of it; instinctively wanted to get
away from everybody till all was over. This must be like waiting
for an operation. She walked out into a fine morning, and
wondered where on earth she should go; thought of the
National Gallery, and decided that pictures required too much
mind given to them; thought of Westminster Abbey and the
girl Millicent Pole. Fleur had got her a post as mannequin at
Frivolle's. Why not go there, look at the winter models, and
perhaps see that girl again? Rather hateful being shown dresses
if you were not going to buy, giving all that trouble for nothing.
But if only Hubert were released she would 'go off the deep
end' and buy a real dress, though it took all her next allowance.
Hardening her heart, therefore, she turned in the direction of
Bond Street, forded that narrow drifting river, came to Frivolle's,
and went in.

　'Yes, Madam'; and she was shown up, and seated on a chair.
She sat there with her head a little on one side, smiling and
saying pleasant things to the saleswoman; for she remembered
one day in a big shop an assistant saying: 'You've no idea,
Moddam, what a difference it makes to us when a customer
smiles and takes a little interest. We get so many difficult ladies
and – oh! well—' The models were very 'late', very expensive,
and mostly, she thought, very unbecoming, in spite of the
constant assurance: 'This frock would just suit you, Madam,
with your figure and colouring.'

Not sure whether to ask after her would harm or benefit the girl Millicent Pole, she selected two dresses for parade. A very thin girl, haughty, with a neat little head and large shoulder blades came wearing the first, a creation in black and white; she languished across with a hand on where one hip should have been, and her head turned as if looking for the other, confirming Dinny in the aversion she already had from the dress. Then, in the second dress, of sea green and silver, the one that she really liked except for its price, came Millicent Pole. With professional negligence she took no glance at the client, as who should say: 'What do you think! If you lived in underclothes all day – and had so many husbands to avoid!' Then, in turning, she caught Dinny's smile, answered it with a sudden startled brightness, and moved across again, languid as ever. Dinny got up, and going over to that figure now standing very still, took a fold of the skirt between finger and thumb, as if to feel its quality.

'Nice to see you again.'

The girl's loose flower-like mouth smiled very sweetly. 'She's marvellous!' thought Dinny.

'I know Miss Pole,' she said to the saleswoman. 'That dress looks awfully nice on her.'

'Oh! but Madam, it's your style completely. Miss Pole has a little too much line for it. Let me slip it on you.'

Not sure that she had been complimented, Dinny said:

'I shan't be able to decide today; I'm not sure I can afford it.'

'That is quite all right, Madam. Miss Pole, just come in here and slip it off, and we'll slip it on Madam.'

In there the girl slipped it off. 'Even more marvellous,' thought Dinny: 'Wish I looked as nice as that in undies,' and suffered her own dress to be removed.

'Madam is beautifully slim,' said the saleswoman.

'Thin as a rail!'

'Oh, no, Madam is well covered.'

'I think she's just right!' The girl spoke with a sort of eagerness. 'Madam has style.'

The saleswoman fastened the hook.

'Perfect,' she said. 'A little fullness here, perhaps; we can put that right.'

'Rather a lot of my skin,' murmured Dinny.

'Oh! But so becoming, with a skin like Madam's.'

'Would you let me see Miss Pole in that other frock – the black and white?'

This she said, knowing that the girl could not be sent to fetch it in her underclothes.

'Certainly; I'll get it at once. Attend to Madam, Miss Pole.'

Left to themselves, the two girls stood smiling at each other.

'How do you like it now you've got it, Millie?'

'Well, it isn't all I thought, Miss.'

'Empty?'

'I expect nothing's what you think it. Might be a lot worse, of course.'

'It was you I came in to see.'

'Did you reely? But I hope you'll have the dress, Miss – suits you a treat. You look lovely in it.'

'They'll be putting you in the sales department, Millie, if you don't look out.'

'Oh! I wouldn't go there. It's nothing but a lot of soft sawder.'

'Where do I unhook?'

'Here. It's very economic – only one. And you can do it for yourself, with a wriggle. I read about your brother, Miss. I do think that's a shame.'

'Yes,' said Dinny, and stood stony in her underclothes. Suddenly she stretched out her hand and gripped the girl's. 'Good luck, Millie!'

'And good luck to you, Miss!'

They had just unclasped hands when the saleswoman came back.

'I'm so sorry to have bothered you,' smiled Dinny, 'but I've quite made up my mind to have this one, if I can afford it. The price is appalling.'

'Do you think so, Madam? It's a Paris model. I'll see if I can get Mr Better to do what he can for *you* – it's *your* frock. Miss Pole, find Mr Better for me, will you?'

The girl, now in the black and white creation, went out.

Dinny, who had resumed her dress, said:

'Do your mannequins stay long with you?'

'Well, no; in and out of dresses all day, it's rather a restless occupation.'

'What becomes of them?'

'In one way or another they get married.'

How discreet! And soon after, Mr Better – a slim man with grey hair and perfect manners – having said he would reduce the price 'for Madam' to what still seemed appalling, Dinny went out into the pale November sunlight saying she would decide tomorrow. Six hours to kill. She walked North-East towards the Meads, trying to soothe her own anxiety by thinking that everyone she passed, no matter how they looked, had anxieties of their own. Seven million people, in one way or another all anxious. Some of them seemed so, and some did not. She gazed at her own face in a shop window, and decided that she was one of those who did not; and yet how horrid she felt! The human face was a mask, indeed! She came to Oxford Street and halted on the edge of the pavement, waiting to cross. Close to her was the bony white-nosed head of a van horse. She began stroking its neck, wishing she had a lump of sugar. The horse paid no attention, nor did its driver. Why should they? From year's end to year's end they passed and halted, halted and passed through this maelstrom, slowly, ploddingly, without hope of release, till they both fell down and were cleared away. A policeman reversed the direction of his white sleeves, the driver jerked his reins, and the van moved on, followed by a long line of motor vehicles. The policeman again reversed his sleeves and Dinny crossed, walked on to Tottenham Court Road, and once more stood waiting. What a seething and intricate pattern of creatures, and their cars, moving to what end, fulfilling what secret purpose? To what did it all amount? A meal, a smoke, a glimpse of so-called life in some picture palace, a bed at the end of the day. A million jobs faithfully and unfaithfully pursued, that they might eat, and dream a little, and sleep, and begin again. The inexorability of life caught her by the throat as she stood there, so that she gave a little gasp, and a stout man said:

'Beg pardon, did I tread on your foot, Miss?'

As she was smiling her 'No', a policeman reversed his white sleeves, and she crossed. She came to Gower Street, and walked rapidly up its singular desolation. 'One more ribber, one more ribber to cross,' and she was in the Meads, that network of mean streets, gutters, and child life. At the Vicarage both her Uncle and Aunt for once were in, and about to lunch. Dinny sat down, too. She did not shrink from discussing the coming 'operation' with them. They lived so in the middle of operations. Hilary said:

'Old Tasburgh and I got Bentworth to speak to the Home Secretary, and I had this note from "the Squire" last night. "All Walter would say was that he should treat the case strictly on its merits without reference to what he called your nephew's status – what a word! I always said the fellow ought to have stayed Liberal."'

'I wish he *would* treat it on its merits!' cried Dinny; 'then Hubert would be safe. I do hate that truckling to what they call Democracy! He'd give a cabman the benefit of the doubt.'

'It's the reaction from the old times, Dinny, and gone too far, as reaction always does. When I was a boy there was still truth in the accusation of privilege. Now, it's the other way on; station in life is a handicap before the Law. But nothing's harder than to steer in the middle of the stream – you want to be fair, and you can't.'

'I was wondering, Uncle, as I came along. What was the use of you and Hubert and Dad and Uncle Adrian, and tons of others doing their jobs faithfully – apart from bread and butter, I mean?'

'Ask your aunt,' said Hilary.

'Aunt May, what *is* the use?'

'I don't know, Dinny. I was bred up to believe there was a use in it, so I go on believing. If you married and had a family, you probably wouldn't ask the question.'

'I knew Aunt May would get out of answering. Now, Uncle?'

'Well, Dinny, I don't know either. As she says, we do what we're used to doing; that's about it.'

'In his diary Hubert says that consideration for others is really consideration for ourselves. Is that true?'

'Rather a crude way of putting it. I should prefer to say that we're all so interdependent that in order to look after oneself one's got to look after others no less.'

'But is one worth looking after?'

'You mean: is life worth while at all?'

'Yes.'

'After five hundred thousand years (Adrian says a million at least) of human life, the population of the world is very considerably larger than it has ever been yet. Well, then! Considering all the miseries and struggles of mankind, would human life, self-conscious as it is, have persisted if it wasn't worth while to be alive?'

'I suppose not,' mused Dinny; 'I think in London one loses the sense of proportion.'

At this moment a maid came in.

'Mr Cameron to see you, Sir.'

'Show him in, Lucy. He'll help you to regain it, Dinny. A walking proof of the unquenchable love of life, had every malady under the sun, including black-water, been in three wars, two earthquakes, had all kinds of jobs in all parts of the world, is out of one now, and has heart disease.'

Mr Cameron entered; a short spare man getting on for fifty, with bright Celtic grey eyes, dark grizzled hair, and a slightly hooked nose. One of his hands was bound up, as if he had sprained a thumb.

'Hallo, Cameron,' said Hilary, rising. 'In the wars again?'

'Well, Vicar, where I live, the way some of those fellows treat horses is dreadful. I had a fight yesterday. Flogging a willing horse, overloaded, poor old feller – never can stand that.'

'I hope you gave him beans!'

Mr Cameron's eyes twinkled.

'Well, I tapped his claret, and sprained my thumb. But I called to tell you, Sir, that I've got a job on the Vestry. It's not much, but it'll keep me going.'

'Splendid! Look here, Cameron, I'm awfully sorry, but Mrs Cherrell and I have to go to a Meeting now. Stay and have a cup of coffee and talk to my niece. Tell her about Brazil.'

Mr Cameron looked at Dinny. He had a charming smile.

The next hour went quickly and did her good. Mr Cameron had a fine flow. He gave her practically his life story, from boyhood in Australia, and enlistment at sixteen for the South African war, to his experiences since the Great War. Every kind of insect and germ had lodged in him in his time; he had handled horses, Chinamen, Kaffirs, and Brazilians, broken collar-bone and leg, been gassed and shell-shocked, but there was – he carefully explained – nothing wrong with him now but 'a touch of this heart disease'. His face had a kind of inner light, and his speech betrayed no consciousness that he was out of the common. He was, at the moment, the best antidote Dinny could have taken, and she prolonged him to his limit. When he had gone she herself went away into the medley of the streets with a fresh eye. It was now half-past three, and she had two hours and a half still to put away. She walked towards Regent's Park. Few leaves were left upon the trees, and there was a savour in the air from bonfires of them burning; through their bluish drift she passed, thinking of Mr Cameron, and resisting melancholy. What a life to have lived! And what a zest at the end of it! From beside the Long Water in the last of the pale sunlight, she came out into Marylebone, and bethought herself that before she went to the Foreign Office she must go where she could titivate. She chose Harridge's and went in. It was half-past four. The stalls were thronged; she wandered among them, bought a new powder-puff, had some tea, made herself tidy, and emerged. Still a good half-hour, and she walked again, though by now she was tired. At a quarter to six precisely she gave her card to a commissionaire at the Foreign Office, and was shown into a waiting room. It was lacking in mirrors, and taking out her case she looked at herself in its little powder-flecked round of glass. She seemed plain to herself and wished that she didn't; though, after all, she was not going to see 'Walter' – only to sit in the background, and wait again. Always waiting!

'Miss Cherrell!'

There was Bobbie Ferrar in the doorway. He looked just as usual. But of course he didn't care. Why should he?

He tapped his breast pocket. 'I've got the preface. Shall we trot?' And he proceeded to talk of the Chingford murder. Had she been following it? She had not. It was a clear case – completely! And he added, suddenly:

'The Bolivian won't take the responsibility, Miss Cherrell.'

'Oh!'

'Never mind.' And his face broadened.

'His teeth *are* real,' thought Dinny, 'I can see some gold filling.'

They reached the Home Office and went in. Up some wide stairs, down a corridor, into a large and empty room, with a fire at the end, their guide took them. Bobbie Ferrar drew a chair up to the table.

'The *Graphic* or this?' and he took from his side pocket a small volume.

'Both, please,' said Dinny, wanly. He placed them before her. 'This' was a little flat red edition of some War Poems.

'It's a first,' said Bobbie Ferrar; 'I picked it up after lunch.'

'Yes,' said Dinny, and sat down.

An inner door was opened, and a head put in.

'Mr Ferrar, the Home Secretary will see you.'

Bobbie Ferrar turned on her a look, muttered between his teeth: 'Cheer up!' and moved squarely away.

In that great waiting room never in her life had she felt so alone, so glad to be alone, or so dreaded the end of loneliness. She opened the little volume and read:

> He eyed a neat framed notice there
> Above the fireplace hung to show
> Disabled heroes where to go
> For arms and legs, with scale of price,
> And words of dignified advice
> How officers could get them free –
> Elbow or shoulder, hip or knee.
> Two arms, two legs, though all were lost,
> They'd be restored him free of cost.
>
> Then a girl guide looked in and said . . .

The fire crackled suddenly and spat out a spark. Dinny saw it die on the hearthrug, with regret. She read more poems, but did not take them in, and, closing the little book, opened the *Graphic*. Having turned its pages from end to end she could not have mentioned the subject of any single picture. The sinking feeling beneath her heart absorbed every object she looked upon. She wondered if it were worse to wait for an operation on oneself or on someone loved; and decided that the latter must be worse. Hours seemed to have passed; how long had he really been gone? Only half-past six! Pushing her chair back, she got up. On the walls were the effigies of Victorian statesmen, and she roamed from one to the other; but they might all have been the same statesman, with his whiskers at different stages of development. She went back to her seat, drew her chair close in to the table, rested her elbows on it, and her chin on her hands, drawing little comfort from that cramped posture. Thank

Heaven! Hubert didn't know his fate was being decided, and was not going through this awful waiting. She thought of Jean and Alan, and with all her heart hoped that they were ready for the worst. For with each minute the worst seemed more and more certain. A sort of numbness began creeping over her. He would never come back – never, never! And she hoped he wouldn't, bringing the death-warrant. At last she laid her arms flat on the table, and rested her forehead on them. How long she had stayed in that curious torpor she knew not, before the sound of a throat being cleared roused her, and she started back.

Not Bobbie Ferrar, but a tall man with a reddish, clean-shaven face and silver hair brushed in a cockscomb off his forehead, was standing before the fire with his legs slightly apart and his hands under his coat-tails; he was staring at her with very wide-opened light grey eyes, and his lips were just apart as if he were about to emit a remark. Dinny was too startled to rise, and she sat staring back at him.

'Miss Cherrell! Don't get up.' He lifted a restraining hand from beneath a coat-tail. Dinny stayed seated – only too glad to, for she had begun to tremble violently.

'Ferrar tells me that you edited your brother's diary?'

Dinny bowed her head. Take deep breaths!

'As printed, is it in its original condition?'

'Yes.'

'Exactly?'

'Yes. I haven't altered or left out a thing.'

Staring at his face she could see nothing but the round bright-ness of the eyes and the slight superior prominence of the lower lip. It was almost like staring at God. She shivered at the queer-ness of the thought and her lips formed a little desperate smile.

'I have a question to ask you, Miss Cherrell.'

Dinny uttered a little sighing: 'Yes.'

'How much of this diary was written since your brother came back?'

She stared; then the implication in the question stung her.

'None! Oh, none! It was all written out there at the time.'
And she rose to her feet.

'May I ask how you know that?'

'My brother—' Only then did she realise that throughout
she had nothing but Hubert's word – 'my brother told
me so.'

'His word is gospel to you?'

She retained enough sense of humour not to 'draw herself
up', but her head tilted.

'Gospel. My brother is a soldier and—'

She stopped short, and, watching that superior lower lip,
hated herself for using that cliché.

'No doubt, no doubt! But you realise, of course, the importance of the point?'

'There is the original—' stammered Dinny. Oh! Why hadn't
she brought it! 'It shows clearly – I mean, it's all messy and
stained. You can see it at any time. Shall—?'

He again put out a restraining hand.

'Never mind that. Very devoted to your brother, Miss
Cherrell?'

Dinny's lips quivered.

'Absolutely. We all are.'

'He's just married, I hear?'

'Yes, just married.'

'Your brother wounded in the war?'

'Yes. He had a bullet through his left leg.'

'Neither arm touched?'

Again that sting!

'No!' The little word came out like a shot fired. And they
stood looking at each other half a minute – a minute; words
of appeal, of resentment, incoherent words were surging to her
lips, but she kept them closed; she put her hand over them. He
nodded.

'Thank you, Miss Cherrell. Thank you.' His head went a

little to one side; he turned, and rather as if carrying that head on a charger, walked to the inner door. When he had passed through, Dinny covered her face with her hands. What had she done? Antagonised him? She ran her hands down over her face, over her body, and stood with them clenched at her sides, staring at the door through which he had passed, quivering from head to foot. A minute passed. The door was opened again, and Bobbie Ferrar came in. She saw his teeth. He nodded, shut the door, and said:

'It's all right.'

Dinny spun round to the window. Dark had fallen, and if it hadn't, she couldn't have seen. All right! All right! She dashed her knuckles across her eyes, turned round, and held out both hands, without seeing where to hold them.

They were not taken, but his voice said:

'I'm very happy.'

'I thought I'd spoiled it.'

She saw his eyes then, round as a puppy dog's.

'If he hadn't made up his mind already he wouldn't have seen you, Miss Cherrell. He's not as case-hardened as all that. As a matter of fact, he'd seen the Magistrate about it at lunch time – that helped a lot.'

'Then I had all that agony for nothing,' thought Dinny.

'Did he have to see the preface, Mr Ferrar?'

'No, and just as well – it might have worked the other way. We really owe it to the Magistrate. But you made a good impression on him. He said you were transparent.'

'Oh!'

Bobbie Ferrar took the little red book from the table, looked at it lovingly, and placed it in his pocket. 'Shall we go?'

In Whitehall Dinny took a breath so deep that the whole November dusk seemed to pass into her with the sensation of a long, and desperately wanted drink.

'A Post Office!' she said. 'He couldn't change his mind, could he?'

'I have his word. Your brother will be released tonight.'

'Oh! Mr Ferrar!' Tears suddenly came out of her eyes. She turned away to hide them, and when she turned back to him, he was not there.

Chapter Thirty-seven

W—hen from that Post Office she had despatched telegrams to her father and Jean, and telephoned to Fleur, to Adrian and Hilary, she took a taxi to Mount Street, and opened the door of her Uncle's study. Sir Lawrence, before the fire with a book he was not reading, looked up.

'What's your news, Dinny?'

'Saved!'

'Thanks to you!'

'Bobbie Ferrar says, thanks to the Magistrate. I nearly wrecked it, Uncle.'

'Ring the bell!' Dinny rang.

'Blore, tell Lady Mont I want her.'

'Good news, Blore; Mr Hubert's free.'

'Thank you, Miss; I was laying six to four on it.'

'What can we do to relieve our feelings, Dinny?'

'I must go to Condaford, Uncle.'

'Not till after dinner. You shall go drunk. What about Hubert? Anybody going to meet him?'

'Uncle Adrian said I'd better not, and he would go. Hubert will make for the flat, of course, and wait for Jean.'

Sir Lawrence gave her a whimsical glance.

'Where will she be flying from?'

'Brussels.'

'So that was the centre of operations! The closing down of

that enterprise gives me almost as much satisfaction, Dinny, as Hubert's release. You can't get away with that sort of thing, nowadays.'

'I think they might have,' said Dinny, for with the removal of the need for it, the idea of escape seemed to have become less fantastic. 'Aunt Em! What a nice wrapper!'

'I was dressin'. Blore's won four pounds. Dinny, kiss me. Give your Uncle one, too. You kiss very nicely – there's body in it. If I drink champagne, I shall be ill tomorrow.'

'But need you, Auntie?'

'Yes, Dinny, promise me to kiss that young man.'

'Do you get a commission on kissing, Aunt Em?'

'Don't tell me he wasn't goin' to cut Hubert out of prison, or something. The Rector said he flew in with a beard one day, and took a spirit level and two books on Portugal. They always go to Portugal. The Rector'll be so relieved; he was gettin' thin about it. So I think you ought to kiss him.'

'A kiss means nothing nowadays, Auntie. I nearly kissed Bobbie Ferrar; only he saw it coming.'

'Dinny can't be bothered to do all this kissing,' said Sir Lawrence; 'she's got to sit to my miniature painter. The young man will be at Condaford tomorrow, Dinny.'

'Your Uncle's got a bee, Dinny; collectin' the Lady. There aren't any, you know. It's extinct. We're all females now.'

By the only late evening train Dinny embarked for Condaford. They had plied her with wine at dinner, and she sat in sleepy elation, grateful for everything – the motion, and the moon-ridden darkness flying past the windows. Her exhilaration kept breaking out in smiles. Hubert free! Condaford safe! Her father and mother at ease once more! Jean happy! Alan no longer threatened with disgrace! Her fellow-passengers, for she was travelling third-class, looked at her with the frank or furtive wonderment that so many smiles will induce in the minds of any taxpayers. Was she tipsy, weak-minded, or merely in love? Perhaps all three! And she looked back at them with a benevolent compassion because they were obviously not half-seas-over with happiness. The hour and a half seemed short, and she got out on to the dimly lighted platform, less sleepy, but as elated as when she had got into the train. She had forgotten to add in her telegram that she was coming, so she had to leave her things and walk. She took the main road; it was longer, but she wanted to swing along and breathe home air to the full. In the night, as always, things looked unfamiliar, and she seemed to pass houses, hedges, trees that she had never known. The road dipped through a wood. A car came with its headlights glaring luridly, and in that glare she saw a weasel slink across just in time – queer little low beast, snakily humping its long back. She stopped a moment on the bridge over their narrow twisting little river. That bridge was hundreds of years old, nearly as old as the oldest parts of the Grange, and still very strong. Just beyond it was their gate, and when the river flooded, in very wet years, it crept up the meadow almost to the shrubbery where the moat had once been. Dinny pushed through the gate and walked on the grass edging of the drive between the rhododendrons. She came to the front of the house, which was really its back – long, low, unlighted. They did not expect her, and it was getting on for midnight; and the idea came to her to steal round and see it all grey and ghostly, tree-and-creeper-covered in the moonlight. Past the yew trees, throwing short shadows under the raised garden, she came round on to the lawn, and stood breathing deeply, and turning her head this way and that, so as to miss nothing that she had grown up with. The moon flicked a ghostly radiance on to the windows, and shiny leaves of the magnolias; and secrets lurked all over the old stone face. Lovely! Only one window was lighted, that of her father's study. It seemed strange that they had gone to bed already, with relief so bubbling in them. She stole from the lawn on to the terrace and stood looking in through the curtains not quite drawn. The General was at his desk with a lot of papers spread before him, sitting with his hands between his knees, and his head bent. She could see the hollow below his temple, the hair above it, much greyer of late, the set mouth, the almost beaten look on the face. The whole attitude was that of a man in patient silence, preparing to accept disaster. Up in Mount Street she had been reading of the American Civil War, and she thought that just so, but for his lack of beard, might some old Southern General have looked, the night before Lee's surrender. And, suddenly, it came to her that by an evil chance they had not yet received her telegram. She tapped on the pane. Her father raised his head. His face was ashen grey in the moonlight, and it was evident that he mistook her apparition for confirmation of the worst; he opened the window. Dinny leaned in, and put her hands on his shoulders.

'Dad! Haven't you had my wire? It's all right, Hubert's free.'

The General's hands shot up and grasped her wrists, colour came into his face, his lips relaxed, he looked suddenly ten years younger.

'Is it – is it certain, Dinny?'

Dinny nodded. She was smiling, but tears stood in her eyes.

'My God! That's news! Come in! I must go up and tell your mother!' He was out of the room before she was in it.

In this room, which had resisted her mother's and her own attempts to introduce aestheticism, and retained an office-like barrenness, Dinny stood staring at this and at that evidence of Art's defeat, with the smile that was becoming chronic. Dad with his papers, his military books, his ancient photographs, his relics of India and South Africa, and the old-style picture of his favourite charger, his map of the estate; his skin of the leopard that had mauled him, and the two fox masks – happy again! Bless him!

She had the feeling that her mother and he would rather be left alone to rejoice, and slipped upstairs to Clare's room. That vivid member of the family was asleep with one pyjama-d arm outside the sheet and her cheek resting on the back of the hand. Dinny looked amiably at the dark shingled head and went out again. No good spoiling beauty sleep! She stood at her opened bedroom window, gazing between the nearly bare elm-trees, at the moonlit rise of fields and the wood beyond. She stood and tried hard not to believe in God. It seemed mean and petty to have more belief in God when things were going well than when they were instinct with tragedy; just as it seemed mean and petty to pray to God when you wanted something badly, and not pray when you didn't. But after all God was Eternal Mind that you couldn't understand; God was not a loving Father that you could. The less she thought about all that the better. She was home like a ship after storm; it was enough! She swayed, standing there, and realised that she was nearly asleep. Her bed was not made ready; but getting out an old, thick dressing-gown, she slipped off shoes, dress, and corset belt, put on the gown and curled up under the eiderdown. In two minutes, still with that smile on her lips, she was sleeping . . .

A telegram from Hubert, received at breakfast next morning, said that he and Jean would be down in time for dinner.

'"The Young Squire Returns!"' murmured Dinny. '"Brings Bride!" Thank goodness it'll be after dark, and we can kill the fatted calf in private. Is the fatted calf ready, Dad?'

'I've got two bottles of your great-grandfather's Chambertin 1865 left. We'll have that, and the old brandy.'

'Hubert likes woodcock best, if there are any to be had, Mother, and pancakes. And how about the inland oyster? He loves oysters.'

'I'll see, Dinny.'

'And mushrooms,' added Clare.

'You'll have to scour the country, I'm afraid, Mother.'

Lady Cherrell smiled, she looked quite young.

'It's "a mild hunting day",' said the General: 'What about it, Clare? The meet's at Wyvell's Cross, eleven.'

'Rather!'

Returning from the stables after seeing her father and Clare depart, Dinny and the dogs lingered. The relief from that long waiting, the feeling of nothing to worry about, was so delicious that she did not resent the singular similarity in the present state of Hubert's career to the state which had given her so much chagrin two months back. He was in precisely the same position, only worse, because married; and yet she felt as blithe as a 'sandboy'. It proved that Einstein was right, and everything relative!

She was singing 'The Lincolnshire Poacher' on her way to the raised garden when the sound of a motorcycle on the drive caused her to turn. Someone in the guise of a cyclist waved his hand, and shooting the cycle into a rhododendron bush came towards her, removing his hood.

Alan, of course! And she experienced at once the sensation of one about to be asked in marriage. Nothing – she felt – could prevent him this morning, for he had not even succeeded in doing the dangerous and heroic thing which might have made the asking for reward too obvious.

'But perhaps,' she thought, 'he still has a beard – that might stop him.' Alas! He had only a jaw rather paler than the rest of his brown face.

He came up holding out both hands and she gave him hers. Thus grappled, they stood looking at each other.

'Well,' said Dinny, at last, 'tell your tale. You've been frightening us out of our wits, young man.'

'Let's go and sit down up there, Dinny.'

'Very well. Mind Scaramouch, he's under your foot, and the foot large.'

'Not so very. Dinny, you look—'

'No,' said Dinny; 'rather worn than otherwise. I know all about the Professor and the special case for his Bolivian bones, and the projected substitution of Hubert on the ship.'

'What!'

'We're not half-wits, Alan. What was *your* special lay, beard and all? We can't sit on this seat without something between us and the stone.'

'I couldn't be the something?'

'Certainly not. Put your overall there. Now!'

'Well,' he said, looking with disfavour at his boot, 'if you really want to know. There's nothing certain, of course, because it all depended on the way they were going to export Hubert. We had to have alternatives. If there was a port of call, Spanish or Portuguese, we *were* going to use the box trick. Hallorsen was to be on the ship, and Jean and I at the port with a machine and the real bones. Jean was to be the pilot when we got him – she's a natural flier; and they were to make for Turkey.'

'Yes,' said Dinny; 'we guessed all that.'

'How?'

'Never mind. What about the alternative?'

'If there was no port of call it wasn't going to be easy; we'd thought of a faked telegram to the chaps in charge of Hubert when the train arrived at Southampton or whatever the port was, telling them to take him to the Police Station and await further instructions. On the way there Hallorsen on a cycle would have bumped into the taxi on one side, and I should have bumped in on the other; and Hubert was to slip out into my car and be nipped off to where the machine was ready.'

'Mm!' said Dinny. 'Very nice on the screen; but are they so confiding in real life?'

'Well, we really hadn't got that worked out. We were betting on the other.'

'Has all that money gone?'

'No; only about two hundred, and we can re-sell the machine.' Dinny heaved a long sigh, and her eyes rested on him.

'Well,' she said, 'if you ask me, you're jolly well out of it.'

He grinned. 'I suppose so; especially as if it had come off I couldn't very well have bothered you. Dinny, I've got to rejoin today. Won't you—?'

Dinny said softly: 'Absence makes the heart grow fonder, Alan. When you come back next time, I really will see.'

'May I have one kiss?'

'Yes.' She tilted her cheek towards him.

'Now,' she thought, 'is when they kiss you masterfully full on the lips. He hasn't! He must almost respect me!' And she got up.

'Come along, dear boy; and thank you ever so for all you luckily didn't have to do. I really will try and become less virginal.'

He looked at her ruefully, as though repenting of his self-control, then smiled at her smile. And soon the splutter of his motorcycle faded into the faintly sighing silence of the day.

Still with the smile on her lips Dinny went back to the house. He was a dear! But really one must have time! Such a lot of repenting at leisure could be done even in these days!

After their slight and early lunch Lady Cherrell departed in the Ford driven by the groom in search of the fatted calf. Dinny was preparing to hunt the garden for whatever flowers November might yield when a card was brought to her:

Mr Neil Wintney,
Ferdinand Studios,
Orchard Street,
Chelsea.

'Help!' she thought; 'Uncle Lawrence's young man!' 'Where is he, Amy?'

'In the hall, Miss.'

'Ask him into the drawing room; I'll be there in a minute.'

Divested of her gardening gloves and basket, she looked at her nose in her little powdery mirror; then, entering the drawing-room through the French window, saw with surprise the 'young man' sitting up good in a chair with some apparatus by his side. He had thick white hair, and an eyeglass on a black ribbon; and when he stood she realised that he must be at least sixty. He said:

'Miss Cherrell? Your Uncle, Sir Lawrence Mont, has commissioned me to do a miniature of you.'

'I know,' said Dinny; 'only I thought—' She did not finish. After all, Uncle Lawrence liked his little joke, or possibly this was his idea of youth.

The 'young man' had screwed his monocle into a comely red

cheek, and through it a full blue eye scrutinised her eagerly. He put his head on one side and said: 'If we can get the outline, and you have some photographs, I shan't give you much trouble. What you have on – that flax-blue – is admirable for colour; background of sky – through that window – yes, not too blue – an English white in it. While the light's good, can we—?' And, talking all the time, he proceeded to make his preparations.

'Sir Lawrence's idea,' he said, 'is the English lady; culture deep but not apparent. Turn a little sideways. Thank you – the nose—'

'Yes,' said Dinny; 'hopeless.'

'Oh! no, no! Charming. Sir Lawrence, I understand, wants you for his collection of types. I've done two for him. Would you look down? No! Now full at me! Ah! The teeth – admirable!'

'All mine, so far.'

'That smile is just right, Miss Cherrell: it gives us the sense of spoof we want; not too much spoof, but just spoof enough.'

'You don't want me to hold a smile with exactly three ounces of spoof in it?'

'No, no, my dear young lady; we shall chance on it. Now suppose you turn three-quarters. Ah! Now I get the line of the hair; the colour of it admirable.'

'Not too much ginger, but just ginger enough?'

The 'young man' was silent. He had begun with singular concentration to draw and to write little notes on the margin of the paper.

Dinny, with crinkled eyebrows, did not like to move. He paused and smiled at her with a sort of winey sweetness.

'Yes, yes, yes,' he said. 'I see, I see.'

What did he see? The nervousness of the victim seized her suddenly, and she pressed her open hands together.

'Raise the hands, Miss Cherrell. No! Too Madonnaish. We must think of the devil in the hair. The eyes to me, full.'

'Glad?' asked Dinny.

'Not too glad; just – Yes, an English eye; candid but reserved.

Now the turn of the neck. Ah! A leetle tilt. Ye—es. Almost stag-like; almost – a touch of the – not startled – no, of the aloof.'

He again began to draw and write with a sort of remoteness, as if he were a long way off.

And Dinny thought: 'If Uncle Lawrence wants self-consciousness he'll get it all right.'

The 'young man' stopped and stood back, his head very much on one side, so that all his attention seemed to come out of his eyeglass.

'The expression,' he muttered.

'I expect,' said Dinny, 'you want an unemployed look.'

'Naughty!' said the 'young man': 'Deeper. Could I play that piano for a minute?'

'Of course. But I'm afraid it's not been played on lately.'

'It will serve.' He sat down, opened the piano, blew on the keys, and began playing. He played strongly, softly, well. Dinny stood in the curve of the piano, listening, and speedily entranced. It was obviously Bach, but she did not know what. An endearing, cool, and lovely tune, coming over and over and over, monotonous, yet moving as only Bach could be.

'What is it?'

'A Chorale of Bach, set by a pianist.' And the 'young man' nodded his eyeglass towards the keys.

'Glorious! Your ears on heaven and your feet in flowery fields,' murmured Dinny.

The 'young man' closed the piano and stood up.

'That's what I want, that's what I want, young lady!'

'Oh!' said Dinny. 'Is that all?'

Maid in Waiting:

Additional material

John Galsworthy writing the third chapter of *Maid in Waiting*

Reading-group questions

↲ Discuss the character of Dinny. How does she compare to Fleur Forsyte? Who do you like more and why? Are family ties a positive influence in her life, or do they hold her back?

↲ The Cherrels are an old, titled family from the country in contrast to the city-based, commercially minded Forsytes. How do the opinions and ideals of the two families differ?

↲ Galsworthy once commented, 'It might be said that I create characters who have feelings which they cannot express'. Consider this in relation to the main characters. How far does this mould and distort their happiness?

↲ Written at the end of Galsworthy's life, the last three books of *The Forsyte Saga* have been seen to give a rather bleak view of love and marriage. Do you agree? How had attitudes to divorce changed since Soames and Irene's separation at the beginning of *The Forsyte Saga*?

↲ The thirties were a time of rapidly shifting morals and crumbling traditional values. Discuss specific ways in which Galsworthy captures this clash of the old and new. How do you think he viewed the developments of his day?

THE FORSYTE SAGA

FLOWERING WILDERNESS

John Galsworthy

'It was like no other hour she had ever spent, and at the end of it she knew she was in love.'

Dinny Cherrell has been proposed to numerous times. But no one has ever come close to capturing her independent spirit – until she encounters Wilfred Desert. They had met briefly at Fleur Forsyte and Michael Mont's wedding and the spark of attraction felt all those years ago flowers into a deep, all-consuming passion. But Wilfred, made cynical by the war, is a complicated and tortured soul. When his past actions come back to haunt him, and the disapproval of Dinny's family work against them, their love is tested to the very limit . . .

Honour, family loyalty and a heart-wrenching love story – *Flowering Wilderness* is the poignant, utterly engrossing penultimate episode in *The Forsyte Saga*.

Since it first appeared in 1906, *The Forsyte Saga* has enthralled generations of readers, and been adapted with huge success for both film and television. These sumptuous new editions of each individual novel include reading-group questions and exciting, exclusive material to introduce them to a whole new audience.

'Such a cracking good story . . . compulsive, as well as very modern and outrageous' *The Sunday Times*

978 0 7553 4092 7

headline
review

THE FORSYTE SAGA

OVER THE RIVER

John Galsworthy

'Every memory she had of him came to life with an intensity that seemed to take all strength from her limbs.'

As *The Forsyte Saga* draws to a close, the future of the Cherrell family, cousins to the Forsytes, seems uncertain. Clare Cherrell has come home, fleeing the clutches of her violent, abusive husband. When he pursues her she vows she will never return and sets about fighting him in vicious divorce proceedings. Dinny supports her sister all the way, but she has her own heartache to conquer, a grief which threatens to embitter her life for ever. Will the sisters make it safely over the river, or is the stream of painful memories destined to engulf their lives?

Over the River is the dramatic, moving and stunning conclusion to John Galsworthy's unforgettable masterpiece, *The Forsyte Saga*.

Since it first appeared in 1906, *The Forsyte Saga* has enthralled generations of readers, and been adapted with huge success for both film and television. These sumptuous new editions of each individual novel include reading-group questions and exciting, exclusive material to introduce them to a whole new audience.

'The satire is sharp, the dialogue, elegant and witty, and the characterisation – dazzling' *Scotsman*

978 0 7553 4093 4

headline
review

Now you can buy any of these other bestselling books
by **John Galsworthy** from your bookshop
or *direct from the publisher*.